# THE LAST ROAD TRIP

## JENNIFER KLEPPER

The Last Road Trip
Red Adept Publishing, LLC
104 Bugenfield Court
Garner, NC 27529
https://RedAdeptPublishing.com/

Copyright © 2025 by Jennifer Klepper. All rights reserved.

Cover Art by Streetlight Graphics[1]

No part of this book may be reproduced, scanned, or distributed in any printed or electronic form without permission. Please do not participate in or encourage piracy of copyrighted materials in violation of the author's rights. Thank you for respecting the hard work of this author.

This is a work of fiction. Names, characters, places, and incidents either are the product of the author's imagination or are used fictitiously, and any resemblance to locales, events, business establishments, or actual persons—living or dead—is entirely coincidental.

---

1. http://StreetlightGraphics.com

*To the Fellas. Especially the Fun One.*

# Chapter One

# 2019

# Lisa

**H**ypocrite. Derived from the Greek *hypokrites*, meaning "pretender or actor," no relation to *Hippocratic* of the medical oath. Most days, Lisa Callihan, MD, didn't conflate the terms. In the past week, however, ancient-Greek derivations had taken up residence in her Northern California brain.

Home but still on call, Lisa muted her phone, slid it into her pocket, and stepped over the pile of kids' shoes, four backpacks, and—she cocked her head—a coconut. She puffed a sigh and closed her eyes.

The clutter shouldn't bother her. She never let it bother her.

*Doctor, heal thyself.*

She pushed the phone deeper into her pocket, but the week-old message from some reporter still burned through the fabric and triggered Greek thoughts. She pressed her temples with her fingers to drive the images away.

As she rounded the corner into the kitchen, the smell of butter and melted cheese—Zander's double-secret cheestastic grilled cheese—and a cacophony of voices and music thickened the air.

She'd barely set her bag next to the fridge when Zander and their two youngest swarmed her.

"Looking beautiful, love." Zander, his soft middle hugged by a T-shirt featuring his latest album-cover-design client, clasped her waist with his hand that wasn't holding a spatula.

Lisa squeezed Julia, four years old and wearing precisely nine animal-shaped barrettes, and spiky-haired Cole, six, who had joined the hug. Jordan, Lisa's fourth-grade doppelgänger from her thick brown hair to her crooked incisor, was setting the table, where Olivia hunched over a geometry book and squinted through blue-rimmed glasses.

"Coconut?" she asked Zander.

"Ha!" He returned to the stove. "Jordan notified me on the way to school that today was the fourth-grade food festival and she signed up to bring a coconut. We snagged one at Safeway, but we didn't think about the fact she had no way to open it. You look beat. Do you need a tropical fruit yourself? Or maybe a tropical drink?"

"Wish I could after today's schedule, but I'm on call."

Cole and Julia pulled on Lisa's arms and legs as if she were a Jurassic-sized wishbone, and Olivia begged for help calculating the volume of a cone. The distractions of chaos blessedly did the job of pushing acting, oaths, and reporters' messages away.

The shrill ring of the landline joined the melee.

Zander, seeing Lisa was still held captive by two small humans, pulled the skillet from the stove. "I've got it."

Lisa peeled off the two small humans and pointed at their backpacks. "Show me what you did in school today." As Zander answered the phone, Lisa turned toward the table. "Okay, Olivia. Let's see what formula you're using for that cone." She leaned over her oldest child's shoulder and studied the figures in the textbook.

Zander had gone silent. He faced Lisa, his eyes open so wide his forehead crinkled. Her first thought was that the reporter hadn't forgotten about her and was trying her home phone. Worry stampeded across her ribcage, stifling her breathing. But the words of her clinical medicine professor repeated in her head. "If you hear hoofbeats, think horses, not zebras." Look for the likeliest diagnosis, not the exotic one. The phone call was probably the school with some reminder of another event Jordan hadn't told them about. Or an IRS scam. Or some patient who had tracked down her number despite all her attempts to delist it and keep her name off the grid.

Zander approached with his hand over the phone's mouthpiece, his hazel eyes lit with amusement. "It's for you. She sounds like a piece of work."

Light perspiration broke out on Lisa's forehead. *Please be a patient.* She wasn't prepared to explain why a reporter would call her about some Texas businessman-turned-politician. It had been twenty years.

She took the phone and croaked a hello.

It wasn't a reporter. It wasn't a patient. And the voice on the line erased twenty years in five words.

"Hey, sugar! It's Mary Blake!" The sing-song voice dripped with magnolia and memories of a sapphire-eyed Savannah girl leading sorority-rush cheers.

Lisa's lungs filled with an inhale that swept time and hoofbeats along with it. "I'd recognize your voice anywhere. This—this is..."

The kitchen noise, which had been so loud seconds before, became muffled, as if Lisa had been plunged into a water tank. People continued to move around her, but sounds didn't register.

Mary Blake's voice alone came through. "Did I surprise you? How are you?"

"Mom!" Julia's screech pulled Lisa out of the water. Layers of clamor again crowded the room's every square inch.

"Sorry," Lisa said as she shushed the kids and moved into the family room. "It's dinnertime. I just walked in from work. It's a little crazy."

"Oh no! I will *not* interrupt family time. And I can't *wait* to hear all about those kids and your medical practice and that dreamy man who answered the phone! You go eat, and we'll have plenty of time to catch up later. All I need is your email address. I have the most amazing, wonderful, Delta surprise." The mischievous lilt in her voice was so familiar, an echo from the past and a pint-sized girl with a bottomless well of optimism.

Lisa recited her email address, and the call ended as abruptly as it had started. With a shake of her head, Lisa returned to the kitchen table and, on the fuzzy side of numb, sat down.

Zander placed a plate in front of her. "Another patient?"

She took a bite of her grilled cheese, but her tongue had lost all sense of taste. "No. It was an old sorority sister, Mary Blake Bulloch. She's one of the girls who drove across the country with me. There were five of us. Camping, etcetera. I told you about that." She glanced down at her sandwich. Not *all* about that. Not even Mary Blake and the others knew everything.

"Ah, Mary Blake, the two-name first-name one. I thought you haven't been in touch with them."

"We... went our separate ways." She hadn't considered reconnecting in the two decades that seemed to have passed in a heartbeat, hadn't wanted to face the rejection of an attempt. She cut Julia's sandwich corner to corner and tried to clear away the fuzz by calculating the area of the triangles.

"It's still funny to me that you were in a sorority."

"Why?" She stiffened at the defensiveness of her response.

"You're more the studious type. My secretly sexy family doc."

"Dad, ew," Olivia and Jordan said in chorus. The younger two giggled.

"Smart girls can do anything." Lisa smiled at her girls and hoped they didn't see through her.

Zander played with a string of cheese on his plate, turning it into a curlicue that he held up to the kids in a triumph of design. "Didn't you say you had a name? The Spice Girls or something like that?"

Lisa imagined her college friends as the Spice Girls. It wasn't hard. Even the Spice Girls had split up. "We were the Delta Rhoadies because we were *Delta Rhos* on the *road*. Get it?"

Mary Blake had coined the term when she proposed they all accompany Lisa on her drive west to medical school. At that point, the plan comprised miles, adventure, and driving rotations. That was before Lisa lay in a hospital room. Before someone had died.

Jordan scrunched her face in thought. "I think I've heard of the Spice Girls. Is that a cartoon?"

"Spice Girls a *cartoon*?" Zander boomed, faking a heart attack and moving on from the phone call that had sent Lisa through a jagged time prism. He grinned at Lisa and crooned the first line of "Wannabe" in his best Ginger Spice voice.

After Lisa provided an abbreviated rendition of the song's chorus to groans and laughter around the table, dinner ended, and the kids flew out the door.

Lisa's phone buzzed with an email alert.

*Hi Lisa! I loved hearing your voice. I'm soooooooo sorry I interrupted dinner!* Face-palm emoji. Shame face emoji. Speak no evil monkey emoji.

Pangs of regret over her lost sisterhood spiked Lisa's heart.

*We're getting the Delta Rhoadies back together!!! We're gonna finish what we started. Road trip!!!! I'll send you the deets next week!* Heart emoji. Celebration emoji. Champagne emoji.

Lisa's pulse pounded with a fight-or-flight response triggered by the memory of lying on a hospital bed in Texas under the gaze of an oil company executive and his attorney. *Why had that reporter called?*

But this was Mary Blake, and the drumming in Lisa's chest could easily equate to the adrenaline-fueled thrill she'd felt at the start of the original road trip, when she'd been excited about her future and grateful and nervous that the other girls were driving with her. She'd thought she would never see those women again.

"Leese? Everything okay?" Zander peered at her, a dish towel over his shoulder.

"Email from Mary Blake. Baby Spice, if you will. She says she's getting everyone back together, doing another road trip. She used about a thousand exclamation points."

"Girls gone wild. Sounds... spicy."

She shook her head. "Oh, I can't go." She wanted to go.

"Of course you can go."

That was so like him. Leap first—figure out where to land later. If she did that, she would plunge into an abyss and live inside her head with regrets for eternity.

"We haven't even had a family vacation in two years."

"You're allowed to do things for yourself, Leese."

"We haven't budgeted for a vacation." Maybe she *didn't* want to go. There were too many variables.

"It's a road trip. How much can that cost?"

*You have no idea.* An old injury in her shoulder throbbed as if whispering about the irony of a future doctor compromising herself from a hospital bed. *Hypocrite, pretender.*

"I'll take care of the kids tonight." He kissed her on the temple. "You take some time to relax."

Later that night, after paying the bills and assuring a mom that her daughter's earache could wait until the office opened in the morning, Lisa sat with a mint tea and stared into the dusk that shrouded their sliver of a back yard.

A fire pit glowed several houses down, illuminating neighborhood women seemingly unburdened by pasts or futures. Zander would have told her to head over and join them. He also would have known his wife would curl up on the couch instead, not wanting to intrude.

The women were too far away for her to hear voices, but an echo of five sorority girls singing around a campfire rang in her head. She looked at the flames and sought to capture that echo, those girls who'd kept her from disappearing into the stacks in college, the girls she'd left behind after she'd been revealed as naïve and powerless by Clayton Harrison and Glenn Whiteford, Esq.

Sounds of bedtime floated down the stairs. Zander sang a Disney mash-up, water ran in the kids' bathroom, and a bed squeaked from someone using it as a trampoline.

Lisa had put her own past behind her, where it belonged, where she'd never truly felt *she* belonged—always separate, the fifth wheel, the outsider who had somehow slipped in the door but never fully entered the space.

But that was then. She was a different person now. Mary Blake had even mentioned wanting to hear about Lisa's medical career, as if Lisa would beguile the group with a *Grey's Anatomy* version of her life.

A flush of insecurity quickened her breath, and she ticked off the things that proved she was in a new place. She was a doctor, not the high-flying, Tesla-driving surgeon she'd expected to be but respectable and changed enough to mean she was a different person, a more impressive person, than she'd been back then. She had a music-industry-adjacent husband—the others didn't need to know he was mostly a stay-at-home-dad and they owed more on their house than it was worth—and four kids who attended blue-ribbon schools.

The reporter's message on her phone thumped like a heartbeat. *I'm still here. I'm still here.*

Horses not zebras. She clicked on the voicemail with its 202 area code.

The voice was professional, unhurried, the same as it had been every other time she'd listened. "This is Selena May with the *Washington Post*. I'm doing background research on Tripp Harrison, related to his potential senate run. Can you give me a call?"

The reporter was simply collecting information, Lisa told herself for the thousandth time. Reporters had to do that sort of thing with candidates, cover their bases. And the message was seven days old with no follow-up. News cycles were short. The reporter had moved on. Tripp Harrison had moved on. Lisa had moved on.

Zander was right. She was allowed to do things for herself. Her eyes, still framed with the dark lashes of her youth but now highlighted with quotation mark crow's feet, stared back at her from the window glass.

This wasn't just about her.

She opened her laptop and typed a name into the browser. Scrolling past the wrong Parker Harrisons, she found an archived West Texas newspaper notice:

> Parker Harrison, 20, died of blunt-force trauma in an accident resulting from faulty wiring in the car he was driving on the Harrison family ranch. Harrison is survived by parents, Clayton and Cordelia Harrison, and brother, Tripp Harrison.

Except the article was wrong. There had been no faulty wiring. And Parker hadn't been driving. Lisa didn't consider the consequences when she signed away her integrity. And she'd never meant to protect Tripp.

But Mary Blake and the others didn't need to know any of that.

## Chapter Two
## TWO WEEKS EARLIER
## 2019
## Mary Blake

Mary Blake Bulloch Vonmeier rested her hand on the custom-built elm cabinetry below a painting that dominated the dining room. Positioned halfway between the home's vaulted entrance and the view of the Pacific, the alcove bar provided the best spot to make herself available to the open-house visitors who were trickling through the oversized doorway.

The Pacific Palisades home wasn't Mary Blake's real estate listing—she wasn't even an agent. But since her divorce had finalized two months and seven days before, her free days had been hollow more than free. It hadn't taken her more than two seconds to agree to skip her Sunday Pilates class and help Marco, the listing agent who recommended her to his poshest clients when they needed their homes staged for magazine spreads or real estate sales.

Standing below the focal point of the dining room, Mary Blake knew she looked like a prop. Her breezy white blouse with ruffled sleeves and her sand-colored skirt breathed the calm of the beach that stretched in the distance, while her sparkling Manolo Blahnik stilettos tugged the eye to the wide-plank sustainable wood floors. Mary Blake couldn't pull her own eyes from the wall art.

Swirling blues reflected the dappled ocean beyond the deck. The acrylic on canvas held a simplicity, as if a precocious child had seen a Monet lily-pad painting and recreated the memory with no sense of depth or perspective. Freedom and a sprinkle of audacity lived in five red-splotched flowers that hovered asymmetrically distanced from the painting's center. The audacity drew her in, but she struggled to pinpoint what spoke to her through the canvas.

"Looks like a kindergartener painted this one." The booming voice behind her stripped the open-house smile from her face and pulled her heart into at least five pieces.

She recognized the volume more than anything, and she closed her eyes. Her newly-ex-husband was nothing if not loud. He wasn't a *major* movie producer, but Frank Vonmeier was big enough that his photo could end up in the tabloids, especially if he was canoodling with an Instagram influencer-turned-cable-channel-reality-TV-host who wasn't his wife.

Mary Blake turned and forced a smile. "Frank. How lovely to see you here with..." She eyed the tall redhead with the Brazilian blowout and silently thanked morning Mary Blake for choosing the stilettos. "Petite" was Mary Blake's brand—she might have said it defined her character and amplified her voice—but she kept a row of power heels in her closet for a reason.

"Mary Blake, this is Monica," Frank said without a hint of sheepishness.

Glamorous in a girl-next-door way on the small screen, Monica radiated effortlessness. Mary Blake could see why the woman had achieved social media stardom and been snatched up by TV. What Mary Blake didn't see was what Monica did for Frank that Mary Blake hadn't known to do.

After Mary Blake offered a polite greeting, Frank pulled Monica toward the kitchen. When he grabbed Monica's hand, Mary Blake saw the rock. It was as big as Frank was loud.

Mary Blake's phone buzzed with an incoming text, allowing her to look away from the carats. Eight? Ten?

*Annesley*: Hi! You free?

Gratitude washed away the tension anchoring Mary Blake's smile. After twenty-four years of friendship, the telepathy between Mary Blake and Annesley spanned the continent.

*Mary Blake*: Helping with an open house. Gorge house in Palisades

*Annesley*: Love the Palisades

*Mary Blake*: Guess who showed up?

*Annesley*: ...

*Mary Blake*: One "loud" guess

*Annesley*: No he didn't

*Mary Blake*: Yes he did

*Mary Blake*: gtg

*Annesley*: CALL ME!!!!!!!

Mary Blake tucked her phone into her pocket just as Frank and Monica returned from the kitchen.

"Can she use the ladies' room?" Frank asked.

Mary Blake gestured toward the powder room and couldn't help but say, "The designer incorporated single-panel porcelain walls. They're stunning. You'll have to see how they did the primary with the same elegant simplicity."

Monica smiled and excused herself. Her lack of disdain or any level of airs in front of the ex was a sign Frank wasn't tomcatting and maybe he had something sustainable this time. Though it could be a sign that a twenty-something didn't feel threatened by her boyfriend's—or was it fiancé's?—forty-something ex-wife.

With a touch of surprise, Mary Blake realized that the forty-something ex-wife didn't feel threatened either. Her marriage to Frank—the island junkets, the yacht parties, the unexpected extravagances—had fueled her for years, but that fire had diminished over time and indiscretions, which was why she wasn't lying in a puddle of pathos on the shiny sustainable flooring.

She wondered if Monica would get the friends.

Of course Monica would get the friends.

The friends—the ever-morphing collection of industry up-and-comers and seasoned veterans—had come with Frank, and Southern charm notwithstanding, Mary Blake did not have the connections or the professional pull of Frank Vonmeier.

Those friends had floated the platitudes, the "I'm simply *devastated* about you and Frank," and "Hollywood can be *so* cruel," and "You'll rise stronger from this. *Screw* him." Hollow sentiments all, the kind Mary Blake's grandmother called "catfish whispers." The friends were now likely ingratiating themselves with the small-screen darling. *That* fact did threaten to leave Mary Blake in a puddle on the floor.

"So, that's her?" Mary Blake asked.

"Pretty, right?" The eagerness in Frank's eyes would have been appropriate coming from a child asking his mother if she liked the macaroni necklace he made for her, but not from a man who had humiliated his wife one too many times.

Still, Mary Blake softened. "Frank." He knew the tone, and Mary Blake was pleased to hear her terseness with him had regained levity or at least hadn't dipped into bitterness. Bitter was ugly.

"My bad. Sorry. Listen…" He leaned closer and turned toward the painting, his voice lowered. "I had no idea you'd be here. Believe me. Are you looking for a new house? I thought you just closed on that place in Malibu."

"Helping a friend."

"Of course you are." His aren't-you-just-the-dickens smile reminded her of their early years, when she'd delighted in delighting him with her spontaneous escapades and when he had glowed at her ease with his cynical friends.

Mary Blake patted his arm. She hadn't touched him tenderly since he'd cheated on her too publicly and Annesley had insisted, *insisted*, that if Mary Blake didn't stand up for herself once and for all, Annesley was going to fly to California and open a can of country club whoop ass. As much as Mary Blake would have loved to see that from a friend who had never opened a can of any kind of whoop ass—unless one counted savagely passive-aggressive glares—Mary Blake had stood up by stepping away in her tallest heels.

She hadn't considered that standing up for herself meant leaving the social circle that had surrounded her for fifteen years.

"This painting is dreadful, by the way," Frank said. "You like it, don't you?"

She nodded, still puzzled by what it did for her.

"You always had more culture than me." His voice trailed off, and Mary Blake followed his eyes to the other side of the room.

Monica had emerged from the powder room and was walking toward the deck's open doors to take in the view. In the light breeze, her gauzy dress cupped a slightly rounded belly.

Mary Blake took in a sharp breath that caught the hint of salt in the breeze. "Is Monica...?" A quick gesture toward her own taut midriff resulted in the reddening of Frank's face. "Changed your mind?"

"Not... exactly. But"—he held up his hands—"listen. It happened after you and I decided to get divorced. The pregnancy, I mean."

Mary Blake waited for a wave of regret or sadness. She knew her friends with kids would expect one to hit, but no wave swelled. After she'd learned in her early thirties she couldn't carry to term, she'd accepted it as part of who she was and embraced the people in her life even more. It had been the blessing that allowed her to drop everything to be with Annesley during her cancer treatments years ago, to take care of her mom in Savannah before she moved in with Mary

Blake's oldest sister, and to make sure no one around her ever felt like they weren't wanted. And Frank had told her he "never really wanted kids anyway."

Frank motioned toward the stairs. "I'd better look at more of the house with Monica. She's not loving the places we've seen so far. Maybe that 'elegant' primary bath will click with her."

With Frank and Monica heading to the master suite, Mary Blake exited to a side balcony. She tapped the edge of her phone with a manicured nail. As welcome as Annesley's interruption had been during Frank's appearance, Mary Blake didn't want to unload on her. Annesley had been her divorce counselor from afar, her one constant, and Mary Blake didn't want to take advantage of her sympathy.

Annesley picked up on the first ring, but Mary Blake spoke first. "How're you doing, honey?"

"I can't believe Frank had the gall to show up there." Living in Connecticut had tempered Annesley's already mild Atlanta accent, but emotion triggered the rounding of her vowels. Mary Blake pictured her friend's strong jaw tensed to withhold what she really wanted to say about her least favorite movie producer, one who'd pushed her buttons from the very beginning by calling her Annie instead of Annesley.

"He didn't know I'd be here. He had the Instagram girl with him. They're engaged." Mary Blake tried to hear the crash of the waves, but they were too far away. "She's pregnant."

"What? So help me..."

Mary Blake tried to feel angry, if only to validate Annesley's emotion, but the sense that bloomed was a desire to befriend the woman. "She seems nice."

"*You're* nice. Stop being so damned nice."

"I know you don't mean that."

"Wouldn't it make you feel better to be mean to him, just this once? Be mad."

"I am mad." At least, she had been.

"It doesn't sound like you are."

Mary Blake cocked her hip, feeling her command of the moment return. "And how, exactly, do I sound when I'm mad?"

Annesley paused. "Fair point. You sound the same as you always do. You talk fast, and you say nice things. But you get that pinched look on your face, right around your nose, and a crooked little line between your eyebrows."

Mary Blake's nose twitched. It wouldn't do to have a pinched face for the open house. "He's moved on. I've... moved on." She sighed and leaned over the metal railing.

"We need to get you out of California."

Mary Blake picked up on the "we" first. Mary Blake's visits to Connecticut had slowed to a trickle after Annesley's cancer went into remission years earlier. "Oh yes. I'll come visit. I miss the girls."

"No, no, not here. Let's do something different."

A flutter of insecurity interrupted Mary Blake's excitement. Of course Annesley would want to keep her time with her husband and two daughters to herself. They'd been her number-one focus since treatment ended and doctors gave the all-clear.

Mary Blake's brain shifted to discussions the two had had over hours of chemo, to the "Carpe Diem List" transcribed by Mary Blake and checked off by Annesley and her family over the intervening years. *Learn how to make sushi. Get the girls a puppy.*

"I don't do *buckets*," Annesley had said from the chemo chair, her dark eyes channeling the spirit that her body struggled to exude. "But there are things I want to do while I'm alive."

There'd been one item that Annesley's family couldn't help her check off that list.

Mary Blake spun on her heel and saw the painting through the slider. The five red flowers hovered. No. They were dancing. The flowers spanned the canvas, but their trajectories were centered, as if they were reconvening.

And there it was. A flash of five college friends dancing at a fraternity party, another flash of the five of them racing down the quad in their pledge jerseys, another of them laughing about absolutely nothing in an off-campus living room.

"I wish we had a do-over for the road trip," Annesley had said one afternoon while poison dripped into her body. She looked fragile, with a floral headscarf that offset her pale face like the hand-painted rim of fine bone china. Mary Blake had squeezed her hand and written "Delta Rhoadies" under "Take the girls to Disney World," something Annesley and Jameson did two years after Annesley's double mastectomy.

Mary Blake leaned against the railing to think. The Delta Rhoadies trip had ended in disaster. Literally.

But two decades had passed. Annesley had survived cancer, and Mary Blake had lived through a public divorce. Who knew what the others had experienced?

And Mary Blake had a knack for finding sunshine in a thunderstorm. "How about...?" She considered the puffs of white clouds drifting eastward. "There was one thing on the Carpe Diem List..."

"Oh" was all Annesley said.

Mary Blake's mind raced as she pulled together ideas for lodging—luxurious—a vehicle—spacious—and getting together with old friends—all of them. Adrenaline gushed, and every nerve fired.

"That was a long time ago." Annesley's voice sounded far away and fleeting.

Mary Blake's frenzied thoughts stalled, and the pieces of her heart smashed into each other. She'd misread the moment. "Of course, of course. We can figure something else out. Maybe you can come out here. My calendar is always open."

"No." Annesley's voice sounded present again. "Sorry. You caught me off guard. I hadn't been thinking about that. But... yes. Yes, let's do it. What can I do to help?"

"Absolutely nothing. You focus on your honey and your sweet girls." Through the open door, Mary Blake's real estate friend Marco caught her eye. "Sorry, Annesley. I need to get back in there. It appears we have some looky-loos who need some Mary Blake!"

"Go give it to them. But save some for the Delta Rhoadies."

# Chapter Three
# 2019
# Annesley

Annesley Wright, née Cannon, placed her phone on the marble kitchen island, her hand hovering as she debated whether to call Mary Blake back. She owed her friend the truth of why she'd called. It certainly hadn't been to revive a cross-country road trip.

The abandoned agenda had included one item and one item only. The phone call, had it gone as anticipated, would have been concise:

*Annesley (tentative)*: I didn't tell you earlier because you had so much going on and I didn't want to worry you. I went to the doctor because I was having respiratory issues. She said it was just a cold.

*Mary Blake (caring)*: Oh, good, honey. We need to keep you healthy.

*Annesley (firmly)*: But I still don't feel right. Something's off.

*Mary Blake (concerned)*: Oh no. Tell me what you need.

*Annesley (determined)*: I need to go in for a second opinion.

*Mary Blake (practically out the door already)*: I'll be right there, and we'll go together.

Now she didn't feel right in a different way. She craved her friend's nurturing. But the shift in Mary Blake's tone from bewilderment in the wake of Frank's appearance to enthusiasm at the reference to the Delta Rhoadies deserved protection from talk about second opinions and that twenty percent chance of recurrence her doctors had warned about years ago.

During treatment, adding the road trip to the Carpe Diem List had been a cathartic pull from the past, a diversion from the chemo. Something easy to say but not to do.

Annesley frowned. Mary Blake didn't need a disaster served up on a Texas-sized platter so soon after her divorce. But then she remembered the tearful reunion she and Mary Blake had shared two years after the road trip split. Annesley had let go of her resentment and hurt at Mary Blake's betrayal, and they had eased into a friendship that distance hadn't marred. And thank God, because Annesley didn't know what she would have done without Mary Blake.

Her daughter Cora, the one about to turn thirteen and with a birthday to plan, burst into the kitchen and beelined for the tray of pralines they'd made earlier. "Were you talking to Aunt Mary Blake? Is she coming for my birthday?"

The seventh grader had Annesley's narrow nose and pointed chin and the same upward tilt of her head when she asked a question and thought she knew the answer would be in her favor. She also had her dad's thick dark hair and love of animals, the latter of which Annesley hoped would give her a strong sense of humanity and open-heartedness Annesley worried wouldn't be inherited naturally from her side of the family. Better to be born with that than to have tragedy jolt her into plotting a new direction.

Annesley let the spring breeze from the open windows fill her lungs. She soaked it in for an extra moment and looked at Cora's expectant face. "Yes and no." Annesley broke off a jagged piece of a praline and let it dissolve on her tongue. "It was Aunt Mary Blake, but she's not coming. Send her a Snap. She loves your silly filters."

Cora thrust her lower lip out in a pout. Mary Blake had become family over the years, particularly during Annesley's mid-thirties, the fuzzy yet stark block of time when Annesley fought breast cancer while her local friends attended mommy boot camps to lose their baby weight. To be fair, those local friends had done all the things: meal trains, playdates, and Hashtag AnnesleyStrong T-shirts, but it had been Mary Blake's presence that allowed Annesley to find wellness at a time when she'd lost control of her body.

In the intervening years—the healthy years, the "all clear" years, the "no evidence of disease" years—Annesley had corrected that loss by way of yoga, meditation, and diet. She had thrived. She still thrived.

And here she was, once again making things all about herself, exactly as she didn't want her daughters to do. Telling herself she owed Mary Blake "the truth" didn't make hypochondriacal fears fact.

The new cough was a shadowy irritation that, as she reconsidered it now, was likely some allergy tied to the spring breezes, an evolving inflammatory overreaction that had migrated from cats to pollen to dust and back since childhood. Allergic didn't mean dying. And she hadn't even mentioned it to her husband or daughters.

"Okay. Back to your birthday." Annesley grabbed a notepad from the counter. "I haven't heard from Josie's mom. Is she coming?"

Cora took a bite of a praline and mumbled, "I didn't invite her."

"Has my memory glitched? I thought she was part of the group?"

"She is." Cora's blank face didn't reflect any middle-school drama. "I just don't want her here. All she talks about is Norse mythology, and she still wears Crocs, and she does this weird thing with her fingers." Cora rolled her eyes. "She's annoying. I mean, *you* know."

Did Annesley know? Instead of picturing the girl who thumbed through Rick Riordan books on the sideline at soccer practices, Annesley's mind flashed with an image of the bookish and med-school-bound Lisa Davis. The memory of her Delta Rho sister was surely compliments of Mary Blake's road-trip resurrection. Annesley had often wondered what might have gone differently if she'd embraced Lisa's assertiveness on the ranch instead of digging in her heels as queen-in-waiting and pushing everyone away.

The timer on the stove sounded, and Annesley stood to get a batch of snickerdoodles out of the oven. "You're not inviting everyone but her."

Cora looked up from her phone with an arched eyebrow and vapid impatience that caused an uncomfortable prickling in Annesley's gut. The expression was one she suspected her old friends would recognize on her own face—that of a queen-in-waiting.

"I'm not in grade school, Mom. Josie is Emily's friend not mine." Cora returned to her phone.

Annesley wrote Josie's name in neat letters at the bottom of the invitation list and added a period for permanency. And maybe to drive home to Cora who was in charge.

"Mom." Cora stiffened in a way that made her appear taller, older. "You can't make me invite someone I don't want to come."

The prickling in Annesley's stomach darted up through her chest and sharpened her tongue before she could stop it. "You'll do what I say." Annesley started at the velocity of her words and the familiarity of her imperious tone.

The look on Cora's face hovered at the intersection of shock, resentment, and an unwelcome recognition she wasn't the boss. Her chin jutted forward, and the silver of her braces caught the sunlight. Still so young.

"I'm sorry." Annesley set her hand on Cora's and ignored the swell of power she'd felt in the moment. "I'm not saying you need to be best friends with her. But you have to include her. She's a part of your friend group for a reason. Once you cut someone off, it might be permanent."

Annesley reached to straighten Cora's necklace and stopped herself when thoughts of her mother intruded again. She touched her own collarbone, where a string of pearls was absent. As much to herself as to Cora, she said, "What would Aunt Mary Blake do?"

Cora's posture lost all rigidity, her rebellious stance falling into a slump of resignation. "Fine."

Annesley knew exactly what Mary Blake would do. Mary Blake would focus on Annesley in the aftermath of her own public divorce. Mary Blake would convince four women to reunite near the scene of a tragedy because Annesley had hinted that it had been one of her great regrets that the group had not held together on that trip. Mary Blake would not have blamed the tragic end of that trip on everyone else, as Annesley had: Mary Blake for her lies, Helen for stealing the keys, Lisa for daring to make nice with Tripp's brother, Charlie for bringing that car, and all of them for ruining the future Annesley had planned, when it had been Annesley who had fixed her focus on bitter prizes.

Twenty years ago, when she was grieving and angry, Annesley's regret had been that she'd trusted the other women. Today, regret rose from spending any day—any moment—with a focus on perceptions instead of on the people she was with.

She looked at her phone lying on the island. There was no need to worry Mary Blake. She owed her friend happiness and nothing else.

Annesley rubbed Cora's back, warm and kid-strong, a body ready to transform and move into its next phase. That vibrancy of youth commingled with Annesley's own renewed vitality from setting a plan in motion. She only hoped she hadn't set Mary Blake, or any of them, on a road to disappointment.

# Chapter Four
# 2019
# Charlie

Charlie McKay's feet pounded the treadmill, causing it to shudder in a percussion that drowned out the June rain pelting the windows. She wasn't running hard enough if thoughts gained primacy in her head. And the fight for primacy had been fierce for weeks.

Three weeks, to be exact. Mary Blake's first phone call had been a stun grenade that triggered foggy memories of girls in ponytails, posing at state welcome signs and scenic overlooks. Those memories mingled with darker images of soldiers standing at attention beside a wintery grave and of twisted metal smoking in the desert.

"I'm organizing a reunion," Mary Blake had said. "We're getting the Delta Rhoadies back together."

Mary Blake's optimism clashed with dark memories, and Charlie didn't articulate a response other than "I'll get back to you. Maybe."

What the "maybe" meant, Charlie left undecided. In the aftershock of the call, she struggled with the question of what she had to show for the twenty years since her brother, Brent, died, twenty years since she promised to do his cross-country trip for him, twenty years since she and her college friends defiled his memory.

After hanging up with Mary Blake, Charlie had sought to clear her head the only way she knew how, with an intense run along Chicago's Riverwalk. And then another.

Her head still wasn't clear, and Chicago's weather had forced her into the office gym every night that week. She turned up the speed again. Her watch buzzed with another alert, and she stumbled enough to catch a toe on the belt and fall onto the rubber mat in a jumble of endorphins and sweat.

At nine p.m., she was alone in the gym, a small room infused with the musky scent of physical exertion and lemon anti-bacterial spray. Even though she used the gym as a perk to dangle when cherry-picking financial analysts off her competitors, its true purpose was to be Charlie's personal refuge when long workdays kept her from her regular routes. The convenience meant she wasn't home as much as she might have been otherwise, but she had a reliable dog walker, and her last half-hearted attempt at a relationship—this one with a real estate investor who traveled more than she did—had ended in mutual ghosting four months earlier.

Charlie downed a bottle of water and picked up her phone to see who'd knocked her off the machine. She brushed past the work emails and assorted text messages then landed on a lone voicemail from Mary Blake.

She dragged a hand across her forehead and wiped the dampness off on her shorts.

A death had triggered that first road trip. She could still smell the peaty scent of upturned earth that nearly felled her when she stood at her brother's casket and made a promise to fulfill his dream. Another death had cut the road trip short and left Charlie directionless and deep in mourning for failing her brother.

What Charlie hadn't told Mary Blake on that first call was that, more times than Charlie cared to count, she'd planned a solo attempt to complete the trip and fulfill her promise.

Sometimes, she planned her solo attempt to start where the five of them had left off in Texas. Other times, she considered a complete do-over, starting from Virginia. Once, she even charted a reverse route, as if that wildcat move might confound the specters that had conspired to hold her back from the commitment she'd made.

If anyone had asked, Charlie could have pointed to an unassailable list of reasons for bypassing each iteration of her trip plans: launching her own consulting firm, onboarding new legal counsel, competing in her first Ironman Triathlon, or scrambling to keep the business together during a bear market so she didn't have to fire anyone.

Brent would have understood. He'd been easy with her, the scruffy little sister who insisted on helping him recondition the sun-fried and rusted 1976 International Harvester Scout II that he pushed into the driveway on his sixteenth birthday. She'd never seen anything like the minimalist truck with its convertible top and Mad Max vibe.

"I'm going to drive this girl across the country, sleep under the stars, and pull right up to the edge of the Grand Canyon," he said. His sandy hair was streaked from the summer sun and his eyes filled with the adventure he always sought.

Charlie's adventure had been a summer of trips with Brent to the salvage yard to find parts for the Scout and lessons in everything from driving a stick shift to hocking a loogie. In payment for her grease monkey services, Charlie made Brent shake on an agreement to give her the Scout when he got tired of it.

"You drive a hard bargain, sis," he said with a fake gangster accent. "But you'll be sadly disappointed when I never get sick of it and you're driving some *loser*mobile."

Brent satisfied his end of the bargain, in a way. He'd left her the Scout. Charlie, though, had failed Brent time and again. First twenty years ago and again each time she set aside new plans to complete his trip.

None of that—a trip revisited, a canyon edge, a promise—would bring Brent back. Besides, he had dreamed of doing it in the Scout, and that car was long gone, a gnarled wreckage of steel and dreams.

Mary Blake's original call and a follow-up email injected with emojis and exclamation points had shaken that regret loose. Each subsequent message thwarted Charlie's best efforts to tuck it away. Instead of feeling resentful, she found herself eager to hear Mary Blake's voice and to imagine her friend scrunching her face as she chose the perfect emojis to punctuate her email entreaties.

Her hand still slick with sweat, Charlie clicked to listen to Mary Blake's latest message as she made her way through the empty hallways to her office.

"Hi! It's Mary Blake!" Roadway noise filled the background. "Again! Has anyone ever told you how positively *impossible* you are to get ahold of?"

Charlie's laughter echoed in the emptiness.

"I'm finalizing plans for the trip and need to confirm you are a definite for next week." Mary Blake had slipped into a clipped tone that pulled Charlie back to college, when Mary Blake would transition from cheerleader to drill sergeant as the situation demanded, whether during a study session gone late or a football tailgate that ran out of wings. "Which I'm sure you are. No more maybes. Call me." *Click.*

Back in Charlie's office, the phone buzzed. Her heart thumped, and she half-hoped it was her old friend. But the name on the screen paused Charlie's hand: Lillian, her stepmother.

Even from the beginning, Lillian seemed to consider it part of her role to facilitate a connection between Charlie and "the general"—Charlie hadn't referred to him as her father since she was ten—first by reaching out a day after the no-nonsense courthouse wedding five years ago that Charlie hadn't attended. If Lillian wasn't so damn sweet, Charlie would have resented her, but the general's second wife had the inquisitive voice of a kindergarten teacher, one so supportive and uplifting that Charlie couldn't dismiss her.

Charlie answered, guarded. "Hi, Lillian. What's up?"

"Charlie, dear, I'm calling because your dad's birthday is coming up. It's his seventieth, you know."

"Big number." Charlie leaned back in her chair and swiveled toward the window. Fat raindrops on the glass blurred the streetlights below.

Lillian continued, her excitement about her plans leveled audibly by a sense that she needed to be seriously convincing with the difficult stepdaughter. "I'm putting together a party a week from Sunday. Nothing too fancy. You know your dad, Mr. Practical. We're celebrating down at the Officer's Club with some of his army buddies. Old faces and old memories. Don't tell him this, but he's getting up there." She laughed, the levity again taking center stage. "I'd love for you to be there. *He'd* love that."

Charlie spun back toward her desk. How many of her birthdays had he missed? A heavy silence grew until Charlie began clicking a pen for the distraction.

"Charlie, I was going through some old boxes... old pictures, to put together a collage for the party, you know? I found one photo I simply adore. Your dad was holding you. You were probably about four, I'd guess. And you were wearing your dad's dress jacket and cap. It's precious."

What felt like a gloved hand squeezed Charlie's heart. She hadn't seen that photo in years. In fact, she was shocked the general had kept those boxes after her mom passed. As a child, she'd taped that picture to her headboard and looked at it every night, wishing her dad were there, even when he was physically at home.

Charlie could still feel the weight of that jacket with the striped ribbons she'd thought so pretty, the sleeves extending past her small fingers and her ear being folded over by the cap. "My little general," her dad had said as he spun her through the air, sending the cap flying across the room and her into a fit of laughter. She shivered at the memory of the thrill that shot through her when the cap flew off, though that shiver could have been the air conditioning against her still-sweaty skin.

Her life with the general had been a series of snapshots. Deployments were long and frequent, and he'd jumped at every opportunity that promised to advance his career, even if it meant another move or another long absence. The man in the photograph wasn't the man who kept coming home. The man in the photograph would have protected her brother. The man in the photograph would have used his position to ensure Brent didn't deploy to a hot spot and come home in a casket.

An email alert appeared on the monitor. Mary Blake again, this time emailing a single photo with no message. Fuzzy memories of the first trip came into clear focus on the screen: two blondes and three brunettes wrapped up with one another and hanging out of an emerald-green convertible Scout, the shade of paint Charlie had helped her brother select at the end of a perfect summer a long time ago. She couldn't tell which arms belonged to which girl, but from the way the sunlight amplified the glow on their faces, anyone could tell the shot was taken in a moment of unadulterated freedom. It had been easy to forget that the trip had been more than its beginning, more than its ending.

Lillian's voice broke through. "I know you and your father haven't had much of a relationship for a long time. But he loves you. It would be special if you could make it. It's going to be a surprise."

The general and surprises didn't mix. Charlie considered what his reaction to the surprise might be, his reaction to seeing her there. She shuddered.

Lillian's kindergarten round-up demeanor masked her hound-dog persistence. She and Mary Blake would make a formidable pair.

But Lillian's calls meant the general would continue to command space in Charlie's mind, a constant reminder of how she hadn't fulfilled her promise to her brother.

Charlie clicked to enlarge the photo and zoomed in on her own face, positioned next to Helen's, her then-roommate. The upward tilt of her head threw her hair into the breeze, and her mouth was open in song as if beckoning the world to join in.

Time blurred her vision enough that the square forehead and prominent eyebrows she saw on herself melted into a memory of her brother, frozen forever in time at twenty-five and, in that moment on-screen, perhaps as close to her as he had been since before he died.

He had always been there for her. She needed to show up for him.

"I'm sorry, Lillian. But I'll be traveling with some old friends. Send me pictures." Charlie softened her tone. "It's nice of you to do this for him."

Charlie took a moment after the call ended. With each breath, the grip of guilt and resentment loosened until her chest rose and fell with strength rather than effort. She opened her recent calls list and dialed the California number.

Mary Blake answered after one ring. "Charlie!"

There was that sound of comfort and acceptance she remembered from college. "I'm in. I assume you've wrangled everyone else."

Mary Blake squealed. "I knew that photo would do the trick. Good to know I haven't lost my touch."

"Anything I need to know that's not in the emails?"

"We're gonna finish what we started, Charlie. We started that trip together, and we need to finish it together."

Charlie looked back at the monitor. Helen's face was open with the honesty that had drawn Charlie to her their first year in college. That face had morphed into a mask of shame and anger, sadness and fear, in a dark hospital room twenty years ago. In the years since,

Charlie had forgiven her. Helen hadn't known what would result from what she'd done that night. But forgiveness went both ways. And Charlie had known exactly what she was doing the last time she'd spoken with her old roommate. She'd intended maximum pain.

# Chapter Five
# 2019
# Helen

Helen Hughes squeezed the diazepam bottle with both hands, her elbows hugging her sides in the middle seat of a flight that was not the one she'd booked. She stared at the seat in front of her and tried to will away the thrumming beneath her skin.

As the captain's voice came over the intercom, scratchy and indecipherable, a flight attendant wearing a red jacket that made Helen's gray cardigan feel drab and chaste checked seatbelts and overhead compartments. The decision not to check a bag had worked in Helen's favor, considering the last-minute flight change. Everything else seemed to be falling apart.

Flying standby because the airline had cancelled her later flight from Richmond to Texas happened quickly enough that Helen hadn't had time to react, but not getting an aisle seat sent cortisol flooding every capillary.

She released one hand from the bottle and opened the leather planner she'd brought, even though Mary Blake had been in charge of the itinerary. Her notebooks had been her diazepam for years, she supposed, going back to the college-era spiral-bound versions from school, which had been replaced by the monogrammed upgrades she dutifully filled and filed nowadays. The planning and documenting centered her, grounded her.

But no planning could have anticipated Helen being trapped between a mouth-breathing man already asleep against the window and a wiry teenager wearing Beats headphones and breakfasting on Flamin' Hot Doritos that he pulled haphazardly out of a party-sized bag. Helen brushed his crumbs off her black pants only to watch them cascade downward to become orange flecks on her white Tretorns.

Perhaps it should be no surprise that things had already gone off course. Though she wasn't sure if it was an echo of the last road trip or a reflection of her current life.

She didn't know when the arguments with her husband, Derek, became punctuated by raised voices or when dismissive comments muttered while walking away escalated to face-to-face accusations. The stability she'd gravitated toward when she reconnected with the man with the thoughtful brow over kind brown eyes at a high school reunion had become a force she increasingly resisted.

When Mary Blake had called with the unexpected invitation to reunite in Texas, it had been the life preserver Helen needed at a time when she hadn't even realized she was wet.

"Helen, honey. It's Mary Blake."

Helen had almost burst into tears on hearing a voice from someone who had never once judged her. She'd said yes before Mary Blake provided a date.

That date was today, and the plane was pulling away from the jetway.

Helen twisted the safety cap and pulled the thick cotton from the pill bottle. She'd hidden the meds in her pocket while Derek loaded the car. He—a general contractor who worked out his frustrations with pushups and kettlebells—had suggested couple's therapy only weeks before, and she'd lashed out at him, not knowing whether she was scared of the prospect of opening up to a therapist, to Derek, or to herself. But she'd asked her general physician for something to help with "flight anxiety," not revealing her need to help leaven her racing heart and the uncontrollable mind-spin that had been coming more frequently while on the ground.

The pills rattled in the bottle as the plane rumbled along the tarmac.

In the initial excitement over the pending trip, Mary Blake's enthusiasm had suppressed Helen's consideration of the break with Charlie. Charlie, who had been Helen's stalwart for four years. Charlie, whose unconditional trust in Helen had proven to be misguided. Disquiet seeped in too late, now that the airplane door was closed, the terminal was behind them, and her middle seat was shrinking by the second.

Despite academic demands, social disruptions, and immature infighting, the Delta Rhoadies had always fallen back together over those four years, as if there had been homing devices implanted in them when they first met. When they were together, they were strong. She was strong. But when they fell apart, bad things happened. That strength could lie at the end of this flight. And that just might be the start of the path forward with Derek.

She'd convinced herself that Mary Blake's invitation was a sign that maybe Helen had to backtrack to fix the torn relationship of the past as a model to fix the relationship of the now. If Helen and Charlie were able to put things behind them, there was hope for Helen and Derek.

The flight attendant held up an oxygen mask with the practiced deftness of a magician, her hand manipulating the device to drop as she exhorted passengers traveling with children to place their own masks on before giving assistance to others.

Where else was it okay to look out for yourself first? Had the girls on the road trip only donned their own masks, and was that why things had fallen apart?

She ran a finger around the rim of the pill bottle, a plastic representation of betrayal—or maybe an admission. Helen moved the bottle to her right hand to tap out a single pill. The plane braked, and the sleeping giant next to her readjusted his posture, flinging his arm over the armrest and knocking the bottle from Helen's hand. Tiny yellow pills flew, a hailstorm following the earlier shower of crumbs. One pill landed on its edge and rolled out of sight down the aisle.

Close quarters in a metal tube suppressed the urge to scream, and Helen's ribs constricted. The plane bumped along the asphalt, interior lights dimmed for takeoff, and the pills popcorned around Flamin' Hot Doritos Boy's Vans and her own under-seat carryon.

Like a bum finding a half-smoked cigarette on the sidewalk or a junkie—she imagined—scavenging to fill a syringe, Helen reached to the floor to gather the few visible pills scattered among the crumbs. Doubled over with a single pill in her hand and staring at the drab airplane carpet, she slumped. This did not look like the path to any kind of fresh start.

"I think it's terrific you're getting together," Derek had said when he pulled her suitcase out of the trunk at the airport. He squeezed her hand, likely thinking about the stories she'd told him early in their marriage, when she'd talked up her fun college years and the Delta Rhoadies. When she'd laughed about flat tires in Mississippi and sorority songs around campfires. She'd long before carved the horrific ending of the trip out of her memory bank and locked it in a cell deep inside where it could do no harm. Telling him someone had died and that she'd been complicit had never been on the table. Derek had no stake in it, and she didn't need his judgment. She'd done the judging herself just fine.

The steady voice of the pilot came over the speakers, clear this time. "Flight attendants, please take your seats." His practiced calm before launching a multi-ton vehicle into the air pulled her upright.

She tightened her seatbelt securely. The five were reuniting.

She let the lone pill fall from her palm and leaned over to put the empty pill bottle into her bag. Unzipping the main compartment, she saw a flash of black leather, something she hadn't put in her bag when she'd packed it the night before. Her hands froze in place, and a welcome warmth sprouted in her chest.

The plane braked softly as it positioned for takeoff.

Helen pulled the leather item from the bag and set it atop the planner on her lap. It was a twin. But the new planner had a yellow sticky note on the cover where her monogram would normally be.

On the paper, in Derek's comforting block lettering, was written "I hope you finish it this time."

The plane's engines rumbled like a dragon ready to spray fire. She peeled off the yellow paper, and her breath caught. Instead of her "HGH" monogram, the embossment on the cover read "ROAD TRIP." She ran her hand over the cover's textured surface and eased it partially open, almost expecting the past to pour out in full color, full action, and full emotion. Her hand held for a split second then completed the reveal.

Inside was a simple outline-style United States map. A red line extended from the east coast westward but didn't make it to the west coast, where a red triangle—a delta—dangled, lonely and disconnected, next to the Pacific Ocean. Below the map, five names—alphabetized, as if she'd designed the planner herself—pulled the past into the present:

Annesley<br>Charlie<br>Helen<br>Lisa<br>Mary Blake

She flipped through the empty pages: no calendar, no templated budgets, and no inspirational quotes. Just empty pages waiting for her—for them—to add plans and memories, to finish an incomplete year, and to fix what had broken that continuous line.

The dragon engines roared, and the plane lifted from the asphalt, pushing Helen against the back of her seat. Her eyes welled with tears, dampening the heat in her chest.

She followed the red line on the page with her finger, backtracking from the trip's fateful end to its exuberant launch.

# Chapter Six
# 1999
# Helen

Helen couldn't have been happier. Her mom had delivered her diploma for framing, a fall position at PricewaterhouseCoopers awaited in New York, the June sun shone on the Virginia farmlands alongside I-64, and—hallelujah!—her best friend was cranky.

Even Charlie's usual posture had returned, a casual slouch that molded her into the black leather driver's seat, as they made their way west from Richmond to start their trip.

Any normality was welcome after a senior year unfit for the pages of a college yearbook. The Delta Rhos had kicked off the school year under the shadow of university-imposed probation in response to a report of alcohol violations. Forget Homecoming floats, fraternity mixers, winter formals, and participation in the capstone events they'd anticipated. Without the pull of a social calendar, Helen's core group of five had wandered farther apart than they had the prior three years. Maybe that would have happened anyway, seniors de-anchoring for the things that came after college, but it happened too soon. Even graduation had been incomplete when Mary Blake missed it to be with her sick dad.

One anchor that dropped and broke through the individual diversions, including Helen's own unraveling, was the death of Charlie's brother just three months prior. None of them had met the young army lieutenant, but they knew from his military photo that he had Charlie's thick blond hair and dark eyebrows, and the excitement Charlie displayed the year he came home for Christmas was proof Charlie could be sentimental. When news of Brent's combat death arrived, Charlie had turned to stone.

Helen had offered to join Charlie on a cross-country road trip in his honor. And after Lisa got accepted to UCLA Medical School and landed a prestigious summer research position there, Mary Blake proposed that they all accompany Lisa on her drive to LA.

"We'll be the Delta Rhoadies. Get it?" Mary Blake's trademark enthusiasm tugged them from the gloom that lingered after the funeral.

Now, after not much more than a week apart, they would be back together in fifty-five minutes, if Helen's calculations were correct. She leaned against the coolness of the bare metal door.

Charlie's face, tanned from the early summer sun, had regained some of its typical ease, a softening around her eyes and jaw, like the stone cast had fallen away. She'd never been the talk-therapy type, but she had begun to open up Charlie-style.

"So help me, Helen, if Annesley turns this into a production, we're going off on our own." Military-family Charlie and country-club Annesley were often at cross-purposes. Helen had never been sure if the animosity was for real or for the fun of the conflict.

Helen laughed, but she knew that if left to her own devices, Charlie would take the trip solo. After Charlie had gotten kicked out of the sorority their first year for refusing to wear the designated sorority T-shirts and jerseys on the assigned days, Helen kept her connected with the other girls as a sort of honorary Delta Rho, even if Charlie refused to embrace the title.

"We have two cars for five people. I've never understood your issue with her." Actually, Helen could name a few reasons, like Annesley's insistence that only BMWs and such got the prime parking in front of the sorority house and her facial tic when she disapproved of someone's attire.

Helen couldn't imagine the group without Annesley, though. The five didn't have a sense of direction without Annesley around, even when Helen was the one figuring out how to get where they were going.

Charlie groaned. "I've attended ten schools. There's been an Annesley Cannon at every one of them. I only tolerate her because the rest of you are marginally okay." She shot Helen a sarcastic side-eye.

"The trip will be fine," Helen said. "No drama. Just adventure. We do have the car for adventure."

Charlie had told Helen they would be taking her brother's convertible. To Helen's surprise, Charlie had pulled up that afternoon in a Wizard of Oz green vehicle that looked vaguely like an extended Jeep Wrangler, only more truck-like and built for someone who had zero interest in comfort.

But Helen liked it: sturdy, spare, utilitarian, and fun in a rugged way. The only part that didn't look like a military-issue fitting of steel and black plastic was a Toshiba cassette player and, beneath that, a CB radio. She couldn't help but see the Scout as part Charlie and part the brother Helen only knew through the snippets of letters Charlie read aloud when she was particularly pleased with one of her brother's sarcastic turns of phrase.

It was rustic, though. The bare metal interior alone seemed unfinished, like this particular unit had skipped the last few guys on the assembly line.

"This... car..." Helen ran her fingers along the point where the canvas roof met the metal framing. "Is everything in, um, working order?"

"I've never driven it before this week." A devilish smirk animated Charlie's face, and she grasped the gear shift like it was a mallet. "But I helped Brent fix it up. Anything could happen."

Helen laughed but tried to ignore the "this car will fall apart before Mississippi" vibe.

A familiar landscape of tidy Virginia farms swished by and pulled the past with it. The eager green of early summer burst from the soil in neat rows, soybeans that would be harvested after she and Charlie were established in New York at summer's end, with Helen launching her job at PWC and Charlie attending law school.

Unfolded on Helen's lap, a road map made promises that were outlined in a ruled notebook that listed each campground, each road, and each point of interest, starting with the truck stop where they were meeting the other three. With each mile marker, the car's rattle sounded more like a call to the future, and things unworthy of remembrance drifted further away.

By the time the truck stop came into view, the rustle of the Scout's soft top had become white noise, and fears of the car falling apart on the highway had receded.

Tractor trailers stood bumper to bumper alongside a building bright with neon signs: Cigarettes. 24-Hour Breakfast. Hot Coffee. Hot Showers. Helen saw no signs of the other Delta Rhos or any highway civilians.

"I think we've found the Club Med of the long-haul trucker world," Charlie said.

As if in response, a heavyset man with a salt-and-pepper beard emerged from a semi. His dark-wash jeans hung loose below a belly that spilled over his waistband. Hopping off the running board onto the asphalt, he was lighter on his feet than his girth would have suggested.

Charlie nodded toward the man. "What's his story?"

Helen considered him. "Father of four girls. The youngest just graduated high school. Almost home after a four-day run. Watches Clint Eastwood videos on the VCR in his truck at night while he fantasizes about his alter ego living as a desperado." Charlie whistled the refrain from *The Good, the Bad and the Ugly*. "Hopes they have some prepackaged flowers for his wife."

The backstory game had started between Helen and her dad when he took her to kindergarten dropoff and the unfamiliar faces frightened Helen. They didn't know these people yet, her dad had said, but they could create stories about them. "That tall lady looks like she grew up next door to a zoo and helped take care of the zoo babies," and "That little girl's favorite cereal is Lucky Charms because she's secretly good at finding four-leaf clovers."

The game survived beyond her kindergarten jitters. And Charlie had been the audience for Helen's divination of the secret lives of strangers since they were first-years and Helen correctly outed Charlie's roommate as having a pet ferret back home in Roanoke. What had been a coping mechanism for her childish homesickness had become part of the glue that bound Charlie and Helen together.

Charlie steered the Scout around an errantly parked semi and pulled toward the restaurant entrance. Without warning, she slammed her foot on the brake. "Brakes work," she said without a sniff of sarcasm. Seeing Helen's shocked face, Charlie pointed toward the curb.

"Oh! It's them." Helen waved at Mary Blake, who was swinging her arms in the air, and Annesley, who stood primly in a white blouse and seersucker skirt at the curb as if waiting for a Town Car to transport her to a garden party.

Fog filled Helen's head, and a light tingle crawled across her scalp. Seeing the duo felt unsettlingly nostalgic, like she was in the body of her future self attending a ten-year reunion. It took her a moment to shake away the grayness of that discomfort and reassure herself that this trip was proof they would stay connected. The power of the five was strong.

Charlie parked next to Lisa's white station wagon, aka the White Whale, an old but reliable hand-me-down from her mom. The windows were obscured by blankets, stuffed black plastic bags, milk crates, and stray suitcases. A blue tarp latched to the roof by a maze of bungee cords hid a jumble of shapes that looked like they wanted to break free.

Notebook in hand, Helen emerged from the Scout at the same time Mary Blake ran forward and squealed, "Delta hi!"

Charlie sighed. "Are we really doing that, MB? Surely graduation relieved you guys of your sorority obligations." Charlie might have been happy to be an ex-Delta Rho, but Helen loved the frilly traditions as tangible proof of the sisterhood she had with the others.

"But we're sisters forever!" Mary Blake, always a flirt and not afraid to push Charlie's buttons, winked conspiratorially as she pulled away from her hug with Helen.

Helen looked around. "Where's Lisa?"

When the five were together, the straight-A student from Pittsburgh could sometimes slip to the edge. Helen wasn't sure if that was intentional on the part of the contemplative future doctor or a byproduct of the other girls' pairings.

Lisa emerged from the other side of the wagon. "Present." Her angular limbs contrasted with her heart-shaped face and full lips in a pleasant way, like there was a fantastical backstory that created that physical combination.

But Helen didn't need to "backstory" her friends. She knew Lisa sometimes watched people as if she was trying to decode their every action and word. She was also one of those waitresses who could take complicated orders from a table of ten without writing anything down, as she'd proved more than once when a group of Delta Rhos sat in her section at the Commonwealth Bar & Grill and put her to the test.

Lisa smacked her hands on the wagon's hood. "I didn't think I had that much stuff. But add in Mary Blake's and Annesley's things and..." She shrugged, eyeing the squished interior.

"And now," Annesley murmured, her terse smile speaking volumes about the depths to which a situation might fall if she wasn't in charge, "we look like the Beverly Hillbillies."

Punctuating Annesley's statement, a mud-splattered pickup truck rolled past, and the goateed driver whistled and tipped his camouflage hat at the girls. Mary Blake curtsied while Annesley rolled her eyes, both reactions triggering laughter from within the truck's cab and a farewell honk. As if by instinct, Mary Blake needed only to make a gesture to offset Annesley's flippant elitism. Helen speculated that Annesley intuited this and that's why she gravitated toward her petite friend, the two having a yin and yang of traits that could be too much when they were by themselves.

Mary Blake floated her hand toward the Scout's roof as she walked. "I do like your car, Charlie."

Charlie, hovering like the car's bodyguard, nodded in appreciation.

Mary Blake stopped at the passenger door. "What. Is. That?"

Helen peeked through the window to see the object of Mary Blake's interest. "It's a CB radio. We're a little retro here in the Scout."

Mary Blake turned, a sparkle in her eyes. "We should get another one so we can stay in touch the whole trip."

Lisa pointed toward the deep blue green of Virginia's mountain range along the horizon. "We're almost on the edge of nowhere. Where are we supposed to get a CB?"

Mary Blake spun and flung her hands in the air to frame the building. "Lisa, you're supposed to be the smart one. We're at a truck stop, sugar! Do you think they sell anything *other* than CBs here?"

Lisa eyed the neon signs. "I'm going to go out on a limb and guess they sell cigarettes, coffee, breakfast, and showers."

"Smart *and* a smart ass," Mary Blake said with a smile that belonged in a toothpaste commercial.

Lisa blushed and tugged at the hem of her denim shorts.

"Where are we staying tonight, Helen?" Annesley asked without moving her narrowed eyes from the truck until it pulled onto the highway.

Helen opened her notebook. "Day 1: We stay along the Blue Ridge Parkway at a KOA." She looked up, knowing that would be Greek to Annesley. "It's a campground. We'll set up our tents—"

"*Tents?*" Annesley turned her gaze to Mary Blake. "You didn't mention *tents*." When no one responded immediately, Annesley kicked into alpha mode. "I can call my travel agent. There are some nice hotels on the way."

Charlie sighed. "Here we go."

Annesley flipped her head to eye Charlie. Annesley wasn't afraid to snap back, and she reveled in the wins she achieved when she and Charlie disagreed.

Helen's feet felt leaden against the asphalt, but her mind raced to figure out how to head off the impending clash.

Annesley preferred things her way, yes, but she'd also driven the five of them to Brent's funeral and sat next to Charlie at the service, her own face shadowed in sadness over a man she'd never met.

"Brent's plan was to camp," Helen blurted.

Annesley held eye contact with Charlie for several seconds, unmoving. With a huff, her shoulders loosened from the iron grip that held her posture erect. "Fine. We camp." She rolled her eyes and turned to Helen. "By the way, I spoke with Tripp and confirmed we're a go to stay at the Harrison ranch. You have the address, right? We won't have to camp there."

Prompted by a finger pressed into the small of her back, Helen turned, ready to face the music for her calculated omission, this one about the stop at Annesley's boyfriend's home in Texas.

"Tripp? Seriously, Helen." Charlie was whispering, even though Annesley had returned to the other girls at the curb. "Did you forget to mention something?"

"I know. He's an entitled asshole, we're not Team Tripp, Annesley's either a pushover to put up with him or she knows something we don't, blah blah blah." Helen bobbed her head back and forth. "It wasn't a definite until this very moment. Anyway, what's the concern? You afraid in these close quarters someone might find out you hooked up with him freshman year?"

Charlie grunted. "I clearly made some horrific mistakes freshman year." She flashed a devilish grin. "Possibly including becoming friends with you. Hey, maybe if I *accidentally* tell Annesley that Tripp and I—"

Helen's stomach tightened, and she clapped her hand over Charlie's mouth. "Don't you dare." She checked over her shoulder to be certain Annesley hadn't heard. "Those two were made for each other. Why stir the pot?"

The Annesley Cannon-Tripp Harrison pairing radiated the confidence and flawlessness of a Ralph Lauren ad, so much so that the latest university admissions booklet featured a photo of them lounging on the quad. The relationship had gotten serious and pulled Annesley away from the rest of them when they were seniors—yet another chink in the group's armor—but Helen saw the stop at Tripp's home as an inclusion of the group in the couple's future.

Charlie rolled her eyes. "This isn't about Tripp. He's just another douchey frat boy, but whatever. I don't want any drama. We don't need this to turn into another beach weekend."

The air pressure seemed to bottom out in an instant, stealing Helen's breath.

Charlie's eyes opened wide. "Oh shit. I'm sorry. I meant all Annesley's dumb drama, not the—" Concern tightened her face, and she stretched out a hand.

Helen pulled her arm back before Charlie's fingers could fall on her wrist. "It's fine." But the rotting sick in her stomach and the burn of shame at the back of her throat proved she hadn't yet exorcised the weekend—That Night—from her system. It still sometimes crept out of its shadowy cave, reminding her that everything would have been fine if they'd all stayed together on what was supposed to be a fun beach weekend to kick off their last year of school.

Mary Blake's lilting voice took over where the tractor trailer engine trailed off, mercifully pulling Helen from the shadow of the cave. "Almost forgot! I have presents!" She turned the word "presents" into a song as she dived into the wagon and pulled out an oversized white designer purse. "It's a little thing, but I made a mixtape. Here's one for the green car." She handed Helen a cassette tape case and moved over to pass one to Lisa. "And one for the white car."

Helen turned the case over. Mary Blake had written "Delta Rhoadies" on the edge and listed song titles on the back in alternating shades of blush and cornflower blue. Triangles embellished a song list that ranged from a sorority bid night anthem to their communal break-up song, from the song Lisa sang at graduation to the song the house band at the Green Elephant Bar dedicated to Charlie on her twenty-first birthday—before she threw up from the tequila shots.

Deee-Lite, Chris Isaak, Sarah McLachlan, AC/DC, the Neville Brothers, Garth Brooks. Pavarotti. Helen ran her finger along the edge of the case. It was perfect. She soaked in the knowing grins of the others, Charlie nudging Lisa to point out one of the songs, Annesley rolling her eyes at something but laughing out loud.

That list only existed in their group, the five of them. No other mixtape would ever have that exact playlist. They were better together, even when they didn't seem like a perfect match.

Mary Blake was already moving, fueled by the reaction. "Annesley, come on. Let's go get that CB thingamabob. I bet they use them out on the ranch. You can get some practice and impress your honey."

Annesley conceded. "Fine. I've got my dad's credit card. Might as well use it."

The two strutted into the building arms linked, balance in the universe restored.

Lisa tossed the cassette onto the driver's seat in her car. "I don't have the heart to remind Mary Blake the White Whale doesn't have a cassette player." She reached to open the door to the back seat. "Gotta move more things up top. It's pretty crowded back here." Lisa disappeared into the wagon headfirst, her pale legs trailing and not looking ready for sunny California.

Charlie nudged Helen and peered at her through narrowed eyes. "You okay?"

The plastic case dug into Helen's palm. She smiled, as much to convince herself as Charlie that she was good. "So long as I've got my Deltas together."

Charlie rolled her eyes. "Don't include me in that. Half a pledgeship doesn't count."

Helen relaxed. "Maybe not, but it was all we needed to rope you in." She grabbed Charlie's hand. "This is going to be perfect."

"Don't get ahead of yourself, Helen. We haven't spent a night together yet."

# Chapter Seven
# 2019
# Lisa

Lisa fidgeted in the taxi's air-conditioned chill and smoothed creases that hadn't been on her skirt when she'd boarded her flight that morning. Overdressed? Underdressed? She couldn't decide.

The parched scrubland of West Texas flashed in splotches of taupe and green outside her window. She stared at the navy pleather of the taxi's interior as if a reunion-success formula was encoded in the grain. Realizing she was fiddling with her phone, she stopped herself from scrolling to the reporter's message, now pushed deep in her voicemail archive but still there, a reminder of how the last trip had ended.

The past, emboldened by her physical presence in Texas, extended its wispy tendrils and pulled her into that hospital room where she'd lain in a backless gown under a thin sheet, her friends replaced by two men, a non-disclosure agreement, and a check.

"Darlin', it's simple," the lawyer, Glenn Whiteford, Esquire, had said. "You say nothing. Nothing about what happened last night, nothing about the existence of an NDA."

His client, the bombastic Clayton Harrison, Tripp's dad, had leaned in close enough that she smelled cigarettes mixed with stale hospital coffee. "And if you ever say one word about any of this"—his nostrils flared—"I will be on you like a coyote on a calf separated from the herd."

The faux leather of the seat back came into focus not as a formula for success but as an unhelpful tangle of lines and creases.

Too soon, the taxi slowed, and the Rancho Verde resort appeared like an oasis at the end of the winding highway offshoot. The organic Frank Lloyd Wright-style resort sat nestled into the bend of a river lined with incongruously rich greenery that Lisa wanted to appreciate. Instead, she ordered herself to breathe deeply like she told her anxious patients to do before she stuck them with a needle.

She was not in a hospital room. *Inhale.* She was not here to see the Harrisons. *Exhale.* No one knew what happened. *Inhale.* That was the past. *Exhale.*

The taxi driver's tenor twang interrupted her, each prolonged vowel stealing the time remaining before they arrived. "Nice resort y'all have here. You must be someone. Quarterback for the Cowboys stayed here after the season ended. Him and his wife... at least, I think it was his wife. Good tipper, anyhow."

Of course Mary Blake chose a place where celebrities stayed. Lisa regarded her scallop-edged skirt and ruffled blouse with renewed dismay. She'd allowed herself too many distractions and needed to focus on the now. Flicking through her messages, she found the one from the reporter—area code 202 stood out on the list like an abscess—and deleted it. She let out a puff of air, lightened by something she should have done weeks ago.

The taxi pulled into a circular drive shaded by a pergola that extended like a low cliff from the building. Lisa stepped out of the cool of the car into a punch of heat, the architectural prairie-style oasis a mirage, at least when it came to the arid climate of West Texas. As she reached into her bag for the fare, she wondered how much the quarterback had tipped.

"Lisa?"

The voice caught her unaware, and she fumbled a handful of bills to the driver. It was probably too much, but at least she wouldn't look cheap.

Next to a thick wooden pillar stood Charlie McKay. She wore a semisheer button-down and loose slacks in a washed-out olive green. Her hair still extended just past her shoulders, with a hint of a wave captured in the wheat-colored layers.

The weight of the heat vanished in a cool burst of familiarity followed by a spray of gratitude. Lisa was grateful that Charlie was the first person she saw, grateful that Charlie had come at all, despite everything that had happened.

Neither moved to hug the other. Charlie wasn't a hugger. But the left side of her mouth curved up, and that was as good as an embrace.

"Doc, you look fantastic."

Lisa tugged on her collar. Why had she gone with a ruffle? "These are just travel clothes. I'm going to change when I get to my room."

Charlie shook her head and laughed, a reminder that Charlie never cared about name brands or comparisons. She valued loyalty. To her brother, to friends. They hadn't all lived up to the standard. Regret and guilt tumbled in Lisa's stomach. Dry heat pressed against her exposed arms.

Charlie peered through the pergola slats. Her hazel eyes had enough of a green tint to remind Lisa of Charlie's car from the last trip and enough amusement to suggest Charlie wasn't here on a revenge mission. "Hottest architect in the country right now, high-end spa, art curator on retainer," Charlie said. "Never any surprises from Mary Blake."

Lisa hiked an eyebrow.

That evoked a laugh from Charlie. "Sometimes surprises. I stand corrected. Anyway, I guess I have to go in now that I've been spotted."

Charlie's barest of smirks made Lisa feel as though she were part of a secret. She'd found Charlie first. Somehow, that helped her gain her footing.

Lisa glanced at Charlie's black and otherwise nondescript carry-on bag. "Do you want to wait for your other bags?"

"This is it." Charlie nodded toward Lisa's luggage, not designer but a matching set that included a large suitcase, an expandable carry-on, and a foldable garment bag, all of which a bellman had loaded onto a gold-framed cart. "It's only four days, right? You guys aren't doing a return trip to Virginia without me, are you?" She held up her hands. "I won't take offense."

Lisa stifled nervous laughter and tried to replicate Charlie's nonchalance with a flip of her hand. "Wouldn't that be something? No, I wasn't sure what to bring, so I threw in all sorts of things. At random." She turned her back to the luggage cart. "I don't even know what's in the bags." Not true. She'd scoured the hidden corners of her closet and used precious credit card swipes to assemble the right outfits for any contingency. And she'd already screwed that up this morning.

Suddenly, twenty years didn't seem long enough.

Cool air engulfed Charlie and Lisa as a doorman wearing a bolo tie opened the heavy wooden doors of Rancho Verde. The faint scent of lavender traced with cut wood evened her nerves. Lisa planned a quick check-in and wardrobe change before she had to face the others.

"Lisa! Charlie!" The melodic call came from the direction of a walk-in-sized fireplace flanked by oversized chairs. Mary Blake, in a whirlwind of bangle bracelets and buttercream highlights, flew across the lobby like a fairy godmother who'd had one too many mimosas. Her embrace was greedy and generous, a long squeeze held for an extra moment, as if to sync heartbeats.

When Mary Blake moved to Charlie, Lisa spotted Annesley walking across the open space, her steps perfectly aligned with the floor's wooden planks. She appeared elegant, as always, with her dark hair in a chic chin-length cut shorter than before, and that dancer's body was even thinner than it was in college. *Who gets thinner after college? And who has breasts that look like that after having kids?*

Lisa knew "work" when she saw it. She wasn't sure why it mattered, why she felt smug. Her face flashed with heat. No, she knew. It was because it made her feel better about her lack of muscle tone and her sagging, four-baby belly. She pulled at the embarrassing ruffle on her shirt, and all smugness vanished.

"Lisa." Annesley's eyes glistened, and her arms spread.

Lisa hesitated. Annesley, typically so cool and detached, appeared to be caught up in the moment, or perhaps she'd been primed by Mary Blake's display. Lisa went in for a polite hug and found herself in an even more fulsome embrace than the one from Mary Blake. Awkwardness stiffened her shoulders, emphasizing the moment's asymmetry. Lisa forced herself to relax in an attempt to match Annesley's reunion etiquette.

Annesley pulled away, eyes bright. "Mary Blake is something else, getting us together like this, isn't she?" Her gaze settled on the petite blonde, who had an arm wrapped around Charlie's waist.

It was as if Annesley didn't remember she'd been the haughty one in college. Her face glowed with a smile that didn't harbor social calculation, and she didn't stand at a distance that allowed her to disassociate from anyone the high-end patrons in the lobby might have deemed undesirable.

Doubt rushed through Lisa's mind. Maybe her memory was faulty, clouded by years of late nights on-call, her growing family, and an NDA that had stalked her into disconnection.

When Annesley approached Charlie, she didn't impose a hug. "Charlie. You look—" her eyes appeared to mist. "It's great to see you."

Even that jarred Lisa in a weirdly positive way. In college, Annesley would have acknowledged Charlie's arrival with a visual once-over that signaled her lack of surprise that Charlie had underdressed for whatever occasion it was. But they weren't twenty-year-olds anymore.

Annesley turned to Lisa, her eyebrows raised in a "So here we are. Isn't it exciting?" prompt. Lisa stammered, trying to formulate a comment that balanced cavalier wit with nonchalant intelligence.

Rescuing Lisa from her inexplicable failure to string words together, the resort's heavy doors opened and sent the artificially conditioned air into a tornadic swirl.

"Helen! You're early!" Mary Blake flew from Charlie to Helen, whose mouth hung half open in apparent surprise at finding all of them in the lobby.

Lisa commiserated. It was one thing to romanticize a reunion. It was quite another to walk in and wonder, *Am I who they remember?*

Helen was slight in a gray boatneck tee and black capris, the simplicity a callback to college, when she'd been the perfect mix of lighthearted fun and actuarial precision. Her words spilled like marbles across a waxed floor. "My original flight was cancelled, so everything fell apart." Plan disruptions were college Helen's kryptonite and likely explained her unsteadiness. "I flew standby on an earlier flight. Last minute. There were two connections. Sorry, I—"

"We are complete!" Mary Blake squealed as she pulled Helen close to her side.

Complete.

Here they were, their voices melding with the same consonance Lisa remembered, from Mary Blake's soprano to Charlie's alto. The visual wasn't the same. Mary Blake still leaned in, but Helen's stance was guarded, and Charlie's slouch, now that Lisa examined it further, looked more like a crouch, as if she stood poised to spring through the big wooden doors the next time they opened. Initial awkwardness was to be expected. It had been so long.

With everyone's attention on Helen, Lisa found herself alone beneath an oversized chandelier. Detached already. Clayton Harrison's warnings of being a calf separated from the herd echoed. Her heart ticked up its pace.

The others continued their overlapping chatter about late arrivals—"You haven't aged a *minute*"—and how much hotter it was here than on the east coast.

Lisa tugged at her shirtsleeves to free her clammy armpits. "I'm going to go check in," she called to the others. She looked for the bellman to urge him to get her bags to her room so she could reassemble.

"No need to, sugar!" Mary Blake's face lit up with a firecracker smile that was even whiter now than it had been in college. "I've got wonderful news." She touched a shiny pink fingernail to her lips. "I upgraded our reservation, and we'll be in the Sam Houston Suite. It'll be like sharing Charlie's army tent, only the complete opposite."

Charlie closed her eyes at the reference to their first night camping on the last road trip and laughed as if she'd been had.

Lisa held her shoulders rigid and didn't let her smile drop. She wasn't going to have her own room. She couldn't remember if she'd brought cute pajamas. "Let me at least give them my credit card so they have it on file," she said, pulling out her wallet. She mentally calculated which card had the most available credit, wondering how much an upgraded Sam Houston Suite must cost.

Mary Blake put her hands on Lisa's. "Oh no, you don't. Gotta put that divorce settlement to good use. This is all on me. *My* treat for *my* Deltas." She glanced at Charlie, who had tilted her head and hiked her eyebrows. "And that includes you."

All together. The whole point of the trip. So why the catecholamine surge that had her squeezing her hand into a fist to slow her pulse? She glanced at Helen, who stood twisting her wedding band, and wondered if she wasn't alone.

# Chapter Eight
# 2019
# Charlie

Mary Blake chattered as she led the newly reunited group Pied Piper-style past the front desk, the Serenity Spa, and the Longhorn Coffee Bar.

Charlie kept her eyes on Helen. Once upon a time, Charlie could read Helen like she now read a room full of venture capitalists. In college, the flush on Helen's face, depending on the rise and the intensity, had communicated joy, excitement, nervousness, or anger. She and Helen hadn't needed that talk-talk-talk, sharing stuff.

But on a beach weekend their senior year, Charlie had wanted to talk. Truth be told, she hadn't exactly wanted "talk." She wanted to know whose dick she should sever and why they couldn't call the police after Helen had woken up in a strange bedroom disoriented and unclothed, with a used condom discarded next to the bed.

Helen's face was a weathered whitewash, almost gray, and she was unsettlingly still as she stood opposite Charlie in the drab living room of their beach rental. "No police, please." She shook her head almost imperceptibly. "I-I don't remember anything much after I told Lisa to leave the party without me. I was drinking and... I don't know what happened. I don't want to think about it, let alone talk about it. I just... promise me we leave it in this room." She locked eyes with Charlie. "Promise." She looked lost, in need of a beacon to assure her there was a way home.

Charlie knew that need, the survival instinct to move away from pain. And it wasn't Charlie's call whether to report it, regardless of her fury. She'd agreed because Helen's pallor, like that of a corpse coated in ash, was utterly unnerving, and Charlie needed to see life in her friend's face again.

Charlie had broken that promise, and it felt like yesterday rather than twenty years ago.

Helen's face now, in the hotel hallway, was inscrutable. She was smaller than Charlie remembered. Not fragile. More like folded in. She hadn't made eye contact since they'd squeezed in hellos when Mary Blake wasn't talking in the lobby. But the fact that Helen had come to Texas at all showed she didn't harbor DEFCON 1-level animosity toward Charlie.

Even in towering heels, Mary Blake kept up her quick clip through the minimalist hallway and ensured an uninterrupted monologue with a recounting of her morning, from her Uber ride to her first-class seatmate. "And then," she said, "the dear old thing—he was seventy-five if he was a day—told me to call him when I was of legal age. Bless his heart."

Helen laughed in the right places.

Once in the suite, the group convened in a sunlit space decorated for the resort's upscale clientele.

Mary Blake spun like a car-show model, arms splayed in brokendoll angles. "Welcome to the Sam Houston Suite, ladies."

White leather chairs surrounded a round table centered under a large metal chandelier. Pink and white flowers spilled from vases on every table and counter, contrasting with the rough-hewn wood beams that framed the room. Three open doors revealed bedrooms.

Mary Blake opened gauzy curtains to show the low-lying river and the undeveloped expanse beyond, the horizon flat and placid. "The concierge promised us a gorgeous sunset tonight, so let's get pretty for watching it." She pivoted and settled her gaze on each of their faces in punctuated succession. "I guess we're all ready!" The comment was so genuine, so Mary Blake, that the release of tension was palpable.

In a throwback to college, Mary Blake looked like she was having all the fun in the world and her only challenge in life was to find enough people to share it with. Still, Charlie felt a hesitancy hanging over the group. This trip didn't fit the usual blueprint of an annual girls' trip or even a class reunion. Not that Charlie had participated in either type of event, but she knew the run of show.

"Helen and Charlie, you get the Longhorn Room." Mary Blake gestured toward the bedroom closest to the entrance, and Charlie held a poker face. "Lisa, we California girls are going to take the Lone Star Room so we can catch up. Annesley has the master. If you get lonely, my dear, you let us know, and we'll all do a sleepover in that big bed with you."

Mary Blake left no opening to question room assignments or ask if this was the right way to start the trip, so close together after being apart for so long. She clapped her hands three times. "What are we waiting for, ladies? Go freshen up, and let's get this trip started!"

And just like that, the superficial chatter of new arrival ended, and Charlie found herself in the Longhorn Room with Helen. While Helen positioned her carryon atop a wooden luggage rack, Charlie stepped to the window and took in the green along the river she hadn't noticed before. During the approach to the hotel, she'd been neck deep in market analysis for work, something she hoped would keep her grounded for the next few days.

The view reminded Charlie of the hikes she'd led during their first trip. She chuckled at the memory of Annesley slipping on mossy rocks in her ridiculous designer sandals and Helen panting but too excited over the natural beauty to complain about Charlie's escalated pace.

"Everyone looks the same," Helen said wistfully.

Charlie's focus drifted to her hands on the windowsill. Her nails were trimmed, and prominent blue veins like a web of waterways ran across skin bronzed from sun and time.

"Except Annesley's hair," Helen continued. "I love it short."

"It's good to see everyone." Though a platitude, Charlie meant it.

"And Mary Blake went all out. I mean, the peonies. Wow." Helen shook her head, obviously impressed.

Charlie had seen the flowers. She hadn't processed that they were peonies. "Um, they were lovely."

Helen froze, her eyes wide. "The Delta Rho flower? Don't tell me you forgot that." Helen loved that sorority stuff: official flower, house colors, secret handshakes.

"Ah, right." Charlie set her travel pack on the counter, next to a pen and notepad stamped with the resort's riverbend logo. She picked up the pen and twisted it until it clicked.

Helen's face was gaunt, but the apple cheeks still emerged when she smiled. Charlie recalled Mary Blake's photo of the five of them atop her brother's Scout. "It's been a long time," Charlie said. She searched Helen's eyes for pain, sadness, anger, hurt, forgiveness—some sign to help her decode the moment, some indication to help her determine if an apology would be enough. "Listen, about—"

Helen shook her head. No anger marked her face, but her posture was rigid. "Can we be okay? The two of us?" The pleading in her eyes matched the softness of her voice.

Charlie straightened. Of course they could, but she was thrown. For the first time, Charlie wondered if Helen remembered their discussion—their argument—at the hospital at the end of the last road trip. Or perhaps Charlie misremembered, her synapses misfiring from grief compounded by grief. "Of course. If you're okay, I'm okay. It was a long time ago."

She and Helen had done that before with a painful moment, making an agreement to move on. The ploy had worked for a while, until it hadn't.

Helen exhaled, and her stance relaxed. She gave Charlie a smile—closed mouth but cheeks glowing a soft pink—and slipped off her shoes. "Mary Blake said we have thirty minutes 'til dinner. I might be awhile." She cranked her neck in a demonstration of chiropractic disarray. "You still good with the army shower—in and out?"

Relieved at Helen's lightened tone, Charlie reciprocated. "One of my personal indulgences anymore is a long scorching-hot shower. But I can get by on a quickie tonight. Take your time."

Helen entered the bathroom, pulled a plush white towel from a glass shelf, and closed the door.

Charlie stretched her arms and felt blood pulse into muscles that had been tense all day. So far, the reunion hadn't been as fraught as she'd had expected. She'd traipsed across the minefield of the reunion as easily as she ran along Chicago's Riverwalk at dawn.

After catching up on emails and a business development proposal she'd been unable to review on the plane because the Wi-Fi failed, Charlie checked her watch. Helen hadn't been kidding about Charlie only having time for an army shower.

Her phone buzzed, and Lillian's name popped onto the screen.

Even thinking about the army had been a bad move. The general's birthday was in four days, and it would be classic Lillian to remind Charlie to phone her dad on his big day. "He'd be thrilled to hear from you," she would say, her voice tinkling with optimism that maybe this time Charlie would call.

Even a fraught reunion in Texas with an inscrutable former best friend was better than one with the general. Charlie answered and cocked her shoulder to hold the phone while she unpacked. She pulled her pajamas out and placed them on the pillow, part of a business travel routine fixed in muscle memory.

"Charlie, dear, it's about your dad." Lillian didn't use her kindergarten-teacher voice. Muffled words from other people and what sounded like metal scraping across metal carried through the phone.

Charlie's pulse quickened. She adjusted her pajamas, as if moving them to the center of the pillow would shift the moment, dodge the hidden mine in Lillian's words. "Yes?"

"He's had a heart attack." Now it was Lillian's voice that sounded like metal scraping across metal. Straining, raw.

Ice gripped Charlie's throat. She pulled her fingers into a fist and focused on her carry-on.

"The doctors..." Lillian inhaled then resumed, her voice calm. "They had to intubate, and he's unconscious, sedated. They don't know much, but he's stable."

Charlie lifted out her toiletries bag and unzipped it. Shampoo, hair ties, Tums, and lip gloss. She shuffled the contents as if there might be a better order to things. She couldn't picture the general in a hospital bed, helpless. She zipped the bag and placed it at the foot of the bed.

From the other end of the phone came sounds of movement. Charlie envisioned Lillian rearranging the blanket on the general, tucking things in just so, and checking the hospital corners but mostly concerned with her husband's comfort, even if he was incapable of recognizing her efforts. How the man had found a woman so respectful of his standards of precision yet so compassionate baffled Charlie.

Steam seeped through the cracks of the bathroom door, ghostlike. Charlie cleared her throat. "Lillian—"

"One minute, hon. I'm sorry. The nurse just stepped in."

Charlie moved back to the window and stared out at the hazy horizon. Pressure in her throat ached with a familiar grip, but this call wasn't the same as the one she got when her mother died. That call had come too late and from a neighbor she'd hardly known. Her mother had already passed. And when the call had come her senior year, the general—the reason Brent was in danger in the first place—had phoned to tell her Brent was gone. "We met with the casualty notification officer," he'd said, as if he'd just inked a loan at the car dealership rather than accepted condolences from the US Army. She hadn't been able to express her grief on the phone, not with him.

Fear, anxiety, sorrow, and anger swirled in her gut. She exhaled to push the emotions out, release the pressure.

"I know you're on your trip with your friends, dear," Lillian said. "There's not really anything you can do here." Her voice was firm, as if Charlie had offered to come back.

Lillian had confirmed the general didn't need Charlie. He never had. Anyway, what was she supposed to do? Go sit by his bedside and wait for him to open his eyes to find her there? She hadn't seen the general in years. If he knew she was here with women from college, he would scoff and brush it off as some midlife boondoggle. If he opened his eyes and found her sitting next to him, he would ask why she didn't have something important to do.

The opening words of "When I'm Gone" wafted from the bathroom. Helen's voice started small but grew into a porcelain-amplified croon, off-key and lyrics-be-damned. The performance came across as a little more crackling fireside karaoke than polished audition, but her crooning held comfort, an escape buried in her imperfection.

"Lillian, I'll keep my phone on. Email if you can't reach me."

Charlie had no doubt Mary Blake had plans that would keep them distracted that night. She tossed the toiletries bag across the room and into her suitcase, where it belonged.

# Chapter Nine
# 1999
# Mary Blake

A towering canopy of trees filtered the diminishing light that glowed yellow green through the leaves. Mary Blake hadn't noticed it had gotten so late as they'd followed the Scout through the mountains along Virginia's Blue Ridge Parkway.

The lack of a cassette player in the White Whale had been more than made up for by Lisa singing every song she could think of that had the word "mountain" in it, her bluesy rasp too Janis Joplin for the school a cappella group but perfect for the road. And listening to Annesley belt out Diana Ross's part in "Ain't No Mountain High Enough" made Mary Blake laugh so hard she almost peed her pants.

"You think we're almost there?" Mary Blake asked, even though their navigator was in the Scout two car lengths ahead of them.

Annesley reached for the new CB jammed under the dash. "I'll CB them and ask."

Before Annesley pressed the talk button, the Scout's wonky blinker lit up. Blink, blink, pause, blink, pause, pause, blink—as if sending a message in Morse code to halt Annesley's imminent 10-4. Beyond a road-crowding tree, a yellow KOA sign appeared.

Annesley replaced the mic. "There's no way they'll get our camp set up before it's pitch black out here." She turned to face Lisa. "They *will* set up our tent and all for us, right?"

# THE LAST ROAD TRIP

Lisa flicked on her blinker and followed the Scout off the main road. "I don't think that's how it works."

The two might not be able to see it, but they were a lot alike. Lisa, who had been elected to Phi Beta Kappa, and Annesley, whose social connections stretched from Atlanta to Washington, DC, and now out to Texas, were the most singularly focused women Mary Blake knew. Sure, Annesley never appeared in public without her heirloom pearls or a manicure, and Lisa hadn't known the difference between cocktail dress and black tie when they started getting invited to Greek parties, but each had entered college, knowing exactly what they wanted to do in life, and Mary Blake had no doubt they would achieve their goals.

Mary Blake ran her thumb over her own manicured fingernail. She'd gotten good with the brush. A person would never know she hadn't been to a salon in nearly a year.

Having goals and ambitions seemed so grown up. She wasn't there yet. First, she needed to make up for a school year that had crumbled for reasons she couldn't share with the others, and this trip was that chance.

On the hardened gravel road, the wagon lurched awkwardly past a concrete restroom facility and on to the campsites Helen had secured for them.

Once they parked, Mary Blake emerged from the car and caught the chorus of a Garth Brooks song playing at a distant campsite. The tune mingled with the fading light, crushed leaves, and charred wood, creating an organic feast for the senses. She met the other girls behind the cars and surveyed the adjacent plots, uncertain what would distinguish suitable from unsuitable.

"These'll work," Charlie said.

That was good enough for Mary Blake, not that she knew of Charlie having any particular outdoor expertise. But Charlie had proved her chops when they were juniors and the Delta Rho

"Lemonade for Lymphoma" fundraiser had encountered a minor crisis in the form of a collapsed lemonade stand. At Helen's urging, Charlie made ugly structural changes with spare wood parts and covered them with flowy curtains she "borrowed" from the sorority house. With Helen at the cash box, Lisa stacking cups, and Mary Blake and Annesley directing traffic to Mary Blake's "lemonade," aka redneck margaritas—a mix of beer, tequila, Sprite, and frozen limeade—they'd raised more money than any prior fundraiser.

That was before the probation and, now that Mary Blake thought about it, had been the group's last day of unclouded joy. Someone had reported the Delta Rhos for selling spiked lemonade, a violation of county liquor laws and no fewer than three university rules, two Panhellenic regulations, and four Delta Rho International Guidelines.

Mary Blake leaned toward the car. "What's next? What can I do?"

Lisa held up a hand. "Stand back in case everything goes flying." She inserted her key in the tailgate lock and inched the hatch open.

Nothing launched out of the White Whale's wayback, but the blankets and plastic bags full of soft things that had molded to the wagon's interior fought to regain their original shape.

Lisa rifled around, pushing aside squishy trash bags. A green Coleman tent box peeked from behind a plastic bin filled with books. "Voila!" She slid it from the car and onto the ground.

The blue tent in the photo on the box was set up on a picture-perfect, lush campsite, next to a picture-perfect family that was laughing and holding red mugs full of some sort of camping beverage.

Annesley said exactly what was on Mary Blake's mind. "The whole tent in that picture is in that little box? And three of us are supposed to sleep in it?"

"That's the plan." Even Lisa didn't seem convinced that Coleman was accurate in advertising that the tent *Sleeps 3-4*. "I'm sorry. This one was on sale, and—"

Charlie didn't try to suppress her amusement. "I'll assume you guys are all set with your pretty little pup tent. Helen, can you give me a hand?"

They struggled with the box, Mary Blake at one end while Lisa and Annesley tugged the innards until they stumbled backward. The tent flew like a cooked turkey, and the accessories skyrocketed every which way.

Mary Blake held up the box like a trophy as she dodged the strewn plastic and metal parts. "Where should I put this?"

Lisa glanced from the box, which seemed even smaller now that they had extracted the tent, to the assembled pieces and parts scattered across the sparsely grassed area behind the wagon. "There's no way we're fitting all of this"—she waved her hands in resignation over what looked like a tent struck by a tornado—"back into that." She pointed at the box.

"I'll take it to the dumpster," Mary Blake said. "I saw one over by the bathrooms at the entrance." She grabbed the box and some stray trash from the car then skirted around an evergreen tree that separated the two plots.

Standing behind the Scout, Charlie pulled on a pile of faded green canvas. White rope bound poles to the folded fabric, and a nylon bag held a collection of metal stakes that poked out of the cinched opening. A whiff of musty garage betrayed the tent's recent whereabouts.

Helen cringed and glanced longingly at the freshly unboxed pile of blue nylon then back at Mary Blake. "Wanna swap?"

"It'll air out," Charlie assured Helen. "I'll get the tent up. Can you unload the sleeping bags and the food?" She tossed the bundle onto the campsite. "MB, if you're heading to the dumpster, I've got a bag."

Mary Blake shoved Charlie and Helen's fast-food leftovers into the tent box. She threw a wide smile at Annesley and Lisa, who both grimaced. Annesley was out of her element and likely devising ways Mary Blake could make things up to her.

People thought someone that tall and that pretty—that self-assured—had no worries, no boundaries. But Mary Blake had seen the caged look in Annesley's eyes on admitted students' day, when her mother seemed determined to micro-manage Annesley's way through college. Since then, the two had been best friends and roommates. They'd joined the same sorority, double dated, and visited Mary Blake's family lodge in Aspen. Although they'd shared an apartment, they'd seen little of each other the last school year. A trip seemed like a way to make up for it, a chance for Mary Blake to be present in a way she hadn't been for months. But Annesley puzzling over a crumpled tent didn't bode well for the next twelve days.

Mary Blake tripped over an exposed root, nearly tumbling face first onto the dirt pathway. A rusty dumpster sat behind the green restroom facility and, based on the sweet smell of rot, was due to be emptied.

No, this wasn't Aspen. But she had to make this work. After all, this had been her plan: the five of them on a grand trip, a grand adventure.

A grand diversion.

# Chapter Ten
# 1999
# Charlie

Charlie chuckled at Annesley and Lisa circling the blue pile of nylon in confusion. The French major and the premed honors scholar held stakes at various angles and tugged at the tent's corners to make it square.

Helen rammed her shoulder into Charlie's. "We're not all rugged outdoorsmen. Maybe you've been camping a gazillion times, you and your tent. For some of us, it's our first time."

Charlie opened her mouth to correct her, but she unfolded the canvas tent instead, probing the recesses of her brain to remember how to set the damn thing up. The general had never asked Charlie to join him and Brent on their camping trips. But the summer she turned ten, she'd decided she would do whatever it was her big brother did and prove to her dad she belonged with them.

Some brothers might have told her to bug off, but Brent had been game. "This *is* Dad we're talking about, though," he said. He led her to the garage and pointed at a pile of canvas in the corner. "Do you know what to do with that?"

He guided her through unfolding and laying out the canvas, arranging the ropes, and finding the right stake placements and angles. Her first solo attempt produced a wobbly funhouse version of a tent. She spent afternoons after school getting the sides straighter, the stakes deeper, and the floor tauter, until Brent told her a real army man couldn't have done it any better.

After a discussion between her mom and dad—seen but not heard through the kitchen window, because even when her parents had disagreements neither raised their voice—her dad wordlessly motioned for a gleeful Charlie to join him and Brent in loading the truck.

When they reached their campsite, Charlie did exactly as she'd practiced with the tent. As she unfolded the canvas, she heard her dad beckon Brent to help him gather firewood. Charlie had looked up with a start, worried about being left behind. Brent shot her a reassuring smile, as if telling her to keep at it and her dad would be wowed when they returned.

But he wasn't. When the two trudged back to camp, her dad didn't seem to notice the tent, with its taut anchor lines and canvas edges perfectly perpendicular to the ground.

Brent did. "Hey, looks like we don't need to put up the tent." He plucked an anchor line. "Pretty sure I couldn't have done it all by myself this well. Right, Dad?"

Her dad glanced at the tent and grunted, a dream-crushing dismissal. "Thought we'd sleep out on the ground tonight, son. Toughen you up. We'll go hunting early." He nodded at Charlie. "You get the tent. And you can sleep in."

The kindness in Brent's face couldn't compete with the alienation of her dad's words. When Brent encouraged her to join them by the campfire, Charlie instead climbed into her sleeping bag and pretended she was camping solo, a ten-year-old wunderkind who could pitch a tent and survive in the wilderness all on her own.

When Charlie poked her head out the next morning, hoping to convince her dad to let her join the hunting expedition, the charred scent of campfire burned like acid in her lungs, and smoldering embers were all that greeted her.

She hadn't asked to go on any more camping trips. And she hadn't put up that tent again until this night in the Virginia mountains, when the canvas, ropes, and stakes seemed to assemble themselves. She hadn't realized she was almost finished until Lisa, Helen, and Annesley hovered around her, their eyes wide in wonderment. An electric current raced from the tips of Charlie's fingers to the base of her skull.

Lisa gaped. "Damn, it's like *M\*A\*S\*H*."

Mary Blake appraised Charlie's tent, grazing her fingers along the canvas and testing the tightness of the ropes. "Was this in a war?"

"Oh, sure," Charlie said. "Korea, Nam, the Gulf."

Annesley's eyes grew wide.

Charlie laughed. "No, don't be ridiculous."

"Charlie, how in the world did you learn to do this?" Mary Blake asked.

"Army kid." Charlie huffed as she raised her mallet and made one last swing at a stake, probably unnecessary and definitely more *intensely* than necessary, but it pushed away the pride she was embarrassed to be feeling. "You pick up things."

"I'd like to see you with a sniper rifle," Lisa deadpanned. Then she cringed, clearly worried she said something insensitive to the grieving sister.

"I might be able to arrange that." Charlie tossed the mallet aside and brushed her hands off on her shorts.

"So," Lisa said, "maybe you can help us with... that?" She gestured toward the other campsite, where the pup tent lay unfolded and the poles and stakes lay out like a game of pick-up sticks.

Charlie adjusted her ponytail and bit her lip to suppress a grin. "What's the problem? Wasn't the box big enough for instructions?"

"They must have been stuck in the box, because we couldn't find them in any of that mess down there. Oh, Mary Blake, you're back."

Mary Blake hopped up next to Charlie, startling her. "Sorry it took so long. I met the sweetest gentleman over by the dumpster. He's a fisherman!"

"Sounds like you may need to go back to get the box, MB."

Mary Blake's face shifted from joy to severe apology, her lips pouting. "Oh, I don't think that's such a good idea. That fisherman I mentioned? He was kind enough to let me put our trash in the dumpster before he threw in the scraps from cleaning the trout he caught today. The dumpster smelled bad enough *before* the bucket of fish guts."

"It's getting dark, y'all." Annesley's reasoned voice didn't mask the wheels turning at the potential of diminished enthusiasm for camping. "I'm sure there's a hotel nearby. Let's put everything back in the cars and find a hotel. We can start over tomorrow. These OK Corral places—"

"KOA," Helen said, her finger raised like a schoolteacher.

"Whatever. I don't think these are right for us. I mean, hunters and guts? And we don't know any of these people, and we have to sleep on the ground even if we're inside a tent. There are no locks, and what about bears and mountain lions?"

Charlie shook her head. This was going to get old. "You guys do that. I'm good here with the bears."

Mary Blake folded back the flap to Charlie's tent and disappeared inside.

Helen engaged in damage control. "Tomorrow, we can stop earlier. I'll update the route again. For tonight, I'm sure Charlie can figure out how to put up the other tent." She patted the taut canvas, generating a soft thud. "I mean, she did this."

Mary Blake exited the tent and let the flap fall across the opening. "Charlie, this is amazing! You know, this tent is big enough for all of us. Just sayin'."

The instinct to shut down that train of thought rose like a locomotive, but a ten-year-old's memory of a cavernous tent and a dark night alone inside dampened the coals. The deep shadows of dusk gave cover to the internal battle Charlie was sure would have been broadcast on her face in full daylight. "Fine," she said, infusing reluctant resignation in her voice. "We can all sleep in this one. And I'll figure the other one out tomorrow."

"Yippee!" Mary Blake's ebullience gave Charlie further cover. "I don't know about y'all, but I'm dying for some s'mores. I think I saw Helen pull a bag of marshmallows and some graham crackers out of the Scout. And I bet Charlie knows how to set up a campfire, being an army brat and all."

Charlie forced herself to roll her eyes and caught Lisa grinning at her. Some things were just preordained when Mary Blake was around.

# Chapter Eleven
# 2019
# Lisa

Lisa's arrival in the wrong outfit felt ages ago, a dress rehearsal for the real reunion after everyone showered and changed. There'd been no time to catch up in the suite, especially since Mary Blake had dashed off to make sure dinner plans were in place. But there'd been time to switch to a coral sundress that swung loosely at her knees and gave at least the impression of being carefree. It was time to leave behind the awkward reminder of her younger self that had emerged earlier.

Ahead of Lisa in the lobby, Charlie and Helen seemed to have fallen into their college cadence, an ease with each other that translated into hands in pockets and no need to fill silences. Businessmen in cowboy boots and women with big hair and jewelry to match postured with cocktails in front of the fireplace. Lisa picked up her pace so it was clear she was with the two in front of her, and the feeling struck her that she'd often trailed the group like this, had never wanted to appear pushy lest she get pushed out.

Helen glanced over her shoulder and moved to her right to make room. Lisa hesitated long enough to dismiss the concern that Helen had overheard her thoughts then moved forward.

Helen slid her hand through the crook of Lisa's elbow. "Do you think we'll be able to keep up with Mary Blake on this trip?"

"She's incredible," Lisa said, feeling linked again. "I didn't have that energy at eighteen, let alone at forty-one with kids and a job."

"Our own personal cruise director," Helen mused.

Everyone had played a role in college. Having Helen steer her and Charlie past the concierge desk and the stenciled glass door of the hotel's Serenity Spa reinforced that. Always the navigator.

The spa-adjacent restaurant opened to an expansive view of the Texas plains. A raised floor and a wall of windows gave the sensation of floating above the prairie grass. And beyond the green riverbank, the horizon stretched forever.

Mary Blake stood from behind a table at the center of the broad view and opened her arms, greeting Charlie, Helen, and Lisa as if the resort were her personal summer villa. She'd changed into a white shift dress tied at the waist with a silk scarf that matched her blue eyes. Directing her attention to Lisa, she smiled. "Is everyone refreshed?"

"I could have stayed in the shower for an hour." Lisa motioned toward Charlie's damp hair. "Looks like Charlie's still army showering."

Annesley sipped water from a tall glass, her long fingers showing off a narrow gold wedding band. She'd never been flashy like Mary Blake. "I seem to recall Charlie didn't take a lot of showers on our trip." Annesley's tone was light, no hint of the fire of the last memorable exchange between the two when they were younger.

Charlie shook her head. "I only shower at fancy hotels, not places crawling with hunters and bears."

"Touché." Annesley raised her water glass in salute.

Despite the quip, part of Charlie didn't seem to be fully with them. In place of the alert ease from earlier, a distracted tension showed in the set of her jaw, something Helen had called "the Mt. Rushmore-ization of Charlie" back in school. Serious, focused, impenetrable. It hadn't been there outside the hotel when Lisa arrived in her taxi. Lisa looked at Helen and wondered if she'd misread their return to form, if Charlie might hold resentment for any or all of them.

Mary Blake placed two fingers on Lisa's bare shoulder. "I love your dress, Lisa." She dragged out the word "love" in a way that filled her whole body with the word. "Coral complements your skin tone."

Lisa flushed and managed a "Thank you," worries about Charlie all but forgotten. She squirmed under the strapless bra that had shifted an inch too far to the left.

With the arrival of their server, each woman put in a drink order. Lisa's "Bourbon and ginger, please" raised eyebrows. She didn't normally drink the hard stuff, but she needed to take the edge off.

"I see you've gone over to the dark side," Annesley said.

Heat burned Lisa's ears, and she wasn't sure if she was being mocked. "I wasn't exactly a teetotaler in college."

"You were more of a wine-cooler girl. Safe." Lisa didn't hear condescension in Annesley's words, but she thought she heard the tone Mary Blake had used when talking about the elderly Texan who hit on her in first class. Bless his heart.

They held off on more chatter while they perused the menus. Annesley was gluten-free: "Helps with the allergies." Charlie, organic: "Don't act so surprised."

Drinks arrived just as Lisa was rising from her chair to run to the bathroom and fix her bra. All eyes landed on her, frozen in an awkward half-standing, half-sitting crouch, a fresh highball next to her bread plate. The expectant smiles fueled the muscle power she needed to stand upright. Heat rose to her face, and she steadied herself by staring into Mary Blake's eyes. "Um"—she raised her glass, the power rising from her legs through her core and into her flexed arm—"to Mary Blake. For bringing us together."

The women echoed the toast, and crisp clinks of rims kissing rims filled the air. Lisa tapped her highball against Helen's wine glass enthusiastically. The sound of glass shattering muted the celebratory words. Inches from Lisa's hand, Helen held a bowl-less glass stem. Blood-red drops of pinot noir licked Helen's fingers, and a crimson pool of wine seeped through the white tablecloth. Hot pink flushed across Helen's face, but the pink was mild compared with the searing flame constricting Lisa's throat. The table—the entire restaurant—was quiet.

Charlie's wide-mouthed laugh sliced through the silence, her earlier calcification giving way. Helen followed, haltingly at first, a chuckle she held close in her chest. But sound burst loose, and she snorted. Her eyes opened wide in surprise, and she covered her mouth and nose with her hand. She snorted again, and Charlie laughed louder then took a drink. Lisa joined in, releasing the binding pressure that made her chest hurt. The resulting group laughter was more cleansing than any shower.

It didn't take long before conversation topics leapt like currents, jumping from one component to another, and any time the conversation forked into two, the separate branches merged back to one for fear of missing out on some tidbit, joke, or anecdote. Mary Blake led the show, a maestro who directed the waitstaff when drinks needed refreshing and pulled women into the conversation when they drifted into the wings. While her hair hardly moved, animation illuminated her face, and her hands fluttered to emphasize every point.

At the latest hypnotizing swish of Mary Blake's bejeweled hand, Lisa gestured toward the Liz Taylor-worthy, diamond-encircled sapphire. "Your ring is beautiful. Wedding ring?"

"Oh, this little thing?" Mary Blake swirled her hand and light reflected through the stone like sunlight reaching into the deep of the ocean. "Frank never would have given me costume jewelry."

Fire burned Lisa's cheeks. She knew from an internet search that Mary Blake had recently divorced. "I'm so sorry. I'm—I shouldn't have mentioned it. I know you—"

Mary Blake waved off Lisa's apologies. "All I have to say is that if you can keep your private affairs private, you'll be a much happier person." She wiggled her fingers, and the ring caught the light again. "I found this ring when I was with Annesley, meeting her now-husband, possibly my greatest accomplishment. The finding Annesley a husband thing, not the ring. Though the ring is fabulous."

"I'd love to hear about that." Helen, recovered from the wineglass incident and well into a refill, leaned forward, eyes glimmering.

Annesley lifted her chin toward Mary Blake. "Shall I? Or do you want the honors?"

Mary Blake motioned for Annesley to proceed.

Lisa braced for tales of private jets, movie stars, and piles of Rodeo Drive shopping bags. And her own flush of jealousy.

"Mary Blake invited me to Sundance. She and Frank had just started dating, and she wanted a wingman. And who am I to turn down the Sundance Film Festival?" She raised her wine glass in a mock toast. "Anyway, Jameson was presenting his documentary, and—"

Mary Blake finished Annesley's sentence in her own way, as she always had. "Frank, the idiot, didn't have any interest in him. But Annesley did."

"Not quite how I was going to phrase it, but yes. Frank's an idiot, and missing out on Jameson's talents is one *small* example." Her nostrils flared. "Don't get me started. My interest, though, wasn't in producing Jameson's next documentary."

"Jameson's a hottie," Mary Blake explained, her fingers splayed for emphasis. Her timing jumping in and out of Annesley's tale indicated they'd told the story before, probably to film directors and movie people who thought it was a cinematic meet-cute.

A flush rose on Annesley's cheeks. "He has so much passion. I couldn't have imagined he'd be interested in me. When he mentioned at a meet-and-greet that he'd be heading to Haiti for his next documentary, I blurted that I could come along as a French interpreter."

Annesley took a sip of water, and Mary Blake grabbed the opening. "Annesley didn't know his mother is French. He's fluent." Mary Blake laughed, her light melody harmonizing with Annesley's smile.

"He didn't tell me that until later." Annesley rolled her eyes but glowed.

"So he was interested," Lisa said. Of course he was. Annesley had always had everything. Looks, status, money. Who wouldn't want her or want to be her?

Annesley shrugged. "Got married, moved to Connecticut, had two kids. That's my story." She ran her fingers across the water beading on her glass and seemed lost in the way the light reflected through the ice cubes. Her eyebrows drew together, as if a troubled thought from Connecticut had intruded, but she flicked it away with a shake of her head. She chose Lisa when she looked up from her glass. "How about you? What do you have going on? What kind of medicine are you in? Let me guess. Cardiology? Neurosurgery?" Her eyes sparkled, and she ran a hand across her blushed cheeks. "Dermatology? I've always wanted a dermatologist friend on call."

"General practice." Lisa's words fell like a bag of sand, heavy and unremarkable. No bling, no international film festivals, no French-speaking mothers.

Mary Blake swooped in with a save. "I bet it's fascinating. You get to see a bit of everything."

But Lisa's mouth had gone numb, and she failed to grab the opportunity to spin physicals and well-checks into a compelling illustration of the job she genuinely valued.

Annesley filled the lull before it settled. "We're a pretty impressive bunch." She looked at Lisa then at Helen and Charlie. "We have a doctor, a CPA, a lawyer—"

"I'm not a lawyer," Charlie said drolly. "But I *have* a lawyer. Does that count?"

"Wait," Annesley said. "You were pre-law. Mary Blake said you were in mergers and acquisitions."

"I have a consulting firm."

"Meaning?" Annesley seemed intrigued. She'd moved on, and Lisa had once again failed to be someone interesting.

"We consult on business acquisitions and combinations. Help companies find strategic partners and start-up capital, advise on deal terms, and so on."

Lisa wondered what Charlie would say about start-up capital generated by coverups and an NDA. How about if she learned that Lisa's payoff hadn't even covered two full years of medical school?

The answer to that was easy. Charlie would say Lisa had made a crappy deal and should have asked for more. Except she wouldn't say that, because the whole thing centered on a death and resulted in a devastating loss for Charlie and—*dammit*. Lisa shook her head and tried to pull herself out of the past—like the others seemed to have done—and find her way back into the conversation.

By the time the antelope carpaccio and burrata bruschetta appetizers arrived, the five had settled into a banter that grew in volume and promised to get louder as more wine came to the table. From job titles to babies born, the women relayed their life resumes. Charlie and Mary Blake discovered they'd both been in Montreal for Christmas the prior year—Charlie on business, Mary Blake on a last attempt to stay with Frank. And everyone lamented not having visited campus in years.

The sun neared the horizon, and entrees replaced apps. Lisa set down her fork to rub her jaw. During rush, they'd bemoaned the facial trauma of fake-smiling for hours on end. But the alcohol had done its job, and these smiles were real.

"Refills!" Mary Blake exclaimed as the sommelier arrived with a fresh bottle.

Lisa's phone buzzed. Reflexively, she checked the screen. A 202 area code.

The din around the table gave way to the whoosh of her breath, to the hot pulse of blood in her jugular, to numbers that translated to NDA. The phone buzzed again. She couldn't look away, and she couldn't stop her mouth from hanging open.

"Who is it, honey?" Mary Blake asked.

"The hospital." *What the hell?* Lisa didn't have time to figure out why she'd said that before the phone buzzed again.

"Sounds important. You should answer it." Mary Blake gestured for Lisa to take the important call and save whatever life was in peril.

The others held looks of admiration. The minor panic of ignoring a ringing phone set in and compounded a desire to fulfill the table's collective expectations, sending her heart racing.

Lisa stood, turned away from the table, and answered at the exact moment she realized she could have sent the call to voicemail and pretended to answer. From behind her, she heard laughter, the other women already moving on and making memories without her while they drank expensive pinot noir.

"Lisa Callihan? This is Selena May from the *Post*." Silence filled the line as Lisa dodged diners to speed toward the restaurant entrance and outpace the weights that wanted to crush her chest. "I left you a voicemail. I'm calling about Tripp Harrison. Maybe you saw that he'll be holding a press conference on Saturday regarding the senate seat that's opening up."

*Press conference?* More laughter. Lisa turned to watch what she was missing, and the weights landed, taking the wind out of her lungs and pressing her ribcage perilously close to her spine.

"No, I didn't get the message. I... I think you have the wrong person. I'm not one of his constituents."

"You went to college with Harrison, right? I have a few questions about the night his brother died."

Thoughts swirled, but all Lisa could grab onto was the thought that this could not be happening the first time she set foot back in Texas. "Yes, he and I went to the same college, but I didn't really know him. Like I said, I'm not into politics, and"—she looked longingly at the refuge of the table—"I have to get back—"

"Your name appeared in some medical records."

Her thoughts stopped churning, too ephemeral to compete with the reporter's statement. Lisa slipped out of the restaurant and let the glass door close behind her. She faced a corner by the spa to muffle her voice. "What medical records?" Fog filled her head as she tried to follow the reporter's words to a natural conclusion.

The reporter relaxed into a nonthreatening tone. "From twenty years ago. Were you in the same remote Texas hospital the night Tripp Harrison's brother, Parker, died? That would be quite a coincidence, especially if you 'didn't really know' Tripp Harrison."

Lisa steadied herself with a hand against the paneled wall. "I don't know what records you're talking about, but it sounds like you—"

"The senate seat that's opening is a powerful one. And Harrison is going to face scrutiny by the other side and the press if he announces his candidacy. It's a big deal. Are you sure you aren't willing to answer some questions?"

*Shit shit shit shit shit.* It didn't matter if Lisa wanted to comment. A contract precluded it.

The hospital and police records were supposed to have been destroyed. She pressed her temples with her thumb and middle finger. Maybe they'd missed something, or someone had held onto a file or a notebook.

"The contract is as much to protect you as anyone else," Glenn Whiteford, Esquire, had said.

"Say nothing," Clayton Harrison had said.

She'd already gone off course by responding at all, by blurting the verifiable lie that she didn't know Tripp. The sunset flooded the restaurant entrance with a discordant orange sherbet glow. She pinched the bridge of her nose to will her liquor-addled brain to think logically.

The reporter could be bluffing, fishing. It had been so long ago. Hospital records had been on paper, and they would have been stored in off-site facilities and destroyed as standard operating procedure, even if they hadn't been disappeared as part of the Harrison family's "handling" of the situation.

If the reporter had something she could use, she would have said something by now. Otherwise, she probably had only enough to make a phone call. A rumor maybe.

"I'm sorry, Selena. I'm not involved in this campaign as a voter or a supporter or anything else." Lisa's voice, uneven and rushed, wasn't as strong as she wished it would be. She needed to be blasé. How would Annesley be responding? She probably would have hung up by now. "I don't know what you're looking for, but I have nothing for you, and—"

"Dr. Callihan, I'm sorry." The reporter's voice took on a more conciliatory tone. "We may have gotten off on the wrong foot. But this story—the senate seat opening up and Harrison making an announcement—is happening quickly. The Harrison family's controversial fracking explorations, together with whispers about past indiscretions, elevates the potential national interest in a seat that's being vacated due to a bribery conviction. To be candid, I think it's in your interest to talk with me. When you picked up, it sounded like you were out with friends, so I understand if now isn't a good time. If you talk to me, I can give you a level of confidentiality. But if we find information through other channels before then, I can't guarantee it."

Lisa may not have fully grasped the NDA when she signed it, but she'd learned in the interim. Her NDA didn't mean she could only tell *some* people or that she could only tell people who said they would keep it confidential. It meant she could tell *no one*. Saying anything equaled a breach. And a breach equaled "liquidated damages" in an amount that would wipe out every dime of her savings and likely send her into bankruptcy. That payment she'd received for signing the NDA had seemed like a windfall, one she'd convinced herself she deserved since she wouldn't get to LA in time for her summer internship. She'd rationalized then that it wouldn't be a burden to keep her mouth shut if no one ever asked.

She'd been naïve. Of course someone would ask. But she hadn't had the luxury of lawyers to help her brush off the Harrisons. They'd presented her with a way out and a way up: take the money and go off to medical school with more than the internship would have paid. Looking back, she wasn't sure what other choice she'd had. She certainly had no choice now.

"You have my number,'" the reporter said. "I hope to hear from you soon."

All the women at the table had their secrets back then. Even Mary Blake, whose lies about her sick father had shocked them all, and yet, she and Annesley had reconciled, and Mary Blake sat at the table's head, unscathed. A rogue thought broke through Lisa's jumbled brain and suggested she unleash the truth and tell her friends, consequences be damned. But it wasn't just the Harrisons she worried about.

Lisa leaned her forehead against the meditation room's cool glass door, her heart thumping. Through the vines etched in the glass she read the quotation painted in flowing, under-lit calligraphy on the meditation room wall: Tranquility flows through silence.

# Chapter Twelve
# 1999
# Mary Blake

Mary Blake lingered at the trailhead, reluctant to let go of the expansiveness she'd felt at the peak and its three-hundred-sixty-degree view overlooking Asheville, North Carolina. She spun in a slow circle beneath the pine canopy. She wanted to memorize every shade of green, from the chartreuse mosses to the dark juniper. The trail they'd hiked, with beckoning side paths and trees that reached toward the clouds, gave her room to breathe, a place to leave her secrets behind.

With the tent situation resolved, a regular driving rotation established in the White Whale, and the five of them ensconced in their own little mobile world—destination Golden State!—life seemed simple for the first time in nearly a year.

Steps away, next to a sign that admonished hikers to "Keep dogs on leash," Lisa tied her shoe. She looked content, easy, like she did when she didn't know anyone was watching. Mary Blake considered it a challenge to get her friend to have that same countenance when attention focused on her. Lisa looked up, caught Mary Blake's eye, and smiled. Sometimes, that was all it took. A shooting star of victory sparkled through Mary Blake's chest.

Lisa pulled a small wad of dollar bills out of her fanny pack and counted them. "Do you need anything from the store? I'm getting a postcard to send my parents."

Mary Blake shook her head. "I'm all set. I'm going to call home."

"I hope your dad's doing okay." She placed a hand softly on Mary Blake's forearm.

Mary Blake smiled wanly and turned back toward the trail in time to see a deer at the edge of the woods. Its antlers combing through the green boughs, the buck stared at her with soulful black eyes. Mary Blake's heart whirred like a swarm of butterflies taking flight. The creature's ears perked, and he turned in a single movement. The white flash of tail disappeared into the woods. An omen, a good one. Mary Blake had been distracting herself, but her dad's news had to arrive soon. Maybe today was the day.

She approached the pay phone in time to see Annesley hang up.

Annesley hiked her purse onto her shoulder and swiveled toward a man hovering behind her. "I hope you got off on my conversation, pervert." She noticed Mary Blake, only yards away. "Are you going to breathe on my friend's neck too?" Annesley glared at the man and didn't break eye contact until he slithered away.

"And that's why I try to not get on your bad side," Mary Blake said with a cheerfulness that belied the truth behind the words.

"You could never be on my bad side." Annesley brushed her hands on her shorts. "Good news. The lake house is all set. My dad's in New York for some board meeting, which means my mother will be redecorating the Atlanta house or commandeering some charity league event. No plans for anyone to be at the lake house this week." Annesley tucked her hair behind her ear and stopped mid-tuck, noting the phone card in Mary Blake's hand. "I'm sorry. You wanted to call home. I'll go buy us some water bottles. Tell your parents I said hi and I hope your dad is feeling better."

Mary Blake gave her the soft smile of gratitude and hope that she'd delivered countless times while praying no one would see through the façade. Annesley walked away, satisfied once again, and Mary Blake used the phone to call her parents.

Mary Blake's mom answered, her "Hello" not a question like when most people pick up but a sunny dose of Vitamin D. And it worked. Mary Blake felt like she could float back to the top of the trail.

"How's your trip, Sunshine?"

"It's been perfect, Mama. We camped in tents and slept on the ground." She described the campsites, the singing, and the waterfalls, their trip a memory collage in her mind after only two nights. "Next stop is the Cannons' house at Lake Burton."

"Back in Georgia! It sounds lovely."

Twisting a lock of hair around her finger, Mary Blake turned to watch the others. They were out of earshot, hovering around the Scout and the White Whale. "How's Daddy?"

"He's at a meeting with his business advisors right now. We're delighted you came home to visit before you went on your trip."

Mary Blake hadn't really had a choice about going home during graduation week. Her only other option was to stay at school and be the one person not in a cap and gown, the one person not eligible to walk across the stage, revealing her year-long deception. So she decided to act the dutiful daughter and visit her "ailing" father.

Nearly a year had passed since her parents had hosted Mary Blake and her two older sisters and their husbands for dinner at their historic Savannah home. The heirloom Caughley china lay on the table, but it hadn't signaled the announcement of a new grandchild on the way or the appointment of her father to some distinguished position. Instead, her father told them in his reasoned tone that an "ambitious" assistant attorney general was on a "wild goose chase" through his firm's financials. His matter-of-factness disarmed everyone—"Nothing to worry about here." Her mother's hand resting softly on her father's forearm tempered any fears Mary Blake might have had. The best thing to do, he told them, was to cooperate, keep the investigation under tight wraps, and maintain appearances.

Frozen bank accounts made the latter a challenge, but Mr. Bulloch hadn't mentioned that part until a one-sided conversation with Mary Blake the day before fall semester tuition was due and no check was forthcoming.

Mary Blake glanced toward the trailhead parking lot. Charlie was holding up the hood of her car for a middle-aged man in cargo shorts. Annesley chatted with Helen and Lisa, likely about her well-laid plans, which didn't have roadblocks erected by assistant attorneys general. Annesley smiled supportively when she looked up to see Mary Blake staring in her direction. Mary Blake gave a thumbs-up, and her stomach soured.

The story about her father being ill had rolled off Mary Blake's tongue like any of her honest Savannah tales. The lie had flowed with such ease, in fact, that she questioned how she'd taken to it without a hitch. That part of the deception hadn't been her plan, though she'd never planned to tell them the truth. The others might have understood, but Annesley would have been horrified by the association with potential scandal.

"Daddy can't travel right now," she'd said before parents' weekend in the fall. Her father was on the older side, sixty-eight, and everyone knew that. They assumed he was ill. She let them, convincing herself the deceit was a harmless white lie. He would be vindicated by the end of the calendar year, he'd assured her.

The duplicity carried into second semester and a missed graduation. "I need to visit Daddy because he's having an experimental treatment." The lie had tasted of rot by May.

Mary Blake tugged at the snaky metal phone cord. "Has there been any news? It's been longer than Daddy said it would be."

"Don't you worry, Sunshine. He's got the best people working on this. There's nothing you need to do except spend time with your friends."

Mary Blake held her tongue. Secretly waiting tables to pay the rent she split with Annesley had made it hard to spend time with her friends, though she'd discovered she had a knack for upselling and getting good tips. She just had to be everyone's best friend until the check came.

What started as an obligation to protect the family reputation turned into a deception that pulled Mary Blake away from her real friends. Luck bent in her favor when the university put the house on probation, which meant no more parties, less engagement, and fewer opportunities to be discovered. She'd just needed to get through the year, wait for her dad's vindication, resume normalcy, and pretend none of it ever happened.

Mary Blake lowered her voice and kept her eye on the other girls. "I have to respond to the school by tomorrow about registering for classes this fall so I can complete my degree. I was wondering... if I can sign the tuition contract."

"I think—" The trace of a waver in her mother's voice contrasted with her usual composure, and discomfort crawled across Mary Blake's skin like thousands of mayflies. "I think it would be best that we wait. You'll have plenty of opportunities."

"The school only allows one year off, Mama. I won't be able to graduate." The whine in her voice dragged against the still air. "Not to mention I had to"—she cupped her hand around her mouth—"lie to Annesley and tell her that I lost my credit card. Now, she's covering things for me. You said it would all be fine." Mary Blake never wanted to question her mother, but she wondered if there was something her parents weren't telling her.

"It will, honey. The attorneys think we should hear in about a week and a half. They have the prosecutor in line. Patience. There's always a bright side. You just have to look past the dark clouds to find it. We'll have Annesley out to Hilton Head when this blows over."

Mary Blake deplored hiding things from her friends, and she'd grown frustrated with living life on hold. But her mother was right. She needed to be patient. "Tell Daddy I love him."

"I will. You have fun. And don't worry about a thing."

Annesley whooped and flipped up her long hair. Light caught strands of glimmering gold highlights. Her embrace of freedom and an unlimited future in front of her was exactly what they should all be celebrating, but it was hard for Mary Blake not to worry about dark clouds.

# Chapter Thirteen
# 2019
# Annesley

In the hotel bathroom, Annesley faced the wall-to-wall bathroom mirror—Texas-sized—and smoothed her bangs to the side. She never would have worn her hair so short back in college. The jawline cut with asymmetrical bangs that fell across her face would have been radical, unfeminine, and worse, unexpected.

Laughter from dinner rang in her head. These women were *life*, and she'd wasted so much time, not just the past twenty years, but in college, too, when she didn't appreciate what she'd had.

She removed her earrings and tucked them into her travel bag. The aquamarine solitaire necklace, a gift from Jameson after the birth of Cora, she left on. He believed in Annesley as a mother, despite knowing her own mother.

She opened her texts. Cora had sent a photo of herself and her younger sister flashing peace signs while Jameson snuck into the background for a goofy photo bomb. The knot of tension in Annesley's shoulders untangled. Cora seemed to have come around since the party invitation dispute. She'd been rather lovely over the past couple of weeks, to the point Annesley worried she'd learned the cancer had returned.

The MRI last week had confirmed it. And next week's scheduled port surgery ahead of chemo sealed the sentence. She rubbed the bruise in the crook of her arm from yesterday's blood draw. Stage IV metastatic breast cancer, an almost certain death sentence, had been stockpiling its armaments in her bones and lungs while she made cookies and went to soccer games. As Charlie would have said, mets was a sneaky motherfucker.

Jameson had assuaged her concerns about Cora's behavior. "She's a girl. *Your* girl. She's mercurial. What do you expect? Some uninteresting, predictable child?" Annesley had snuggled in when he wrapped his strong arms around her. "We'll talk to them both when you're back from the trip."

She pulled a prescription bottle from her bag. The new pills helped her general achiness, but they didn't cooperate with alcohol. Fortunately, no one had noticed that she'd nursed that single glass of wine throughout dinner. The soft swish of the bedroom door interrupted her as she was about to twist off the cap.

Mary Blake's voice followed. "Hey, sugar! You need anything?"

Annesley whipped the hand holding the prescription bottle behind her back and leapt out of the bathroom. She felt silly at the motion but more concerned about Mary Blake seeing the bottle reflected in the bathroom mirror.

Backlit, Mary Blake glowed like a sprite, and Annesley held back from trying to draw from her friend's energy. It felt manipulative when Annesley hadn't told her yet. She planned to tell her soon, because she wasn't going to lie.

But first Mary Blake needed to be on an upswing, one Annesley could grab ahold of. Mary Blake had been her lodestar when she'd battled cancer before, helping Annesley regain the sense of control she loathed ceding to the doctors.

Mary Blake stood next to the bed, her hands fidgeting and her jaw tight. "What's behind your back?"

Annesley's legs went weak, like she'd overdone a spin class. She placed her free hand on a chair to steady herself, to conjure an explanation, while sliding the bottle into her waistband. "Chipped nail."

She pretended to examine her nails and pushed a hand into her pocket.

"Don't be silly. No one noticed. I certainly didn't. How do you think it's going?" Mary Blake's eyes pleaded for affirmation.

Annesley relaxed, legs steady again. It wasn't always about her.

Not even four months had passed since Mary Blake had signed the divorce papers and called Annesley, her shine dulled to an unrecognizable matte. "I can't understand what I did wrong," Mary Blake had said during a tearful late-night phone call.

Now, Mary Blake was so hopeful, so eager for this trip to be a success. She needed her own guiding star.

"Dinner was incredible." Annesley puffed her cheeks as if she'd devoured an entire Thanksgiving turkey. "And being with everyone…" Her eyes misted, and she blinked hard to stem the tears that wanted to spill.

"Do you think so?"

"Dinner? Yes, it was fantastic." Annesley focused on the food to divert her attention from the nostalgia wrapping around her heart. "After that Gulf Coast redfish, I don't think I can gloat about New England's seafood being the gold standard."

"Oh, that makes me happy. But I mean everyone. It's good? Do you think everyone's having fun?"

Their dinner appeared in Annesley's mind as a tableau vivant, Mary Blake smiling but holding her hands on the table to still her nerves. She needn't have worried. The women had dived into conversations as if they hadn't been apart, loud, overlapping, and working toward closing a twenty-year gap over three courses. Granted, the conversation had skated along superficialities. And the trip's end hadn't surfaced. But why would they entangle themselves in the complications of the past? Surely, Annesley wasn't the only one who didn't want to sully what could be a lovely reunion. Tonight had been the kind of success that Mary Blake needed.

Annesley held back from an instinct to hug her friend, lest any movement send the bottle down her slacks and out the bottom of her pantleg onto the patterned carpet. It wasn't as though Annesley was never going to tell her. It was perfectly appropriate to wait to tell non-family.

Her legs wobbled again. Mary Blake *was* family. Annesley re-gripped the chair and squeezed.

Family needed to be supported. But telling Mary Blake when the trip was taking off would turn the rest of the weekend into a "farewell to Annesley" funeral dirge. They'd already been on a trip in which Annesley had made things all about her. The results spoke for themselves. Once they had a successful trip as a memory, she would tell Mary Blake, whose shoulders were so tense they hovered near her chandelier earrings.

"Are *you* having fun, Mary Blake?"

Mary Blake exhaled, and her shoulders fell from their perch. "Yes. This makes me happy. I missed you. And seeing everyone is more than I could have expected. There's still one thing, though." Concern clouded her face. "We need to remember Parker."

Annesley ran her hand across her collarbone. "Do you think it's worth bringing up? If no one wants to talk about it, maybe it's best to—"

"We can't ignore it. You and I didn't ignore it."

She was right. When Annesley and Mary Blake had reconnected in their twenties, they had talked for hours, debating their role in Parker's death. They hadn't been at the crash. But it was complicated.

Mary Blake continued. "You and I, of all people, know it's best to put things out there."

Annesley opened her mouth, but no words came.

"I know," Mary Blake said, misconstruing Annesley's concern. "It's still hard to think about. But we'll get through it. Hey, can I get you a glass of wine? Room service sent up a couple of bottles. I'm fixing to call my dog sitter, and then I have a surprise for everyone."

Annesley smiled and moved to usher Mary Blake back to the common room. "Sure. Just a small one, though. I had a lot at dinner. It's only the first night." It was a small lie, but it constricted her throat just the same. "I'll be out in a sec."

The bedroom door clicked shut, and Annesley collapsed, hands on her knees and pill bottle digging into her back.

She tried to convince herself that an omission wasn't a lie, but a question nagged at her. Would she have extended Mary Blake the same grace that last year of college when Mary Blake had hidden her father's legal troubles? Doubtful. She'd wanted life to be easy and predictable, and Mary Blake's scandal hadn't fit into that.

Fast-forward twenty years, and now, Annesley harbored the lies. She couldn't backtrack without imposing a painful hurdle to making this trip work. And it had to work, because it was probably the last one they would take together.

# Chapter Fourteen
# 1999
# Annesley

Annesley fingered the dog-eared corner of the *Marie Claire* magazine that lay open across her and Mary Blake's knees. The two shared an oversized chair covered in a soft chambray that matched the lakeside decor favored by her mother's designer when they rebuilt the lake home. The two-story vaulted ceiling and the water view marked a one-hundred-eighty-degree turn from the last few nights of hillbilly living.

Annesley flinched at the thought of wedging herself into the confines of Lisa's car, sleeping on packed dirt, and peeing in a ditch. To her surprise, though, the rustic approach to travel hadn't been completely wretched. The independence of movement and not knowing where they would stop each night had become an extension of the hints of freedom she'd tasted that year.

Granted, if Annesley could have gone back in time by a few days, she would have made sure Mary Blake didn't throw out the tent instructions, and she would have packed a pair of hiking boots. Still, she didn't regret climbing into the White Whale's back seat, if only because it had brought her here.

The family lake house had been a release valve when she was a kid. Away from their Atlanta home, things were unbound. Above the fireplace hung a mounted elk head. Photos of suntanned children on boats and water skis decorated the walls.

Purchased when it was little more than a rundown cottage, the reconstructed home had hosted long summer days for Annesley and her brother, Davis, the outdoors an escape while their mother did whatever the moms did while their husbands worked the jobs that paid for their vacation getaways. Davis hadn't been there in years, but his presence persisted in child-sized handprints in the concrete on the lower patio and a fist-sized hole hidden in the closet of his old bedroom. The others didn't need to know about the latter.

Mary Blake hummed a nameless tune while Helen gazed out the giant picture window at cotton-candy clouds reflected in the lake's smooth surface. Lisa puttered in the kitchen, and Charlie read a week-old *Wall Street Journal* she'd picked up at the general store when the group went for an early bike ride.

The five of them hanging out wasn't unlike a weekend at the Delta Rho house, ease coupled with anticipation of the next event. But with graduation behind them and another night at the lake ahead, "next" was nothing more than going out on the water. The lack of expectations made the day perfect.

"Is there any more of that banana bread, Lisa?" Charlie called into the kitchen.

Lisa was wiping the counters again, scrubbing as though she didn't want to leave so much as a fingerprint. "Just crumbs," Lisa replied. "But we need more coffee, so we can get supplies, and I can make another loaf before we get on the road tomorrow."

Lisa was reliable. Awkward at times, which was to be expected, considering her dad was a grocery store manager or something like that, but reliable, a rule-follower, something Annesley could appreciate. If Annesley had been into projects, Lisa would have been her project. A fashion fix, a tweak of the makeup, and braces to fix that one crooked tooth would make Lisa a triple threat.

Annesley took a sip of Mary Blake's sweet tea—"The sweeter the better, sugar!"—and turned the page to continue their lazy game.

Mary Blake pointed at the raven-haired model in a jeans ad. "How about her?"

Annesley considered the slouch and the middle-parted, naturally curly hair. "Deadhead. Definitely a Phi Alpha." She flipped the page to find the next ad and determine which sorority the model would have been in.

"Tri-Gam. Straight out of the Hamptons. That girl teethed on sterling."

Annesley might have pledged Tri-Gam herself if her mother and her grandmother hadn't both been Delta Rhos—and if Delta Rho alums didn't practically run the country club where her mother presided over the social season. At college, the Delta Rhos had a reputation for being old-school but with a touch of eclecticism. There must have been an outlier legacy sister a generation ago that steered membership off its straight path. The old-school aspect made their probation all the more scandalous, while the eclecticism took the blame.

The probation had kept her mother away, giving Annesley a taste of her future. The woman who had attended every pledge class initiation, every parent and alumnae weekend, and more on-campus events than Annesley cared to recall had suddenly vanished from Delta Rho's halls, whether because house activities had been throttled by the probation order or due to mortification at the reputational stain. Annesley had gloried in Mother's absence, triumphant though a touch guilt-ridden for feeling that way.

Mary Blake sank deeper into the chair, her bare arm warm against Annesley's. "I wish we could stay here forever. It's like our own little bubble away from the world. Do you think you'd ever want to live in Texas, forsake trees and lakes and beaches and your daddy's big houses?"

"I think I'll have had enough trees and outdoors on this trip to last me a while."

"Maybe Tripp will pop the question while we're there." Mary Blake twisted toward Annesley, her face bright with plans to buy up every bridal magazine at the supermarket. "With all of us at the ranch, that would be perfection."

Annesley suppressed a grin. She was in no rush. She'd set a long-term plan in motion freshman year when she'd seen Tripp at a mixer. "That one," she'd said, pointing at the SAE pledge class president, whose angled stance exuded exclusivity.

She saw in Tripp what she'd honed in herself: ambition and a willingness to go hard for what he wanted. And she wanted him to want her. He'd finally asked her out when they were juniors, but they looked so good together, people assumed they'd been a couple for years. Sure, she'd had to overlook some indiscretions. *Boys will be boys.* Cannon women were resilient, and now that college was over, he would be more settled. She'd make sure of it.

"We'll see. He'll be working for his father over the summer before he heads to an internship on Capitol Hill with some congressman Mr. Harrison hunts with. After that, he'll go to law school, then he'll work for one of his father's companies. They have the largest cattle-breeding business in Texas, plus oil and real estate. Then it's state office then the US Congress for one or two terms then Senate. With my communications work, we'll be the perfect team."

"Senator and Mrs. Harrison." Mary Blake practically purred as she settled into her corner of the chair. "Oh, I like that. You'll have to invite us to the White House."

Annesley liked it too. She especially liked that she was in charge. True, her mother had provided the scaffolding, but this was Annesley's life to build now. Her mother may preside over charity banquets and new member cocktail parties at the club, but Annesley would have her own realm, a bigger one, one that didn't have her mother's claw marks all over it.

"You could be the next Kennedys, another Camelot," Mary Blake cooed.

Annesley sat taller. "Republican Kennedys, of course."

"You do remember," Charlie said without looking up from the *Journal*, "what happened to the Kennedys, right?"

The front door opened, and Annesley turned toward the hidden entryway in surprise. At the sound of heeled shoes clacking in long strides across the tile, Annesley's pulse accelerated to highway speed. She jumped from the chair and aligned the magazines in a stack on the coffee table. She didn't reach the doorway before her mother walked through it.

Her mother's pencil skirt matched her aqua pumps. In true form, her sole adornment was a string of pearls, the twin to the string Annesley wore, both received as part of a family tradition upon turning eighteen. Her mother's severe bob with no strand out of place prompted Annesley to smooth her own hair, which she realized with a rush of anxiety was pulled into a ponytail rendered lopsided from her position on the chair with Mary Blake.

Annesley pasted on the proper smile, one of fealty and gratitude, barely registering the surprised faces of her friends. "Mother!" She kissed her mother on the cheek, wishing she could undo the phone call that alerted her mother they would be at the lake. "I wasn't expecting you." If she'd expected her, Annesley wouldn't have made the side trip to Georgia. She would rather sleep in a tent.

"I hardly saw you over the past year." Mother's eyes narrowed with suspicion. "And it *is* my house."

Like recorded music when the live band takes a water break, Annesley's training kicked in, and that meant introductions. "Mother, you know Mary Blake, Helen, and Lisa from the Delta Rho house."

Mother inclined her head. "Ladies. I trust your"—she pursed her thin lips, shaped in her signature dusty rose lipstick—"little *adventure* has been enjoyable."

Mary Blake bounded to Annesley's side, eyes sparkling. "Hello, Mrs. Cannon."

Mother leaned forward. "How lovely to see you again, Mary Blake." With the drop of a half octave, she shifted her tone to "heartfelt sympathy." "How is your father, dear? Annesley told us he's been ill."

"You're too kind to ask, Mrs. Cannon," Mary Blake replied. "A little more time and I know everything will be back to normal. Just have to be patient." She raised her arms toward the picture window. "Your home is breathtaking! You have the best spot on the lake." It was so like Mary Blake to turn attention away from herself and know exactly what to say.

Mother's sympathy smile relaxed into a genuine one. "Yes, we do." She patted Mary Blake's hand and gazed out the window.

Her mother nodded hellos to Helen and Lisa, both of whom earned a nearly imperceptible eyebrow raise. Admittedly, they looked like public high school kids in their graphic T-shirts and athletic shorts.

Annesley pointed at her other friend. "And this is Charlie McKay. I'm not sure if you've met."

Charlie reached out a hand. "Pleasure to meet you, Mrs. Cannon."

"Charlie," her mother said, trying out the name and looking Charlie over like she would a new horse at the equestrian facility where she rode on Saturdays. "I don't believe we've met. Did you live in the Delta Rho house? Or perhaps you lived off-campus?"

"She's not a Delta, Mother."

Mary Blake's mouth opened as though she was about to dispute that. Annesley cast a warning glare. She didn't want to get into Charlie's expulsion.

"I'm sorry." Curiosity filled her mother's eyes. "Which house are you in?"

"I'm not," Charlie said with emphasis on the first word, indicating she wasn't sorry in the least that she wasn't a Delta Rho. Annesley half-glared, half-pleaded in silence until Charlie clarified. "I'm not in a house, that is."

"I see." Mother wiped her hands on her skirt, causing Charlie to tilt her head in confusion. Or was it amusement? "Well, then. It's nice you could join Annesley and her sisters."

If chastening or condescension had been her mother's intention—and if Annesley knew her mother, it was—Charlie didn't wilt. But she also didn't dismiss Greek life or spin a smug explanation about getting kicked out, which Annesley would have expected from the one most likely to say something just to trigger a response.

Instead, Charlie said, "Thank you for having us here in your beautiful home."

From the corner of her eye, Annesley saw Helen give a mock salute. Of course Charlie would have proper manners after growing up in a military household. In any case, it was enough to satisfy her mother and might even bode well for making a good impression at the ranch.

Mother released the group from attention with a nod and led Annesley into the dining room.

Once they were out of earshot of her friends, Annesley said, "I wish you'd called." If she'd known her mother was coming, Annesley and the others could have loaded the Scout and the White Whale and fled after breakfast.

Her mother disregarded the statement. "There's a fundraiser at Celia Garden's lake house tonight. You remember her daughter, Natalie? Poor thing never did pledge Delta Rho." She passed a hand across the cherry hunt board and frowned at a slight warping in the wood. "Celia's family is from Dallas, you know."

Mother had hated Celia Garden ever since Mrs. Garden had received the Atlanta Order of the White Rose the year Mother had been certain she would be the new inductee. Annesley recalled that Natalie Garden had attended Auburn and been cross-cut during rush, leading to a face-saving transfer to Georgia, which Mrs. Garden proclaimed to all who would listen "had a far superior public-relations program."

Annesley's lips parted. She quickly pursed them and nodded. Now, the surprise visit made sense. Her mother had come to the lake house to crow to the neighbors about her prize show horse of a daughter, who not only got into Delta Rho but who was now off to visit the Harrisons of Harrison Oil in Texas.

"I made some inquiries about Tripp's mother." Mother set her purse on the table and adjusted Annesley's necklace so the clasp was in the back. "Cordelia De Baillon Harrison"—Mrs. Cannon rolled the name like she was admiring a Tiffany chandelier—"comes from a fine Baton Rouge family and was presented at the Beaux Chevaliers Ball." The rare tinge of awe in her voice piqued Annesley's interest. "It's a shame you *all*"—she gestured toward the great room—"have to be at the ranch."

The subtext was clear: Annesley belonged there. Except for Mary Blake, the other girls couldn't possibly. And most of all, don't let anyone get in the way of making the right impression.

She wasn't wrong, and Annesley knew that, but she was offended on behalf of her friends. Their visit would be fine. She would make sure of it. Tripp would make sure of it. A natural politician, he got along with everyone. The thought of him eased the stress building in response to her mother's words. Tripp enjoyed a relaxed bravado that Annesley attributed to the freedom of a ranch, which must be one thousand times the freedom Annesley expected at the lake.

Mother parted the floral curtains, releasing a slice of yellow sunlight that cut the room in two. "He's from a fine family. Fine young man."

Her mother's enthusiasm about Tripp split Annesley in two. There was something uncomfortable about being aligned with her mother on the matter. As she did any time she entertained doubts about Tripp, she thought back to the first night they slept together, when he'd leaned in close, his Texas accent tickling her ear. "Darlin', I want to show you something, my granddaddy's war letters home. I never show them to anyone, but—damn. You look at me and..." He placed her hand on his chest, proving a connection he had only with her, the one woman who broke through his playboy persona. "It melts my heart like a snowball in the desert." She'd nearly melted herself. Heat rose to her face at the memory.

Her mother continued, oblivious to her daughter's sinful thoughts. "I also thought you might like an update on your graduation party. The invitations finally went out after I had them redone. You wouldn't have believed the calligraphy. It was like they assigned a third grader to address the envelopes. The quality has gone downhill since they brought in that *new* girl."

Annesley didn't want to play the gossip game. She would always lose against her mother. Anyway, she wanted to know about the guest list. "Did you invite Davis?" She didn't know if her mother even had her brother's address. The last Annesley heard, he was living near Boston, maybe Cambridge.

Her mother huffed. "If you must know, he called. He wanted to surprise you by coming back. Can you believe that? After being gone seven years, you don't *invite yourself* to a party. I told him we don't need him to come back. He made his bed, and now he has to lie in it."

A bitter burn singed Annesley's heart. Davis had left after high school and swore he'd never set foot in their "bourgeois world" again, but it had been their mother who'd pushed him. So what seared her was the "we." "*We* don't need him to come back."

Annesley's shoulders slumped as she considered her complicity. She clung to the club, the party invitations, the credit cards, and the big houses. She didn't question her mother about pushing him away. She let the matter drift, ignored.

But that March, when she sat in a cold metal chair next to a stoic Charlie while a brother was lowered into the ground, a burst of loss and confusion had washed over her. She didn't know where she stood with her own brother. She wondered if she would deserve to mourn him if he were gone. She'd hid her tears and her shame behind her Gucci sunglasses.

"But let's not talk about that, and stand up straight," her mother continued, apparently not haunted by doubt or misgivings over the severance of family or the fact that her son had willingly left. "About your visit to the ranch—"

Annesley interrupted, causing a fissure in her mother's marble visage. "We were about to go out on the lake."

Mrs. Cannon gave a cursory nod toward the great room. "They can go. We have plenty of things to cover. We can't have you getting to Texas strung out from the road like some drifter among a band of vagabonds. Did you even bring your make-up bag with you?"

"Of course, but—" Annesley stopped herself from saying Tripp didn't care. The times she'd stayed over at his place, which had been an awful lot this year, she'd had a compact and mascara to touch up in the mornings before he awoke. But that was on her, not him. He loved the way people looked at them when they were together, and so did she.

"And I hope you aren't planning on showing up wearing something like that." Her mother gestured at Annesley's ponytail and tank top.

"O-Of course not," Annesley stammered. "We just got back from a bike ride."

"You're not out for a ride now." Mrs. Cannon shook her head in disappointment. "If I've taught you anything, it's to always represent who you are, and you are Annesley Blair Cannon."

# Chapter Fifteen
# 1999
# Annesley

Annesley made her way down the wooden steps behind the lake house and zigzagged through the pine trees toward a hidden pier that had so far escaped her mother's renovation efforts. After dealing with the queen, she needed a moment to herself.

Halfway to the water, she veered off the stone steps and onto an overgrown path that wound through a patch of azaleas ablaze with fuchsia blooms.

Her mother had left for the store, unimpressed with the groceries the girls had bought for their brief stay. Normally, Annesley wouldn't have thought twice about it, but she rankled with personal offense. She was glad the others had disappeared from the great room and hadn't seen her stomp on the entryway's ceramic tile like a petulant child after her mother closed the front door.

Still, it wasn't her mother's intrusion, unwelcome as it was, that caused the roiling sick in Annesley's gut. Mother had dismissed Davis, and Annesley did nothing. She hadn't even asked for his phone number.

Following the Cannon siblings' secret childhood path, she skirted the boat house and headed toward the old fishing dock. She used to sneak down to the dock with Davis for epic rock-skipping competitions or on her own just to watch the sky. A stand of pine trees hid the dock from the house and allowed her to feel like she had her own "best spot on the lake."

She rounded the trees and stopped short. Her stomach dropped. Charlie stood at the end of the dock.

First, her mother, now Charlie.

Just as Annesley was about to turn and walk away, Charlie flung her arm back and whipped her hand forward to send a rock across the water's smooth surface. The whirling arc of Charlie's body was familiar, a pull from youth that wasn't ready to be left behind.

Annesley scanned the ground and selected a single stone, smooth, oval, and flat. She walked the dock's length, her bare feet soundless on the silvery wooden planking. Charlie let another rock fly.

Annesley counted to herself as she sidled up next to Charlie. One, two, three, four. "Four skips. Not too bad. May I?"

Charlie moved aside, accepting the challenge. Annesley rubbed her thumb across the smooth gray rock, flipped it, and pressed it between her thumb and first two fingers. She pulled her arm back and swung, flinging the stone across the water. One, two, three, four, five, six, seven, eight.

Charlie grinned, and Annesley found the sparkle in Charlie's eyes flattering.

"You have home-dock advantage," Charlie said.

They watched the eight dimples in the water dissolve, the only distraction an osprey's high-pitched peal. Annesley moved to the left of a piling and sat, pitching her head back to watch the osprey alight on a dead branch.

Charlie remained facing the water, the fingers of her left hand rotating a pair of rocks. She pocketed one and whipped the other with too much downward force. One, two.

"How'd you find my secret spot?" Annesley asked.

Charlie laughed. "Secret, huh? You sneaking away from your mom?"

Annesley flushed. "It's complicated."

"Try me." Charlie sat on the dock's edge and leaned back to allow the sun to blanket her face.

Annesley wasn't sure if Charlie was inviting her to explain or brushing away Annesley's problems as no comparison to Charlie's own. They weren't exactly heart-to-heart friends. But something about the moment—the lake's calm, the wisps of white making their way across the sky, the anger building inside, and the fact that Charlie wasn't looking at her—allowed words to form.

"It's my brother. Davis." The deep blue water pulsed against the wood pilings like a living organism. "It's been forever since I've seen him. And my mother has decided he's not worthy of coming to my graduation party. To her, he's dead." Instantly, her stomach tumbled with remorse at her words. She wanted to slip into the dark water, let it engulf her, so she could disappear. "Charlie, I am so sorry. That was insensitive."

Charlie turned, pulled her legs up, and wrapped her arms around them. "Tell me about him."

An invisible veil lifted, and Annesley glimpsed why Lisa and Helen were so at ease with Charlie. But still, the Cannon family didn't discuss Davis. His free spirit didn't fit the prescribed narrative of prep-school Southern gentleman. But here on the dock it seemed okay. Charlie wasn't into prescribed narratives.

Annesley chewed on some words and gazed at a flock of Canada geese floating offshore. "Davis was the bad child. I was the good one." She didn't need to look at Charlie to know she'd be smirking. That made Annesley smirk, and she enjoyed a small chuckle. "I'm sure that comes as no surprise." She pushed her hands against the dock, her toes en pointe above the water.

A memory evoked an unexpected laugh, and she sat upright. "Our country club had etiquette classes." She exaggerated her already erect posture and raised her nose for effect. "When I was old enough to take the class, Davis asked to register again. He'd already done two sessions, and let me tell you, that boy had no manners and no intention of ever acting proper. He was clearly up to something, but my mother was oblivious."

She couldn't help but smile at the thought of Davis's rebellion against their mother and everything she stood for, those expectations Annesley had considered goals and had met—exceeded—and prided herself in, even today. It occurred to her that Charlie wasn't unlike Davis in that way. She snuck a glance at Charlie, who was watching the geese, but attentive to Annesley's words. "That first day, I learned why he was dying to take the class. He grabbed my hand and pulled me away from the banquet hall." She'd told no one this story, and the words spilling out seemed to unspool twine that bound her insides, like she was inviting him back in, even though her mother had foreclosed the possibility.

"He knew a secret way into the catering pantry. The Whitmore Country Club is famous for its pecan pralines, 'Whitmore pralines.' You can only get them at the club. Every little girl dreams of having her wedding at the Whitmore and having each guest take home a Whitmore praline in a monogrammed favor box." The sugary, buttery, milky sweetness made people forget the damage they did while eating them. Annesley hadn't had one since she was a kid, but she could almost taste one today.

"I'm intrigued." Charlie had turned toward Annesley, and her eyes lit with the devious glint she showed when one of them acted out of character, like she took vicarious delight in their boundary pushing.

"So we sneak into the pantry. My mother would have killed us—literally murdered us, and I'm not kidding—if we'd been caught.

There were shelves of salt and pepper shakers, silver platters, Bunsen burners, and liquor bottles. Overflow, I guess, for club events. And smack ahead of me was a shelf lined with Whitmore pralines. I imagine there was a wedding scheduled for that weekend."

"You didn't." Charlie's voice carried a hint of admiration.

Annesley responded with silence.

Charlie's eyes shot wide. "Miss Annesley Blair Cannon, breaking into the country club pantry, ruining some poor debutante's dream wedding?"

"I know!" Annesley pulled her knees up to control the buzz of excitement that had replaced the pit of remorse in her stomach. "I was scandalized with myself. What if someone caught us? What if my mother found out? But those pralines..." Annesley closed her eyes and pictured the brown-eyed boy whose hair flopped across his forehead like a beaver's tail. Later, he'd grown that flop into a free-flowing and decidedly not-country-club style and dyed it blue. But in the dark pantry, the floppy bangs had signaled irresistible recklessness.

"So did she ever find out?" Charlie asked.

"Not exactly. I mean, I'm still alive." Annesley scrunched her face. "At the end of the summer, when I had to squeeze into my dance costume, not only did the zipper only go halfway, sequins popped off." *You need to nip this in the bud, young lady, or you are going to have a life of cellulite and stretch marks,* her mother had said, the words stabbing Annesley like shards of ice. She'd been, what, eight years old? "Anyway, my life of eating pastries ended. Alas."

Annesley noticed Charlie staring at her and flushed with the embarrassment of exposure. "What?" Of all the people in the world to tell this story to, she'd chosen Charlie. The mountain air and altitude of the past few days must have gotten to her.

"I'm aghast!" Charlie held her open palm against her chest in mock horror. "I'm sitting here next to a criminal. Breaking and entering, fraud, pastry theft." Charlie's face broke into a wide smile, an invitation usually reserved for Helen or one of the others. But was she lighting up for Annesley then or Annesley now?

Annesley didn't have the space to think about the difference. "Anyway, he's gone, and he won't be at my grad party." She deserved his abandonment, just as her mother had.

Harsh squawks and a flurry of splashes drew their eyes to the water, and the geese took flight.

Charlie's gaze followed the birds as they swooped over the lake. "Maybe it's time for you to go rogue again, break free. We could break into the general store tonight and steal cigarettes, get a mohawk, or maybe shortsheet your mom's bed."

Annesley laughed, but a weight grounded her to the dock. She thought she had already broken free: a school year without her mother, a road trip, tents, dirt, and a dingy station wagon. But the resentment she'd felt in the dining room and the hold her mother had over her emotions said otherwise.

Mary Blake called out Annesley's name from somewhere above and broke the easiness of the moment.

"I guess I should head up before my mother gets back and turns everyone into a Stepford wife," Annesley said.

"I think I'm safe."

"Ha! You've only just now met my mother."

Annesley stood, and Charlie rose with her.

"If you're interested in windsurfing," Annesley said, "we've got a couple of boards in the boathouse. That was Davis's favorite thing to do here, other than get beat by me skipping rocks, of course." Annesley loved seeing Charlie laugh at that. "He said being out on the board was like controlling the wind." Or maybe it was that he wasn't the one being controlled.

"I think I'd like your brother."

"Davis would *love* you, Charlie." She chuckled. "Not that that's a rousing endorsement."

He hadn't even needed to be told to leave. He'd walked away. Annesley loved Charlie for sitting there and not asking questions, for appreciating her brother for that moment in time. But that was enough openness for one day.

Charlie squinted toward the path. She seemed to know Annesley wanted some alone time. "Why don't you stay, and I'll go take care of your mom. Though MB is an expert at diversions. Don't worry. I won't touch your mom's sheets." Charlie reached into her pocket and handed Annesley her last rock before walking away.

Smooth and flat, the rock was a sure-fire nine or ten. Annesley spun it across the water and watched it dribble in a staccato of tiny splashes until it disappeared to join the hundreds of skippers lying at the bottom of the lake.

Charlie's words burned in her ears. *Maybe it's time for you to go rogue again.* Annesley going rogue was about as likely as Mary Blake quitting Delta Rho. Hell, she wasn't sure if she even knew how to go rogue anymore.

# Chapter Sixteen
# 2019
# Mary Blake

While the others said goodnights to their families or checked work emails, Mary Blake chatted with her dog sitter and repositioned the side chairs in the suite's living room to complete a conversation area for five. Annesley's warnings about reviving the past weighed on her, as did the unspoken words and the washed-out fatigue on Annesley's face.

She rearranged the fringed throw pillows on the leather chairs one more time and surveyed the room's neo-Western aesthetic. She closed the loose white curtains and moved to the bar, where she'd set out the hotel's branded glass water bottles along with pretzels, apples, and miniature bags of M&M's in case anyone got the midnight munchies. The sweet smell of peonies melded with leather and wood into a thick scent of sophistication.

She looked approvingly around the room. The only thing missing was the others, their laughter, and their old stories. As long as the old stories didn't end the trip before it got on the road, things would be fine.

The women had avoided discussing the ending of the last trip as if by unspoken agreement, but they couldn't ignore it. She just needed to create the right environment so they could face it and move forward.

Annesley emerged from her room, dressed in a white chemise and pajama bottoms decorated with birds of paradise. The colors popped against the suite's dark wood. Mary Blake put on her happy face and held her breath as Annesley scanned the room.

"You always outdo yourself, Mary Blake. We don't deserve you." The fatigued look from earlier had disappeared. Perhaps it had never been there at all, and Mary Blake was just nervous.

"Anything for my girls."

"Your girls." Annesley seemed to warm at Mary Blake's endearment. "It is something to see everyone." She eased into a wingback chair. "Charlie is about as chatty as she always was. And I'm waiting for Helen to pull out the maps tomorrow. And Lisa—"

Mary Blake followed Annesley's gaze to see what had cut her off. Lisa stood at the bar, looking like she couldn't decide which foot should take the next step.

Mary Blake handed Lisa a wine glass. "Everything okay back home? We got worried when you disappeared at dinner. Emergency stuff?"

"No. I mean, yes. Right. Emergency stuff. But it's all good. I'm sorry if I interrupted." Lisa eyed Annesley and tugged at her pajama top to cover her midriff.

Annesley patted the arm of the adjacent chair in an invitation for Lisa to sit. "We were talking about how nice it is to see everyone."

Minutes later, Helen and Charlie arrived, completing the circle by sharing the couch.

Mary Blake startled at the arrangement, an uncanny remembrance of the five of them in the great room at the lake house or the Delta Rho TV room.

Charlie eyed the space, from the bar to the window to the seating. "Have you been redecorating, MB?"

Annesley lifted her chin. "Mary Blake is a staging visionary. People hire her to stage their houses for televised interviews and magazine spreads. Did you see that pre-Oscars interview with Saoirse Ronan? She didn't win, but all anyone could talk about was how gorgeous her living room was."

Heat rose behind Mary Blake's ears. "It's just a hobby." At least, she'd made sure it was just a hobby back when she needed flexibility to take care of her mother, manage Frank's social world, and be there for Annesley. None of that was necessary anymore. She shook her head to return focus to the women in front of her.

The next phase in the accelerated timeline of the weekend would set the tone for the remainder. Normally, Mary Blake never worried about being "too much," but doubt itched at her now. She'd filled the room with peonies, arranged a delightful menu, and hand-selected the wines. The shared suite had been a bold move, but the women had taken to it. They couldn't avoid the past, though. She couldn't have it hanging over the trip like a thundercloud, like Frank's indiscretions had hung over their marriage until *TMZ* spun in like a tornado and she'd had no control over the fallout.

Back in her room, Annesley hadn't seemed convinced about confronting the past. Mary Blake bit the inside of her lip, second-guessing herself. Annesley was usually on point about things.

Charlie sipped a drink. Lisa fiddled with a button on the front of her pajamas. Helen's foot flickered against the couch's wooden leg. *Tap, tap, tap.* Annesley regarded Mary Blake with an ambiguous smile.

People looked… bored.

Mary Blake clapped her hands once, eliciting wide-eyed looks of expectation from the others. Fueled, she pushed past her trepidation. "I've got something for you."

"Seriously, MB," Charlie said, "you've done more than enough."

"Oh, hush." She pulled a stack of thin shiny books from a bag by the bar. "I made a collection of photos on my Mac, and clickety-click, it turned into a book." She tapped her nails on the shiny white cover and felt her direction recalibrate.

She handed a copy to each of the women. "I should have gotten my pictures to y'all back then. But... well, you know."

Fleeting memories of arriving in California disgraced and without her best friend tempered Mary Blake's bounce. She wasn't the only one. Charlie's face twisted. Helen took in a gulp of air and followed it with a gulp of wine. Annesley watched Mary Blake with what looked like concern. Lisa twisted her wedding band.

Mary Blake squared her shoulders, generating a wave of fortitude that anchored her to the floor. They had been more than that ending, and the book was the reminder. She placed her copy on the table for everyone to see.

The first page was a grid of party pics: keg-eyed frat boys and smiling girls, some with baby fat still plumping their cheeks. A photo of the group at Delta Rho's fated charity lemonade stand, all of them dressed in plaid shirts and cut-offs, took up an entire page decorated with triangles.

"We look fabulous," Annesley said. "Cora taught me how to use photo filters to look like I'm twenty again." She placed her hands on the sides of her face and pulled the skin taut.

"No filter required, sugar," Mary Blake said. "And I guarantee we've all aged better than those fraternity boys." She flipped forward to the first night of camping: an out-of-focus shot of three of them by Charlie's tent and another of Helen by the fire, her face pink and sticky with marshmallows.

Lisa touched a photo of her younger self. "Did we look like that?"

After a collage that included Charlie and Helen holding frogs, Annesley balancing on a stump in a delicate arabesque, and a group of them floating on air mattresses at the lake, Annesley stilled Mary Blake's hand and leaned in. She traced a snapshot of herself leaning against a Coke machine. On the other side of the machine stood a ruggedly handsome guy, hands in his pockets. A smile floated across Annesley's lips as his name slipped out. "Luke."

"The Alabama redneck from the back of beyond," Charlie proclaimed.

Annesley didn't pull her eyes from the page. "He had an agriculture science degree and was taking a year off to help his grandmother." She laughed softly. "Still not someone my mother would have approved of."

"I'll never forget the look on your mother's face at the lake house when you climbed into the Scout with Charlie the morning we left for Alabama," Mary Blake said.

Annesley laughed. "You'd have thought I was boarding a prison bus."

Helen drained her glass. "I guess as detours go, it was a fun one. I remember thinking we left Lake Burton with your secret twin, Annesley."

"Your *more fun* secret twin, I recall you saying," Charlie said. "I liked More Fun Annesley. In fact, I think she's my favorite Annesley."

"Annesley is my favorite Annesley!" Mary Blake refilled Helen's drink. The weight of worry had lightened, but as pages turned from college to North Carolina then to Alabama, she knew they would reach Texas soon. She squeezed her hands together to dampen her pounding pulse, which reverberated the full length of her spine.

When Mary Blake flipped to the final page, the room stilled. The lights in the chandelier cast diffuse shadows against the pale carpet. The peonies even seemed to have withheld their scent. The other women stared in communal silence at the last photo, taken the day they'd arrived at the ranch, a snapshot of when they were poised to soar from some of the greatest nights of their lives to their next grand adventure together. But it hadn't worked out that way, and there were no more pictures.

The time the five spent together had been compressed: a lifetime filling four years, another lifetime filling two weeks, and a third filling the intervening years.

Each breath felt like a lifetime now. Mary Blake clenched her fists until her fingers ached, and she wondered if she'd miscalculated, picked the wrong time or picked the wrong images, and gone about this all wrong.

She stared into her own eyes in the last photo, willing her then-self to change the curve of time, transform that moment into one that didn't devolve into lies revealed and a tragic death.

"Did you guys...?" Lisa's mouth hung open for a beat, then she clamped her teeth together and pinched the bridge of her nose.

Mary Blake could have pulled it out, whatever it was that Lisa wanted to share. Lisa had always spoken more freely when Mary Blake was around to shepherd her into the front. Instead, Mary Blake held her smile. She had set the stage, but the women needed to play their own parts tonight, so the end of the last trip didn't hang a black curtain over the rest of this one.

Helen, mid-drink, removed her wine glass from her lips as if she hadn't realized she was holding it. She set it on the side table, fidgeted with her hands, and picked the glass back up. "Did we what?"

Lisa's eyebrows pulled together. Before Mary Blake could decipher the expression on the doctor's face, the cloud across Lisa's eyes cleared, and she seemed to change directions. She looked back at the photo, where a grinning Parker Harrison held a cowboy hat over Lisa's head. It was probably the last photo taken of Parker.

"I have a lot of regrets about that night. The whole time at the ranch." Lisa's voice was measured, calm, distant.

Mary Blake placed a hand on Lisa's shoulder and squeezed. The most noticeable change in the room was the loss of eye contact. The second was the change in air pressure. It was as if all the air had left the room and extracted the energy of their initial reconnection. The past, that night, had needed an opening to fill.

This was it; this was when they confronted it. A whirlwind roiled in her gut, flipping her organs in loopy somersaults. Mary Blake held her face in relaxed calm, no lines between her eyebrows, no quivering lips.

Lisa turned to Annesley with a suddenness that put Mary Blake on alert. "Did you stay in touch with the Harrisons? After…"

Lisa didn't have to finish her sentence for Mary Blake to know she was asking about the family-only funeral for Parker held the day Lisa and Mary Blake left Texas. Helen and Charlie had already departed, Helen on a plane home and Charlie in a taxi to who knew where. Only Annesley had stayed behind.

Annesley shook her head. "There was no reason."

"I sometimes imagine it was a bad dream," Annesley said.

"Nightmare." Lisa rubbed her shoulder, the one injured in the crash, and shook her head as if to rid her mind of ghosts. "There are some nights you wish you could take back."

Helen stood and set her glass on a side table. "Time for bed for me."

"We don't need to talk about this." Charlie's voice was monotone, her face taut.

"It's okay," Helen said as she walked into their room. "Long day." She closed the door.

"Should I…?" Mary Blake stood and moved toward Helen and Charlie's room.

Charlie held out her hand like a traffic cop. "She did have that flight cancellation, and this Texas heat is a bitch. I'll check on her in a bit."

Annesley's mouth pressed into a contemplative line. Lisa's eyes looked troubled, but she caught Mary Blake's gaze, and she smiled.

Charlie reached for a wine bottle and refilled her glass. "MB, you sure know how to bring a party down. I guess some things never change." Her deadpan delivery hung in the air until she let out a low chuckle.

Annesley grabbed the book from the table. "Very funny, Charlie." She flipped back several pages. "Maybe we should go back to Alabama. That's a side trip I wouldn't mind taking again."

# Chapter Seventeen
# 1999
# Charlie

Alabama I-20's fresh asphalt made the Scout ride like a hovercraft. Since leaving the lake house, Charlie had a new co-pilot, and to her surprise, Annesley in the passenger seat had *not* been irritating. Back at the lake house, Annesley had stared nonchalantly out the windshield while Mrs. Cannon, a Roman statue in linen and pearls, watched them drive away.

"Annesley, why do I suspect that getting in the Scout with me this morning was your way of sticking it to your mom?" Charlie stepped on the clutch and shifted gears to pass an overloaded pickup that spewed debris. A Styrofoam cooler escaped the truck bed as they drove past. The small chest flipped up into the air and smashed into pieces on the road.

"To be candid"—an air of irony lifted Annesley's voice—"it was a difficult decision, choosing which car." She gestured toward the White Whale, three car lengths in front of them. "Something the cleaning lady would drive or"—she patted the Scout's dashboard—"one a serial killer would load with bodies."

"I'm flattered."

"You should be. I do wish I'd turned around to watch her when we drove away. I'm sure it was pure operatic tragedy."

"Based on what I saw in the rearview mirror, I'd say she was torn between relief at seeing the cars gone from her driveway and paranoid the neighbors would see the cleaning lady and the psychopath running off together."

Annesley spat her Evian water onto the dash and wiped at it with her hand, apologizing through her laughter.

Charlie waved off her concern. "The dash is waterproof, which is more than I can say for the roof. Pray it doesn't rain."

The calm of the smooth road and the white noise of the fluttering roof threatened to lull Charlie to sleep, so she locked eyes on the White Whale's rear bumper. Next to the blue "Keystone State" plates was a faded *My Child is a Cliffside Middle School Honor Student* bumper sticker from when the car had been Lisa's mom's. Charlie pictured her own mom's Dodge—only American cars in the McKay house—and the black-and-gold "Proud Army Mom" decal on the rear windshield.

Betrayal rather than pride had erupted within Charlie when her brother enlisted. "You're leaving me?" she'd whined.

He indulged her childish response. "When you graduate," he said, "I'll get leave and we'll do it. Go off-map, take in the local flavor, get lost. Maybe I'll even let you drive. But probably not." He'd never let her off without a brotherly jab.

Charlie found herself gripping the wheel so tightly her knuckles whitened. She relaxed her hold. He would have gotten a kick out of seeing her in the front seat with the girl she'd referred to derisively in her letters to him as "Miss Catwalk" for the way she walked as if on show, her stride long, her shoulders back, and her chin parallel to the floor.

Annesley's French and political science classes didn't overlap with Charlie's business and prelaw. If Charlie wanted to grab a sandwich or walk the quad, she'd ask Helen or go alone. Whatever activities Annesley and Mary Blake engaged in together, Charlie was sure they weren't her thing. Over four years, Annesley and Charlie had never had a reason to hang out together, just the two of them. And here it was, twice in two days. Charlie detected an odd feeling percolating, but she couldn't identify it.

Annesley toyed with the CB cord. "Good idea to bring the air mattresses from the lake to put under our sleeping bags."

"Can't have Annesley Blair Cannon be uncomfortable."

"Ha ha, hilarious. I don't believe for a second that you find the ground comfortable. You're just good at not saying anything about it." Annesley smiled and peered at the passing landscape.

As the miles wore on and Annesley didn't morph into a Lilly Pulitzer-wearing, soul-sucking prom queen, Charlie wondered if her four years could have included more Annesley. Or maybe the road and the context had thrown all sense of normalcy out of whack.

Billboards loomed with faux importance. Personal injury attorneys in dark suits and red ties pointed King Kong-sized fingers at them, MADD mothers warned them about "last call," and a church called for them to "seek Jesus." Alabama, or the interstate at least, formed a vortex of liability and redemption. Probably not the local flavor Brent had imagined.

The cassette reached the end of side one and clicked over to side two. Again.

Monotony needed disruption, so Charlie feigned falling asleep, her right arm following her head as it fell to the left, sending the Scout careening into the passing lane.

Annesley grabbed the wheel and pulled it hard to the right, no mean feat in a car with no power steering. "You're going to get us killed."

"That would really piss your mom off."

"You have a point. Carry on."

Charlie needed to be careful, or she might start to enjoy having Annesley around.

Mary Blake's voice blared through the speaker. "Breaker, breaker. Eight twelve four one. This is White Whale. Scout, do you copy?

Everything okay back there? Y'all seem to be having some difficulty driving between the lines."

Annesley grabbed the mic. "White Whale, this is Scout. Charlie and I are engaged in a fistfight. Please disregard."

Silence from the other car layered on top of Charlie's own speechlessness. Annesley rarely surprised her. The Atlantan's interactions in the world were predictable: Scrunching her nose like she sensed a foul odor when a sorority sister wore cowboy boots with a mini-skirt, having her father contact the provost to arrange VIP invitations to meet visiting speakers—both predictable and things that painted Annesley as a cliché, a younger version of the woman Charlie had seen in the rearview mirror that morning at the lake house.

But there had been moments that transgressed that predictability and put cracks in the statue that was Annesley. The conversation on the dock had been one. Another had been their freshman year, when Annesley spoke with calm patience to a girl in a bathroom stall. Charlie hadn't meant to eavesdrop, but she recognized a pair of shoes as those of a girl she knew by name and by her weight loss that semester. Charlie had seen Susannah's flip flops under the door of a stall before, accompanied by muffled sounds of retching.

That day, however, Charlie recognized her Delta Rho pledge sister Annesley's voice. Its cultured southern accent typically bordered on staccato, but that afternoon it rolled smoothly, comforting even.

"Sweetie," she said, and that was what stopped Charlie in her tracks. Annesley didn't trade in endearments. Her voice held firm but carried a softness, an acceptance. "I've been there. You are beautiful, and you will be beautiful if you do this or if you don't. I can't tell you to stop. But I can tell you I am here for you anytime. My door is always open." She was definitive, yet compassionate.

Susannah hadn't come back to school after that semester, but Charlie hadn't overheard her retching in the bathroom during the time she remained. It was as if Annesley could help someone else recognize the disease of trying to live up to someone else's standards but couldn't treat the problem in herself.

Charlie tapped her finger on the steering wheel.

Annesley lowered the volume on the radio. "Yes?"

Charlie continued tapping. "Remember Susannah? From freshman year?"

"Yes."

Silence returned until Charlie interrupted it again. "I hope she's doing well."

Annesley cocked her head and opened her mouth. She closed it and nodded. "She is."

The percolating feeling swelled, and Charlie recognized it. It was respect.

Miles passed, and Lauryn Hill faded into the Grateful Dead, one of many incongruous transitions that represented their four years.

Before long, the transitions blended into each other, and Charlie got antsy. "The lake house was nice and all," she said, "and Helen has put a lot of work into the planning..."

"But?"

"When Brent used to talk about this trip"—saying his name aloud didn't sting as much as it had yesterday—"the only set thing he had in his plans was the Grand Canyon. Other than that, he wanted to drive. Go wherever the road took him. 'Local flavor,' he said."

"This road is taking us to the Grand Canyon."

"Look around."

Annesley obliged, taking in a blue highway sign advertising a Hampton Inn, a McDonald's, and an outlet mall. "Sweet home Alabama?"

"Ha. This isn't right. It's not how he would do it. Would have done it." The sting she felt now didn't have to do with talking about him.

"So what are you gonna do about it?" Annesley's posture looked cocky, challenging.

"What am I, quote, gonna do about it, end quote?"

"Yes. Since when do you stay on course?"

Charlie caught the spark of conspiracy in Annesley's eyes, accompanied by a sarcasm Brent would have piled on with. A spark of her own crackled and ran across the surface of her skin like a web of lit fuses. Could Charlie have an ally in mixing things up? Helen hated plan disruptions, and while this wouldn't be the first change of plans, it would be the first made while going sixty miles per hour.

Charlie could handle Helen. Hell, Helen might even hand over the maps at the sign of Charlie and Annesley agreeing on something. Practically vibrating in the seat next to her, Annesley looked more than ready to take a new direction.

"When are we going to be in Alabama ever again?" Charlie mused.

"Never?"

"Agreed. How about we make the most of our one-time visit to the Heart of Dixie and actually see the state?" Charlie moved to the left lane and passed the White Whale. "Tell them we're taking a detour."

"Scout Commander going off course," Annesley barked into the CB mic. "Wants to find some, and I quote, 'local flavor.'"

The radio crackled with Helen's voice. "Our next stop is in twenty miles. I'll check the map to see if there's something on the way."

Charlie shook her head. "No maps."

"I'm being told 'no maps.' Sorry, Helen!" Annesley turned off the CB and howled with laughter. "Do you think Helen has her atlas out to figure out how to maintain control of the situation?"

"I am one-hundred-percent certain she does." Charlie exited the interstate and cranked up the volume on "Back in Black," Brent's favorite song, which had played around six times now on this tape but probably a hundred or two when Brent had the car.

As soon as green countryside replaced the chain restaurants, Charlie pulled over to the shoulder. "Top's coming off."

"What took you so long?"

Within seconds of parking the White Whale behind the Scout, the other three girls jumped out of the wagon to rotate drivers. One nice thing about Charlie being the only one who could drive a stick was that no one else could even offer to drive her brother's car. She might be sharing the journey, but she could keep Brent's baby to herself.

Annesley explained Charlie's plan—or rather, lack of a plan—to the bemused White Whale occupants while Charlie removed the soft top. The topless Scout, with the roll bar overhead, screamed summer and off-roading. Charlie glanced at Miss Catwalk and decided against going off-road. She was sure there were limits to Annesley's version of going rogue.

Back on the road, Charlie leaned back in her seat. The Alabama sun bathed them in yellow light, and a blast of wind whipped up and over the windshield. Annesley's hands shot to her hair, shiny and smooth as a wet seal from whatever morning routine got her up early that day.

Charlie squinted in a challenge. "Come now. Is a serial killer going to worry about her hair?"

Annesley seemed to struggle with the question, an internal fight dominated by twenty-two years of composure and compliance. She put on her sunglasses. "Fuck it. Let's go."

The ride was quieter with the top down, which wasn't saying much, except that the Scout hadn't been built for sixty-mile-per-hour highway driving. It had been built for *doing something*. Dry air blew their hair in whirlwinds, whipping it up like tornadoes before the tendrils descended to start over again.

Annesley lowered her glasses. "Seriously, though. Where are we going?"

"Seriously? I don't know."

"Helen's got to be going nuts." Annesley pointed at a sign ahead. "How about we turn there?"

"If there's a sign for it, I don't want to be there."

Annesley sat back. "You know what? Neither do I."

# Chapter Eighteen
# 1999
# Helen

Helen glanced at the Scout's tailgate and back at her atlas. The farther they got from the interstate, the smaller the dots were. Big red dots of cities gave way to black pinpoints of towns, and the distance between black pinpoints grew.

While she burned at getting pulled off the itinerary—the one she'd spent hours preparing and revising to accommodate the addition of the lake house and a stop at the Harrison ranch—there was a sense of order in the dots that somehow made her okay with the situation. Or if it wasn't the cartographical logic, it had been the glee with which Charlie and Annesley de-roofed the Scout.

The group had fallen into a groove. Helen had felt it herself, that soft click into sync with the universe. Her year had been a somewhat solo affair for a time, weighted as she'd been after That Night at the beach.

Brent's death had been when she'd first felt a lightness. She hadn't noticed at first. Charlie had needed help. She never would have said as much, but the vacancy in her eyes told the story. So Helen made travel arrangements, tracked schedules, and did the grocery shopping. The focused activity and the convergence of the five of them to attend the funeral had lifted the weight one feather at a time, until the planning and the launch of the road trip had her hovering and in need only of a place to land.

The White Whale, helmed by Mary Blake this stretch, followed the Scout down an unlined blacktop and past crops of some sort growing close to the sun-dried ditches. Ahead, Helen spied a gathering of buildings that looked like it used to be a town, or maybe once tried to be a town but never pulled it off. She checked her map. No dot. She had some work to do to get them back on track.

Charlie's voice came through the radio after being incommunicado for the last hour. "Tell Helen she might be out of a job. I'm hungry, and the car needs gas."

Helen peered ahead. A gas station stood at the edge of the almost-town. There was a single gas pump and a farm stand with FRESH in fading white paint on its wood-shingled roof.

"Boom!" Charlie said, claiming her position as accidental navigator.

Helen swiveled her head. Empty road ribboned ahead and behind their lonely two-car caravan, and the crossroads they approached bled desolation despite the promise of fresh produce. "It's like *Children of the Corn*," she whispered.

"I don't think anyone's here," Lisa said as Mary Blake maneuvered the car between the Scout and a scraggly strip of shrubbery. "The gas pump looks circa 1957. Geez, it's full service."

Helen hopped out of the car and walked to the Scout. "Charlie, I can't find this place on a map. But if we go back to that last intersection, we should be able to get to a real town about five miles east. You can get your food and your gas there. Better yet, we can head west, toward where we're *actually* going."

"We're looking for local flavor." Annesley squinted at the produce stand, which, to Helen's surprise, had fresh produce on display. "I see watermelons and peppers and..." She nodded and smiled. "Ah... a *local*. See? Local. Flavor."

A young man approached from the stand, wiping his hands on a blue towel that he then shoved into his back pocket. His lips parted in a broad smile. The well-tanned skin above the neckline of his faded ConAgra T-shirt suggested he may have been the harvester. Scruff on his face didn't detract from the humor in his blue eyes nor from his youth. "You ladies lost?" His voice rolled like honey poured over river rocks.

Suddenly, Helen didn't mind being off course.

"Oh, we are found," Annesley said with exaggerated sauciness.

Helen shot a look of alarm at Charlie, and Charlie smirked.

Helen shook her head. *What on earth has been going on in the Scout?*

Mary Blake bounced in front of the car as she pulled her hair into a ponytail. "Hi! I'm Mary Blake." The girl who never met a stranger extended her hand.

The gas-attendant-slash-produce-harvester adjusted the tractor company hat that covered his dark blond hair. "Luke Wylie."

Mary Blake stepped forward again, testing Luke's range of personal space in true Mary Blake form. "We're awfully thirsty. You don't happen to have any sweet tea?"

No one ever squirmed with Mary Blake, and Luke, looking amused, was no exception. "Why, yes, Miss Mary Blake, we have sweet tea. And I think you might like some of my peaches to go with it."

Helen couldn't tell if the grin that crinkled Luke's eyes was devilish or just polite.

"I do like me some peaches," Mary Blake responded in kind.

Luke clasped his hands together and redirected his attention to Charlie, who stood propped against the Scout. "Can I fill you up?"

Charlie arched an eyebrow.

Lisa stage whispered, "You can fill me up."

Luke cocked his head, and Annesley turned toward Lisa with eyes wide with faux horror.

Lisa shrugged non-apologetically. "My tank's empty."

The girls lasted about two seconds before Helen spat a laugh, and the others joined in, from Mary Blake's delightful cackle to Lisa's restrained, full-body shudder. When Charlie rolled her eyes and shook her head but couldn't restrain her own chuckle, Helen lost control and snorted, and they all doubled over.

Helen wiped the tears that blurred her eyes and apologized on behalf of the group. "You'll have to forgive us. We've been on the road awhile."

Luke kept his lips together, but the dimples beneath the scruff betrayed his amusement. He was enjoying the unexpected arrival of a group of women who were acting like high school girls. Helen didn't blame him. It was fun to be free of expectations.

"So," he said, "two fill-ups." He nodded toward the small store behind him. "We have a ladies' room and a shop. Cokes, postcards, whatnot. I'll meet y'all over at the farm stand for that sweet tea and peaches when I'm done."

He motioned toward the Scout, love-at-first-sight filling his eyes in the way Helen had seen on one face or another at almost every stop they'd made on this trip. Not Mrs. Cannon, though, who had stiffened when Annesley slid into the Scout and took two tries to get the passenger door to close.

Luke held the gas nozzle aloft and pointed it at Charlie's car. "Mind pulling that beauty around? The nozzle won't reach."

"Sure thing, Peaches." Charlie jumped in and turned the key.

Nothing happened.

Charlie pulled the key out, turned the steering wheel five degrees to the left, and looked at the gas pedal as if there might be a car-not-starting switch on it. She put the key back in the ignition and turned it.

Nothing.

Helen frowned. "Charlie, is everything all right?"

"Car won't start."

From a silver boom box atop the Coke machine outside the farm store, Trisha Yearwood's "XXX's And OOO's" whispered into the windless heat. In the nearly two hours since Charlie had left with Mary Blake in the White Whale in search of a part to fix the Scout, the station had played everything from Hank Williams Jr. to Reba McEntire.

Lisa drew a giant pound sign in the dirt with the toe of her flip-flop and marked an X in the lower right. Helen marked an O in the middle box. They went back and forth until the inevitable stalemate.

"I hope Charlie finds what she's looking for." Lisa squinted down the road, which shimmered wet-like in the afternoon heat. "We can't get to California if we're stuck in Alabama." She tapped her fingers together like she was counting days.

"I promise we'll get you there in time." If they'd stuck to Helen's plan, they would have stopped at a proper gas station, remained in civilization, and been near a repair shop. She breathed in to the depths of her lungs to stifle the bubbling irritation.

"Thank goodness, there's a junkyard nearby."

Helen fanned herself with her notebook. "Well, it *is* Alabama."

Lisa's light laugh gave Helen a smile. Ever since That Night, when Helen had told Lisa to leave the party and "Go, already. I'm fine. I don't need a babysitter," Helen had struggled not to appear distant.

She told herself she didn't want Lisa to feel guilty for leaving the party, didn't want Helen's poor judgment to fall negatively on another person and compound the consequences, but the truth was that Helen was ashamed enough as it was. The fewer people who knew what had happened or that Helen wasn't even sure what had happened, the faster the memory would fade. There had to be scientific proof of that. But Lisa didn't act snubbed by Helen's distance. In fact, she seemed more gentle, more accommodating than normal. Helen wondered at one point if Charlie had violated her promise, but she knew Charlie well enough to know that Charlie never broke a confidence.

Helen squinted and tried to guess what fruits or vegetables used to be painted alongside FRESH on the farm-stand roof. Only flaking remnants in orange and green remained. "I was kidding before about *Children of the Corn*, but we're in the middle of nowhere, and one of our cars died. This might actually be a horror movie. I'll get us back to the real world."

Lisa brushed away the tic-tac-toe board and glanced over at the stand. "Good luck with that. If this is a horror movie, Annesley dies first because she's flirting with the hot guy."

Sure enough, Annesley leaned against a post, her long legs angled like a pin-up girl, while she watched Luke stack worn wooden crates that looked like they'd been in use since the Great Depression. He grabbed a peach from next to his crate tower and took it to Annesley, getting within Mary Blake-personal-space distance to hand it to her.

"Nah," Helen countered. "She'd have to have sex with him in the first scene. *Then* she'd be the first to die. I think she's safe."

"I don't know. Annesley's tempting fate all over the place today."

"After seeing her mom, I can't blame her. I'd forgotten how uptight Mrs. Cannon is."

Annesley's laughter startled both of them, and they watched her take a bite of the peach then wipe her chin with the back of her hand, decidedly un-Annesley-like and something that would have gone over like a neck tattoo in front of Mrs. Cannon.

"What happened to Tripp and Camelot?" Lisa asked.

"Much like JFK, Tripp is no choirboy. I say good for her. Anyway, Charlie should be back soon. Let's see how we can get back on track." She bent over the side of the Scout and pulled her backup map from the door pocket. She unfolded it on the hood.

Lisa leaned over to trace their route from Virginia, across the whitened creases of the folds of the map, down through North Carolina and Georgia, and across Alabama. She got lost on the interstate. Helen pointed to the spot that approximated their current location, an area devoid of dots, red, black, or otherwise.

"Gotcha. So now we do this." Lisa traced a straight line west to Los Angeles in full violation of navigational protocol. "It's still a long way." It sounded a bit like a question, a plea for confirmation they'd get there before her job started.

Helen nodded. "We have a little cushion. I'd already planned to arrive a couple of days early so we can help you get settled. We'll drive a little later than usual tonight and make up time tomorrow. Sound good?"

Lisa nodded quickly. "Totally fine, I know you'll get us there. I'm glad you guys came with me. Otherwise, this would have been interminable. Faster but interminable."

Helen couldn't have agreed more. Her summer—her life—would have been interminable if they'd ended the school year disassembled and scattered from their disrupted year. "We'll ask Luke for the fastest route—"

Annesley's low laugh rose, piquing Helen's curiosity over what was crinkling the farmer boy's eyes in laughter. The debutante and the redneck seemed oblivious to Helen and Lisa's presence. And Annesley had never looked that relaxed standing next to Tripp.

Lisa smirked. "If we can tear him away from Annesley."

A few minutes after they went back to studying the map, Annesley slid up behind Lisa. "No Charlie yet, huh?" She turned to smile at Luke, who stood behind her. "We may have to stay here."

"She'll be back, and I'm sure she can fix it." Helen waved toward the impotent Scout. "Luke, can you help us get back—"

"Oh, I have no doubt Charlie will have this thing purring," Annesley said. "But I think we can wait to leave until tomorrow, give her plenty of time."

Lisa glanced toward the map. Helen reassured her with a flick of her hand. No way they were staying the night.

Annesley's eyes glimmered like the heat on the road. "Luke was telling me about a big party tonight. Junefest."

Luke adjusted the brim of his hat. "I don't think I'd call it a big party." His white teeth contrasted with the dark stubble on his jaw. "Calling it Junefest is a joke we make anytime we get together. Next month, it'll be Julyfest. But y'all are welcome. It's out at the Shrouder farm, past the old mill."

"Doesn't it sound fun?" Annesley grinned as if she'd always wanted to go past said old mill to some stranger's farm.

Before Helen could explain new routes and a shrinking timeline, the sharp beep of the White Whale's horn pulled her attention away from the strange person who had replaced her country-club friend.

Charlie emerged triumphantly from the wagon. "Thanks for the lead on the junkyard, Peaches. We made it through mostly unscathed." She didn't glance back at the beaming Mary Blake, who had a scratch on her arm and a black smudge across her right cheek. "And I got the part I need." She held up a filthy black cylinder.

Helen had the utmost confidence in Charlie, but the chunk of metal in her hand didn't look promising. "You're going to fix it with that?"

Charlie palmed the piece and opened the Scout's tailgate. "It's an ignition coil. The one in the car is one I helped Brent replace. Not a big deal. Since I couldn't get her to start even after Peaches put in a couple of gallons, it's definitely something with the starter. If I'm right, it shouldn't take me more than thirty minutes." Charlie pulled out a container of tools. "And I have my brother's repair kit. He could fix anything." She glanced at the map spread out on the hood. "We all set for the next stop?"

Helen moved toward the map. "I wanted to check with Luke about—"

"Change of plans!" Annesley beamed. "We're staying here, and you can take your time. There's a party tonight."

Charlie cocked her head at Helen.

"It sounds great and super fun, but we have to get back on the road," Helen said, sounding schoolmarm-y. "We're supposed to be in California in six days."

"Don't be a party pooper." Annesley pouted. "I trust you'll get us there on time. You, too, Lisa, right?"

Helen's jaw tightened. Opening her mouth to push back, she noticed she alone faced the other four girls.

Annesley had thrown her arm around Lisa's shoulder, and Mary Blake was practically bouncing on the balls of her feet. Charlie hung back, relaxed and seemingly amused by all of it. Helen slow rolled putting the map back in the Scout's passenger door pocket. She exhaled hard to force her shoulders to relax.

She was willing to set plans aside if it meant they'd finally regained what had been missing the past year, that sense of freedom and connection that had been restricted by university punishment, death, and nights she planned to forget. "Okay, okay."

"Local flavor!" Annesley sang in a key that both delighted and scared Helen.

With a flourish, Annesley tossed her bare peach pit across the road, major-league-pitcher style. Helen caught Charlie staring at Annesley's chest, where a drop of peach juice perched on a pearl, ready to drip down to the constellation of drips already marring the white shirt. If there'd been any doubt that the trip had taken a new direction, that doubt had vanished.

Helen smiled. Maybe it was finally time for her to let go a bit.

# Chapter Nineteen
# 2019
# Helen

Helen tucked in the flat sheet and pulled the comforter taut across the hotel bed. A hangover had spared her, but lingering dryness from too much wine and old memories stiffened her joints. Her phone bobbled between her shoulder and her ear.

Derek rejoined the line after sending their eight-year-old, Josh, out to camp carpool. "And he's off."

Helen pictured Josh, cast newly removed, right arm skinny and pale because she'd let him climb that tree. She hastily folded the top sheet over the comforter and focused on the purity of white on white.

"Are you making the bed?" His low voice mocked.

She hoped he was being playful. "Maybe?"

He laughed, and she relaxed. "Some things never change. You know, Helen, I hear even Texas hotels have housekeepers."

Making her hotel-room beds wasn't a *bad* habit. Folding in the corners and smoothing the comforter centered her and put things in order, something she needed after a day that started with travel disruption and ended with her unceremonious exit.

Surveying the room, she stepped back, grateful for the space Charlie had given her that morning. Sunlight brought out the gold in the woodgrain floor, and outside, deep green shrubs softened the prairie that extended to the west.

"It hasn't turned into a bunch of drama?" Derek said. "Real Housewives of a Resumed Road Trip?"

The others chatted outside her door, the ease of their reunion apparent in the light, animated tones and the lack of uncomfortable pauses. The ending of the last trip still felt unsettled, a leaning tower that wouldn't topple. But the others seemed at peace about putting the past behind them, her awkward exit from the room last night notwithstanding. Now they were picking up the trail they'd abandoned.

"It's been one day, Derek."

"So there's still time."

Four days didn't sound like a long time, but less than twenty-four hours had made twenty years feel like a blip. "It's been great to see everyone. Annesley—I told you she's the one who looks like a L'Oreal model?—she still does, and she's married to a documentary filmmaker, and we need to watch the one on Haiti because apparently she's in the background of some shots. And Mary Blake was married to a movie producer, and we need to avoid watching anything he's done because he's an asshole."

"So it *is Real Housewives*. Is Lisa a pro-athlete's trophy wife? Who's the other one? Maybe a B-list actress from the nineties?"

Helen burst out laughing, and the pajamas she was folding into a military roll Charlie-style ended up more of a blob than a cylinder. "You're impossible." She embraced the feeling of having a normal conversation with Derek, the joking they'd shared earlier in their marriage.

"No throwing chairs across the room. And definitely don't have too much fun. I want you on that return flight."

"I can't promise anything, Derek." That came out the wrong way, but Helen waited too long to correct it.

Derek didn't seem to take her comment one way or the other and returned to telling her about his latest project, the renovation of an old church in historic Richmond.

Nodding along with his descriptions of unexpected finds behind plaster walls, she grabbed the last thing to pack, the photo book.

She flipped through the pages absentmindedly and stopped at two that were stuck together. When she slid her fingernail between them, they feathered apart and revealed a photo Helen had missed. Her lungs seized. The image showed five girls at the beach, faces overexposed from the flash. The nondescript beige of a borrowed beach condo sat in the background. Helen recognized the red T-shirt with the embroidered neckline on her younger self.

The photo had been taken before an argument over something she couldn't even remember sent Mary Blake and Annesley back to campus early, before Charlie threw up from food poisoning, before she and Lisa went to the party alone, and before she sent Lisa back to the condo. Before.

Mary Blake couldn't have known the photo tied to that "before," tied to anything other than their four years together. Helen's face shone with rosy naiveté, her cheeks still full, though her baby fat had melted away later their senior year like snowflakes on a river. She looked in the mirror at her caved-in cheeks and dull eyes and placed her hand on her chest to feel the rise and fall.

"Have you given any thought to what we talked about before you left, Hel?"

"I'm sorry, what?"

"That therapist Mike and Diane recommended. She has an opening for new clients."

Her fingers pressed into her chest to stifle a response.

"We need our navigator!"

Annesley's voice from the other room snapped Helen's gaze away from the image in the mirror. She slapped the book shut and forced words past the grip on her throat. "I still can't believe you talked to our friends about that. Can we please table this until I get back?" Better yet, forget about it, bury it, never bring it up again, because that deep gray would devour her. "I have to go. We've got a long drive today, and someone's got to navigate."

She hung up, shaking and ready to disappear into a crowded car and let the road take her away. When she went to zip her bag closed, the photo album stared up at her. She swiped it to the floor and kicked it under the bed. The housekeeper could take care of it.

# Chapter Twenty
# 1999
# Annesley

On a back country road, on their way to this thing called June-fest, Annesley had no objection to being squeezed in the back seat of the White Whale. Her bare leg pressed against the rough denim of Luke's faded jeans.

Helen, who had eyed Charlie and Annesley with what looked like gleeful suspicion since they'd left the lake house that morning, spoke through the CB speaker. "I'm trusting you with the navigation, Mary Blake. Please don't land us in South Dakota."

Annesley didn't care where they were headed. The prospect of going somewhere new was exhilarating.

Charlie laughed in the background. "Tell Annesley tonight is all about the pralines."

Luke leaned even closer to Annesley and whispered, "Pralines? Do tell."

Annesley feigned confusion but felt the glow of flattered amusement infuse her face.

After Charlie had fixed the Scout, which had taken all of ten minutes once she had the part, they'd cleaned up at Luke's grandmother's farmhouse.

"Call me Grams. All Luke's friends do," the silver-haired woman in a mint green housedress said before hustling them to the guest bathroom. They could have taken turns, but the girls had crammed into the bathroom together, alternating in front of the mirror as Charlie washed the grease off her hands and Annesley twisted one of her silk scarves into Lisa's hair.

Lisa turned off of Alabama route something-or-other onto an unmarked dirt road lined with metal fence posts. Annesley felt like a character in someone else's story, brimming with excitement of the unknown that lay at the end of a dirt road and the man next to her, who smelled of hay and soap.

Luke waved a hand that held a go-cup of spiked sweet tea. "Keep going around this way toward that barn and silo. Park by the other cars."

The barn gleamed in deep red with white trim. The silver silo towered to its left. As they approached, two chickens fluttered away.

Verdant crops planted in precise rows abutted an open space behind the barn. Vines dotted with flowers the color of ripe watermelon ran wild up and around a corner of the red siding.

They parked along the edge of the field, and Luke introduced the five girls to the dozen or so people already there.

"These lovely ladies had some car trouble at the farm stand and decided to stay the night," he said to a lanky redhead in a "Bama" T-shirt.

"You pulling spark plugs out of cars again when no one's looking?" Bama Guy joked. "Watch out for this one, ladies."

Luke play-punched him in the shoulder. "Remind me never to make you my wingman. How am I supposed to impress anyone when you tell all my secrets?" Luke smiled wide and brushed his hand against Annesley's, sending a shiver up her arm.

The group were all in their twenties, and they welcomed Annesley and her friends with the same ease Luke had displayed at the farm stand.

The sun blazed above a copse of trees to the west, spotlighting a stocky, clean-faced guy in a plaid shirt who sat tuning a guitar on top of a tractor. Junefest felt like the set of a country-music video, complete with trucker hats, cowboy boots, and big hair. The scene was the exact opposite of the refinement Annesley expected of Mrs. Cordelia De Baillon Harrison at the Texas ranch. The reminder of that refinement—confinement—constricted her chest, and she grabbed a can of beer from Charlie's outstretched hand to counter the intrusion. This was her life, not her mother's, not Tripp's, and not anyone else's.

That she was behind a barn with random strangers and drinking—she checked her can: Budweiser—proved she was in charge. Charlie reclined against a rusty axel, eyes on Annesley and her mouth tilted into what technically qualified as a smile. Was she impressed, like Davis had been when Annesley grabbed a praline in the country club pantry without hesitation? Annesley hoped so.

Luke chatted with his friends but was never more than an arm's length away. He wasn't bathing in the attention of fawning coeds or giving "fraternity house tours" to overserved freshman girls like Tripp did, thinking she didn't notice.

The clean-faced guy hit the first five notes of "Brown-Eyed Girl," and the sound carried across the field like a feather on rippling water, washing away unwelcome thoughts of Tripp embarrassing her with his drunken indiscretions.

"I have decided," Annesley announced, "that I am a huge fan of Junefest."

"Is it better than filching pralines?" Charlie asked.

Annesley caught Luke smiling at her. "I'll let you know," she said.

"Can I get you another beer?" Luke asked.

She nodded.

"Don't go anywhere," he said, leaving her scalp prickling.

Attention from guys wasn't new, though she never reveled in it or even encouraged it. But this felt freeing and innocent. She searched her internal warning system and heard no alarm bells, no internal voice in her mother's tone telling her "no" or "stop." She let the purity of the moment engulf her.

Before long, the sun dipped below the treetops, and the Delta Rhoadies had blended in with the locals enough that they moved easily in and out of conversations. They still gravitated back to each other.

"I'm glad we stayed." Lisa said. She seemed more present than usual, like she wanted to be seen rather than stay in the shadows. "After a year of social probation, it's nice to be out with no worries."

Eying the jade scarf in Lisa's hair, Annesley swelled with pride for her part in that.

Charlie hiked an eyebrow. "I wasn't on social probation."

Annesley brushed aside mention of collegiate punishments and ribbed Charlie instead. "Yeah, but did you ever do anything social without us? You can admit you love us."

Charlie sipped her beer, but Annesley saw the smile.

"I'll read into that non-comment anything I want," Annesley said, prompting Charlie to roll her eyes.

A bounce-the-ball-against-the-wall-of-the-barn version of beer pong—"barn pong," the locals called it—took over as stripes of clouds pulled the colors of sunset into a blaze of fire. It outshone any sunset Annesley had ever seen, from the Gulf display at Key Largo to the alpenglow of Aspen.

Annesley still didn't favor sleeping in tents, but if that was the price to pay for a night like this, she would swipe a card at the next KOA and open a tab. She couldn't remember ever not being worried about whether her hair was frizzy from the humidity, if her lipstick matched her manicure, or if standing next to any given person might have a butterfly effect of assumptions and expectations that could lead to being snubbed at the next social event. She stretched out her arms to take up as much space as she could and pull all the world toward her.

Somewhere between "Brown-Eyed Girl" and barn pong, the lone guitarist gained a bongo-playing friend. The duo was less than polished, but their spare "Sweet Home Alabama," with the low sun infusing the sound with an ochre glow, got people dancing. Helen bumped hips with Mary Blake, and Lisa appeared to be urging Charlie to strike a pose, which she stoically did not. Annesley thought of her mother at home, planning her perfect summer graduation party, a dry affair choreographed to be praised and imitated as another Luella Cannon signature social event.

No one had planned this night. Roses running up the side of a barn beat out custom centerpieces. Annesley had already decided that every event needed off-key cover songs and strange drinking games, and the ease of the gathering met every standard of hospitality. She'd attended countless parties in college, but she'd been so focused on not being part of the spectacle and not getting stuck in conversations with the wrong people that they hadn't been more than stops along the way.

The lanky redhead hopped onto a trailer strewn with hay. Urged on by his friends, he raised his hands in a Rocky Balboa pose, turned his back to the crowd, and pushed off into a backflip. His feet landed without a wobble, and he bowed to beer-fueled cheers.

Luke leaned toward Annesley. "He'll be doing that at parties until he can't climb onto a launch point."

A busty girl with curly black hair and a bandana top brushed the dust off the lower part of the redhead's pants.

Luke laughed. "Or until Gevvie there stops letting him."

A short-haired blond girl standing near the guitarist bent over, set her hands on the ground, and kicked her feet up until she held a handstand. Her button-down shirt, tied at the waist, fell to show off her midriff. She tipped over to the side, laughing as her fall threw up a puff of dust.

"Is this a thing?" Annesley teased Luke. "Party tricks at dusk?"

"Feats of physical daring," Luke said solemnly. Then he cracked a smile that sent a thrill through her legs and down to her toes. "AKA 'dumb shit we do when we're drinking.' What else do we have to do out here in the sticks while we're waiting for our turn at barn pong?"

Annesley craved the comfort of enjoying every moment like this, of savoring the dirt and the dusk and the ease of it all.

Helen cleared her throat until she had her friends' attention. She straightened her arms, a beer grasped in one hand, the other hand splayed into a star. With great ceremony, she touched her nose with her tongue and made an exaggerated bow.

Annesley hadn't realized until now that she'd missed Helen's sense of fun. Granted, Annesley hadn't lived in the sorority house that year and had been distracted with extra classes to finish her double major, so she hadn't seen the others as much as prior years. But when they had been together, Helen's presence had seemed shallow, like she'd been distracted. The trip seemed to have re-energized her, just as it had the group as a whole.

"You should have shown that to my mother," Annesley joked.

"Oh, I did!" Helen said, her eyes lighting up. "She and I shared tips. She can put her entire fist in her mouth."

Annesley guffawed.

Helen pointed at Charlie. "Your turn!"

Charlie shook her head. "I can fix a car, but I already did that today."

Luke tilted his head and looked at Annesley, mischief in his eyes. "You must have something." *This guy.* He'd told her at the gas station that he was helping his grandmother get the farm ready to sell before he took a job in Birmingham. He was probably the kind of guy who loved you even more when you woke up messy and bare faced in the morning.

She shrugged. "I'm a simple girl. No tricks. No feats of physical daring." It wouldn't do to embarrass herself, do something that would expose her as not belonging. Her heart pulsed and pressed as if in a cage.

"That's right. Suuuper simple," Charlie said with no attempt to mask her sarcasm. "And Annesley Blair Cannon *never* goes off course." She flashed a smile that said, "You're all right. Now prove I'm not wrong about that."

A guitar solo swelled. Annesley considered whether she had anything interesting she could do, anything unexpected. The urge to participate, to be a genuine part of the moment, rose in her as a force, a need that pushed at her chest. But everything she'd ever done had a purpose, a goal, an expectation. None of this had a purpose. A cheer rose from the barn pong table and the sound of competitive joy overwhelmed her.

A tightness deep within released like a spring. "I have something." The declaration felt bold. She hesitated. "But it's a little derivative."

"Is that your excuse?" Charlie asked. "You don't want to be *derivative*?" The challenge in Charlie's eyes, that gleeful competitiveness she'd seen on the dock and in the Scout, provided the purpose Annesley could grab ahold of.

Annesley slid off her sandals. "Hold my beer." She thrust her can at Charlie and wiped her hands on her shorts. "Bear with me. I'm not warmed up." She breathed in a lungful of air, savoring the aromatic combination of beer, mud, and roses.

Balancing herself with a hand on Charlie's arm, Annesley positioned her feet, raised onto her toes, and lowered into a demi-plié. She rose again then did another. She lowered into a grand plié, her knees pointed outward and her inner thighs pulling tight as her glutes neared her heels. The muscle memory softened her limbs.

She nodded at Luke. Curiosity filled his face, and the fact someone looked at her with no idea of what she might do next gave her a thrill that flowered from flutters in her chest to an expansiveness that tracked each nerve to its end.

After taking her hand off Charlie, she grounded the balls of her feet into the dirt, feeling the dry grit between her toes. She tilted her hips upward to flatten her posture. The contraction of her thighs and calves felt powerful, and she bent her right leg, pulling her knee up and to the right. When her foot reached hip height, she cradled her heel in her hand and guided her leg straight up until it hugged her ear. A full standing split in three-inch seam shorts.

"Well, I'll be." Luke's grin pulled her taller.

Her muscles quivered, warming her skin. The positioning of her hands had been awkward and her form lamentable, but this was not a recital, with her mom sitting stiffly in the front row. Her body could do this, and she would let it. Quivers turned into vibrations. She was out of practice, and she didn't care. She released her leg, smiled at Helen, and fell into a deep curtsy. Then she grabbed the Budweiser from Charlie and downed it.

When she pulled the empty can from her lips, she saw Helen and Charlie laughing, their heads close together. Cicadas hidden in the trees buzzed.

"Anything you two would like to share with the class?" Annesley asked, suddenly worried she'd miscalculated freedom and how one exercised it.

Helen held up her hands. "We're just wondering who you are and what you did with our friend Annesley."

Charlie chimed in, deadpan. "And how *Titanic* may be ruined for us forever. Though I do like your version better than Kate Winslet's."

Annesley flexed her quads again, pulling from their strength. She'd left their friend Annesley back with her mother. And damn, did it feel good. "I told you it was derivative."

"Derivative or not, I love More Fun Annesley!" Helen linked arms with Charlie and beamed.

With a flourish on the bongos, the tractor duo switched songs. The opening riff pricked at Annesley's ears. Before the singer opened his mouth to sing the first words, Lisa caught Annesley's eye.

"Mountain Music!" they screamed in unison. They'd missed that song in their "mountain medley" on the drive through Virginia.

Annesley grabbed a questioning but willing Helen. She knew the others would follow. "Come *on*!" she hollered, willing them all into the topless Scout until the five of them balanced on the seats.

Annesley and Lisa took the lead, singing until the others joined in. Alabama's words became their own. They could have been surrounded by good ol' boys or all alone in the middle of a field, and it wouldn't matter. They were screaming into the night, and nothing could stop them.

# Chapter Twenty-One
# 1999
# Annesley

Birdsong had replaced the cicada serenade from the night before, a soft entry to the morning. No matter how hard she pressed her eyelids together, Annesley couldn't recapture the soft bliss of sleep, so she settled into absorbing the melody that still pulsated from her chest down through her core.

Behind the Junefest barn, she'd leapt from the Scout into Luke's arms. They danced, sang, and explored the fields. Under the light of a high moon, Luke pulled her close and stopped short of a kiss.

"Just passing through," he said.

"Just passing through," she agreed.

Then she kissed him. She'd led things from there.

Annesley eased her eyes open despite a craving to live in the memory of a star-filled night and no tomorrow.

The morning sun pushed pinks across the sky, and Luke's even breathing lent to the serenity. Some farm boy, though, sleeping past dawn. She smiled and shifted toward him on the crumpled wool blanket that lay behind his grandmother's farmhouse. Annesley's movement prompted Luke to roll over and wrap his arm around her.

The last things she remembered from the night before were his arm pulling her close, the stubble on his chin brushing against her neck, and his warm breath as he whispered, "Goodnight, beautiful."

She'd felt it before he said it. Beautiful. She'd spent her life praised for her poise at the piano and admired in designer dresses that emphasized her long legs. But she wasn't sure she'd ever thought, "I'm *beautiful*." Perfect, yes. Her mother made sure of that. Perfect meant following the rules and fitting into a box. She was good at that. But beautiful... that was a feeling free of restrictions and expectations.

Beautiful was vines creeping up the side of a barn.

She'd felt beautiful singing with her friends, chugging a beer, and walking through the fields in a silly game of hide and seek. She hadn't been Annesley Blair Cannon, held to the strictures of expectations and model behavior. No need to set a standard, uphold a legacy, prove anything, or move to the next level. She got to be someone else. And with Luke, she hadn't felt like she was achieving a goal or like she herself was a prize.

Luke stirred again, rubbing his chin across her shoulder and sending shivers down her spine. Her heart thrummed.

"Mornin'," he said. "You made me oversleep."

"I'm terribly sorry."

"No apologies allowed. You're welcome to pass through our slice of heaven any time." As if on cue, a pair of little brown birds swooped past and alit on a cherry tree. "It was a pleasure to spend time with you, Miss Annesley Blair Cannon."

She stiffened on hearing her full name aloud, so formal. His affected tone, she knew, wasn't meant to be mocking and wasn't meant to invoke thoughts of her mother: *Never lose sight of your goals. Always represent who you are.*

A piercing call came from the tree, an outsized scold from a bird no bigger than Annesley's hand. Her heart, so full, sank into her stomach.

As Luke's eyes closed again and his breathing became regular, Annesley refocused on the house. Paint peeled off the wood siding, and a gutter hung loose at a corner of the roof. Chickens strutted near an open shed while a gray-and-white cat watched languidly from a tractor seat. Only a few feet away, T-shirts dangled from clothespins. She didn't need to stand to be reminded that fields lay in all directions with only distant farm buildings breaking the monotony.

Where did she fit in? Dancing on top of a dead soldier's car? Drinking cheap beer? Sleeping on a plaid wool blanket underneath a clothesline? Is that what the girl from last night would do? It most certainly was not what Annesley Blair Cannon would do. The thrumming of her heart now filled her gut, and the nausea of realization bubbled.

Her brother had trained himself on how to break free. He'd teethed on stealing from the posers and matured into punching walls until he simply broke through and disappeared. Her mother's words from the dining room pecked at her memory: "He made his bed and now he has to lie in it." The ground beneath her suddenly felt like the dirt that it was and pushed hard against her pelvis.

She reached to adjust her pearls, and her fingers found only the edge of a T-shirt. An intake of air seared her throat. She scanned the ground around her as panic set in. Her pearls could have fallen off anywhere. The Junefest farm was miles away, and the fields stretched forever.

White curtains covered the windows of the bedrooms where the other girls slept. They'd been there last night. They knew. Maybe not everything but enough. The birds called out a final accusation and flew away.

She'd willfully ignored the purpose of her mother's direction. When you follow the rules, you don't have to think about consequences. When you break the rules—

Annesley bolted upright. *Just passing through.*

Luke sat up and leaned back on his hands, a curious look on his face. "Everything okay?"

"We have to go."

Annesley's face felt splotchy with heat. Miss Eloise's cotillion and the country club's etiquette class didn't teach young women how to be someone else.

# Chapter Twenty-Two
# 2019
# Lisa

The valet waved a thank you, clearly pleased with whatever tip Mary Blake had slipped him before she embraced the concierge outside Rancho Verde's double doors. Lisa adjusted her seatbelt and clutched her phone. Despite last night's diversions, the reporter's call echoed on a loop in her brain.

Perched like Barbie in the pink Mattel truck, Mary Blake took her position in the driver's seat of the rented Escalade. Blond hair in a smooth bun and eyes hidden behind oversized sunglasses, she turned and peeked over the black frames. "Time to finish what we started. Next stop, Albuquerque. First, we need some music." She fiddled with the radio.

"I have a great 90s playlist on Spotify that Zander put together," Lisa offered.

"Perfect! Annesley, can you"—Mary Blake waved at the Bluetooth connection display—"deal with that? And, Helen, how's my navigator?"

Helen, occupying the other captain's seat in the middle row with Lisa, held up a map. A black leather planner lay across her knees. "ROAD TRIP," it said in gold on the cover.

"Hel, you brought a *map*?" Charlie leaned forward from the third-row seat she shared with some of Lisa's unnecessary luggage.

"We have this new-fangled technology now called GPS. Perhaps you've heard of it?"

"We're mocking each other already?" Helen's tone feigned offense, but a hint of a smile illuminated her brown eyes, filling Lisa with relief that Helen's departure from the conversation last night truly was due to exhaustion.

"It's like riding a bike," Charlie said. "Can you still touch your nose with your tongue?"

"Wouldn't you like to know."

As Mary Blake pulled away from the hotel and along the road back to the highway, Lisa opened her phone settings to figure out how to connect to the car. Annesley folded down the mirror and pushed her bangs to the side. She caught Lisa's eye and smiled. "I'm still trying to match your highlights."

Lisa finger-brushed her hair, freshly touched up so the gray roots didn't show. That wasn't what Annesley referenced, though.

In the farmhouse in Alabama, Annesley had reached out to touch Lisa's hair. "My stylist told me I can't get highlights this color. I can't believe you get them naturally."

Annesley twisted a silk scarf and weaved Lisa's hair into an updo of jade silk and highlights. Lisa had ridden the high of the compliment all night.

Lisa frowned remembering what happened with the scarf and returned to the screen, which showed the Bluetooth still attempting the connection. The phone rang, and she startled.

Mary Blake flashed a quick smile in the mirror. "More doctor stuff?"

Zander's name on the screen allowed Lisa to exhale. "No, it's home this time." She tapped the answer button.

Zander's voice blared through the car speakers. "Leese, I need your help."

Annesley, Helen, and Mary Blake sang, "Hi, Zander!" in unison.

Lisa flushed and swiped at her phone, trying to figure out how to redirect the audio. The high-pitched wail of a four-year-old in the background filled the car.

"Our little moppet isn't happy," Zander said. "I have a call with a potential client in ten. Any chance you can help?"

With a couple of frantic taps, Lisa turned off the Bluetooth.

Their youngest, Julia, got on the line and explained the situation in a blubbering ramble that would have been indecipherable to an outsider, save for the "Daddy" and "It's not Mondaaay!"

Lisa put on her bedtime voice, soft and infused with dopamine. "It's going to be okay, Julia." *Just one of those details Daddy doesn't think about.* She didn't begrudge him. She envied her content husband and his ability to look at the big picture and let the little things fall through his life sieve. What she wouldn't give to blot out the details, see only the forest and not every single tree that might fall.

"Daddy didn't know you can't wear Monday panties on Thursday. Isn't he silly? Ask him what day-of-the-week underwear he's wearing."

That prompted a skittering giggle. Tantrum over—crisis managed.

Talking on her cell in a middle row seat was like being on the phone in a dorm room. The reaction in the car to Lisa's side of the conversation ranged from slightly amused—Charlie—to about to burst out laughing—Helen.

Lisa wasn't uncomfortable with the attention directed at her. She hadn't worn white after Labor Day or spoken out of turn. She'd done what moms do, and she'd done it efficiently. Lisa shook her head as if to say, "Kids and husbands, amirite?"

Zander got back on the phone. "You're a goddess. Yesterday was equally crazy, and I forgot to tell you some reporter called—"

Lisa's smile froze, and the thought of her Bluetooth reanimating and connecting to the Escalade again sent a tremor through her whole body. She worked to maintain her capable-mom face despite the sudden burst of panic that made her lips tremble.

For a few seconds, his voice was muffled. "Hey, Julia, sweet, don't climb on Daddy's desk." More clearly, he said, "Sorry. It was the *Post*, or maybe the *Chronicle*?" His next words faded in and out.

Lisa checked her screen. It still showed two bars. "I'm sorry, what was that?" The enclosed space of the cabin was making her dizzy. She pushed her head against the door frame to get the phone closer to whatever cellular signals might be zipping past the car. She needed to know what the reporter had said. It hadn't occurred to her that Zander might be pulled into this.

"Some article. Research. She didn't say. You're a good source for all things medical. And hey, if you can sneak in my name—'the brilliant album cover designer behind the doctor'—a little publicity never hurts. What's the article about, anyway?"

Relief seeped in. Attuned to the continued in-car interest in her conversation, Lisa reinforced her mom face. "Oh gosh, Zander, I don't know. I'll let you know when I do."

As if to rescue her, something crashed in the background of Zander's end of the call. "Oh, Julia, not Daddy's computer! I guess I was due for an upgrade, anyway. Gotta go. Love you!"

Lisa hung up and grimaced, stunned. She became aware of four curious faces. "Julia's got expectations," she said.

"I imagine Helen like that as a child," Annesley mused, "mapping out her week by undergarments."

"Very funny, Annesley, especially coming from someone who flashed her undergarments in a wheat field to impress a boy," Helen joked. "Those were some short shorts, as I recall."

"It was soybeans, not wheat." Annesley's profile maintained an air of elevated levity. "And my mother would not have approved of those shorts."

Strings of clouds stretched to the south like a music scale devoid of notes. Zander's call reminded Lisa that there was literally no one she could talk to about the resurrected NDA. That had always been the case, but sitting in the confines of the SUV with four other women, something about that fact made her feel alone.

She swiped to turn her Bluetooth back on. "Let me pull up that playlist."

"No worries, Lisa!" Annesley turned up the volume, and Shania Twain's voice came over the speakers. "I got things set up."

Lisa sank into her seat, sulking like a child, as though Annesley had taken something from her. Pressing her head against the window, she let the drone of the road run through her body while she considered how she could get the reporter to leave her out of the story.

Zander didn't know what he was asking for when he wanted publicity. If that reporter got ahold of anything from that night, anything to hang a story on, he would not want to be mentioned. She regarded the other women. No one would want to be associated with her. An ugly thought emerged. She hadn't only been hiding what happened from everyone else. She'd been denying to herself what had happened. Nausea rose as heavy heat from her gut infiltrated her chest and crept along her scalp. She adjusted the vent to blow cool air onto her neck.

"Car sick?" Helen asked.

"I'm fine, thanks."

A lone tumbleweed blew past the car and off across the prairie. Lisa wanted to reach out and grab hold of it. She must have dozed off, because she jolted awake when the car swerved, and her temple thumped against the glass.

"Sorry, ladies," Mary Blake said. "Armadillo on the road, in case anyone's playing travel bingo. And up ahead"—she'd adopted her cruise director voice—"we have oil tankers."

Lisa rubbed her head. The nausea had settled into the base of her stomach, mild enough to ignore. She peered around the driver's seat to see the small convoy of trucks.

"That's fracking sand, not oil," Charlie said. To satisfy the curious looks from the others, she continued. "We did some research on sand mines for a deal last year. The regulatory red tape is a nightmare."

Mary Blake moved to pass the trucks. Polished chrome bumpers and hubcaps shone. Centered on each gleaming white cab was a barbed wire logo in gunmetal gray, the signature of a certain Texan cattle and oil family.

A chill crept down the back of Lisa's throat. Harrison Industries had grown since being Harrison Oil, the second largest ranch in Texas.

"Could've been you," Helen said.

It took Lisa a beat to realize Helen had directed her comment at Annesley.

"Thank God that didn't happen." Annesley's profile, sharp nose under a broad brow, was silhouetted against the sky's white blue. "I wish the exit had been under different circumstances."

Lisa wanted to scream her agreement, but the two weren't in the same position. Annesley had no need to worry about the barbed wire or the Harrisons or reporters or anything else.

No one in the car would face the pain of staying silent in a raging spotlight, knowing that speaking up would lead to a massive contractual penalty. "A violation of this agreement," the attorney had said, "would have an incalculable effect on the Harrison family and their enterprises, so if you breach, you will be responsible for paying liquidated damages of one million dollars." That number was as unrealistic now as it had seemed when she lay in a hospital bed.

The Harrison family were the ones, with their shiny trucks and their land grabs and their fancy attorneys, who should have had to figure out how to deal with the reporter, to get her to stop calling

Lisa and her home. What if the reporter called Lisa's office? The cold in Lisa's throat burned like dry ice.

She was a good doctor and a good mom, someone who deserved better than to be weighed down by politics and news reporters. She looked at her phone. Two bars. She googled Glenn Whiteford, Esquire, and there he was at the top of the search results. In the photo, he wore the same navy suit and had the same high and tight haircut, though all gray, as when she had first met him. She wondered if he still owned the gold Rolex that had glimmered under the flickering fluorescent bulbs of her hospital room. Harrison Industries stood out on his client list.

The others joined in a Third Eye Blind chorus, laughing as much as singing. Lisa didn't want to miss any more stories or songs. She copied the email address on the law firm page, tucked herself in against the door, opened a new message in her email, and started typing.

> Dear Mr. Whiteford,
>
> This is Lisa (Davis) Callihan. You may remember me from twenty years ago. I signed a contract with your client Clayton Harrison. I've honored the agreement but have been contacted by a reporter who has called my personal number and now my home. She says she has information from the hospital. My understanding was that no records would be retained. I don't know how you can expect me to honor the contract when you haven't honored your end. Is there anything you can do about this?
>
> Kind regards,
>
> Lisa Davis Callihan

She slid the cursor back to change "Kind regards" to "Sincerely." Two bars changed to one. She deleted "Sincerely" and left just her name. She decided that was too abrupt and unprofessional, so she added "Regards" and wondered what that word actually meant. She switched back to "Sincerely."

The one bar flickered off then back on. She panic-clicked Send and watched the email hang. The single bar disappeared, and there was no signature "swoosh" of the email going through.

"Sorry, ladies!" Annesley said. "No more service. Say goodbye to the '90s." She switched to the radio and searched for a clear station.

Lisa opened her mailbox. The email wasn't in her Outbox, and it wasn't in the Sent folder. The dry ice from her throat traveled down her esophagus and burned a trail into her core. Something about the absence of the email triggered second thoughts, but she had no way to re-read what she'd written, no way to unsend it.

She'd already forgotten the words she'd used. Did she say "Sincerely" or "Regards"? *Shit*. She could just imagine the lawyer laughing at her stupid letter and at the memory of the pathetic girl in the hospital bed. She was an idiot with a terminal degree who didn't even know how to write an email.

Lisa looked out at the New Mexico landscape, an expanse as vast and raw and dismissive as the plains they'd left behind in Texas. Lisa had deluded herself when she thought she'd moved beyond her college self and her younger self before that. She started to wonder if the time for that had passed.

## Chapter Twenty-Three
## 1999
## Lisa

Next to Lisa in the White Whale, Mary Blake paged through one of the "women's" magazines she'd pilfered from the lake house. Since they'd entered Mississippi, she'd quizzed Lisa to determine her "Sass Quotient"—two out of ten—and read aloud enough articles that Lisa now knew how to apply a smoky eye and what ten steps to take to achieve a cover-model body. Annesley had passed on participating.

A driver in the left lane lay on his horn and waved his arm as if swatting them backward. Lisa glanced in the rearview mirror. Suitcases and bags blocked the back window, but she could see Annesley, who had been stiff and unreadable behind her sunglasses in the back seat all morning.

Lisa darted her eyes away and tried to figure out if she'd done something to tick Annesley off. Junefest had been exhilarating. The night had held the promise and freedom she'd expected their last year of college. Annesley had been no exception. She'd cozied up with Luke, sung on the Scout, and done Lisa's hair. But now, she sat rigid in the back seat, like her mother had placed a stack of books on her head and threatened to cut up the credit card if they fell.

Lisa considered the barn pong, the party tricks, and the crowded wagon. Had she made a comment that came off the wrong way?

Annesley had wandered off with Luke late into the night, but Lisa hadn't said a word.

"Scout to White Whale. Yard sale alert." Charlie's words were insistent.

"Can you elaborate?" Lisa asked, appreciating the distraction.

Helen's voice took over. "You're losing things off your roof."

Through the side mirror, Lisa saw a trail of junk along the highway behind them. Then a floral sheet flew like a painted ghost past the back of the car. The junk was Lisa's stuff.

"Shit." She'd made more room for Annesley inside the car that morning by putting more items on the roof. She'd pulled the roof rack bungees tight while Annesley said goodbye to Luke. Everything had been in place when they left the farm.

She parked on the narrow shoulder, but cars zipped past and thwarted each of her attempts to open the driver's door. Instead, Lisa crawled out the passenger door, a small humiliation that made her want to curl up in the wheel well.

More humiliations awaited after the Scout was parked and everyone gathered in the ditch. Lisa's possessions dotted the road and the shoulder behind them as if she'd set out breadcrumbs for a return trip to the east coast. A pair of jeans did the splits astride a fence post. A broken plastic bin lay in assorted pieces like a roadside brainteaser. The Cup O' Noodles and bagged bulk cereal that had been in the bin spilled into the road.

All sound, from the buzz of passing cars to the heckling caw of unseen crows, softened as if she'd duct-taped pillows to the sides of her head. One sound came through from within, a sixth-grade taunt, mocking her. "Clean up in aisle five." Viscous shame rolled in her gut.

Kid Lisa had known she didn't have the right logos on her shirts or the latest sneakers, but she hadn't known that her dad's job relegated her to mockery status until a classmate recognized him working at the grocery store and the kids started calling her "Bags." None of her college friends knew that moniker, but her life on display made her feel like they knew now.

Another car swooshed past and sent a tidal wave of thick air over the shoulder.

Charlie hopped down from the White Whale's rear bumper, a black elastic cord hanging limp in her hand. "A couple of bungee cords broke off completely. These metal bits are angry little fuckers. You're lucky they didn't fly off and break someone's windshield." She said it almost as if it would have made the trip all the more exciting, a true road trip adventure.

Sound roared now, from the caws and the buzzing to Charlie's finger tapping the remaining metal bit. Property damage, injuries, interstate pile-up. Replacing her own stuff would be bad enough. She couldn't be responsible for someone else's.

"Hey, space cadet." Charlie snapped her fingers in front of Lisa's face. "I have some rope we can use to secure things. I'll be right back."

Mary Blake and Helen approached, their arms already filled. Mary Blake handed Lisa a Delta Rho pledge jersey with blush twill letters stitched onto heavy cornflower blue cotton. It had seen a lot of wear, both required—Delta Rho Jersey Wednesdays—and optional—"only if you're looking your Delta best"—and was broken-in enough that a little road rash hadn't caused appreciable damage.

When Lisa had left home as the first in her family to go to college, joining a sorority hadn't been on her syllabus. The principal concern at the Davis house had been whether Lisa would be able to repay her student loans.

But everyone else in her dorm had gone through rush, and Lisa would have stood out by not joining in. A Panhellenic scholarship saved her from the embarrassment of having to turn down Delta Rho's bid due to the chapter dues, but her brief financial anxiety paled next to the blistering fear that the membership committee would discover that somehow Lisa wasn't supposed to have been included on the bid list, that her name had been included in error, a piece of paper put in the wrong pile and in need of correction, because they couldn't let the daughter of a grocery-store clerk and a home health aide wear their letters.

She'd battled the irrational feeling of discovery of some clerical error ever since, worried the others would see behind the blush and blue jersey that allowed her to blend in. By hovering at the edge, she couldn't step on any feet, or at least no one would see her missteps.

And there she was, on the side of I-20, the embodiment of the childhood taunt that had marked her in middle school. "Clean up in aisle five," indeed.

Annesley stood next to the station wagon, still lost in thought. Lisa took some relief in that. She would have been mortified if Annesley had climbed over the fence like Helen had in order to collect her underwear or the biochem notes she'd saved just in case they would be helpful at med school.

Suddenly, Annesley straightened to her full height, her attention captured like she was a hawk that saw a blade of grass move against the wind. She removed her sunglasses and squinted. Lisa followed her gaze and saw a flash of jade. The silk scarf Annesley had woven into her hair for Junefest was woven into a wire fence. A lump lodged low in Lisa's throat as Annesley walked toward the fence.

Annesley untangled the scarf. "You put this on the roof? It's *Hermès*." She shook her head as though Lisa were a child who had disappointed her mother yet again.

"I—" Lisa's words caught in her throat. *What was I thinking?* She had learned over four years to stand back so she didn't do something uncultured, anything that would remind people they weren't supposed to be friends with a girl who didn't know that a colorful piece of fabric was an Hermès that required special care.

Annesley stared at Lisa from behind her Gucci sunglasses. "Can we go now?"

"Don't mind her, sugar," Mary Blake said. "She has a drawer full of Hermès." Mary Blake put her collected items into the back of the wagon and turned to walk east along the highway for the other things.

Lisa waved her off. "It's okay, Mary Blake. We can leave everything else behind."

"No, these are your things, your life. You don't want to leave them on a road in Mississippi."

Mary Blake couldn't have known her words would crush Lisa. If those things were her life—a mismatched set of bedsheets, rubber shower shoes, and a stuffed animal now covered in road grime—Lisa wanted to leave it.

Mary Blake placed her hands on her hips, insistent. Lisa looked at the trail of debris. Her mental calculator went to work on what it would take to replace what lay in the ditch: New sheets, twenty-five dollars. New sneakers, thirty—ten if she got the crappy ones at Kmart, but those never lasted more than a year.

A dump truck flew past, and the tires whipped a rock against the wagon—*thwack*—missing the windshield by an inch. Everyone ducked. Annesley glared as if Lisa had parked the car for maximum flying rock exposure.

Lisa wanted to jump out of her skin. Instead, she closed her eyes and clenched her hands. She needed her stuff, and that meant turning around and heading back. Things could have been flying out for miles. She looked over at the east-bound lanes. The median was deep, as in bottom-out-a-car, you-are-not-doing-a-U-turn-here deep.

"Helen, when's the next exit?" she asked.

"Eight miles."

Another car swished by. "I'll just... drive backward on the shoulder."

"We'll follow you. Be careful," Charlie said.

Annesley didn't hide her exasperation as they climbed into the car. Lisa tried to avoid eye contact in the mirror. Even with the sunglasses, Annesley could fix a glare so direct it made Lisa squirm.

She'd always wanted to be like Annesley, the type of person comfortable in the knowledge that she wasn't going to use the wrong words or the wrong fork. Lisa had taken Annesley's acceptance of her as an anointment. She'd let herself forget an Annesley anointment was revocable.

A tractor trailer sped past, and the White Whale shook. Air displacement from the trailer pushed against the car, and Lisa pulled at the steering wheel for stability. The rear wheel clunked off the edge of the shoulder, jerking everyone to the right as the car tilted like a broken amusement park ride. The front wheel followed with another hard clunk, and rubber ground against asphalt until Lisa steered the tires back up onto the shoulder.

Lisa avoided the sunglasses in the mirror, but she didn't miss the frustration tensing Annesley's face. "I'm so sorry," she whispered. "Just a little further."

Mary Blake rolled down her window. "Do you hear that?"

Lisa listened as she maneuvered the car. *Clunk*, pause. *Clunk*, pause. *Clunk*, pause. She pushed thoughts of repairs out of her mind. She hadn't budgeted for repairs. "I'll grab a few more things, and we can go."

Within fifteen minutes, they'd collected most of what they could see and secured the stuff to the roof. When Lisa hopped down, she saw the source of the clunking. What looked like the metal handle of a window crank was sticking out of the inside wall of her rear tire. Her now *flat* rear tire.

Charlie approached with a pillow covered in dirt. "Found one more—oh, shit." She crouched next to the flat. "Do you have a spare?"

Lisa prayed the answer was yes, but she'd never needed one and hadn't thought to check. She opened the hatch and lined up crates and bags on the dirt, taking care to leave as many of Annesley's precious possessions in the wagon as possible. With the spare-tire compartment clear, she lifted the cover and prayed.

Empty. Her feet were lead weights. All air left her lungs in a whoosh, and she didn't want to expend the energy to replace it.

Annesley removed her sunglasses and swiveled her head. "Do you have one we can use, Charlie?"

"Won't fit."

It looked like Annesley couldn't decide who to blame: Lisa for daring to drive over the hidden remnants of an old accident or Charlie for not having a spare tire that would fit someone else's wheel.

Charlie must have noticed Annesley's flared nostrils and tense mouth. "Did someone wake up on the wrong side of the picnic blanket this morning?"

Charlie and Annesley stared at each other, and Lisa worried they were on the brink of an abrupt dismissal that would undo every moment of joy from last night.

Annesley squinted and broke first. "You're right. Sorry. I'm out of sorts." She turned to Lisa. "Let's get the car reloaded."

"I've got it," Lisa said. "Maybe you can help Helen figure out where we can go to get a tire." She didn't want anyone else cleaning up her mess. And she didn't want them to hear the echoes of her childhood in her head.

# Chapter Twenty-Four
# 2019
# Lisa

Low clouds hung like sandbags over the Sandia Mountains when they arrived at their Albuquerque destination. Mary Blake had once again set them up in one of those hotels that appear in those Top Ten Dream Vacation lists Lisa saw in the magazines in her medical office lobby.

This lodging selection specialized in "adobe chic" and the soft aesthetics of rounded doorways and smooth corners, as if the structure were its own geological marvel grown out of the earth. They emerged from the SUV parched and creaky.

Helen raised her left arm and bent sideways to the right. "I don't recall dealing with sciatica last time." Helen's spine cracked in a crescendo that made Lisa cringe.

"We didn't have gray hair or mortgages, either." Lisa put on her serious doctor face. "My official diagnosis is A.G.I.N.G."

Mary Blake pushed her oversized sunglasses on top of her head. "I've got a cure for that! Margaritas. Over the counter. No prescription required."

Annesley smiled like she'd remembered the name of a song that had been on the tip of her tongue for the last ten miles. She caught Lisa watching her, and her eyes lit up. Lisa's pulse accelerated as if it knew something Lisa didn't and almost swept away her ruminations over her email to the attorney, which now loomed menacingly in her Sent folder but hadn't elicited a response.

The hotel's interior lived up to the low-key luxury façade. The foyer was dim and earthy and lit by copper sconces. A bar beyond the front desk featured a backlit stock of tequila in a monochromatic array from deep amber to crystal clear and margarita glasses the size of goldfish bowls, as if anticipating the women's "ailment" and Mary Blake's cure.

In the hallway to their rooms, Mary Blake distributed key cards, and thank God, everyone got their own room. "Massage in thirty minutes then get ready for dinner on the patio."

"Sounds great, Mary Blake," Lisa said, her muscles relaxing at the thought of massage oils and soft music.

Before Mary Blake entered her room, Annesley whispered something to her and gestured toward Lisa. Lisa turned to see who was behind her, but there was no one. Mary Blake looked at Annesley with suspicion, squinted her eyes, and opened her mouth into a toothy smile. The hairs on Lisa's neck stood up.

Mary Blake handed the valet ticket to Annesley and walked away, a bounce in her step.

Annesley, with a slight hitch in her gait from the ride, approached Lisa. "Are you up for running an errand with me? A secret errand?" Annesley gave an I'm-asking-a-lot-aren't-I look. "You'd have to miss the massage."

"Oh." Lisa bit her lip. She didn't want to look flattered or torn. She was both. Massages existed back home. Not that she would spring for one, but it was a theoretical possibility. Annesley stood in front of her right now, and the idea of a secret errand was intriguing. "Sure! I'd love to. No problem on the massage."

Annesley set a hand on Lisa's wrist. "Meet you at the front in fifteen."

Lisa rushed to freshen up then texted Zander. *Arrived in ABQ! Hope the client meeting went well. Margaritas tonight. Secret errand with Annesley first.* She added a detective emoji and a dancing lady emoji.

There had always been a glamour about Annesley. In college, following in Annesley's wake made walking into fraternity mixers as comfortable as walking into chem lab. When Lisa joined Annesley in the hotel lobby, the copper fixtures and rounded arches amplified that glamour. Walking with Annesley was enough to pull Lisa's mind from emails and "Esquires," especially since Annesley had invited her and her alone.

Lisa climbed into the passenger seat, and they followed the GPS directions away from the hotel.

The tires on the road hummed with a low vibration that an hour ago had lulled Lisa to sleep. Now, it heightened her anticipation. She felt sheepish about asking a question, as if she might cause Annesley to realize she'd brought the wrong person with her, but she asked anyway. "Where are we going?"

Annesley didn't take her eyes from the road. "Margarita supplies." So matter of fact.

"Did you see the hotel bar?"

Annesley gave a dismissive flip of her hand. "Mary Blake insisted on managing this entire trip, and I've been trying to come up with one thing I could contribute. It's hard to do anything for that girl. First, she has everything. Second, she sets the bar too high."

They turned onto a four-lane road lined with low-rise storefronts.

"So," Annesley continued, "we're going to hunt down beer, frozen limeade, Sprite, and tequila." The corner of her mouth turned up in a sly grin.

Lisa barked a laugh. "Redneck margaritas."

"Right! When I saw the photo of the lemonade stand in Mary Blake's book, I was like, bingo! I just wasn't sure when."

Lisa's mind returned to the photo and the annual Delta Rho charity event. The beer-and tequila-spiked limeade had led to their probation and even a cruel whisper campaign among the underclassmen that Lisa had been the snitch because she was worried about academic penalties. But the Delta Rhoadies—before they were so named—had her back when she expressed her devastation at being ostracized as a tattletale, Annesley herself stating, "They'll find some other thing to complain about soon enough. Move on." And that had been that as far as the rest of the girls were concerned. But Lisa had never shaken off the hurt of the rumors.

"It's a fun idea, Annesley. I wonder how Mary Blake's doing with Charlie at the hotel."

"She's in heaven. If she succeeds in getting Charlie to turn off her phone, it's entirely possible Mary Blake will make this car fly to California on the spirit of victory alone."

Twenty years before, when they'd had to leave the other three behind, Mary Blake had accompanied Lisa to California. That leg of the trip had been fueled by regrets and grief. It was the one time Lisa had known Mary Blake not to carry a conversation.

Lisa stared at the dirt and debris that formed a low berm along the curb. "When did you two reconnect?"

"Two years after, when her father died."

"Oh, that's sad. About her dad, I mean. I'm glad you two reconciled. That's not sad." Lisa shook her head. *Making things awkward since 1977.*

Annesley fiddled with the radio, and they passed a collection of clothing strewn along the shoulder: a T-shirt twisted into a knot, a single shoe, and a towel.

Annesley laughed at the dismal still-life. "That reminds me of... where were we when your things went flying?"

Lisa hadn't forgotten the humiliation of her tiny life on roadside display. "Mississippi."

Annesley chuckled at the memory that still turned Lisa's stomach. Lisa wanted to find it funny, so she forced a laugh. It didn't work. On the last trip, Annesley's presence in the back seat while Lisa's life was reduced to dirty sheets and creased academic achievement certificates had amplified the embarrassment. She hated that the feeling still wormed its way through her insides.

The hum of rubber on road grew louder. Or maybe it was the hum of silence. Annesley chewed her lip and screwed her face in thought.

Lisa sat on her hands so she didn't squirm. "That was a long time ago," she reassured herself aloud. "We didn't realize how simple things were back then. What we had."

"Can I tell you something I haven't told anyone yet? Other than Jameson, I mean."

Lisa's pulse quickened.

Annesley didn't wait for a response. "I had breast cancer eight years ago." She shook her head. "Well, people know that."

Lisa blanched. *She* hadn't known. Should she have? Annesley didn't look like she was in treatment. She had short hair, but it appeared straight out of a photo shoot. She was thin, but she always had been.

"I was thirty-four. My girls were practically babies. BRCA positive, triple negative. I had a bilateral mastectomy."

"Annesley." Lisa didn't know where to start. Her doctor self seemed to be on sabbatical. "I'm so sorry. I didn't know."

"Don't worry about it. I hated the attention that came with it. My mom, the micromanager. You can imagine. There wasn't a treatment she didn't push until I was finally like, 'I'm done.'"

Heat rose to Lisa's cheeks. The mastectomy explained the plastic surgery Lisa had silently mocked back when Annesley strode across the lobby in Texas. Lisa wondered if everyone else knew, and she had been the only one to be shut out. She parsed through comments she'd made over the past two days to figure out if she'd said anything that might have come off as insensitive.

Annesley's arms stiffened in her hold on the wheel, but her voice went soft. "It's back. Metastatic. Bone, lungs. Scans last week confirmed it." Annesley's arms relaxed, her elbows falling from their locked position.

A chill passed through the car and needled Lisa's scalp. "Chemo?"

"I start next week. But..." But Annesley's aggressive form of cancer didn't always respond well to chemo, treatment options were limited, and survival rates were low.

"Is there anything I can do?" With relief, Lisa heard her doctor self in her tone: measured, controlled, and sympathetic.

"No. I—well, yes. Don't tell Mary Blake." She turned to Lisa, her eyes wide and filled with trust against a backdrop of her usual knowing confidence. "Okay?"

Lisa stalled between flattery and fear. This was what she'd always wanted, to be on the inside, to be the trusted go-to. But she hadn't considered this sort of inside. Being in the role of confidante outside the clinical setting didn't come naturally. Holding her own secret in the years since their road trip had kept whatever secret-holding space Lisa had at full occupancy, and she'd hated herself for it. She thought of Mary Blake's excited bounce at the hotel after Annesley got the valet ticket from her. "Why aren't you telling Mary Blake?"

Annesley's lips pressed into a thin line. She'd obviously struggled with this. "It's not that I'm not telling her. It's that I'm not telling her *now*. Mary Blake needs this trip." Her hand dropped to her lap. "She did this whole thing for me, you know."

Lisa hadn't known that either. She shook her head.

"When I was in treatment, she sat with me in chemo while Jameson was with the kids. They took turns. She and I drafted a Carpe Diem List. It was a lark to pass the time."

Lisa envisioned Mary Blake perched on the edge of a chair, writing in her happy, loopy script—little hearts and triangles above the i's—while she kept Annesley distracted from what was dripping into her body.

"Jameson and I and the kids have crossed off almost everything. We visited Yellowstone and saw bears, we took a dirty dancing class, and we got chickens." She laughed, and her face lit up, elegance aglow. "At one point, Mary Blake and I talked about revisiting the road trip, but I thought it was selfish to ask everyone. When she resurrected it after her divorce, I heard the hope in her voice. I thought it would be good for her."

Lisa studied Annesley's graven face. She understood the concept, the desire to allow Mary Blake to find her joy by delivering joy. But this wasn't about Mary Blake. Lisa had practiced medicine long enough to see patients cling to their diagnoses privately before bringing others in, grasping at control when control seemed all but lost.

Maybe Annesley had told Lisa only because Lisa was a doctor. College Lisa would have considered herself fully actualized if she'd been included in this way. Today's Lisa wasn't sure if the confidence was a burden or a privilege, if helping Annesley meant hurting Mary Blake, and if Lisa had room for more secrets.

Annesley grabbed Lisa's hand and squeezed it like she didn't want to let go. "Thank you."

The GPS directed them to "Turn right ahead."

Lisa returned the squeeze, grateful for the privilege. "Let's go find some frozen limeade. I can't wait to see Mary Blake's face."

# Chapter Twenty-Five
# 2019
# Charlie

"Hand it over, Charlie." Mary Blake held her hand out, palm up. Since they'd come down to the spa, she'd been like a Pekingese on Ritalin, taking care of Charlie and Helen while Annesley and Lisa were off on some errand that got them out of this ridiculous massage. She'd shoved a full glass of water into Charlie's hands at least three times and called the front desk to send extra towels to all the rooms even after Charlie told her four were enough, thank you.

In the dim light of the massage room, the pixie fixed her eyes on Charlie and not the willowy massage therapist busy with preparations in the corner. "It's time to relax."

"*Me* relax?" Charlie asked. "I'm the paragon of chill."

"You're also inseparable from that phone."

"I do have a company to run, Mary Blake." Though the screen time was more about researching heart attacks and VA hospitals and checking Lillian's regular text updates than reviewing market reports and financials. All the better to maintain a barrier between her and any potential drama on the trip.

"Oh yes, your M&A consulting company that I'm sure you run all by yourself." Faux awe infused her voice. "No need for pesky staff. Right, Helen?"

"Ha! Maybe no one wants to work for her."

"Funny, Helen. I'll have you both know that I have the best team in the business. Total rock stars."

Mary Blake's eyebrows arched. "If they're rock stars, they don't need you." She sang the words in good fun, but the sentiment fell like a boulder and sent dull vibrations through Charlie's ribcage and deep into her chest.

Charlie's stepmother's words replayed in her mind. "There's nothing you can do here."

Since that call the day before, the general's condition hadn't improved but hadn't worsened, either. He didn't need her.

Charlie inhaled the sandalwood and aloe scents that infused the room. Candles along a high ledge emitted an ancient glow, and New Age music drifted in from unseen speakers, the sound making her antsy. "I'm not sure how listening to a kalimba and a rain stick could possibly be relaxing. How about we go for a run instead?"

"I can't believe you ran this morning," Helen said, twirling the terrycloth belt of her white bathrobe. "I would throw up after a hundred yards in that heat."

"I used to run until I puked." Charlie was more disciplined now, which allowed her to compartmentalize. That skill had been disarmed somewhere between Chicago and Albuquerque, allowing thoughts of the general and Helen in a hospital room to twist together in her brain. She didn't like being unarmed.

"I'll change the music," said the willowy woman who stood at a side table, arranging whatever materials massage therapists arranged. "Is James Taylor okay?"

"How about 'House of Pain'?" Charlie made a show of clicking on her screen. "I have it on my phone."

"I'm not sure..." The therapist drew her words out dubiously.

"Charlie." Drill sergeant Mary Blake had entered the building. She put out her hand again for the phone.

"Kidding, kidding. James Taylor is great." But Charlie didn't hand anything over.

"Fine. Keep the phone." Mary Blake acted disinterested and whispered something to the woman.

"Don't try reverse psychology on me, MB."

The woman moved to the door, her feet not making a sound even on the terra cotta floor. "I'll be right back with Esther and Jewel, and we'll get started." Even the names of the therapists seemed designed to soften the sensory stimuli.

Charlie caught Helen watching the woman walk away. "What's her story?"

Helen perked up, receptive to Charlie's own return to old games. "Oh, fun!" She considered for a few seconds and squared her shoulders. "Ex-New York City stockbroker. Loved the excitement but burned out fast and moved on impulse to Albuquerque to pursue a dream of being a jewelry artist. Discovered jewelry artists are a dime a dozen in New Mexico, and she wasn't good at it, anyway. Took a massage class through Groupon. Misses real bagels, and is glad her mother can't visit because of altitude sickness."

"Damn," Charlie said. "Is it possible you've gotten better at this?"

Helen bowed. If Charlie had any concern her old friend harbored grudges or lingering pain from the past, it was gone. The fragility of their senior year, when Charlie had agreed to let Helen heal in silence after the weekend at the beach, and the words Charlie had said out of grief and anger at the end of the trip, still weighed on her. But seeing Helen be Helen allowed Charlie to close that compartment for good.

"And that," Mary Blake said, "is exactly why I keep refilling your water glasses, ladies. You keep me entertained." She busied herself by straightening an errant incense tray and pushing the metal trash can into the shadow of a side table.

"If anything is making me not relaxed right now, it's you," Charlie replied.

Mary Blake glared in her Angry Tinkerbell way.

Charlie found it hard not to laugh. "How about this? If you stop moving and get on the table, I'll give you my phone."

"Deal!"

Helen guffawed as Charlie handed over her phone. "Some deal maker, Charlie. Mary Blake's the one who got what she wanted."

"Doesn't mean I have to enjoy any of this." But she stripped down along with them and got situated while they waited on the therapists.

The three were settled facedown under thin white sheets on parallel tables when the words of "You've Got a Friend" came through the speakers. Charlie grinned into the face cradle despite herself. Mary Blake had probably orchestrated the kalimba music to get Charlie to be the one responsible for the mushy song.

The door swung open, and three pairs of feet padded across the room.

"Ready for our *massage a trois*, y'all?" Mary Blake's hidden smile came through in the upswing of her words.

The willowy woman spread a cool substance in arcs across Charlie's upper back. "The masque is made of dirt from the Sandia Mountains, natural spring water, and a chili-pepper infusion." She had the barest hint of a New York accent, a flattening of vowels Charlie had missed when she'd been in the room before.

Spurred by either the smooth strokes across her back or the heat from the chili peppers, Charlie's focus centered on the tiles below her and pulled her thoughts away from her work, the women beside her, and the general lying on a bed of his own on the other side of the country.

"And what does this magical mud do?" Mary Blake asked, her voice muffled by the face cradle.

The willowy woman's voice blended with the low light and soft music. "It extracts the toxins from your pores and infuses your system with essential nutrients and hydration. You'll feel the benefits most tomorrow, but be sure to drink lots of water. We're fifty-three hundred feet above sea level, which can lead to dehydration and headaches." She smoothed a stroke across Charlie's lower back. "My own mom can't even come visit because of the altitude."

"I'll be here all week, folks," Helen said.

Charlie found it hard to relax when all three of them were laughing. Maybe she didn't need to worry about drama.

# Chapter Twenty-Six
# 1999
# Charlie

Being an early riser had always positioned Charlie for the day, but this morning, it gave her time to herself. She didn't regret being with the others on this trip, but there was together time, and there was *in-the-car* and *in-the-tent* and *by-the-campfire* time. Being first up meant first out and getting a chance to breathe in the Mississippi morning air in solitude.

She skirted the unused fire pit and stepped over a deflated air mattress, a casualty of Lisa's interstate yard sale the day before. Low voices from adjacent campsites mixed with the yips of dogs getting their morning exercise.

Brent would have loved seeing that window crank sticking out of Lisa's tire the day before. "Million to one shot, Doc!" she could imagine him saying.

But ditch diving for Lisa's things and going on an unplanned field trip to find a tire for a 1987 station wagon had threatened the existence of More Fun Annesley.

Charlie had always been able to blow off Annesley's attitude. After the open-book Annesley at the lake and the party-trick girl at Junefest, however, the mere hint of that attitude had Charlie feeling misaligned, like she'd put her shoes on the wrong feet.

She checked her watch. On the east coast, her mom would be awake and waiting for Charlie to check in. Approaching the pay phones along the frontage road, she kicked a crushed cigarette box to the road's edge. A gust of wind lifted it, and the box tumbled against a dead possum lying in the wind-dried weeds. Charlie grunted at the poor soul.

Her mom answered on the second ring and let out a soft exhale the moment Charlie said, "It's me." This reminder of Brent's passing didn't stab Charlie the way it had when her mom first expressed anxiety by worrying about her only living child. What had prompted palpitations even days ago now allowed Charlie to relax and lean against the phone's plexiglass surround.

"Are you in Texas?"

"Mississippi. We're supposed to be in Texas, but we ran into some road trouble."

"I'm sure you handled everything. Speaking of which"—her mom rustled some papers in the background—"we got your tuition bill for Columbia yesterday."

"It's all good, Mom. My personal accountant, AKA Helen, prepared a financial spreadsheet for the next three years, all contingencies covered. I'm having the tuition loan forwarded straight to the school. I'm good to go."

"You two are going to have such a great time. I'm sure she'll have you doing all sorts of things to explore the city."

Charlie hadn't thought that far ahead, but her mom was probably right about Helen. She eyed the possum. Its legs shot straight out in rigor mortis, and its teeth were bared as if to ward off the vultures.

Her mom's light voice continued. "You've got good people in your corner. You know, your father had dinner with the dean the other night."

Charlie pulled her gaze from the dead possum. Or was it playing possum? "Dean? Of what?"

"Columbia Law. Your dad helped the dean's son with his military connections five or six years ago. He's always been grateful."

"I don't follow."

"Your dad reached out to him after you told us you applied. If you ever have any questions, you have an 'in' at the administrative level." Her mom sounded pleased about her father's obtrusion, as if she had no sense that the general had devalued her daughter with a single phone call. He knew what he'd been doing, though.

A refrigerated truck rumbled past. Its diesel fumes mixed with the earthy smell of rural Mississippi. She pushed a hand against her chest and inhaled until it hurt. "I don't want an 'in' at any level, Mom. He had no right to get involved." She pushed harder. "When exactly did he reach out to the dean?"

"Sometime after New Year's. Is everything okay?"

The beginning of the year, before Brent died and before the law school acceptance letter arrived. The general was interfering in her life, directing it. And yet, he hadn't directed his son not to go off and get killed.

She tapped her head against the plexiglass. "Let me get this straight"—tap—"I got into Columbia Law School"—tap—"because my dad"—tap—"is friends with the dean."

"Oh no, honey! That had nothing to do with it. I mean, maybe it made sure your application didn't get lost in the shuffle, but you qualified, and they accepted you on your own merits."

"What you're saying is that he wants me to go to Columbia."

"Exactly. He's so pleased you're going there. We both are."

Charlie stopped tapping her head, clarity achieved. Her mother's voice continued in the background. Charlie heard instead the opening and closing of car doors and the clang of tent poles landing in truck beds beyond the pay phones. She was once again the little girl standing next to a tent, holding back tears while her dad walked away from camp.

The muscles from the base of her skull down through her fingers tensed until they trembled. Why had she even told him where she'd applied? She squeezed the phone receiver until her fingers cracked.

She pictured that little girl trying to impress her father with her achievements. "Look, Dad. I pitched a tent. Look, Dad. I applied to law school."

And he had done what he'd always done. His pride—now, as always—would be in his connections. "Not only can I get a law-school dean's son a prime commission, I can get my mediocre daughter accepted into a top law school." She hated herself for giving him that opportunity. But maybe he'd been right all along.

She wanted to hang up. She wanted to scream. She wanted to run down that road, through the earthy smell, past the roadkill, and away from the campers emerging sleepy-eyed and clueless from their tents, and keep running until all of this, everything she'd known, was so far behind her she couldn't see it and couldn't be reminded of it.

"Mom, I have to go. I might have trouble reaching you for a couple of days. It's getting hard to find pay phones." Her words rushed out, and she barely heard her mother's goodbye.

Heat rose, grew, and pressed with the force of molten iron inside of her. He couldn't let this thing be hers. And now her brother wasn't there to be her backstop, to absorb the pounding threatening to make her heart explode. Another truck rumbled past belching thick exhaust from a broken tailpipe that dangled below Louisiana plates.

The law school acceptance letter had lain unopened on her counter for over a week, oblivious to a too-early death and a void that could never be filled. What should have been a thrill and a moment of excitement to share with Brent—getting accepted at her top choice for law school and one-upping him after their days of driveway negotiations—was instead a box to check. And now even that box had been blackened.

Her brother's letters had encouraged her, his jibes the written equivalent of pulling her in under his arm. "Be sure your law school essay doesn't reveal what a weirdo you are. Seriously, though, any law school will be lucky to have you. Mom and Dad will be proud no matter what."

She wanted to slam her head against the plexiglass as punishment for thinking the general could be a normal human being. This was the man who, when ten-year-old Charlie's dog Herc was killed by a speeding car, had shoveled dirt unceremoniously over the carcass while Charlie cried uncontrollably. The man had no empathy, no regard for others.

A pair of feet wearing expensive sandals stepped into her view of the dusty ground. The red polish on Annesley's big toe was chipped, and something about that lightened Charlie's anger.

"What are you doing up?" Charlie asked.

"Gotta get up early to do my make-up."

"Haha." Charlie knew Annesley had abandoned her multi-step routine in Georgia.

But Annesley didn't laugh at her own joke. She was looking at Charlie with the intensity of a psychoanalyst. "Everything okay?"

Charlie's brother was dead, the emotionless general couldn't stay out of her business, and her mom was oblivious. Heat pulsed in Charlie's face. "Yeah. Just... home."

Charlie felt the look of pity before she saw Annesley's face. The furrowed brow above hazel eyes and the tightened muscles below high cheekbones were a visual platitude she'd hoped to leave behind after graduation. Charlie's brother was gone, and no number of condolences or tiptoeing around the matter would bring him back. But there was compassion in those eyes.

"Why don't you let us tear down camp? Take your time. Give yourself some space." Annesley set her hand on Charlie's forearm. "Okay?"

Charlie nodded and watched Annesley head back to the campsite, her runway walk sidestepping a crushed Natural Light can and clumps of weeds that shot out of the worn pathway like little green landmines. Charlie let out a silent scream and jumped up and down to shake away the hurt from the phone call. Maybe Annesley wasn't the only one who needed to go rogue.

The roadway was clear, and she took off past the tents, past the untended weeds, and past the roadkill, her mind clearing with each stride.

# Chapter Twenty-Seven
# 1999
# Helen

Helen stretched the kinks out of her neck and rolled up her sleeping bag. Dust danced in the light above Charlie's pillow. The inside of the tent hadn't lost its garage smell since Charlie had pulled it out of the Scout in Virginia, but the odor had mellowed and absorbed the scents of clay soil, dried pine needles, campfire smoke, and now the open air of Mississippi.

Her stomach growled, a rumble that reminded her their last meal had been fast food after learning how to change a tire and finding themselves half a day and one state off schedule. She couldn't be angry. The tire incident hadn't been Lisa's fault. A swirl of discomfort made her nose twitch. She pulled on a pair of shorts and a T-shirt, grabbed her travel bag, and emerged from the tent.

The stovetop wasn't next to the empty fire pit, and Charlie wasn't heating water for oatmeal. Annesley and Mary Blake drank from enormous bottles of Evian. Lisa filled a postcard with tiny text.

A mosquito buzzed past Helen's face, and she swatted at it. "Where's Charlie?"

Annesley screwed the lid onto her bottle and squinted toward the entry road. "She was on the phone with home this morning. I told her we'd do tear down."

Home meant reminders of Brent. Helen knew the need to keep to oneself, to let the minutes and hours turn into days, days into weeks, and weeks into months. Brent's death had been less than four months ago. Charlie was only human. But there was a schedule to keep.

She pulled her notebook and atlas out of her travel bag and made a few notes for the updated route. "Easy drive today, ladies, long but straight across Louisiana and deep into the heart of Texas. We might be able to stop to see The Largest Papier-Mâché Gator in the World if we make good time."

"Perfect!" A delighted Mary Blake stood and brushed the dirt off her shorts. "I'm running to the little girls' room."

Once breakfast was cleaned up, Helen directed tear down, following Charlie's standard operating procedure to ensure they left the campsite as neat as they'd found it. They'd come a long way since the tent-box fiasco their first night. She placed the tent into the Scout and checked the camp. Save for a collection of belongings organized around the fire ring, it looked like they'd never been there.

Helen checked her watch. She'd been up for an hour and a half, and Charlie hadn't returned.

"Should we be worried?" Lisa asked.

"I'll go look for her. We can still get to Texas by sundown." Helen set the atlas and her bag next to Mary Blake's purse. "Alas, no time for papier-mâché alligators."

Annesley, seated on a tree stump stool, stood and brushed bits of bark from her shorts. "I'll pack the rest of this stuff so we can leave as soon as she's back."

Helen went by the communal showers. No Charlie. She passed a playground with a lone seesaw and a swing set devoid of swings. No Charlie. A wave of worry quickened Helen's pulse. A young woman last seen alone on a pay phone by a highway was the start of a tragic news article.

She headed toward the campground entrance, where trees occluded the view of the road. Movement above made her look up.

Three giant turkey vultures circled above the trees. Helen scanned the road. Something fell on her shoulder, and she jumped.

Charlie, face flushed and streaked with dust and sweat, panted and pulled away her damp palm.

"Charlie! You scared the crap out of me. The vultures and…"

Her sweaty friend jerked her head toward the ditch, where a fat dead possum lay. "Circle of life."

"What the hell?" Helen whacked Charlie on the shoulder. "You can't run off by yourself. I was getting worried. What if something happened to you?"

Charlie stared at the possum for a beat too long. "I can take care of myself."

Back on the road, Helen gauged her friend's status: focused and intense.

Charlie tapped the steering wheel. "You guys got everything packed up, right? Got all the tent stakes?"

"Chill, Charlie. It's all good. Lisa and I did the tents, and Annesley and Mary Blake put everything else in the cars. We're seasoned outdoorsmen. But now, we need to be seasoned travelers and get back on schedule. No more side trips. Just drive west. We're expected at the ranch in two days, and we're already going to be getting there pretty late at night."

"Okay, okay. Where are we landing tonight?"

Helen unbuckled her seatbelt and leaned to the side to reach behind her seat. No bag. She looked behind the driver's seat. Nothing. She didn't see it in the rear of the Scout, either.

Helen picked up the mic. "Scout to White Whale. Do you have my bag?"

"White Whale here," Annesley said. "Don't you?"

Helen's neck tensed. "No, unless you buried it in the back of the Scout?"

"Hold on. We'll check."

Helen pictured the campsite when they'd left. Nothing had been on the ground. But maybe the bag had fallen behind a log or a rock. "Charlie, we may need to go back." She swallowed, and the knot in her throat rebelled.

Annesley's voice came through the CB. "Found your bag. Mary Blake packed it in the Whale."

Relief flooded Helen's system. "Thanks, Annesley. I think I died for a moment there. Charlie, we need to pull over—"

"Chill, Helen. We'll be fine. We don't need your notebook. 'Just drive west.' We're seasoned travelers, remember? Plus, don't you have like eighteen more maps?"

"I have one other map. I just don't like not having my bag." Helen pulled her back-up map from the side pocket. The paper had been folded and unfolded so many times that fibers spiked from the worn white folds that crisscrossed in a grid. She ran a finger along the raised creases. As soon as they had an empty tank, they would have to stop. She peeked at the dash. The gas gauge was on F.

Rain started the moment the two-car caravan crossed the Louisiana state line, passing the Bienvenue en Louisiane sign. Raindrops plinked against the soft roof, and the wipers thumped with every cycle.

Over the next hour, the light drizzle turned into a bayou-style deluge. Rain pounded against the windshield like a drum line, ran along the metal framing, and flowed directly into the cabin, smooth sheets of water punctuated by soft splatters each time the Scout hit a seam in the asphalt. Dark clouds had turned the day to night, and the view of the wagon in front of them was intermittent between the swipes of the windshield wipers.

Helen half expected a shrimp boat to pull alongside them. "Laissez les bons temps rouler," she murmured as she pushed a squashed roll of paper towels against the roofline, where the rain had established a steady flow. With the Scout bumping over the uneven road at fifty miles per hour, Helen clambered over the seats to position the canvas tent as a giant tarp over their things while praying they didn't careen off the highway.

The Scout, which had seemed so spacious compared to the White Whale only the week before, closed in on them. A tear in the roof near the driver's side flapped open, and a drop of water fell from the rearview mirror onto the CB mic. Helen slid back in her seat, her bare legs stuttering across the damp leather.

Visibility diminished, and Charlie's grip on the wheel tightened. A crack of lightning startled them upright, and they shared nervous laughter when the thunder followed seconds later. Charlie lifted her left knee. Water that had pooled beneath the pedals dripped from her left sneaker.

"I guess this is why Brent always kept it in the garage." Charlie grabbed the mic and held it close to her lips. "White Whale, we're getting a hotel tonight."

The silence at the other end of the transmission spoke loudly. Helen imagined the confusion at Charlie's about-face but also the relief on Annesley's.

Mary Blake's voice crackled through the speaker. "Y'all don't want to camp in the rain?"

Water pooled in Charlie's tent-turned-tarp. The blue tent in the wagon wouldn't hold more than three of them. But Charlie loved a challenge and could go any direction if prodded.

Helen grabbed the mic from Charlie. "It's raining in the Scout. Literally. We're not camping tonight unless we want to be one with the bayou. I'll check the map and figure out a place to stop." She reached down for the back-up map. What she extracted was a sodden mess of pulp that pulled apart at every fold. Bits of Louisiana dotted her fingers. Apparently, the side of the door leaked even worse than the roofline. "Shit. We don't have a map."

Annesley responded. "We'll check your atlas."

Murmuring ensued, followed by bits of "I don't have it," and "I'm not the one who packed it." The sound clicked off, and Helen's heart rate clicked up.

Mary Blake finally said, "The atlas isn't in your bag—"

"What do you mean it's not in my bag? How could you leave it behind, Mary Blake?" Anger at Mary Blake was a hot lump of coal filled with discomfort. "I put it in there." She thought back. No, she'd set the atlas next to her bag when she went to look for Charlie. The lump of coal lodged in her throat.

"Helen, honey, I'm so sorry." Mary Blake said. "We'll find a hotel. Follow us. I have a good feeling."

Helen opened her mouth to offer to pull over and search the car herself but reconsidered. The windshield wipers were fighting against the torrent, and Charlie's white-knuckled grip on the wheel matched her iron gaze on the road.

Helen tried imagining lush Louisiana landscapes that hid gators, pelicans, and swamp creatures, but the soggy splotches out her window disrupted the fantasy. So she kept her eyes on the brake lights ahead and tried to let the cacophony of rain lull her into a state of acceptance.

Lisa turned left onto a two-way road that wound into the green splotches. The trees loomed closer, with branches that waved like the arms of crazed demons, and Helen's head pounded from not knowing where the hell they were. She needed her notebook in the way a scuba diver needed an oxygen tank.

She dared to breach the quiet. "Do you think we could—"

Lisa's brake lights blinked on, and the wagon swerved toward the left side of the road. Charlie cursed while slamming on her own brakes. Helen screamed, expecting the Scout to hydroplane into an unseen swamp filled with the creatures hidden in the shadows. They barely missed clipping the wagon and stopped at the edge of a gaping chasm in the asphalt, where a torrent of water rushed across what used to be a road. Helen's heart pounded. Thank God Charlie had been paying attention.

"I have no words," Charlie said.

"I do. But I'm not going to say them." Her breathing was heavy, in time with her speeding pulse, as she considered the near miss in the middle of nowhere.

Helen turned to check the wagon behind them, which now faced the opposite direction. Next to the road stood a weathered blue sign: Pelican Ridge Motel – 2 miles.

## Chapter Twenty-Eight
## 1999
## Mary Blake

"Y'all got caught in that toad-soaker, yeah?" The Pelican Ridge Motel clerk passed his unlit cigarette from hand to hand. His dark hair had that just-groomed look, like he kept a small comb in his back pocket and brushed his hair to the side as a nervous habit when he couldn't hold a cigarette in his hand. "Musta threw you off course. Bad luck."

"I like to think I'm a glass-half-full kind of girl." Mary Blake waved a hand around the empty wood-paneled office, where she and Annesley had checked in for the group a half hour earlier. "We found this charming motel. The rain stopped. You were so kind to let me use your phone to call my daddy just now, *and* you gave us extra towels." She spied an atlas next to the room keys hanging on hooks behind the man. "Say, can I buy an atlas?"

"Ten ninety-nine."

Her brow furrowed as she opened her wallet. Her secret waitressing money had gone from a healthy wad of cash to a thin line of protection from discovery. She handed over a precious five and a clump of ones like she was parting with her Louis Vuitton Chantilly crossbody bag.

"Ya seem nice enough." He gestured toward a fishbowl filled with matchbooks. "There ain't much goin' on around here, but there's Billy's Air Boats. Should be lots of gators after the storm. And

Jethro's Fish Fry, but I'd stay away from the hushpuppies if I was you." He eyed her up and down, his cigarette tracking his visual scan. "Five girls, right? Tooloulou's got music and dancing."

She grabbed a Tooloulou matchbook to be nice, but her mind wasn't on excursions.

Her father's words from the phone call repeated in her head. "Sorry, Li'l Bit. I know we thought today would be the day, but the other side told us they have some paperwork to complete. Everything will be back to normal soon."

She'd been hearing that for ten months, and her half-full glass had been draining drop by drop the whole time. Her charm hadn't made progress with the school bursar, who refused to extend the date past next week's deadline. Worse, she felt an ugliness she could only term resentment.

She waved goodbye to the desk clerk, who was still talking and swirling his cigarette, but he didn't seem to mind talking to the empty room. As much as she told herself she was protecting her family by lying to her friends, she knew it was more than that. In truth, she hadn't wanted to see the look of "Who are you?" in Annesley's eyes if her friend learned Mary Blake's dad was under federal investigation. She hadn't wanted to find herself alone in a room, talking to no one.

She didn't know if she could maintain the façade much longer. But at least the group was out of the rain and the confining cars. After the treacherous drive through the storm and the near crash, they all deserved a chance to dry out and relax.

With a tower of scratchy maroon towels balanced in her hands, Mary Blake stepped over the muddy rivulet that divided the motel parking lot in two. She pushed her shoulders back to crush the kind of negative thoughts that led to empty glasses and bounded through the open door of Room 1-C. Feeling the squish of her wet shoes, she stopped short and looked from her muddy sneakers to the brown and yellow carpet.

Lisa, splayed on one of the two beds, noticed Mary Blake's indecision. "I don't think it matters."

Mary Blake took off her shoes anyway and set the towels on a table by the window. The room smelled like a water pipe had leaked in the middle of a heat wave while the air conditioning unit was broken.

They had adjoining rooms, 1-C and 1-D. Annesley had insisted on two rooms despite Lisa's offer to sleep on the floor if they split a single five ways, thereby adding even more to the debt Mary Blake owed Annesley. With the drenched contents from the Scout and the White Whale's roof spread out across the floor and over the furniture, the room looked like a news photo of a post-hurricane trailer park.

Annesley held the corner of a rust-colored coverlet between two fingers like she was holding a cricket by the leg. "When do you think they last washed the bedding?" She pulled the coverlet toward the foot of the bed. "This is going to do wonders for my allergies."

"The sun's coming out, y'all," Mary Blake said. "It'll be setting soon, but it's out." She put on her biggest smile, the one that pulled her whole body taller. "And I got you a new atlas, Helen. I am so sorry about losing the other one."

"I'm sorry I snapped. It wasn't your fault." Helen hugged her before accepting the atlas. "I should have double checked. Even if it's not raining, though, we can't really get back on the road to try to make up time. Everything's soaked." She opened the atlas to a two-page spread that included Texas and Louisiana. "But if we leave early tomorrow, we'll be able to get to the ranch by dinner."

Annesley let out a tiny sneeze. "What I know is that I can't sit in this mildewy room any longer than necessary. Benadryl can only do so much."

The four girls looked at Mary Blake, bored, desperate, or both. "Tooloulou," Mary Blake offered.

Helen cocked her head. "Too what what?"

"Tooloulou." Mary Blake dug in her pocket for the matchbook. "The nice man at the front desk said there's a bar down the road called Tooloulou. Music and dancing, he said. I thought everyone might be too tired, but under the circumstances..."

The coverlet fell to the floor, forming a crumpled, rust-colored puddle of polyester on a rug that matched the muddy water snaking through the parking lot.

Annesley sighed. "This motel, this area... it's all a little sketchy. But I trust you."

That was all Mary Blake needed to refill her glass.

# Chapter Twenty-Nine
# 2019
# Mary Blake

"It's margarita time!" Mary Blake pulled Charlie onto the open patio of the Albuquerque hotel. "That mud masque should have us primed for tonight."

Charlie grunted, which made Mary Blake laugh.

The mountains' slumbering silhouette merged into the blue-black sky, and twilight embraced the patio. High-backed couches hugged private fire pits. Voices of patrons enlaced and rose into the night air.

She'd plotted every element of the trip for impact, for the reaction she sought from her Deltas. She lived for that sharp intake of breath, followed by eyes widening, pupils dilating, and the sensory awareness of the setting. Her efforts made people feel special, redirected them, and swept them forward. She'd seen the response from Annesley at Rancho Verde, Helen in the massage room, and Lisa when Annesley pulled her away on some secret mission. She would get Charlie yet, and the five of them, now mature and settled, would be those red-splotched flowers coming together like she'd seen on the canvas in the Palisades.

"We've certainly upgraded our accommodations this trip," Charlie said. Fairy lights along a pergola haloed her hair.

Mary Blake couldn't help but see a younger Charlie, despite an even sharper jawline and the gray strands of hair that shone in the light. Helen and Charlie's banter during the massage had taken Mary Blake back to the time when friendship had been easy, when they'd all had nothing but sunshine in their futures. Her smile fell as she remembered herself in a wedding gown with her gregarious groom, his face covered in cake. He'd been uncharacteristically nervous about the "proper Southern" wedding guests, triggering a facial tic she hadn't seen before. Smashing the cake on his mouth squashed the tic, and he looked at her with those brown-and-gold-speckled eyes like she was the answer to his every prayer. She'd believed him.

A thread of sadness wound through the hollow of her stomach. She grabbed Charlie's arm. "About those drinks."

Mary Blake put an order in at the bar, and they moved to an unoccupied curved couch that faced the sleeping mountains. Large planters with leafy bushes abutted the ends of the high-backed settee. Flames danced above a copper fire pit filled with a sparkling sea of crystals.

"Just you and me tonight, MB?" Charlie's finger tapped on the casing of her phone.

"Everyone's running a little late. We get some alone time."

*Tap, tap.* When Charlie had handed her phone to Mary Blake back in the spa, a text had popped up on the screen. Mary Blake hadn't been snooping, but it was impossible not to see. *Numbers aren't improving. But your dad's a fighter.* With Helen in the room, she hadn't wanted to ask what Charlie's dad was fighting, and Charlie wouldn't have seen the text until after the massage. "Charlie—"

A server, crisp in his starched white button-down, arrived with five colossal margaritas on a tray. He raised an eyebrow at seeing only two women at the table.

"We're thirsty! Don't judge." Mary Blake winked and arranged the heavy glasses around the table.

Charlie's distracted gaze alerted Mary Blake to the arrival of the others. Mary Blake alchemized her concerned curiosity into her trademark pep. "Oh good, they're all here."

The three emerged from the restaurant's amber glow, Helen casual in a pair of walking shorts and a loose blouse, Lisa grinning like a naughty schoolgirl, and Annesley carrying an enormous umbrella-striped bag Mary Blake had never seen.

Annesley flashed a look of mischief. A kaleidoscope of butterflies fluttered in Mary Blake's chest, a thrill like she'd felt when Annesley did her party trick at Junefest in Alabama.

Lisa and Annesley scanned the table and shared a laugh. They maneuvered so Annesley sat on the end.

"I ordered everyone—" Mary Blake snapped her mouth shut when Lisa lifted Charlie's glass and set it in front of Annesley. Lisa did the same with Mary Blake's then Helen's then her own.

Annesley picked up the first margarita and tilted the glass toward the planter on her right. Mary Blake gasped. The contents splashed out and disappeared into the dirt, leaving only a wet mound of ice cubes.

"Annesley!" Mary Blake said, peeking over the back of the couch to be sure no one on the patio had seen. The butterflies burst free from her chest like sparks of light.

Annesley ignored her, and Lisa's smile widened. Annesley picked up the second glass and poured it after the first.

"Lisa and I thought we should do this Delta Rho-style," Annesley said.

"But those are top shelf margaritas," Mary Blake said while Annesley dumped the last glass.

Annesley gave the glass a shake to urge the last drop to fall. "Apologies, my top shelf friend. But these, my dear Deltas"—she smirked at Mary Blake and reached into her bag to pull out two containers—"are redneck margaritas." She handed the larger container to Lisa, who took over as server and refilled the margarita glasses.

Like a Polaroid picture magically emerging on film in real time, the image of the five of them at the Delta Rho fundraiser appeared in Mary Blake's mind. Gone was the nervous anticipation from the day before. Tucked away was the sorrow from their remembrance of Parker last night and questions for Charlie about a text message she shouldn't have seen.

"Annesley, I never would have expected," Charlie said.

Annesley's face shone under the fairy lights. "You only live once."

Lisa blinked from Annesley to Mary Blake, as if pulling herself out of a daydream.

Charlie lifted her glass. "To lemonade stands and not getting to have one senior year. Not that I would have been involved. I never did figure out who reported you all. So many mysteries."

Mary Blake and Helen batted names back and forth: a jealous ex, a cross-cut freshman, or a college administrator who accidentally got served the spiked lemonade.

Annesley put her hands in the air. "I suppose I can come clean." She took a long pull from her glass. "I was the one who reported the house." She said it like she was revealing she was Mrs. Peacock and had done it with a candlestick in the library.

"What?" Lisa's question came out like a bark.

Annesley's hair fell across her forehead and covered part of her right eye. "I was done with my mother visiting and asking about the social schedule. Were we having mixers with the right fraternities? Was our new pledge class up to par?" She held up a finger as if scolding them. "No. She would make that determination herself." She brushed her bangs aside, and they fell again. "I just... couldn't anymore. I mean, I wasn't expecting a full-scale shut-down, maybe a slap on the wrist that would shut her up for a while. But honestly"—she waved her hand dismissively—"we were fine without the parties."

"That is true." Mary Blake nodded vigorously. Probation had shielded her own ruse from discovery.

Lisa's brows had tightened, and three lines ran in parallel roads across her forehead. "People were saying it was me. The juniors wouldn't even talk to me first semester."

"Oh, that's ridiculous." Annesley carried on with her margarita, but Lisa continued to look at her until Annesley supplemented her comment. "I'm sorry, really." She sounded cavalier, using the Annesley posture that anything that didn't upset her shouldn't upset anyone else.

Lisa obviously wasn't mollified, and tension started to edge out the evening's delight, sending a wave of prickles from Mary Blake's toes up to her spine.

"I was mortified," Lisa said. "You told me to ignore it all." Her voice had dropped to a whisper. Light flickered against the now-black sky. The chatter at the other tables had grown louder, glasses clinked, and hoots of laughter layered over the patio.

"I'm pretty sure the statute of limitations has run." Annesley's voice had lost its bravado.

She wasn't the only one. Lisa's mouth hung open. Charlie cocked her head. Flames flickered and cast liquid shadows across their faces.

The prickles amplified, and Mary Blake could feel every hair at the base of her neck. For the first time, she envisioned the trip not working. Her throat dried, making it hard to swallow. She hadn't considered what would happen if the five of them weren't able to click, if they went their separate ways anew, just as they had twenty years ago. Her separate way would be back to her new bungalow, her two dogs, and a stunning ocean view. An empty, stunning ocean view. She sank into the cushion.

This trip was about rising. Rising from divorce, rising from cancer, and rising from the past. To do that, Mary Blake needed the five of them to reconnect. She hadn't known that when she'd first suggested the trip, but she saw it now. She also saw Charlie tapping at her phone again. "Charlie, how's your dad?"

"What? My—the general? Why?"

Mary Blake gulped. "I-I saw a text on your phone."

Charlie tucked her cell under her thigh. "When did we start looking through each other's phones?"

"Oh, I wasn't peeking, honey. It just popped up earlier when you handed—"

"Whatever. Fine. Alive. Remarried. Retired. Anything else you want to know?"

The words shot like darts across the table. College Charlie hadn't talked about family, and apparently, New Charlie didn't either.

Lisa drained her margarita and set the glass down a bit hard, almost as if trying to replicate the prior night's glass breakage. Annesley's pursed lips held in words Mary Blake craved to know, while Helen hastily refilled Lisa's glass and then her own.

Mary Blake found herself babbling, searching for the thread that would take them back to where they should have been. But whatever words came out of her mouth weren't distracting them, and they weren't distracting Mary Blake from her private pity party.

Annesley coughed. She apologized then coughed again.

Mary Blake emerged from the one party she didn't want to attend. "You okay?"

Annesley shook her head but said, "Yes."

"Nothing that a margarita can't fix, right?" Mary Blake accepted the soft pleading in Annesley's voice.

A cryptic look passed between Lisa and Annesley.

"I think I'll be the first to turn in tonight," Annesley said. She gave Mary Blake a wan smile. "Altitude, I think. I'll leave the margaritas for you all." And Annesley was gone.

Mary Blake glanced from Lisa to Charlie to Helen, trying to determine which to focus on to correct the momentum.

"Well, ladies," Charlie said, "looks like more margaritas for the rest of us. We might as well get some food."

# Chapter Thirty
# 1999
# Charlie

Mary Blake's head popped into the motel room every five minutes, as if a countdown would generate excitement about going to a random bar after a shitty day. "Ten minutes!"

Hip cocked and arms folded across her notebook, Helen stared at Charlie, who sat in a thinly cushioned chair. "This room makes your army tent smell like a Bath & Body Works." She lifted the edge of a damp sleeping bag from the brown and yellow carpet with her toe. "I know you don't really want to stay here by yourself while we go out."

Charlie didn't know what she wanted. The phone call with her mom that morning felt like it had been days ago, as if the rainstorm had softened time and pulled it like taffy. But the drumbeat of humiliation in her chest marked time unabated.

"Well?" Helen said.

The shower turned off, and Lisa's hand reached out from the bathroom to grab a towel from the counter.

Charlie stared at the fake wood paneling and followed a seam up to the ceiling. A water stain shaped like a tank shot a water stain missile toward the door. She blinked, and it was just a water stain.

If she stayed at the motel, the general would haunt her. She needed to move, hear some noise, knock back a few drinks, and expel the interfering general from her head.

"I'm in."

Tooloulou had seen better days, or maybe it had never been fully painted. Clear Christmas lights lined the building's frame, and a sign topped with a giant fiddler crab capped the entrance. The parking lot overflowed with cars and pickup trucks, mud from the deluge apparently no deterrent to a night out in rural Louisiana.

"Looks like we picked a good night!" Mary Blake chirped.

Charlie trailed the group into the bar. Mounted alligators and voodoo masks adorned the walls. Dollar bills stapled to wooden beams fluttered as the girls walked past a T-shaped stage. A sea of Mardi Gras beads hung from the ceiling, swaying in the heat rising from the throng of drinkers. A group of men waved the girls over to take their high top.

Mary Blake flashed her wide smile. "Why, thank you! Such gentlemen."

Helen grabbed Charlie by the elbow and steered her toward the table. "See," Helen said. "I told you this would be better than staying at the motel by yourself."

The rancid smell of cigarette smoke competed with the damp dragged in from the day's rain. "I'm not convinced yet." But the walls weren't closing in on her.

A round of tequila shots magically appeared, presented by an auburn-haired waitress wearing a "Tooloulou" T-shirt cut around the neckline to display her freckled décolletage. The bar's name separated into three lines down her chest:

TOO

LOU

LOU

The *o*'s in TOO were strategically placed, with a fiddler crab reaching his one large claw suggestively toward the center of the second one. Annesley, looking in her pleated shorts like an out-of-place mannequin, froze, her expression somewhere between embarrassed and confused.

Charlie laughed. "We're totally getting you one of these shirts, Annesley. They'd be perfect for the lake house."

"Very funny." Annesley bumped Charlie's shoulder.

The waitress—Jules, according to a pin above the fiddler crab—doled out five shot glasses. "Compliments of Big Red and the fellas over there." She leaned in conspiratorially. "Don't worry. They're harmless. They won a fishing tournament today, so they're feelin' flush."

Mary Blake batted her eyelashes. "We'll take all the free drinks they want to send us."

"I suspect they'll oblige if one of you competes." The server smirked and raised an eyebrow above her thickly mascaraed lashes.

That got Charlie's attention. "Competes in what, exactly?"

The waitress pointed at a laminated sign on the table's shadowed edge. "I'll warn you, though. No one wins if they don't take it off. It's the only way to get a shirt." She winked and sashayed away.

Helen moved the sign closer. "Ah... it's amateur night."

Annesley's eyes widened. "Is this a strip club?" She looked toward their waitress, whose lower back tattoo of a winged crown showed above her waistband. "Mary Blake, seriously."

Charlie tilted the sign to catch the light. "Not exactly. Stripping is *encouraged* but not required. The winner gets fifty dollars and one of those"—she pointed at a fiddler crab T-shirt that hung above the bar—"fancy T-shirts. I could even cut it in half like our waitress did."

Annesley's eyes narrowed. "You wouldn't."

"Win it or cut it in half?"

Roars from the crowd pulled their attention to the stage, where a hairy guy in a plaid shirt introduced a woman stumbling in black cowboy boots, Daisy Dukes, and a shirt unbuttoned to mid-cleavage.

She strutted to the offbeat of "Boot Scootin' Boogie," using a clumsy two-step and parts of assorted line dances. The crowd ate her up. Beads flew to the stage, and she obliged by undoing the remaining buttons.

Helen and Mary Blake shared a look of shock, and Lisa blushed.

Annesley sniffed. "I'm not sure this is really our kind of place. Mary Blake, was there somewhere else?"

"You, uncomfortable?" Charlie challenged Annesley. "I thought you could hold your own anywhere."

Annesley squinted like she was trying to count the points on the buck antlers on the wall. She picked up her shot glass. "I'll stay..." She sipped the tequila like it was tea at Buckingham Palace. "If you dance."

"You're the dancer, sister. Not me."

"I already showed off my dance moves at Junefest, *sister*. In fact, as I recall, you wimped out on doing anything that night." She slouched and shoved her hands in her pockets, an exaggerated posture that lowered her height by half a foot. "'I can fix a car, but I already did that today.'" Her voice didn't sound remotely like Charlie's, but the tone of disinterest and the eyebrow lift made them all laugh. Annesley downed the rest of her shot and reestablished her debutante posture. "Not up for the challenge? Okay. Ladies, shall we find another place to go?"

Charlie downed her own shot and slammed it on the table. "You're on."

Before she could lose her nerve, Charlie whispered in the DJ's ear then jumped up on stage. The lights glowed low enough that she saw bodies but not faces. The Delta Rhoadies raised their arms and whooped.

She turned her back to the room and flared her arms away from her hips. A catcall from a dark corner set off a wave of whistles.

The opening notes of the theme song of *Titanic* floated from the speakers. The Irish penny whistle confused the bar's atmosphere, but the other four girls howled their approval, and Annesley's voice rose above the rest. Charlie felt herself blush, and it made her smile.

Holding out her arms as if she were a prima ballerina, Charlie turned and cast a beatific glance toward the Delta Rhoadies. Before Céline Dion started singing, the wail of horns and the thumping bass of "Jump Around" blasted the room. Charlie's hip punctuated the thick hip-hop beat. The tequila seeped into her limbs, and every cell vibrated with the heat. She spun around and owned the stage.

Every step felt like a kick against the general. As she reached the end of the stage, she grabbed a grubby hat from the crowd and slapped it on her head.

She tugged at her T-shirt, exposing her belly. Beads flew, and she laughed. The smell of beer and cigarettes was intoxicating.

The crowd whooped and yelled, "Show yer tits!"

She inched the hem upward slowly to expose the black edge of her bra. A hand grabbed her by the upper arm.

"Hey!" Charlie twisted around to whack the perpetrator.

The crowd booed as Annesley pulled Charlie's shirt down.

"The song's not over, Annesley. I'm killing it up here."

"We don't need to throw fresh meat to the wolves, Charlie. You've proved your point."

"You're not the only one who can show off. They love me." She waved to the crowd, which hollered in solidarity.

Annesley stared at her, eyebrow raised and lips pursed.

Torn between the odd comfort of feeling like a petulant child and the mature understanding she saw in Annesley's eyes, Charlie relented. "Fine, fine."

Annesley waved to the crowd with her other hand and bowed. "That's all, folks!"

A few patrons threw plastic cups at them as they left the stage, but the crowd was quickly distracted by the next contestant.

Charlie tossed the hat back to its owner then dragged the hem of her shirt across her sweaty forehead. Her breath caught like a grappling hook in her throat. A memory of the general tossing his hat to her when she was still enamored with him threatened to obliterate the moment.

"Not too bad!" Annesley grinned and gave her a golf clap. "I mean, it wasn't Julliard material, but it wasn't bad."

"I'm next!" Helen struck an awkward pose just as the other four all yelled, "No!" Their laughter drowned out the new song heralding the next contestant on stage.

*Fuck the general.* She had these guys.

# Chapter Thirty-One
# 2019
# Lisa

Lisa's head pounded, and dryer lint lined her mouth. Dehydration? *Check.* Nausea? *Check.* Jackhammer to the skull? *Check.* Diagnosis: beer and tequila did not mix.

Finishing the pitcher with Charlie the night before and adding another round—or was it two?—of obscenely large margaritas from the bar after the other three peeled off had lessened the sting of Annesley's confession. With four hundred ten miles left to get to the Grand Canyon, however, a hangover remedy was in order.

Emerging onto the patio, she lowered her sunglasses and ran smack into Helen. Helen regarded her with one eye closed. Knowing she wasn't alone in her hangover misery provided Lisa a modicum of relief.

To their right, a sixty-something Hispanic gentleman stood from his chair and placed his napkin on his empty plate. Lisa and Helen took a seat at the free table.

Lisa flagged a waiter. "Coffee, please. Black." Helen held up the peace sign, making it an order for two cups.

The waiter cleared the table. "Shall I..." His hand hovered over the newspaper the older man had left behind.

"You can leave it. He may come back to get it."

Unlit fairy lights swung in the light breeze, and sunlight bathed the patio in a buttery warmth. Hotel patrons seemed to glide from table to buffet and back.

"Kind of a bummer last night with what Annesley said," Helen said. "Are you okay? I'd totally get it if you are still pissed."

Lisa's stomach turned but not from the beer and tequila she'd drunk the night before. It was her pettiness at being upset by rumors from twenty years ago. She tried to shake it off. "To be fair, I might have burned the sorority house to the ground to get rid of Mrs. Cannon if she was my mom."

Helen deadpanned, "I might have provided the accelerant."

"It's just... Annesley caught me off guard." She waved her hand and pushed away resentment that Annesley had that very same day asked her to keep a heavy secret. "Totally not a big deal." Lisa couldn't help but think that if she told them about the NDA, she wouldn't get a pass. Lisa had allowed a twenty-year-old kid to take the blame for a tragedy.

A white mug with steam rising from the dark roast appeared in front of Lisa. She let the liquid sear her tastebuds and wished she could mainline the caffeine.

"What's the plan today?" Lisa asked, almost wishing it was to get on a flight and be home by lunchtime.

"Mary Blake gave me free rein on the next leg. I need to decide whether to go north, south, or central." Helen pulled out her phone and opened a map app. "Mary Blake's a little less peppy today. That little dust-up with Charlie about the text messages was unexpected."

A minor social glitch, forgetting Charlie didn't like to talk about family, was nothing. Mary Blake would get over that. Lisa was the one who could crush Mary Blake's joy and single-handedly ruin this trip in more than one way. One inkling of Annesley's cancer or Lisa's own secret, and Helen's map skills would be useless in keeping them on track.

Lisa's mouth puckered with dryness. She gulped a glass of water and reached for the newspaper as a distraction. She unfolded the paper then removed her sunglasses, hoping they were making her see things. They weren't. The muscles of her neck pulsed with aggression. Next to a small news piece was a photo of Tripp Harrison. He had the same prominent nose and square chin she remembered, but fine lines now etched his face. Lisa's throat thickened as she read the column.

*Oil Scion Forms Senate Exploratory Committee*

Regarded in Austin for political loyalty, the Harrison family is also known for their privacy. "Impenetrable," remarked longtime State Senator Jake Tenley (R-Houston) when asked his impression of the Harrison dynasty.

Scion of the oil and cattle family, Tripp Harrison is an unlikely candidate, having never run for political office. Some campaign experts see this as an asset for a US Senate candidate, as Harrison has no voting record to be used against him. However, this will be a hotly contested seat, and opposing candidates will attempt to pierce the veil that has cloaked the Harrison family's personal and business activities for decades. The Harrison family's legal team, led by Glenn Whiteford, Esq., has quashed whispers of scandals over the years, dismissing them as attempted "money grabs" and "sour grapes."

Harrison is President of the Parker Harrison Foundation, named after his brother, who died in a car crash due to mechanical malfunction in 1999.

Lisa gripped the seat of her chair. No oilman's hand squeezed her throat, but the phantom pressure on her pulse point made her dizzy. She didn't know what scandals had generated whispers and wondered if the crash at the ranch had wound its way into the rumor mill.

"Who died?" Helen asked with a hint of a laugh, gesturing toward the paper. "You went pale."

Lisa passed her the paper without a word.

Two decades ago, the lawyer had said the whole thing would be "tucked away." She shuddered to think what would happen to her if these opposition candidates dug deep enough. If she got dragged into the news, she would have no way of responding, because she'd signed away her right to speak. Perhaps this news explained the lack of response to the email she'd sent the attorney.

Helen raised her eyes from the article and squinted against the sun. She reached for sunglasses on her head only to find nothing there.

"Do you think about"—Lisa frowned—"the ranch?" She didn't like revisiting that night and suspected Helen didn't either. But Helen was the only other one of them who'd been in the car, who'd been with Parker in the last hour of his life.

"It was so long ago. Everything from back then is hazy." She looked away. "Most things."

Memories from the ranch were so vivid in Lisa's mind it was hard to grasp that it wasn't so for Helen. "The night of the crash?"

"I don't remember much after we left the bar. I barely remember being back at the house. Then I was waking up in the hospital."

Grateful that at least Helen was free from the scenes of those last moments, Lisa wrapped her hands around her mug. Tripp's face stared up from the newspaper. The reporter hadn't reached out to Lisa since Texas two nights before. She imagined the reporter following a new lead and getting her scoop. Lisa's face would be plastered all over the news with the headline: California Doctor Covered Up for Oilman's Son in Tragic Death. Nausea swelled.

Lisa's hangover headache throbbed into something caffeine and hydration couldn't fix. "I'm going to pack."

# Chapter Thirty-Two
# 1999
# Lisa

Lisa turned away from the passing Texas landscape and back to the Tooloulou postcard on her lap. She'd opted for the card that didn't feature cleavage. Instead, the photo was a collage of taxidermy from the bar: a bobcat, a deer, a boar, and a jackalope. Mary Blake had been convinced that last one was a real animal. Putting the pen to the card, Lisa wrote about the storm and the dancing but avoided the part about the strip contest.

The CB crackled with Mary Blake's approximation of a long-haul trucker's road-hardened voice. "Breaker, breaker. White Whale to Scout. Ranch ETA five minutes. Copy."

The Scout's air conditioning managed a whisper of lukewarm air through industrial-looking vents. She paused her writing to pull at her thin T-shirt, which stuck right back to the mist of sweat on her chest. Drops of condensation clinging to the inside of the speedometer remained the only evidence of the rainstorm the day before.

"Telling her a good story there?" Charlie flicked on the blinker and passed a tractor driving half on and half off the road.

"Just the basics. You know, Annesley hooking up with a farmer, you stripping on stage."

"Hey, now. I kept my clothes on."

"Only because Annesley dragged you off."

"She's such a killjoy."

Lisa still felt the vibrations from the bar, the thrill of being together. "I had no idea you had moves like that. Funny that it was Annesley who got you up there."

"Ha. Yeah. At this point, anything could happen."

The cassette tape reached the end with a clunk. Lisa ejected it before it started over at the beginning again. Her stomach growled to remind her she was starving. She reached into the crumpled McDonald's bag.

"Sorry, Leese. I ate the last fry."

"No worries. Just disregard the rumbling coming from my side of the car."

The incoherent flutter of the roof tear whispered goodbye to Louisiana. She added a note about exotic roadkill. There were no armadillos in Pennsylvania, but they appeared to be the Texas state animal, based on smashed banded armor on the highway shoulder.

Beyond the White Whale in front of them, the road was an unmarked black slate that led to the future. Not long ago, the future had been a brochure and a career counselor's words of encouragement. Now it was a glowing orb inside, filled with potential. Medical school offered a chance at reinvention, a chrysalis for Lisa to enter and emerge in four years as something new. She could be a Mary Blake, all bubbles and rainbows, someone who swooped in and made everything right. Or she could be an Annesley and act like it wasn't her first rodeo and let people come to her. With a dash of Charlie's bravado and Helen's resilience, Lisa envisioned herself showing up on her first day of her internship confident. She'd earned her way into UCLA. Impressed physicians and researchers would marvel at her efficiency and talent.

More scrubland passed, oil wells churning on some, cattle dotting others, but most open and empty. Lisa tucked the postcard into her bag and adjusted the radio. Gospel channels alternated with classic country and the occasional fire-and-brimstone preacher on the AM they were able to get on the long stretches.

She sighed and glanced at Charlie, whose face relaxed into a serenity unbothered by the miles or the weather.

Signs of civilization grew on the horizon. A single sprawling estate squatted among the flatlands. At first, rooftops dominated: a large building, a barn, and some side buildings. As they neared, a house emerged from behind an outbuilding. The house sprawled like only a house in a state with limitless acreage could. Marked by an unassuming sign with a dark gray barbed wire logo, the property didn't have a grand entrance, despite Annesley's claim that it was one of the largest ranches in Texas.

"Looks like this might be it," Lisa said. Unbidden, a trickle of anticipation set the hair on her arms on end.

Charlie stepped on the clutch and downshifted as she followed the wagon onto the long driveway.

They parked on the circular drive in front of the house. The two-story residence served as the centerpiece among tight but meticulous landscaping of broad-leafed shrubbery and bright pops of low flowers. White buildings stretched left and right. Auburn dust coated every surface.

Near a closed garage were two golf carts. A butterscotch cat darted under a Gator utility vehicle. Beyond, the flat expanse stretched each direction. Scattered upshots of rough green scrub and compact fireplugs of trees provided the only sense of perspective.

Lisa exited the Scout and turned in slow motion while she stretched out the kinks from the road. She tried to think of how a person who'd been places would react to the ranch. How a *Doctor Lisa Davis* would react. Impressed, because she knew how much all this must cost, maybe. Or perhaps unimpressed because she knew how much all this must cost. She didn't know.

Annesley, wearing shorts and a Delta Rho T-shirt, emerged from the wagon. She frowned as she brushed at creases dotted with dark spots of sweat. "You can't even see the full ranch from here," she said, not bothering to look around. "It's over a quarter million acres." She peered into the wagon's side-view mirror and flinched as if she saw an ogre staring back at her. She smoothed her hair, full and wispy from driving with the windows down. She plunged a hand into her purse, pulled out a tube of mascara, and swiped the wand across her eyelashes.

Her eyes passed over each of them, from Helen in a button-down camp shirt and khaki shorts to Lisa in a party tee and jean shorts to Charlie in cut-off khakis. Annesley frowned like she'd walked into a room and forgotten why she'd entered it. Lisa wanted to yank Future Lisa into the moment. She would know how to act, how to look.

Annesley grabbed Mary Blake's arm and led her to the wide wooden door with stained glass inserts. She reached to adjust her necklace. Her hand froze, clenched, and dropped to her side.

She didn't have her pearls. Lisa had never seen Annesley without her pearls. Lisa glanced at Charlie with mild alarm. Something about the moment tripped an instinct to be on guard, but Charlie didn't seem to have noticed.

"How big is a quarter million acres?" Mary Blake whispered to Lisa.

Before Lisa could answer, Annesley responded sharply, "Bigger than Manhattan."

Annesley tugged Mary Blake's attention back to the front door and reached for the doorbell. Before she pressed the button, the doors opened, and a woman in a gray and white maid's uniform greeted them. She led them through an art-filled entryway into a formal living room then excused herself to find Mrs. Harrison.

Lisa was once again in a house she had no place in. The lake house had wowed her, but nothing in Lisa's background provided context for hired help in uniforms.

Shadowy paintings in gilded frames hung on the walls. She'd envisioned longhorn skulls and leather-upholstered furniture, not brocade side chairs and shiny wooden tables with clawed feet.

Annesley seemed in her element. They'd walked through a portal and left the rest of the trip behind. Whether the set was the desert of West Texas, the lush green of Lake Burton, or a debutante ball, the role was the same. This was Annesley's stage. She didn't even scold Charlie for poking around the books on the shelves.

"I hope there's a pool," said Helen, who was fanning her underarms. "I'd jump in right now if I could."

Lisa leaned over to admire the intricately carved fireplace. "I'll need about an hour in the bathroom first. I haven't shaved my legs since Georgia."

"Pool's getting cleaned today."

The low voice startled Lisa upright, and she bumped her head on the mantel. The Texas drawl was too strong to be Tripp's. Lisa flushed and turned to see a softer version of Annesley's boyfriend. Whereas Tripp had sharp features and a long neck that lent to his air of superiority, this man was more compact with smoother edges.

"The pool will be open later today. After you shave your legs, of course." His smile showed off white teeth when he nodded toward Lisa. "I'm Parker. My big brother's out with Daddy and Representative Benedict about a job on Capitol Hill, so y'all'll have to settle for me." He walked toward a coffee table, his dusty cowboy boots landing quietly on the plush rug. "We had a dust storm come through yesterday. Big one. It was so thick the rabbits were digging holes six feet in the air." His drawn-out words pulled Lisa closer until she felt like she would lose her balance. He turned toward Annesley. "You must be the Annesley I've heard about. You're even prettier than Tripp said."

Annesley blushed appropriately. Lisa looked down at her feet to hide the jealousy she was certain showed in her eyes. Her toenails, gnarly from hikes, campgrounds, and general disregard, mocked her. She curled her toes into the foam of her K-Mart flip-flops.

Annesley introduced them, already acting as ranch hostess. Turning away, she pulled a tissue from her purse and dabbed at her nose.

Lisa rolled her eyes at the prim gesture. What was next? Swooning onto a fainting couch?

The group fell into easy conversation, uncovering the fact that Parker was a rising senior.

"Texas A&M, where my Daddy went," he said. "But Tripp wanted to go to college closer to DC. He thought he could gain more political capital out there." He checked his watch. "He should be back any time. Daddy has to meet with the foreman in thirty minutes to get a ranch report. By the way, whose green International Harvester is out front? Sure would like to drive that girl."

"That would be Charlie, who was runner-up at the strip club competition last night," Helen said, earning an eye roll from Charlie.

"Is that why you're a day late? Strip clubs?" The crisp voice of a woman whose erect bearing could only mean she was Mrs. Harrison caused them all to turn their heads toward the door.

Annesley looked mortified, her mouth open in a silent O. Seeing the condescension on Mrs. Harrison's face, Lisa wilted on Annesley's behalf.

Tripp's mom wore loose linen slacks, a white blouse with a flared collar, and a sand-colored scarf around her neck. She was narrow, as if she could turn sideways and slide between the stair railings in the entryway. Not far behind her, a housekeeper carried a pitcher and a silver platter of small sandwiches.

"Mother, this is Annesley Cannon."

Lisa's stomach growled loud enough to turn Helen's head. Lisa's face burned. Annesley shot Lisa a warning glance, flushed, and realizing Mrs. Harrison's eyes hadn't left Annesley, rushed her greeting and fumbled through introductions.

Charlie had also seen the warning glance and looked questioningly at Annesley.

"Please make yourselves at home." The acoustics allowed Mrs. Harrison's soft words to carry beyond what their decibels should have allowed. "Help yourselves to the sandwiches. Marcela will show you to your rooms." She turned back to Annesley. "I hope you'll pardon me. I was expecting you to arrive two days ago and had already scheduled an appointment for after your departure. Dinner is promptly at seven. We dine casually." She eyed Annesley's attire. "It looks like you're prepared for that." As quickly as she'd arrived, she left.

Parker grabbed a sandwich and a napkin. Lisa leaned awkwardly against the mantel and bobbled, her curled toes failing her.

Parker checked his watch again. "Sorry to leave you ladies, but I have to go take care of some chores." He dipped his head before he left the room.

Lisa could have sworn he paused an extra beat when his eyes landed on hers.

Annesley ran her fingers along the piano keys, ending on a low C. "I think Lisa has a crush." Annesley said the last word as if she were flicking it with a spoon.

Ordinarily, Lisa would have laughed along with Annesley's jibe. "Well, he is cute."

"Hmm," Annesley said blandly. "I don't imagine you're his type. No offense." She turned to follow Marcella to her room.

Lisa's face burned from the insult.

Charlie leaned in close, like a quarterback setting up the next play. "I don't know what crawled up Annesley's ass, but I saw Parker staring. He's totally into you."

The pressure released. It had been a long drive, and Annesley was tired. Still, Lisa didn't like the dismissiveness that seemed all too familiar coming from Annesley.

# Chapter Thirty-Three
# 1999
# Annesley

Annesley exhaled as she entered the guest bedroom. It was chaste, with white linens and a four-poster bed. The light scent of lily of the valley made her nose tickle.

Alone for the first time in days, she finally had space to disperse the haze that had settled in somewhere along the interstate highway system. She pulled at her damp T-shirt. Sweat-stained creases were not her hallmark, and she'd blown the moment with Mrs. Harrison in more ways than one. She brushed aside her self-flagellation for not changing into something appropriate before arrival, marking that as the last bad decision of the trip.

She squared her shoulders and looked out the window at the pool, where a dark-haired worker scrubbed the mosaic tiles. She was there to see Tripp. She'd lost sight of that, had let her mother and Charlie—a most unusual combination—get into her head. She sneezed and quivered at the compounded discomfort, her focus lost. Being on the road was not the same as the real world, and the real world resumed right now.

After finding some Kleenex in the bathroom, she dabbed her eyes and blew her nose. She splashed water on her face, and the coolness lowered her temperature.

She unzipped her suitcase and winced. Everything smelled of campfire, Alabama fields, and Louisiana mildew. Individually, each scent beckoned her to return, but together, they formed a noxious cloud.

Two arms grabbed her from behind, spun her around, and threw her into a dip.

Annesley tilted her head up to see his face. "Tripp!"

They'd only been apart since graduation, but his skin was tan, and the white strip around his hairline marked a fresh haircut. His blue eyes shone, and Camelot whispered.

She stifled a sniffle and hoped her nose didn't drip. "I thought you were with your dad. Why didn't you come down to see everyone?"

He smothered her words with a kiss and swung her upright. "I wanted you all to myself. Can't have my heart melting in front of everyone. Missed you."

His cinnamon-orange polo made her think of sunset in an Alabama field. She flushed at the memory and hesitated in confusion because she didn't feel a speck of remorse for that decision.

"Darlin', are you so happy to see me that you're blushing *and* tearing up?"

Annesley wiped her eyes. "Allergies. It's all the dust. That must have been one heck of a dust storm. And there was no AC in Lisa's car. You cannot imagine what I've been through." She didn't want him to try. "But yes, I'm happy to see you." She pressed on her eyelids to staunch the irritation and hoped her mascara hadn't run. "I think I botched things with your mother."

"She's tough. But I'm sure you'll be fine. Unfortunately, I've gotta hop." He squeezed her butt somewhat vulgarly, making her wince. "You get that pretty face pulled together, darlin'. Your mascara is running. My mom is going to love you. You two are a lot alike. High standards. I mean, you are dating me, after all." He laughed and planted another kiss on her lips before he left.

She wiped hard under her eyes. She'd lost her bearings over the past several days, and it was time to reclaim them. The first step was washing up and getting dressed for dinner. The rest of her life started now, and she had no plans to stray off course again.

After a hot shower, Annesley felt dust-free and ready to put one thousand miles behind her. She reached into her makeup bag for her Benadryl and pulled out an empty blister pack. Her stomach dropped like a rock in a pool. She'd taken the last pill at that godforsaken, mildewy motel. She thrust the pack back into her bag and returned to the bedroom to get dressed.

Ignoring Mrs. Harrison's "casual" dress code, she put on a butter-yellow chemise and a flared floral skirt, a pairing Mary Blake had picked out on a shopping excursion in Savannah the prior summer, their last such outing together before what had been an odd and busy year that saw them more apart than previous years.

She stood at the foot of the bed with her eyes closed and envisioned herself walking into the dining room. Confident and polished, she would approach Mrs. De Baillon Harrison and erase the initial impression of sweaty exercise clothes and references to strip clubs. "I recognized the painting in your foyer as a J.L. Crier," Annesley would say.

"I'm so pleased," Mrs. Harrison would say. "Most people aren't familiar with the artist."

They would share a knowing smile, and Annesley would continue. "We had a private tour of his works at the High Museum in Atlanta. My mother—" She brought her hands to her collarbone, where a loop of pearls should have curved in parallel with the neckline of her top. Smoky thickness clogged her throat.

A knock on the door pulled Annesley from her fractured fantasy.

Mary Blake peered into the room. "You are *gorgeous*!" The petite dynamo looked like she'd come off a weeklong relaxation retreat. Sparkling eyes, natural color in her face, and unbound energy repudiated the day's slog in ninety-degree heat.

Gratitude flowed over Annesley like a cool breeze, and the grip on her throat loosened. "Did you get ahold of your parents?"

"No. They must be out." Mary Blake's wide smile indicated she expected good news about her dad. It had been almost a year, and Mary Blake hadn't complained a whit about her dad's medical struggles. "I'll call tomorrow."

They headed toward the dining room. In the hall, Annesley ran her hand along a side table then paused. Photos of Tripp, Parker, and a man who must be their father—all three relaxed in cowboy hats and athletic postures—filled heavy silver frames. Sepia daguerreotypes showed soldiers in uniform, and a simple wood frame displayed a scrap of gray cloth. Back at school, Tripp's tales of home had taken on a veneer of cinematic fantasy. He talked of cattle roundups and roughnecks, private fireworks shows to celebrate oil strikes, and the lawlessness of the landscape. The crafted narrative of an oil dynasty was on full display.

"Girls!" A large man in jeans and a button-down, broad like a bear and with a round face to match, startled Annesley and Mary Blake.

The bear-man engulfed Annesley in a hug at the same time Tripp rounded the corner. "As you can see, Daddy doesn't need introductions," Tripp said.

When Mr. Harrison moved to Mary Blake, Annesley tried to reconcile the giant bear-man with the ice-queen wife. Somehow, the two had produced Tripp, and the combination unsettled her.

Mr. Harrison led them into a dining room that smelled of roasted garlic and butter. Lisa chatted with Parker while Charlie stood off to the side. Helen was admiring the food displayed on a stout hunt board: blood-red tenderloin, balsamic green beans and onions, baskets of steaming bread, roasted new potatoes with rosemary, and a green salad. Annesley's stomach felt bloated at the sight.

Helen smiled when she saw Annesley and Tripp. "There's enough food for an army."

Tripp laughed. "Welcome to the Harrison ranch. We don't do anything small."

"Especially this one." Mr. Harrison pounded Tripp on the back. "We've got big plans for this guy."

Annesley swelled at the comment. Tripp had big plans, and she was part of them.

Marcela, in her gray and white uniform, poured water and delivered glasses of wine to the table.

Tripp's father invited Annesley to sit next to him. Seeing Mrs. Harrison at the opposite end, Annesley hesitated. She didn't know if it be more advantageous to get in with Mr. Harrison or to try again with Mrs. Harrison. She sneezed. *Dammit!* One thing she knew was that she needed to shake whatever this was. She picked the bear-man over the ice queen when no invitation came from the other end of the table.

Chatter filled the air, but Annesley's head buzzed, and she struggled to follow the conversation. She reached for her water.

Mr. Harrison scanned the table. His gregarious smile dropped. Without the crinkle around his eyes, he looked menacing. "Marcela," he barked, "you missed one." He gestured toward Lisa, who didn't have a glass in front of her.

"Oh, I'm fine," Lisa said. "I—"

"Marcela, get her a glass of the merlot."

Lisa sat mute. All she needed to say was that she didn't care for any, thank you so very much. But she sat there like she'd never had dinner with real adults before. Annesley found it embarrassing to watch. She wanted to speak for her but was afraid her voice would come out as scratchy as her throat felt. Plus, Lisa should have been able to take care of herself. Annesley took a sip of water to clear her head.

"Impossible to find good help," Mr. Harrison said.

Once Lisa had a glass in hand, Mr. Harrison smiled, eyes crinkling again, and raised his bourbon. "To pretty girls on a ranch." He took a healthy drink and set the crystal glass on the table. "Now, tell me about your trip."

Navigator Helen proceeded with a turn-by-turn recap. She made the last week and a half sound as benign as a drive to the salon. "South of Asheville on Highway 280, we ran into some traffic. We found an off ramp and used 191 instead and still made it to Lake Burton on schedule. Charlie got a part at a junkyard to fix the Scout."

Annesley rubbed her eyes. Her head was fuzzy. She took another drink while Helen continued glossing over events best not shared.

Mrs. Harrison took the travelogue as her cue to confer with Marcela in soft tones regarding the platters of food, which she announced would be served family style.

Annesley dabbed at her blurring eyes with her napkin. Feeling a tickle in her nose, she sneezed daintily into the pressed linen.

"You okay?" Tripp asked.

Annesley nodded. She wanted the sneezes to be charming but worried they made her look weak, as in *Tripp's little girlfriend can't handle the dust*.

"And then Lisa's air conditioning conked out, and we drove straight through to the ranch," Helen said in conclusion.

Mr. Harrison regarded Lisa. "So you're the one from Pennsylvania. I saw the plates on that station wagon out there. Surprised that old car made it this far."

Parker stepped in. "She's heading to UCLA Med School."

Annesley stared at a beaming Lisa, wondering when Parker and Lisa had gotten each other's life histories. She blinked, and her eyelids scraped like sandpaper across her corneas. She added dust to her list of annoyances, and the likelihood that she and Tripp would ever live in West Texas was getting slimmer by the moment.

Mr. Harrison took the tray of beef from his right and served himself a large cut. "Tripp tells me y'all will be here two nights. You young ladies can sleep in tomorrow, but on Friday, plan to get up early. We'll have a big crew coming in to brand the calves. We'll show you girls some real Texas cattle ranching. Make a day of it. We can't have you leave the ranch without a big shindig, can we?"

"Sounds wonderful," Annesley lied.

"Branding as in—" Lisa held up an invisible branding iron and poked it at the air.

Parker and his father laughed like her gesture was the most adorable thing ever. Annesley rolled her eyes then froze when she saw Charlie's puzzled stare. Annesley looked away.

"Exactly. We need to keep track of the livestock. Sometimes cattle will get separated from the herd and disappear for days, weeks even. But we can find them." He forked a slab of steak and placed it on Annesley's plate, where it landed with a wet thud.

Mr. Harrison's words appeared to trouble Lisa, and Annesley had to dismiss thoughts of baby cows being singed with red-hot iron. Mrs. Harrison looked bored. Annesley adopted the same countenance and suppressed a sniffle.

"Charlie," Mr. Harrison said, "I hear your dad's in the army. I did four years in the Marines. Tripp says he's a general?"

"Ah, no, not a general. He's a colonel."

Annesley shifted in her seat. Charlie had always referred to her dad as "the general," like he was a Ray-Ban-wearing, cigar-chomping, battle-plan-constructing colossus. She wondered why Tripp had been talking to his dad about Charlie.

"He can't be happy you refer to him with a higher rank." Mr. Harrison tilted his head in interest, eyes narrowed.

Charlie's eyes narrowed right back. "That's the point."

Mr. Harrison guffawed and took a slug of his bourbon. "I like this girl."

Annesley sipped her drink, and the tannins stripped at her throat. She reached for her water. None of these conversations had a point, and she was excluded from all of them.

Dinner rolls came from the right, and Annesley passed them without taking one. Too much bloat already.

Mary Blake was regaling the table with tales of a great-great-grandfather, "a colonel or maybe a sergeant but maybe a general," who rode a horse right into his beloved's house to propose marriage, a grand gesture that introduced a strain of moxie into the family line.

Annesley gulped more water to soothe the alcohol's sting. She remembered the pictures in the Harrisons' hallway, the old military photos and memorabilia. She needed to take control of the conversation. "Mary Blake's family is rooted in American Revolution history. Her mother has a direct tie to Yorktown. The loveliest woman you'll ever meet. And her father—"

"You're too kind, Annesley." Mary Blake's interruption sparked a new irritation. But Mary Blake turned toward Mrs. Harrison and proved she had a plan, the same as Annesley's: show they were one of them. "Helen didn't tell you about the Cannons' lake house." She sighed luxuriously. "It reminds me of your ranch. Exquisite design in a beautiful setting."

Annesley felt her chest constricting. She stared at her plate, where red blood pooled next to a filet on the south side of medium rare. Her stomach roiled with nausea.

"Darlin', are you all right?" Mr. Harrison looked at Annesley with concern as he handed her the platter of balsamic green beans and sweet onions.

His "darlin'" blurred in her ears. The same word Tripp used. "Yes, I'm fine. Thank you." She focused on Tripp slicing into a blood red steak on her left and not on Mrs. Harrison reigning at the other end of the table. Sandpaper scraped across her eyes again, and nausea from the mucus draining down the back of her throat rose like a snake uncoiling at the scent of prey.

*Focus.* She'd been trained in decorum. Dancers didn't feel pain, and Cannons didn't break down. She dabbed at her nose with her napkin.

A butterscotch ball of fur shot from under the table, and Annesley inhaled with a rasp. She felt a tickle in her nose, and she was thrown out of her body, like her body belonged to someone else.

The body at the table was not Annesley Cannon. Annesley Cannon was watching from the corner as tears flooded this other person's eyes and her sneeze shot mucus all over the green beans and sweet onions.

Everything after that happened in a blur. Mary Blake jumped out of her chair in alarm and nearly knocked over Mrs. Harrison. Mortified, Annesley rushed up the stairs to her room. Her four friends followed and crowded around her.

"Here, sugar." Mary Blake handed Annesley a cool, wet hand towel.

Annesley buried her face in it. She didn't want to look at them. A quick glance confirmed Tripp hadn't followed them, thank God. But the humiliation had.

"It's so not a big deal," Helen said. "Only a sneeze."

"Impressive amount of snot in one sneeze, though," Charlie said. "Shit, it's probably the most exciting thing to happen out here in the desert in ages. Let's get back to the dining room. We'll all go together." Charlie's voice held pity but also something like a challenge, as if the statement contained a test.

Someone set a hand on Annesley's forearm, an invitation to join them as their charge, their protected friend. She recoiled and pulled the towel from her face. She could accept their help and be at their mercy—a needy, dependent child accepting pity—or she could reclaim herself.

She pressed the fabric of her skirt and felt her quads flex. She didn't need their pity. "I'm fine. Please go. Finish your dinner."

Mary Blake grabbed her hand. "I'll get you some tea with cinnamon and honey. My nana—"

"I said"—her words came out with more force than intended as she pulled her hand away—"please go."

Mary Blake ushered them out of the room like a nanny hurrying her wards off to school. She didn't even have the dignity to act offended. "Annesley will be fine. Just needs her beauty sleep. We'll start our Texas visit fresh in the morning. Clean slate."

# Chapter Thirty-Four
# Lisa
# 2019

Back in her Albuquerque hotel room to pack up, Lisa opened her phone. No response from the lawyer. Her head still pounded, but she could no longer blame the booze. Not for the first time, she fantasized about an alternative reality where she hadn't signed the NDA. Where she'd said, "I'm going to tell my friends what I told the police," and the Harrisons hadn't been able to "disappear" the records because too many people knew what the records said.

She zipped her luggage and took a last visual sweep of the room. She knew for certain she would have survived without the payout. She'd been dropped from the paid internship after missing the mandatory orientation and being hobbled by her injury, but she would have made it work, even if Alternate Reality Lisa had ended up in even more debt than Reality Lisa. And the five Delta Rhos might have banded together, finished the last trip, and not even been here today. The thought of that made her head hurt in a different way.

Lisa hauled her baggage out of the lobby and over to the curb next to the Escalade. She still didn't have it in her to give her luggage to a porter, even if it made her look cheap.

The others were already out front, facing away to admire the daytime view of the mountain.

Her phone pinged. Hot breath filled her throat as she opened the email.

> From: Glenn Whiteford, Esquire
> Subject: **PRIVATE**

Residual limeade and beer in her stomach turned like compost. She spun away from the SUV and clicked on the email. The buttery sun from breakfast was now a fiery inferno. A thin film of sweat glazed her neck.

> Dr. Callihan,
>
> I am in receipt of your email, timed opportunely with recent news regarding Mr. Harrison. While we are not your attorneys, I advise you not to speak with the press.
>
> If it is additional compensation you seek, I recommend you obtain your own counsel.

Lisa's heart pounded harder than her head. She hadn't been seeking compensation. She just wanted them to make the journalist go away. She scrolled and froze.

> A Cease and Desist Letter is attached. You are treading in dangerous waters.

"Everything all right?" Annesley, pink-cheeked and not hungover because she'd surreptitiously drunk straight limeade the night before, looked at Lisa with innocent eyes.

Mary Blake stood beside her, beaming, apparently recovered from Charlie's snapback about her dad and demonstrating that other people in the world were capable of not falling into sucking whirlpools of regret and social disaster.

Lisa opened her mouth, but she could think of no words that would pull her out of the dangerous waters.

# Chapter Thirty-Five
# 1999
# Mary Blake

Early morning after the truncated dinner, Mary Blake walked with Annesley through the Harrison's entryway. Before they had to encounter anyone else, they would go into town, buy some Benadryl, and pretend yesterday hadn't happened. Mirrors reflected their faces as kaleidoscopes of blues and greens from the stained glass-filtered light. Mary Blake's "done" hair added a couple of inches to her height, the result of hard water, a hair dryer, and the first spritz of hair spray she'd used in days.

Annesley didn't look like she'd had the luxury of a good night's sleep. Bloodshot eyes, nostrils ringed in red that looked aggravated by repeated nose blowing, and a pallor dulled her friend's vibrancy from earlier in the trip. Annesley's physical appearance was countered by the steeliness in her posture. It had only been a sneeze—granted, it was all over the green beans—but Annesley's expectations of herself were nearly unattainable as it stood. And she wasn't used to being out of control. "I'm so sorry about last night. I shouldn't have yelled at you all. It wasn't my best moment."

"Sugar, don't give it a second thought." The whole episode had been a distraction that allowed Mary Blake to forget, for at least a time, about the fact that she owed Annesley money, that the bursar's office needed her response about fall registration by next week, and that she hadn't heard from her parents since the call at the Pelican

Ridge Motel, when they told her they'd ring the ranch when things were finally settled. She was prepared to grant Annesley grace.

Mary Blake wouldn't have said Annesley was embarrassed. That wasn't a word she associated with Annesley. Discomfort was a better term, and even that never lasted long. Annesley tended to shift from discomfort to anger, and from there, to determination, which was where she thrived.

Marcela wished them a good morning and stacked the day's newspapers on a leggy table by the stairs. "I'm sorry we weren't able to find any medicine for you, Miss Cannon," she said. "Miss Bulloch, your mother called. You were in the shower. Would you like to call her?" Marcela gestured toward the sitting room.

Mary Blake's heart jumped. "Thank you!"

Annesley eyed the entrances to the rooms off the foyer, where any one of the Harrisons could be lurking, ready to catch her in her puffy state. "I can go alone. You call your mom."

Mary Blake turned to Annesley with enough energy for both of them. "I'll call when we get back."

"Are you sure? It could be important."

"Let's take care of you first."

For now: Benadryl. Then she could check in with her parents and learn the legal mess was over so she could tuck the last year away as a passing cloud.

Outside, Annesley glanced up at Tripp's bedroom window.

Mary Blake grabbed her by the elbow and dragged her to the carport. "Stop it. He's out riding fence with his dad. They'll be hours." She jangled Lisa's keys. "Come on."

It had to be over a hundred degrees inside the White Whale. Even the cloth driver's seat burned the backs of Mary Blake's bare legs.

Annesley fumbled with the climate controls and huffed in frustration. "I forgot there's no air conditioning. Unbelievable." She sneezed. "And how in the world did I not know Tripp had a cat? Plus a dust storm right before we arrived?"

"Oh, honey, I am so sorry. You've had a time of it here. But you are going to wow Mr. and Mrs. Harrison, and they are going to beg Tripp to spend the rest of his life with you just so they can have you around."

Mr. Harrison had seemed to adore the five visitors, even as his wife maintained a frosty distance. Still, Tripp's dad was more than he let on. His type—brash, charming, fawning over pretty girls while diminishing the help—had frequented Mary Blake's home in Savannah, seeking her father's investment money or the reasoned gentility of his conversation. Her father was always the calm in the storm. Men like Mr. Harrison were always the storm, complimenting the women in the room before deciding which competitor to eviscerate. But Daddy had a knack of bringing men to reason, getting them to redirect their money or other intentions, like he was doing with the assistant attorney general. Mary Blake had his pluck, and the Harrisons were her target.

Annesley continued her tirade as they drove down the highway, windows down and vents open. An oven flying across the desert. "I get it. We were late, and we showed up looking like a bunch of vagrants. I can't give her anything else to count against me. But I know her type."

Mary Blake wondered if Annesley was picturing Mrs. Cannon when considering the "type," though Mary Blake would never have said that aloud.

"Thank God you're here with me, Mary Blake."

"No place I'd rather be."

After parking next to the line of pickups and SUVs in front of the drugstore, Mary Blake took advantage of exiting the oven-slash-car to change the subject. "It must be nice to get to see Tripp. Ranching has been kind to that boy."

Inside the store, they headed straight for the "Colds and Flu" aisle.

Annesley left her sunglasses on and blithely ran her fingers along the row of boxes. A lightness in the way she glided down the aisle indicated she had completed her full cycle of anger. "I'm hoping we can finally spend some alone time together tonight."

"Then maybe you should get some of those." Mary Blake pointed at the condoms behind the pharmacist counter.

"Don't be ridiculous," Annesley whispered, harsh as a brick. Maybe she hadn't moved on from her anger. "Everyone here knows everyone else, and I couldn't buy those without word getting back to the ranch." She snapped her fingers to emphasize the wildfire spread of gossip. "I can't mess anything else up at this point." She selected a box of allergy medicine and approached the check-out line that extended to a candy stand on one side and a newspaper stand on the other.

Mary Blake reached for a bag of M&M's and turned to ask Annesley if they should grab some beer or maybe some flowers for Mrs. Harrison. She would figure out how to crack that woman. Calla lilies, perhaps. Elegant, yet foreboding. She could picture them in a glass vase in the entryway. Finding calla lilies in West Texas presented a problem, though.

Mary Blake saw her friend's reaction before she realized what had triggered it.

Annesley lifted her sunglasses, and her puffy eyes squinted in confusion. Her jaw dropped and she turned slowly, as if the store had motion detectors she didn't want to set off. "Mary Blake?" she whispered.

In front of them, the headline on the *Dallas Morning News* screamed out loud. At least that's how it felt.

*Financial Titan Indicted for Fraud*

Mary Blake's limbs went cold. She checked the surrounding store patrons and workers to ensure they didn't notice her reaction, that they didn't know it was her father in the photo under that headline. Of course they didn't know, and there was a shred of relief in that. But the subhead fractured her.

*Family Empire a Shell Game, Coffers Empty, Feds Move In*

She wouldn't be going back to school in the fall. She wouldn't be going back to any kind of normal. She clutched her purse tight against her chest, her stupid, four-hundred-dollar Chanel purse.

"This must be a mistake, right? He's sick." Annesley looked from Mary Blake back to the newspaper, her voice rising and tightening the icy grip that squeezed Mary Blake's chest. "Right?"

It was all Mary Blake could do not to grab the entire pile of papers and shove them in her stupid purse. "I—no—I don't know. I mean, no, he's not sick." The fact that she wished in that moment that he was sick and not in handcuffs made her ill. The M&M's bag crinkled in her hand and fell to the floor.

She needed to call her father. Was he even reachable? In the photo, his face was inscrutable and his suit impeccable. He could have been on his way to a board meeting instead of central booking. Central booking, is that where they would take him? All Mary Blake knew of these things she'd learned from *Law and Order*. "I-I knew they were investigating, but—"

"Miss..." A voice from the back of the line prodded them to step forward, despite the fact that there were still three people in line ahead of her. Mary Blake wondered how a store in such a desolate part of the state could be Grand Central Station on the very morning her shame was scrawled across the front page for everyone to see.

Annesley lowered her whisper another notch but ratcheted up the irritation. "What? Why didn't you *tell* me?" Now it was Annesley who scanned the store. Her reputation was about to be sullied by association. She was looking for an exit from the wildfire.

"I thought it was a regular government review." Mary Blake knew that wasn't entirely how she'd understood things. Frozen family assets didn't seem "regular," but she hadn't questioned her father. "He told me the government was on a wild goose chase, some rogue prosecutor looking to brownnose his superior. He was supposed to close the case as soon as he got the promotion he wanted. I talked to Daddy when we were in Louisiana, and he said it would be over soon."

"This"—Annesley jerked her head toward the newspaper almost imperceptibly—"does not look *over*." She huffed at a woman holding things up at checkout by counting out nickels and pennies, put her sunglasses back on, checked to be sure no one had associated her with the white-collar criminal on the front page, and exited the store, leaving her Benadryl on top of the newspapers.

Mary Blake followed her in silence then climbed into the car.

With all four windows down and the Texas wind racing through like a brush fire, Annesley kept her focus straight ahead. After a searing ten minutes of silence, she spoke. "It's best not to tell Mr. and Mrs. Harrison anything about this." A reasonable tone had conquered the irritated bite from earlier, and the lack of emotion triggered a buzzing that relayed through the frame of the car into Mary Blake's body.

Annesley was in damage-control mode, like when the sorority had been suspended and Annesley volunteered to speak to the student newspaper on behalf of the house. "The Harrisons are quite prominent," she said. "And with Tripp's own political plans, well, you know, they can't be associated with anything like this. I'm sure it will all blow over, but let's be quiet about it."

It didn't feel quiet. It felt thunderously, murderously loud.

# Chapter Thirty-Six
# 1999
# Annesley

Annesley stepped onto the smooth asphalt of the circular drive at the ranch. Freshly power washed of the auburn dust, the house gleamed white, like it was trying to outshine the sun by deflecting every ray. She ignored the sound of Mary Blake exiting the car behind her, as simmering anger had her hands clenched in tight balls.

She'd allowed herself to be pushed into a corner. She'd endured an awkward and late arrival at the ranch, a disastrous incident at dinner, and now the kind of scandal that could taint everyone it touched. She strained to push aside the fact Mary Blake had lied about an ill father and how she had to go home to see him and miss graduation.

Annesley couldn't shake the prickling question of why Mary Blake hadn't told her. She was her best friend, for God's sake. Annesley would have been supportive. Quietly and privately supportive, at least. Supportive in a way that didn't drag everyone around them into the funhouse mirror maze she'd felt like she was in at the grocery store.

She wouldn't have brought everyone to the ranch. She wouldn't have gone on the trip to begin with, in fact, meaning she wouldn't be in this position now. That set off a new plume of fire in her chest.

Mary Blake stepped softly next to her. Annesley tried to picture the friend who'd handed her a wet towel the night before instead of the one standing in a drug store, holding proof of her lies. Fists still clenched, Annesley ticked through a plan. She would act normal, try for a third impression with the Harrisons, and deal with the Bulloch family scandal later, just she and Mary Blake.

"Let's... pretend this didn't happen for now," Annesley said without making eye contact.

Mary Blake quickstepped to keep up. "Of course, of course."

The housekeeper was sweeping the hallway when they entered. "There's coffee by the pool," she said.

"Perfect." Annesley strode to the tall table to get the newspapers Marcela had left there earlier. She didn't want the Harrisons to see the headline and make the connection. Also, she wanted time to think things through before the other girls knew.

The table stood bare. Annesley's heart plunged into the hollow of her stomach.

Mary Blake was engaged in friendly banter at the doorway, something about the woman's children and "Isn't this Texas heat simply blistering?"

Mary Blake had just learned her father was going to prison, and she was now one-hundred-percent rainbows and roses. Mary Blake's positivity usually amused Annesley. Sometimes, it made her roll her eyes at the sincerity of it all. But at this moment, it was a charade that made her skin crawl. Mary Blake was concerned about some stranger's life, but she couldn't share her own life with her best friend.

Options tangled in Annesley's mind, and she pulled the strongest thread loose. She needed to stay on course. And that meant deciding that the Harrisons wouldn't make the connection. If they did, Annesley would distance herself. *None of us knew. What a horrible situation.* Annesley sneezed, and the mortification from the night before resurrected itself as a vile taste she couldn't swallow.

She blinked hard in an attempt to repel her body's inflammatory response.

Approaching the back door, Annesley hesitated before stepping out of the air conditioning and back into the heat. The tickle in her nose and a craving for a big mug of coffee prompted her to turn the knob. She could have kicked herself for leaving the drugstore without the Benadryl.

The pool shone Tiffany blue after the post-dust-storm scrubbing, and soft ripples caught the sunlight like diamonds. Charlie, Lisa, and Helen lounged in patio chairs under a gargantuan white umbrella. A side table displayed remnants of a breakfast spread of coffee, orange juice, and muffins. Annesley realized she hadn't eaten since yesterday morning, not since before last night's bloody filet and balsamic green beans. Her stomach gurgled in both revulsion and hunger.

"Hey, Annesley." Lisa scooted over to make room for Annesley and another chair under the umbrella. She looked comfortable—or was it smug?—in her UCLA Medical School T-shirt.

"Just getting a coffee," Annesley said. Her nerves glitched like a TV whose antenna had broken loose.

The slider opened and closed, and Mary Blake joined the group with a high-pitched "G'morning, y'all," as if being chipper could erase front pages and lies.

Annesley ignored Mary Blake and focused on Lisa. Was she glowing? Annesley wondered about Lisa and Parker being together last night when this visit was supposed to have been her chance to be with Tripp. On a different day, she would have been happy. But it wasn't fair.

From the corner of her eye, Annesley saw Helen gesture toward Mary Blake. Helen pulled a folded newspaper from under her thigh and held it low, as if it were a cache of government secrets being handed off in a train station. Mary Blake shook her head lightly, lips pursed to convey, "Let's not discuss this now."

"What's that?" Annesley asked, knowing full well what it was.

Helen shot a shocked gaze from Annesley to Mary Blake and back again. She inched the newspaper back under her thigh.

Annesley barked at Mary Blake, and she didn't care that she sounded like a shrew. "*She* knew?" Annesley turned back to Helen, the less complicated target. "You knew?"

"I..." Helen looked to Mary Blake.

Annesley moved to stand between the two, to force Helen to reckon with the treachery.

"I knew *something*," Helen said. "I didn't know about this."

Annesley's face burned from the sun, from the cat, from the betrayal. But the cat was no competition for the humiliation. Her eyes watered, and her chest heaved. A trickle of sweat ran down her temple as she directed her gaze at Charlie and Lisa. "And you?"

They shook their heads.

Mary Blake stood in the full light, her teased hair glowing like she'd been blessed by the sun. She lifted her sunglasses, folded them carefully, and slid them into a case. She held her purse in front of her, arms folded through the straps, as if the bag were her armor. "This isn't about Helen. She was house treasurer and knew I didn't pay dues last year. She kept it a secret that I had to deactivate as a Delta Rho. But she didn't know about my dad's legal issues."

Mary Blake pursed her lips as if trying to decide whether to let the next words out of her mouth. It was so quiet that Annesley noticed the absence of nature sounds. No birdsong, no leaves rustling in the wind, all the sounds that had become a sort of soundtrack over the past days absent.

Mary Blake nodded almost imperceptibly and directed her words to Annesley. "Or that I had to withdraw from school. I worked last year while you were in class. You practically lived at Tripp's, so you didn't even notice."

Annesley's mouth fell open. At least this time, she wasn't alone. Helen and Lisa shared looks of shock, but Charlie, who had seemed disinterested and distracted up to that point, twisted her mouth into a sly grin.

"Wait," Charlie said, directing her smile at Mary Blake. "Are you saying you're not a Delta either?"

*Leave it to Charlie to make this a joking matter.* The trouble was that Annesley felt like the joke. Wilted, she regarded Mary Blake. "You bitch." Her words came out as a breath more than a sound, a sulfurous exhale that stilled the other four girls.

"Whoa, whoa, whoa." Charlie's chair scratched across the concrete. "Don't take your issues out on MB. From what we read, she's got a lot to deal with."

"*My* issues?"

"Yeah." Charlie made a circling motion to take in Annesley's face then waved at the ranch, indicating—Annesley didn't know what, but she didn't like whatever implication it was.

And Annesley didn't like the way the others were looking at her, as if she'd drowned the Harrisons' cat. Defensiveness warmed her face. She swallowed the bitterness that filled her mouth, but it lingered, blossoming into a caustic flower. "Charlie, you are just too cool. So chill. Nothing bothers you—nothing holds you back. Some of us have lives. No one's keeping you here, you know."

Charlie brushed at her shorts. A cascade of crumbs tumbled to the deck. "Annesley is as Annesley does. And the rarified air of this million-acre ranch has turned you into your mother once and for all. I guess you were on some sort of Rumspringa, and we should have known you would climb right back up on your pedestal."

"I don't need a pedestal. But I'm not like you, with no rules and no standards."

"Standards? Ha! We're making a special stop in Texas for you to see Tripp. You make him out to be a prize. At least *I* didn't lower myself to that standard."

The anger rising in Annesley's chest stalled in confusion.

Helen placed her hand on Charlie's wrist. "Charlie, don't you think that's enough?"

Charlie shook her hand free. "No, I'm good. No rules, right?"

"*You* lowering yourself to Tripp? Please." Annesley's words didn't sound as certain as she wanted them to.

Charlie smirked. "I don't know what those standards are, but he clearly thought I met them when we were freshmen."

"Charlie!" Helen hissed.

Annesley's nostrils flared slightly, her eyes narrowing.

When Annesley didn't respond, Charlie asked, "You didn't know?" She rolled her eyes. "He seemed fun for about a minute. And then he pulled this whole 'Darlin', I want to show you something.'" She shifted into an exaggerated Texas accent. "My granddaddy's war letters home. I never show them to anyone, blah, blah, blah. You look at me, and it melts my heart like a snowball in the desert." She faked gagging.

At the mention of snowballs in the desert, humiliation bubbled in Annesley's gut like an oil well about to burst. She felt her cheeks quiver.

Charlie dropped the accent. "I'll give him points for originality, but the sleaze factor was truly impressive. Oh, wait. Did he say that to you too? Did he show you his granddaddy's letters? Did the frosty princess think she'd melted his heart? That's when you should have known it was a line. Anyway, I wonder if that means I meet his high standards. Or even better, you sank to his low standards. I'm so confused. In any case, you're the bitch here. No wonder your brother left."

Charlie, eyes on fire, glared at Annesley. Helen, Lisa, and Mary Blake were frozen in place, mouths open in shock.

Annesley turned away and stared into the pool, so crisp and clean. There was no sign of a storm or dust or the fact that anything had ever happened to sully the ranch's pristine setting.

# Chapter Thirty-Seven
# 2019
# Lisa

"I didn't understand it all back then," Mary Blake said, making eye contact with Lisa in the rearview mirror. Mary Blake had carried the conversation from their New Mexico hotel into the Arizona desert and was discussing her dad's business dealings after Charlie informed her that she couldn't tell her about the deals she was working on right now unless they all wanted to be facing insider trading charges.

"They teach his case in business schools now, or so I hear," Mary Blake continued. "All it took to blow it open was a junior accountant with a conscience. Comparable to Enron, except Daddy had been weaving in phantom trusts and real estate in British protectorates, turning it all into an international kerfuffle. That's why the prosecutor allowed it to stay quiet for so long. It didn't make the regulators look good."

Lisa hadn't followed the fallout of the investigation. She'd had other things on her mind back then, things she'd tried to force *out* of her mind after the last trip, but she hadn't missed the news that the elderly Mr. Bulloch had died in prison only two years after his arrest, away from the sunshine his daughter had always held in her petite palm.

And here Lisa was again, mind heavy with lawyers and threats. "Charlie, what do you know about NDAs? I mean, like in that situation. The junior accountant must have had an NDA, right? You must deal with this. I mean, I'm just curious. Like, could a person, that junior accountant, go to jail for violating an NDA?"

"No jail. It's a contract dispute. Put that junior accountant aside, though, because there was no way in hell that company was going to sue him for breach for reporting fraud. But I've seen corporate acquisitions blow up because someone gets too gabby. Sometimes, there are millions in damages. And going up against these big companies, even if you win, can drain the bank. What's the sudden interest in contracts and corporate secrets? Do you have a side hustle in corporate espionage?"

"Ha ha. Just curious." What would her friends think if they knew the truth? Mr. Harrison had warned her about being separated from the herd. What if the herd turned against her? She recoiled at the thought of their disgust.

A lull overtook the car, giving them a chance to check their phones, count the telephone poles, or in Lisa's case, piece through moments to find the point at which she could have changed the course of time. There had to be a way out of this mess. She turned back to Charlie, about to ask a follow-up question about cease and desist letters.

"What's going on up there?" Charlie pointed ahead through the front two seats.

Lisa peered through the windshield. The horizon billowed with sepia clouds, as if a photo filter lay across the windshield. "Rain?"

"Rain's not rust-colored," Helen said.

Lisa checked her phone. The weather app reported sunshine and ninety degrees. "It's not supposed to rain." She'd seen plenty of forest fires in California. Dark clouds of smoke had taken up residence for what seemed an eternity the prior summer. "I'd guess a forest fire, but this is straight-up desert. Plus, the color's not right."

Mary Blake continued to drive toward the billowing mass, which as they neared it, looked more like the dusty aftermath of a building implosion, a horizon's worth of building implosions. "Do we keep driving?" She leaned toward the steering wheel and peered into the cloud.

Charlie responded matter-of-factly, "It's coming right at us. I'd keep driving through to get to the other side faster, like going through a downpour."

The cloud looked impenetrable, and that one time they tried to drive through a downpour—in Louisiana, twenty years ago—things hadn't turned out so well. No one else objected to Charlie's suggestion, though, so Lisa said nothing.

Tumbleweeds charged at them in platoons, hopping across the center line and back again. One vaulted over the car like an acrobat in a demented circus.

The cloud didn't have a definitive entry point. First, Lisa heard tiny pecks against the windshield, small grains of dirt and sand flicking the glass. Mary Blake slowed the SUV and turned on her windshield wipers, which did nothing other than add a rhythmic *thwack thwack thwack* to the new soundtrack.

The cloud transformed into a whirling sandblast that engulfed the SUV. In an instant, there was no road before them, no road behind them, and only murkiness on either side. The earth had literally closed in on them.

"Well, shit. I wasn't expecting that," Charlie said.

Helen fumbled with her phone and muttered something about having no service. "This wasn't in the forecast. I checked. We should have taken a different route." She squeezed her phone until her hand shook. "I'm so sorry. We should have gone south." She pulled her map from the seat back pocket and struggled to unfold it. She flipped the map as she smoothed out a bent corner and it tore. "Shit."

"Sugar, it's gonna be all right. I think it's safer to pull over. I can't see a doggone thing." Mary Blake moved the car off to the right until the wheels hit dirt.

The headlights cast an eerie glow through the dust, illuminating nothing but monochrome. Grit peppered the car. Mary Blake turned off the wipers, and the only sound was the arhythmic percussion against the exterior of their metal tomb. Lisa pushed into her corner against the door.

"I guess we wait for it to blow over," Mary Blake said. She turned and gave them a wide-eyed smile. "Remember when we arrived at the Harrison's ranch—"

Charlie made a low sound, close to a growl. Lisa was Team Growl on that. There was no need to talk about the Harrisons.

Mary Blake rushed out her words, and her sunshine faded. "There had been a dust storm. Remember? That's all I was going to say."

"Ah," Annesley said. "Now I get what Parker meant about rabbits digging holes in the air. Remember when he said that?" She laughed as a swirl of dust whipped the windshield.

Lisa chilled at the mention of Parker and his colorful explanation in the Harrisons' parlor. She tried to focus on his charm and not the guilt she'd spent years trying to suppress about the night he'd died and the decisions she'd made both that night and the morning after. It didn't work. It was impossible to evade her complicity.

When the police had released the report stating that it had been Parker driving and the car had failed due to some wiring problem, Lisa had said nothing about their lies. She'd confirmed herself as a person of no importance, someone who simply existed while the world went on around her. The fact that she signed the warrant that would lock her in that cage forever seemed wildly appropriate. If her old friends had known, she never would have made the guest list for this trip.

A giant tumbleweed struck the windshield, and they all jumped. Annesley coughed. She apologized then coughed again.

Mary Blake pulled a water bottle from the center console. "You okay?"

Annesley took a sip. "Dust, I guess."

Mary Blake started flipping the vents closed then pressed the window buttons to be sure the windows were all the way up.

"Allergies?" Lisa asked, recalling the ranch. "Cats and dust?" Her words felt rehearsed, a doctor checking boxes, hiding her worry that the coughing might crack a rib weakened by metastases.

"Lisa, I'm—" Annesley turned toward the back again. Her eyes widened, and an orange glow illuminated her face.

By the time Lisa realized the orange glow was coming from headlights approaching from behind the car, it was too late to brace for the impact.

The Escalade lurched, sending Lisa face first into the seat in front of her. She felt the thud of the collision internally, like her organs had smashed into each other, a spongy, twisted mass. Disorientation set in, as did the spray of stars that accompanies a hit to the nose. For a moment, a filament of time grabbed her, and she was in an emerald-green Scout.

Lisa tried to squint away the stars, but they sparkled through memories of a dark Texas sky carpeted with the Milky Way, a low tree lit by yellow headlamps, a police officer's flashlight that pulled her from the darkness, and a desperate plea to know what had happened to her friends.

A low whine broke her daze. Helen shook in the seat next to her.

Lisa unbuckled her seatbelt and fumbled with the strap when it caught on her shoulder. She kneeled between the two captain's seats. "Are you okay, Helen?" Lisa placed her hand on Helen's knee.

"I'm sorry." Helen was sobbing and shaking and shrinking into her seat. "I'm so sorry."

Helen's comments stilled Lisa and pulled Charlie from her seat in the rear.

"Helen, are you okay?" Charlie asked while kneading her own neck.

"I'm fine. I'm fine."

Charlie squinted as if in pain.

"Did you hit your head, Charlie?" Lisa asked.

"I'm fine," Charlie snapped, but it seemed like she was chastising herself.

Helen waved Lisa and Charlie away, but Lisa forced eye contact and searched for signs of shock. After satisfying herself there were no significant injuries in the back seat, she moved to the front, where Mary Blake was holding back tears and Annesley sat stone-faced in concentration. No broken bones, no blood. The Escalade was a tank, but the sense of dislodging was unsettling.

Annesley opened her mouth and faltered. She didn't present as okay. She looked at Lisa, not for help but for silence.

Annesley turned back to Mary Blake. "It's all good, Mary Blake. Everyone's okay. We're fine. This will all be fine."

Lisa had heard that line before from any number of patients. A mantra. But Annesley wasn't fine, and she wouldn't be able to keep it a secret much longer.

A knock on the driver's side window made them all jump. A person wearing goggles and a towel wrapped around his face held a torn piece of paper with writing on it up to the window:

SRY. U OK? UR CAR LOOKS NOT BAD. HAVE SATELLITE PHONE IF NEED CALL.

He slapped a business card next to it that simply said, "@STORMCHASERTX"

"A storm chaser?" Lisa said. "Are you kidding me?" At least she didn't need to worry about injuries in the car behind them. The storm chasers could take care of themselves.

Helen's sobs continued. "I don't know why I'm crying. I'm sorry." She blubbered and blew her nose into a tissue. "It caught me off guard. I'm sorry. I'm fine."

Mary Blake was fine. Annesley was fine. Charlie was fine. Helen was fine.

None of them were fine, though, and it didn't take a doctor to know that. But there had to be a way to power through this. It didn't have to be like at the ranch, when Charlie's plans changed, Annesley decided to stay, and everything escalated.

# Chapter Thirty-Eight
# 1999
# Helen

Helen emerged from the house to search for Charlie and almost tripped over the cat. The feline allergy factory slipped past her and through the door as it was closing. "Hey!" she called without putting much effort into it.

Annesley and Charlie going at each other by the pool that morning as they never had before and Helen not having known Mary Blake's full truth had given Helen a sour dose of reality. Maybe they weren't all going to be Delta Rhoadies forever. She shielded her eyes against the sun. There wasn't a cloud in the sky.

She opened her notebook, brittle from the dry heat like the pages were from ancient tomes, and reviewed the new schedule. The cattle branding thing, which sounded dreadful, took up most of the next day, so she'd had to reroute the drive. Unfortunately, that meant bypassing the side trip to the Grand Canyon. More unfortunately, Helen had to break that news to Charlie.

Even without the mishap in Louisiana, they would only have had one night at the canyon, hardly more than a bathroom break. The new itinerary would get Lisa to her internship on time, and Charlie could take the return trip and spend as much time as she wanted at the canyon and anywhere else she chose to visit. And maybe Helen could do the drive back with Charlie instead of flying home from LA.

The Delta Rhoadies may not have a future, but she and Charlie had New York. They had accounting firms and law school.

The sun was high. Only the sound of the air conditioning unit by the house broke the quiet. She walked past the carport, the only rectangle of shade in sight. The Scout, topless again, sat next to the White Whale and a shiny black Ford pickup.

Charlie sat to the side of a nearby white shed, the Scout's fabric roof spread out in front of her, repair kit against her thigh. She loved that car, her tie to her brother. In a way, he'd accompanied them the whole trip. Helen hesitated to approach, but Charlie looked up with a smile when she saw Helen's short shadow cast on the ground next to her.

Helen shuffled her feet and felt fine dust settle onto her toes. "You get it all stitched up?"

"The storm in Louisiana ripped the crap out of it, but I think it's good to go."

Helen nodded. A soft wind pushed grains of dirt along the ground, creating tiny trails. "I was getting lonely in the house. I think Lisa's out on a Gator ride with Parker. Mary Blake hasn't left her room since she finally got ahold of her mom. God knows where Annesley is. I've never seen her so pissed."

Charlie clicked the mini-scissors back into the red casing of her Swiss Army knife. "I have to admit, I'm impressed. You and MB and your secrets." The slight smile on Charlie's face suggested admiration but could easily have been distrust.

"I didn't know much. And I promised her I wouldn't tell anyone."

"Wasn't my business." Charlie smoothed out the Scout's top like she was arranging a sacred cloth.

"Annesley's convinced Mrs. Harrison knew about her allergies and—I don't know—planted cat hair in her room. Like a Princess and the Pea thing. I think she's gone off the deep end."

"Tripp's mom doesn't give a rat's ass about Annesley. But what do I know? Maybe that's how these women play. Mrs. Harrison has to show she's alpha dog somehow. Or alpha cat. People don't change." She flicked the scissors back out of the red casing and back in.

Helen bristled at the memory of Annesley fleeing the dinner table in tears. It wasn't often Annesley showed vulnerability. With her dining room humiliation compounded by the discovery that her best friend had been lying to her for nine months, maybe Annesley landed in the justifiable position of deserving pity.

"You may not even see Annesley after tomorrow, Charlie. My money is on her staying here, cat or no cat. She can't even look at Mary Blake." That, more than the Charlie-Annesley fight, unsettled Helen.

"I've got no sympathy for Annesley. She can have this ranch, her douche of a boyfriend, and his brittle twig of a mother." A hot gust of wind whipped up the dirt beyond the irrigated landscaping.

"It's just a pit stop," Helen said. "I was working out some plans for New York City—"

"Listen. About that..." Charlie flattened her palms against the fabric and pushed herself up.

Helen stiffened. No good conversation in the history of the world started with, "Listen. About that..." Those were words earmarked for crushing a two-left-feet child's expectations she would make the soccer team all her friends played on or for the news that the friend who promised to attend prom with you ended up asking someone else after you bought your dress.

Charlie jerked her head and stared beyond the maintenance shed. "I'm not going to Columbia." She spouted the law school's name with bitter pomposity.

Helen twitched. "Of course you are." A line of sweat ran down the inside of her upper arm. "What do you mean?"

"I mean I'm not going to law school. There's no way in hell—"

Helen followed Charlie's gaze. She saw only smudges of unruffled brush on arid land. It was a wonder anything could survive in this part of the country. "But you have to go." The pleading in her voice sounded scratchy in the dry air.

A short laugh escaped Charlie. "I don't *have* to do anything."

"But it was *your* plan. Why are we doing this"—Helen waved at the cars in the carport and the miles behind them—"if you aren't going to do what you planned to do?"

"*Us* being on this trip has nothing to do with *me* going to law school."

"It has everything to do with it. We have a three-year plan."

"My plans changed. They don't need a spreadsheet, and they are *my* plans. No one else's."

Helen gripped the map, but it didn't provide her the power she needed. "What do you mean? What plans?"

Charlie took a step and clasped her hands behind her head. "All I know is that I'm going to the Grand Canyon tomorrow. After that..." She spread her arms wide.

Helen shook the notebook at Charlie. "We told Mr. Harrison we were going to the branding party tomorrow. We don't have time for a side trip to the Grand Canyon. It's too far north. We're going through Tucson instead, so we can reach LA by Sunday."

"It's not a *side* trip." She glared at Helen. "It's *the* trip."

It wasn't Charlie's fault she'd had to re-route again, but Helen used words to stab her anyway, perhaps fueled by Charlie's own tirade earlier. "You can do the Grand Canyon on the return trip. I was going to offer to come with you, but you clearly prefer to be by yourself, so that works out even better." Desperation had seeped into Helen's tone as she tried to add a bitter bite to her words.

"What is your problem?"

"My *problem*? You're abandoning me."

"You're a big girl, Helen. Sometimes you have to be responsible for your own life."

Helen flinched. Was that what Charlie thought? That she was irresponsible? Shame from That Night pushed like a stone into her throat and blocked the air. Sharp edges dug into her windpipe when she swallowed. "I cannot believe how selfish you are."

Dust billowed in the distance. Perhaps Lisa was on her way back with Parker, but they were too far away for the Gator's rumble to reach them.

Charlie's raspy exhale broke the silence. Her eyes went blank. She pulled her car keys from her pocket and tossed them to Helen.

"What are these for?" Helen asked.

"To open the tailgate. Make sure you get anything else that's yours out of my car. Leave the keys under the front seat. Sounds like Lisa will have room in the White Whale if Miss Catwalk is staying. I'm on my own from here on out."

Helen looked at the keys and back at Charlie, whose back and shoulders were solid, unwavering. Charlie was already on the road ahead of them all.

If anyone felt on her own, it was Helen.

# Chapter Thirty-Nine
# 1999
# Annesley

Annesley unzipped her makeup case and removed her compact. She ran her fingers over the engraved script of her monogram. *ABC.*

"Elegance is simple," her mother always said. "And elegance stands alone."

Overhead lighting reflected off white tile and Carrara marble, all the better to see her face. Annesley sighed in disgust.

That very week, she'd done a jeté over an irrigation pipe and brushed bits of hay out of her hair. Messy and beautiful. Or so she'd thought. What looked back at her from the mirror now was sobering. She'd let herself go off track, followed people who went off track.

She was not a follower. An hour ago, she'd run into Mary Blake in the hallway.

"You look so much better, honey," and "Let me know when you're ready to talk," and "Can I get you a cup of tea with lemon and cinnamon?"

Annesley didn't make eye contact. Anger armored her against the hurt that fought to wind its way into her heart.

Mary Blake had humiliated her. The two of them had always been the pair others watched with envy. She'd pretended not to see the stares, the girls who wanted to make it a trio to be part of the glamour, the guys who couldn't decide between the blonde and the brunette but would have been thrilled if either of them had glanced their way. Part of that allure was the mystery of what it must be like to be one of them, the image of a perfect life.

That shattered image bore edges that cut through layers Annesley hadn't known existed, a sense of belonging she never knew she'd needed before this trip. All the rest of them now knew that Mary Blake hadn't trusted her to tell her. And yet Mary Blake had told Helen, the other liar in the house.

Annesley refused to focus on that. She needed to get this trip—*her* trip—back on track. Her mother was right about choosing who to surround yourself with. Lesson learned. And she refused to let any of them hold her back.

She ran her fingers across her cheeks. There was only so much she could do to cover the red splotches around her nose and eyes, but she'd learned from the best. While Annesley's mother had likely never faced allergen-induced gargoylism, she'd armed Annesley with the confidence to do so with her head held high. Tonight was her night; Tripp owed it to her. In fact, Parker had free rein to entertain the other girls. She could deal with the Harrisons, and the "friends" would be gone tomorrow.

She powdered her nose and added highlighter to her brow-line. *Pull the eye away from what you don't want people to see.* The diamond earrings from her father, the ones her mother had said were too big, too gauche for an eighteen-year-old, sparkled.

Annesley curled the corners of her lips slightly, mimicking her mother's perpetual almost-smile, gave her glowing nose one last puff of powder, and exited the room. She glided across the hallway's tile floor, earning the nickname, Miss Catwalk, Charlie had derisively bestowed upon her. Why it got under her skin, she couldn't say.

Thinking of Charlie brought heat to her face. Annesley wasn't naïve. Tripp had a history. Charlie, though? Sure, Charlie was pretty, but she embodied roughness, an unappealing grittiness. She wasn't a woman who would walk into a reception on the arm of an executive or share a clever joke with the matriarch of an important family.

Charlie wasn't competition, and Annesley could dismiss Tripp's passing interest. What was harder to erase was being diminished in front of her friends. Charlie had tried to expose Annesley as a fool with a perversion of Tripp's grandfather's war letters and talk of melting hearts.

Annesley refused to accept that Tripp had used the same words with Charlie, that it was a cheap line. Tripp lit up every time he saw Annesley. She'd *seen* his heart melt. Charlie might have a sort of dangerous vibe, but she didn't melt hearts. And Annesley had held those letters, airmail from the Pacific theater addressed to "Dora, darling." Charlie hadn't specified details.

In fact—and Annesley's posture straightened at the thought as she descended the stairway into the empty foyer—she would not put it past Charlie to have gotten the story from Annesley herself during some late-night Delta Rho gab session and then pulled it out this morning as a cruel joke.

When Annesley emerged onto the flagstone walk in front of the house, Tripp grinned. "Hey, darlin'." His approving gaze, which dipped to her toes and slid up her body, fortified the confidence that had withered since her arrival.

"Man, that cat sure did a number on you." He grimaced slightly, his eyes lingering on her face, and it was all she could do not to collapse. "Hope it clears up soon. I suppose it'll be dark at the Ranch Hand." Sweet bourbon hung hot on his breath.

"The what?" Annesley asked.

"The Ranch Hand. The bar we're going to. You missed the preparty."

"But"—she cringed at the plea laced through the word—"I thought it was going to be you and me tonight. Alone."

Then Annesley noticed Parker, Lisa, and Helen, who must *not* have missed the unadvertised preparty, judging by their laughter and the bottle of Dos Equis Helen finished off before giving a bow. The group stood behind the White Whale, where Lisa's pitiful life pressed against the wagon's windows.

"No big deal. When we get back, you and I can sneak off by ourselves." He searched her eyes, which were saying "absolutely not" but might be unreadable in their swollen state. "I have to be a proper host, right? Can't leave those two with my underage brother. Plus, you clearly need to get away from the house and the cat."

Annesley's core tensed. The sun was low, but heat from the day still rose from the asphalt in a steady pulse that seeped through her sandals and bloomed through her feet.

She saw in Tripp's eyes that he had the inertia for a night out, and once Tripp was on a mission, he achieved it. That drive was something they had in common, something she'd relied on to pull them together and propel them to the next stage of life. She held her head steady. One thing she'd learned was patience. Hell, she'd driven eighteen hundred miles, slept on the ground, and ridden in a back seat next to God-knows what kind of trailer park detritus. She was a Cannon, and one night out wasn't going to kill anyone. And Tripp was right. She needed to get out of the house.

"Fine." Her word wasn't loud enough for Tripp to hear. "Fine," she said louder and followed him to the cars.

Parker ran his hand over the driver's door of the Scout. "This is to die for. Think we can take this? I'd love to give it a spin."

Tripp leaned over the passenger door to look inside. "We could do some serious damage in this thing. Four on the floor. Nice. I like a girl who can handle a stick. Parker's right. Let's take the Scout."

"Charlie's not coming," Helen said dismissively.

That was a good omen. Maybe the night could be salvaged by losing one person at a time. Mary Blake wasn't making an appearance, either, so that was two down.

Helen's tone indicated an irritation with Charlie. Mild curiosity surfaced. Maybe Helen finally saw Charlie's true colors during her display by the pool. Anyway, Helen was already buzzed. She would probably drop out early and pass out in her room when they got back. If Parker and Lisa spun off, Annesley would finally have Tripp alone.

"Then Parker's truck, it is," Tripp said.

Lisa climbed into the front seat of the black Ford, and Annesley and Helen got into the backseat, with Tripp sitting between them. He unrolled a brown paper bag as Parker pulled onto the main road.

Helen laughed a little too loudly, further proof of the preparty. "What's in the bag?"

"Wouldn't you like to know?"

"What's in the bag, Tripp?" Annesley echoed, her eyes narrowing.

"Popular question from such curious little girls." Tripp opened the bag to reveal a bottle of whiskey and a Ziploc baggie with white powder in it. "Something for everyone, and both for me." He opened the baggie and took a hit off the base of his thumb. At least in college he'd been discreet.

Helen's eyes went wide. "Is that—" Her voice dropped to a whisper. "Cocaine?" The naiveté would be endearing if it weren't coming from someone Annesley wished was back in the main house.

A poultry truck flew past, chicken feathers fluttering behind it as if celebrating escape from captivity.

"Maybe you should keep it down, Tripp," Annesley said, trying not to sound like a scold. "Do you really need to do that tonight?"

"Chill, darlin'. We're out in the middle of nowhere. Gotta make things fun."

A police car appeared ahead.

"For God's sake, Tripp." Anger had crept into her voice.

"Don't get your panties in a bunch, Annesley. My dad owns this county, and he owns the local police. We can do whatever we want. We always do. You wouldn't believe some of the shit we've gotten away with. Am I right, Parker? Get used to it, darlin'. It's the Harrison way."

Nonetheless, Tripp stuffed his stash into his pocket and held the bottle low while the police car passed. Annesley blew her nose and felt as crumpled as her Kleenex.

"Sorry about the cat, darlin'." He laughed and squeezed her knee then leaned in and kissed her. "I'll make it up to you later. Promise."

She turned her gaze out the window, wondering how Tripp could make up for what had become the road trip from hell.

# Chapter Forty
# 2019
# Helen

The sky showed no trace of the orange cloud that had inhaled the women and spat them out after the storm chaser rear-ended the Escalade. Without the storm chaser's satellite phone, they would have been hitchhiking. Instead, the women rode in a rental shuttle driven by a quietly jocular man who'd insisted on moving all the luggage from the Escalade himself despite Charlie's vehemence.

Helen barely remembered getting into the van, but there she was, belted into the back seat next to Lisa. Annesley, helped into the van by Charlie due to what she called "a stitch in my side," sat next to Charlie in the middle.

With the impact reverberating in her bones and the past seeping through microscopic fissures, Helen's head bobbed in tiny shakes. Lisa put her hand on Helen's. The warm pressure stilled her enough that she could focus on Mary Blake, whose animated movements in the front passenger's seat made her look like she was under the control of a coked-up puppeteer. The peaks of Mary Blake's phrasings reached new heights, and her sentences ran together to the point Helen worried that if the van braked too hard, one sentence would smash into the next and the next and the next.

"A storm chaser, can you believe it? He walked right up to the driver's side door with a towel wrapped around his face like he was on Mars. That red dirt swirling all around us, it was like *The Martian*.

Did you see that movie? So nice of him to wait there until you arrived. I'll have to find his YouTube channel. I'm glad we had such a big car. I love the Escalade. I drive a Tesla at home. Have you ever ridden in one? You have to try it sometime."

The taste of iron in Helen's mouth recalled memories too muddled to reveal faces or words. There was pressure on her chest. Her own voice, was she screaming? There was darkness and anger, and she was flying. Why were events blending together?

"Any of you wonder if we're cursed?" Charlie's voice was casual, as if she were asking if everyone liked her new haircut, which she would never do.

"It's bad luck, Charlie," Annesley said. "Sometimes, it's just bad luck." She turned toward Helen and was unable to hide the wince as her torso twisted. "Are you doing okay? You were a little peaked before."

Helen's skin no longer held her together, and she was a collection of particles expanding like the stars in the universe. She clenched her hands to feel substance. She needed a sense of order, but emotions flowed from all directions and no direction at once. "Yes. It was a shock. That's all."

She'd had these fissures and time leaks—emotion leaks—before. Her father's roast a few years back was supposed to have been a night of laughs to celebrate a milestone birthday. Helen had stood in front of friends and family and "backstoried" her father to raucous laughter. Everything was fine, though maybe she'd had too many drinks. Then he stood to counter-roast, and instead of clapping back at everyone, he gleefully announced his early retirement. It shouldn't have been anything other than a lovely reveal. She'd known he would eventually retire, and she would take over the firm. But she exploded like her insides were a shaken bottle of soda and someone had twisted off the top. She'd gone from stone-faced to unstoppable tears in a flash.

She still couldn't explain it, and Derek's face haunted her. She'd never seen him look so helpless.

She blamed stress and latched onto upgrading the firm's record-keeping system and overseeing new renovations to their home, making things her own. Derek seemed to go along with it, and she was fine until Josh's fall only days before Mary Blake's call about the trip. His cry still rang in her ears. And the memory of the panicked look of fear in her son's eyes had been like looking into her own eyes.

She turned to see Lisa studying her, more empathetic than diagnostic. Helen looked away and leaned her forehead against the window. She grabbed her planner with both hands and opened it, but her eyes refused to focus.

Maybe she needed to hear Derek's voice, to be pulled back to earth by something that had grounded her in the past. She pulled her phone out and—no. Despite the dust storm and the storm chaser, she needed to feel safe with these women. Safer. Like she was in a cocoon. She would stay with her friends, stay on course, and her world would stay woven and snug. That had been the plan.

She texted instead. *We'll be getting to the GC late. Minor accident.*

Derek's response was quick. *You OK?*

If he'd seen her emotional breakdown in the Escalade, essentially a reenactment of the scene she'd made at her father's retirement announcement and more times in the last couple of years than she cared to remember, he would probably have—she wasn't sure. Left her? Committed her? Insisted again they start therapy? *You have to let me in*, he'd said then, without understanding that the only way she'd survived the past twenty-one years was by not letting things get out. And she'd spent the past hour convincing herself that the reunion's excitement and the dust storm's creepiness created the perfect moment for a fender bender to send anyone into tears.

*Everyone is fine,* she texted. *I'll call you when we get to the rental place.*

She didn't want him to hear her voice while dark memories spun unchecked in her brain. She focused on Mary Blake's words instead.

Mary Blake's rambling monologue took on the veneer of white noise like rubber on road, but her words didn't silence the judgmental whoosh of Helen's pulse.

At about the time the five of them were supposed to have been wrapping up a pre-sunset hike at the Grand Canyon had they not been waylaid, the women crowded into a satellite car rental location ninety-three miles from their destination.

Helen stood against a white wall adorned with a faded print of Arizona's Coconino National Forest, phone in hand and torn between calling a husband who had just sent a fourth text and watching Mary Blake's performance at the rental counter.

The clerk, sturdy in a blue uniform blazer and purple-rimmed readers, offered Mary Blake a Nissan Maxima and a credit for a future rental.

Mary Blake leaned over the counter and pointed at the keyboard. "You're a gem. Thank you! But can you check again for something bigger? An SUV? Y'all can even let us keep the Escalade. It barely had a scratch on it."

The woman shook her head and said that damaged vehicles had to be removed from service then excused herself to hunt down an alternative. Mary Blake turned with a pre-emptive smile of victory, and it was enough to embolden Helen to make the phone call.

Derek answered on the first ring. "Are you okay? What happened?"

"Just a fender-bender. We're in Winona, outside of Flagstaff, getting a new rental. Everyone's fine. Only Mary Blake could have a run-in with a storm chaser in the middle of nowhere. Crazy, right?" Derek didn't laugh, so Helen laughed for him. She twisted her shoulders to get her spine to pop but felt only tightness. "Lisa said we need to watch for signs of whiplash, but we're all good."

Annesley sat in a plastic chair by the door, her eyes closed. Helen imagined her reciting a meditation mantra that guaranteed eternal glamour and health. Not far away, Charlie stood while Lisa not-subtly checked her pupils and offered a bottle of water and what looked like ibuprofen. Charlie rolled her eyes, then she took the pills and swallowed them without drinking the water.

The clerk returned and proved immune to Mary Blake's charms. "I'm sorry, ma'am. We don't have any SUVs available, unless you can wait until tomorrow afternoon."

Helen's mouth went dry. The itinerary didn't have flexibility for a night in Flagstaff. Tonight's hotel was still an hour and forty-six minutes' drive north. Malibu kept looking farther away, as did finishing what they'd started. Helen checked to see if Charlie had heard and would flip out about the schedule being botched again, but Charlie's face betrayed nothing.

Helen had missed what Derek said. "I'm sorry, bad connection. Can you repeat that?"

"The connection is fine at this end. I asked if you wanted to talk to Josh. He's excited he got to swim for the first time since getting his cast off. Are you sure you're okay? You sound distant and not because you're on the other side of the country."

"Yes, I'm fine." Her jaw tightened, clipping her words. "I was in a crash."

"I know. That's why I'm concerned."

"We have a doctor on board. I'm fine." Helen envisioned him stroking his chin, concerned and serious, but having no clue what she was going through and still trying to box her into talking about it.

At the counter, Mary Blake persisted, her voice crackling with sharp spikes of desperation. "I'm sure you have something that will work for us. What do you have that we can get tonight?"

The woman's fingernails clicked against the keyboard. "Let me check one more... Yes, here we go. I can get you a white passenger van. Seats twelve."

Derek's voice came through loudly. "Helen, are you there?"

She flinched and stumbled while inching backward toward the wall. "Yes. Sorry, we've got a lot going on here."

"You sound stressed."

*I'm sorry. I'm sorry.* "Of course I'm stressed. We got hit by a jacked pickup truck."

"But you said it was no big deal. Watching out for whiplash. You were laughing about it. Am I missing something? You're giving *me* whiplash."

"No, it wasn't a big deal." Her voice had crescendoed.

From across the room, Charlie regarded her with a look of concern.

"Babe, is everything all right? Did something else happen? Can we FaceTime? I want to see you."

Helen rubbed her eyes. She didn't want to be someone people thought they needed to take care of. Someone who wasn't responsible, who couldn't take care of themselves, be trusted with anything. "No. I'm okay. I shouldn't have even told you. This is what happens."

"What are you talking about? Just... calm down. All I am is concerned. I'm starting to think there's more going on than you're telling me. You have to let me in."

*You have to let me in.* The words felt like she was being flayed, her skin pulled away from her body to expose everything inside. "Calm *down*? I'm okay. Can *you* get us a car that isn't a church van? No? Then I don't need your help." Helen stood wedged in the corner now, and all eyes were on her. Pressure in her temples surpassed the pain of her morning hangover. She pressed her eyelids closed against the pounding and the tears. "Tell Josh goodnight for me. We're hours behind schedule, and we need to get back on the road."

A pull at her chest felt like a bungee cord had let fly, a tether lost. But she wasn't falling yet. The other women stood together, Annesley up from her chair, meditation interrupted. Their shared gaze created a thrum that rose into Helen's throat, where a mix of emotions tangled into a lump she couldn't swallow.

Lisa approached with the water bottle. "Here, drink this."

They needed to change the trajectory they'd started on when they were younger. One decision here, one there, and everything changed, and they all smashed together.

*No, Josh, you can't climb that tree. Yes, Lisa, I'll leave the party now. No, Tripp, I don't know where the keys are.*

# Chapter Forty-One
# 1999
# Lisa

Lisa let her hand flutter out the window as Parker sped down the highway, heading back to the ranch. The night air pushed her hand in an oscillating wave that sent electricity from her fingertips to her toes. She wanted to absorb everything: the warm desert wind, the field of stars in the black sky, and the leathery-dusty smell of the truck. In two days, her summer would end. But tonight wasn't over.

She wished it were only she and Parker on the open road. The bickering in the back seat between Tripp and Seething Beauty continued to interrupt Parker's stories, and Lisa could have listened to Tripp's brother all night.

Parker was nothing like Tripp. He was self-deprecating rather than arrogant, accommodating rather than demanding. And when he said Lisa's name, he made it sound as if it was a privilege for him to string the sounds together.

When Tripp said Annesley's name, tonight anyway, it sounded like a taunt. Lisa couldn't remember why she'd thought of Tripp as a prince for so long, the perfect half of a perfect couple. Yes, the two commanded attention and admiration. But the miles and the extended proximity since the start of the trip, or maybe just her own clear eyes, had cracked the veneer, and she now saw what was behind Tripp's Ray-Bans and Annesley's Dior lipstick.

Loud from whiskey and beer, Tripp disrupted their conversation again, right when Parker was telling Lisa about birthing calves. "C'mon, Annesley," Tripp pleaded. "Why you gotta be so uptight tonight, darlin'?"

Tripp had grown brasher and looser at the bar. He'd tossed back Patrón shots and glad-handed with the locals like he was mayor. All the while, Annesley had hardened into a glacier, her smile disappearing after the first game of pool. Tonight's Annesley held her judgmental stare for longer than a split second. Tonight's Annesley muttered under her breath instead of pursing her lips and flaring her nostrils.

Lisa had given up on engaging with Annesley by the third round of darts, which Lisa had turned out to be surprisingly good at. Helen, on the other hand, couldn't get the dart to hit the board. Every Helen miss prompted a curtsey or a swirl of the arms, followed by the requisite drink. She seemed untethered, released from the past year's pain. A little reckless, though. As a result, Lisa had nursed a single Bud Light the whole night. She thought it best to stay sober and keep an eye on her friend.

Helen had drunk more beers than Lisa could count, and now the navigator drowsed peacefully in the back seat. That left Lisa free to enjoy the night and the attentions of Parker.

"As I was saying before I was so rudely interrupted," Parker said, rolling his eyes and grinning, "we use this stuff called J-lube to help birth calves. It's a powder, and when you mix it with water, it gets super slimy. Helps get the calves out, but it's a bitch—pardon me, a pain—to get off your hands."

"Okay..." Lisa said. "What does this have to do with a homecoming week prank?"

"Imagine you're in the shower."

"Oh, I can imagine that," Tripp said.

"Don't be disgusting," Annesley snapped.

Parker continued. "You're soaking wet, shower on full blast. What happens when someone leans over the stall and dumps a bunch of powder over your head?"

Lisa cringed as she imagined the gooey cascade. "You look like you got slimed?"

"Let's just say it's not a prank to pull on someone who holds a grudge, or you might wake up one morning with genitalia drawn on your face in Sharpie... or so I've heard."

Lisa laughed and leaned as close to him as the center console allowed. "That's hilarious. Harmless fun, I guess."

A rustle of paper suggested Tripp had broken away from Annesley to take another swig of whiskey. "You two talking about lubricants? A little early in the evening for that, I'd say." A smash of glass on the highway indicated he'd rid the truck of the bottle. "Or maybe not. Whaddaya think, Annesley?"

"I think I'm ready to head in."

"Laaame. The night, as they say, is young."

Helen, apparently revived from her micronap, joined in, her voice wobbly. "Yeah, Anneshley. Come on! Lasht night in Texas."

They parked in front of the house and spilled out into a night devoid of motion. Annesley pulled her purse onto her shoulder, looking more like a woman returning from a church meeting than from a bar with bras nailed to the ceiling.

Annesley ignored Lisa, who stood close enough to Parker that she felt the rise and fall of his shoulders as he breathed. "Let's go, Helen."

Helen squinted and pointed at Annesley, her arm locked but wavering back and forth. "Time to rally, Annesley! It's early!"

With a directed look that bore an uncanny resemblance to Mrs. Cannon, Annesley addressed Helen. "You have a schedule for tomorrow, right?"

Helen's face hardened. "No one else cares about schedules. Why should I?"

Tripp nodded approvingly at the rallying Helen and looked back at Annesley. "Just cuz you're a butterface tonight doesn't mean Helen needs to go in too." Tripp used his hands to squish his cheeks until his eyes squeezed shut.

Lisa flinched. That was too much. Solidarity—the concept of solidarity anyway—called. They were friends, sisters, and Tripp was being an asshole. But before Lisa could pull away from Parker's side and detangle her fingers from his, Annesley glared at her as if Lisa was the one out of line, as if Lisa's mere presence—the taint of her commonness—demeaned the rich, elegant, perfect Annesley who, Lisa decided, was a perfect match for her asshole boyfriend.

Annesley's nostrils flared. "You know, Tripp. There are plenty of other guys who will treat me better. In fact"—her shoulders squared—"I may have met one earlier on this trip." Her eyes locked on Tripp's. Neither wavered. "We're done." She looked at Lisa, who couldn't get her jaw to cooperate and stood with her mouth wide open, and then at a wide-eyed and swaying Helen. "We're *all* done." She stormed into the house, slamming the door behind her.

Lisa's facial muscles came back into action as her gut absorbed a punch she realized she'd been bracing for for years. "Wow."

"Fuck her," Tripp grunted. "Prima donna."

Parker wrapped his arm around Lisa's waist. "Want to go after her?"

"She clearly wants nothing to do with any of us."

Parker's strong hold and the carpet of stars nudged away resentment, and a sense of freedom seeped into its place. Apparently, the antidote to rejection was not being the lone target.

"Now what?" Helen asked, bobbing like a wobbly top.

Tripp made a show of checking his watch. "Time to patrol the ranch." He stumbled and caught himself with a hand on the truck.

Helen squinted at Tripp. "Wait a minute. Don't you have people for that out here on this fanshy ransch? Your rich daddy has people." She emphasized *people*, spraying the word more than saying it.

It was like watching a TV show. Lisa was dying to know what would happen next. The air felt electric, the breeze tickling her ears.

Parker pulled his arm tighter around her waist and whispered, "I take no responsibility for my brother. But you're guaranteed a night to remember when he's around."

"We have people for everything," Tripp said. "But sometimes, I can do a better job. And sometimes"—he moved toward the Scout—"I want to drive Charlie's car."

"Ha!" Lisa and Helen barked in unison.

"No way Charlie's going to let you drive the Scout," Lisa said.

"Plus," Helen said, spitting the hard *p*, "Charlie's being a bitch." Her words filled her mouth the wrong way and slushed together. She stretched the muscles of her jaw to reorient them. "Not gonna let us. Nope. Even though I know where she keeps the keys." Those words came out clearer, which she seemed to think meant she could have another drink because she raised the bottle again. She clamped one eye shut, the definitive sign Helen was full-on blitzed and couldn't see straight.

Lisa's mind shifted to the night at the beach house party, when she'd left Helen, only to see Helen talking with Charlie the next morning in their condo. In her memory, the condo had a dimness to it, as if light couldn't penetrate. Lisa had slept in and went out into the hallway when she heard voices. Helen stood in front of Charlie, her eyes ghostlike in their lack of focus. Lisa didn't remember why she'd held back unseen in the hallway, but she had.

Charlie's voice had teetered on anger. "I'm not going to just sit here. Tell me what you remember, and I'll take care of it."

"No." Helen's admonition sounded firm, even though her voice was low. "I don't want to talk about it, and I don't want you to talk about it or do anything."

Lisa had run the night through her mind. The party with a bunch of rugby players and assorted college kids had gone late, and being the sober one at a party had gotten old. Helen had seemed in control when she'd left. They knew the people there or were at least familiar with them.

Lisa took a step and opened her mouth to let them know she was there.

Charlie put a hand on Helen's shoulder. "We should at least tell the others—"

Helen jerked back and shook her head. Lisa froze in the shadows.

Helen raised her hands. "Please. I... I can't. I don't want to... I need to get it out of my head. Promise me you won't tell anyone and don't mention it again." Her cheeks trembled.

Charlie didn't move.

Helen swallowed. "Promise me." She squeezed her hands into fists at her sides. "It'll only make it harder."

Charlie exhaled and took a half step back. "When have I told anyone anything? But I need to know you're okay."

"I'm fine. I'll be fine."

Lisa had retreated to her room and berated herself for leaving the party early.

Parker nudged Lisa, knocking her out of the memory. "This could be fun," he said.

"Nah, it's Charlie's baby," Lisa said, still cloudy with the memory of Helen in pain. She didn't mind pissing off Annesley, not after Annesley had made her feel less-than, but Charlie always seemed to have her back.

"It's just harmless fun." Parker leaned in and nuzzled her face. He kissed her, and the electricity from the night split into a thousand sparks.

She looked up at the house's dark windows. There was nothing for her there. Out here, she could look after Helen. Parker ran a hand up Lisa's back and grazed a finger along the curve of her neck.

"I'm not so sure," Lisa said.

Tripp jumped up onto the driver's door. "Let's do it."

"She'll be so mad," Helen said, wavering on her feet. "She's leaving tomorrow all by hershelf. I'll be riding with Lisha. I love you, Lisa." She lurched toward Lisa with her arms out for a hug.

Lisa grabbed Helen by the arms. "What do you mean Charlie's leaving by herself?"

"She's leaving us all." Helen waved her arms around. "Because she doesn't like us anymore."

Of course Charlie was leaving by herself. Lisa needed to learn that this trip was every woman for herself.

"Well, now," Tripp responded, plopping into the seat, "that means we have to take one last ride. Where did you say the keys were, Helen?"

# Chapter Forty-Two
# 2019
# Lisa

The white passenger van—the "Great White Whale," as a sardonic Charlie termed it when climbing into a rear seat like she was a brooding bass player boarding a tour bus—lumbered north, hours behind schedule.

As much as Lisa hated to admit that a dust storm car crash and a series of medical situations comforted her, a focus on observation and diagnosis had been a balm for her fractured conscience. The doctor had answers. Whiplash this, cancer that. The others listened to her as though she had keys to a world they didn't. The admiration in their eyes was genuine and a reminder of what she'd achieved.

Lisa had sought separation from her old world for years. She earned more now than both her parents combined, but she still clipped twenty-cent coupons and watered down the last of the shampoo to make it last longer. Her life today was twenty years and fifteen hundred miles from the ranch, but the past's grip on her persisted. A thousand miles, a million miles. It didn't matter. She'd deluded herself by thinking the past would slip away into oblivion.

Tired, sore, and spaced in the van like prison inmates kept apart for safety—but really, so they could stretch their legs and spread out—the five pulled into Grand Canyon Village under darkness.

"I had a sunset dinner planned." Mary Blake pouted with a lilt that would have typically injected levity into the moment.

"Not hungry," Charlie said. She seemed more distracted than disconnected, fiddling with her phone and glancing at Helen, who had been wordless since her call with her husband.

No one else expressed a desire to eat.

Mary Blake shepherded the group through check-in at the El Tovar, an incongruous Swiss hunting lodge-style hotel at the rim of the Grand Canyon. "I'll text about meeting up at the restaurant next door. We can get some food and decompress. We deserve that." Her hair hung flat, and her voice lacked vibrancy. But she opened her eyes wide in an apparent effort to generate the enthusiasm her words usually carried. "And don't crash into bed. Lisa said it was best to keep moving. Right, Lisa?"

Lisa nodded, torn between the allure of Mary Blake's admiration and the safety of privacy.

Annesley smiled. "Thanks, Mary Blake. The hotel is beautiful."

In her room, Lisa didn't bother unpacking. If she'd been paying her own way, she would have collapsed on the bed and never come out. The air conditioner motor filled the air with a guttural drone, and she tried to focus on that and not the email that had been pushing back into her head in the hours since the crash.

On the nightstand, her phone buzzed. The dread of another message—lawyer or reporter, it didn't matter—soured her gut. She checked it anyway.

Mary Blake had sent a group text: *Snagged us a corner booth. Ordered apps.* Cheese emoji, bread emoji, wine glass emoji, heart emoji, triangle emoji, and a road emoji.

Lisa closed her eyes and tried to picture a different trip. A trip Lisa herself documented in strings of emojis. A trip without lies, without crashes, without lawyers. A trip where she wasn't balancing on a high wire. Fall to one side, and the lawyers would get her. Fall to the other side, and her friends would shun her. Guilt and sadness bubbled and burst inside her like lava. It was hard to maintain balance above a trembling volcano.

The phone buzzed again. The new text included a photo of Mary Blake alone in a booth, fake pouting. *Come down, y'all! I'm lonely!* Cry emoji. Laugh emoji. Heart emoji.

Lisa rolled off the bed, feeling every bit the emoji with no mouth. She looked in the mirror above the dresser to see if the boiling inside showed on her face. Almost disappointed that it didn't, she surrendered to the limp hair and the blue-purple half-moons under her eyes.

Lisa took the stairs to the lobby and walked the paved path to the restaurant. The canyon was out there in the dark, hiding.

She was once again the last to arrive. This time, she didn't care. Her eyes drifted to a bus boy wiping down tables. He had that end-of-shift droop restaurant workers and medical professionals got after being on their feet all day. Invisible weights pulled the shoulders forward, and gravity compressed the lower spine. She felt the same. Quasimodo in a sundress.

"It'll be an early night for me, Mary Blake," Lisa said when she slid into the booth.

Charlie raised a hand without looking up from her phone. "Same."

Mary Blake wasn't having it, her demeanor upbeat and joking but brittle, as though the dust storm had leached her vivacity and left only desiccated undertones. "You must not be too tired, Charlie. You're still working. What's going on tonight? Leveraged buy-out? Surprise IPO?"

Charlie sighed and closed her eyes. The weight of her response seemed to speak for everyone. They were exhausted, and they had no desire to put on a charade, even for Mary Blake. No one stepped into the pause in conversation.

But even a tired Mary Blake couldn't bear empty space. "Annesley, how are you, sugar? You were limping."

Annesley took a breath. Lisa held hers. A light above the adjacent table flickered. Lisa was certain Annesley would reveal her diagnosis after the maelstrom of excitement that day. She had to, because Lisa's double deception was swirling inside, and she didn't think she could contain it any longer without bursting.

Face placid, Annesley ran her fingers across the chain of her necklace. "Just sore from that crash."

"Annesley," Lisa pushed down the boiling of her own secret as she attempted to extract her friend's. "Don't you think—"

"I know I'm not the only one who's sore." Annesley folded and unfolded her paper napkin and managed the barest of smiles. "We can't let a little car crash ruin our trip."

Lisa tried to force her face into placidity but managed only an awkward twitch.

"A car crash *ended* our first trip," Charlie said, causing another twitch.

Mary Blake rushed to blunt Charlie's statement, her words spilling like water from an overturned bucket. "But that one wasn't our fault. Parker had never driven your car, and the wiring was bad. It was an accident. Even so, if we'd been more—"

Lisa blurted, "It wasn't Parker," at the same time Charlie said, "It wasn't the car."

Their words floated above the table like a clump of helium balloons. Other words, fancy lawyer words like "liquidated damages," flashed in front of Lisa's eyes. The others looked past Charlie's comment—they'd heard her defense of the car before—and leaned in to stare at Lisa.

"Of course it was Parker," Annesley said. "What do you mean, Lisa?" She looked to Mary Blake for confirmation. Mary Blake, for a change, said nothing.

Lisa was shaking her head, trying to redirect their attention from her words. She didn't want to see their reaction, their rejections, their judgment that she was never one of them. But Charlie's focus had sharpened, and her eyes reflected vindication and validation that it hadn't been her brother's car that caused the crash. It hadn't, after all, even though that was the story the Harrisons and their bought-and-paid-for police chief had told. Lisa didn't want to look at Helen, the only other one of them who'd been in the car, but she did. Helen's look of pure horror poured ice water on the fire inside Lisa, and her stomach rolled with icy explosions.

"It was in the paper." Mary Blake's face twisted in confusion. "Parker was driving, and the car malfunctioned. The Harrisons said it. You said it."

Lisa's words came out fully formed, but still somehow out of her control. "No, I didn't. I didn't say anything." That was exactly why she shouldn't have come on this trip and why none of them would ever want to see her again. Now they were all looking at her, in the corner booth of an emptying restaurant. She felt herself shrinking, like she'd done when Clayton Harrison and Glenn Whiteford, Esquire, had cornered her in her hospital bed. "I don't want to pull you guys into this."

"Lisa," Annesley said, grasping Lisa's hand, "what are you talking about?"

Charlie regarded Lisa with curiosity and a touch of skepticism, Mary Blake with utter confusion. Helen's face revealed nothing but trepidation. No knowledge, only fear. No warning, only something dark and deep.

At the table next to theirs, the bus boy wiped down the booth. Lisa closed her eyes and let herself return to Texas.

# Chapter Forty-Three
# 1999
# Lisa

With Lisa and Helen in the back of the Scout and Tripp in the passenger seat, Parker pulled away from the carport. He took it slowly, testing the car like it was a newly broken horse. The engine growled.

"Easy, girl." He shifted into a higher gear.

Parker took a sharp turn out to the road, and Helen, head lolling, smashed into Lisa. She rubbed her face and looked at her hand as if she just discovered she had fingers.

"Yeah, easy, girl." Lisa put her arm around Helen and felt their hair twist together in the wind. Warm and dry, the air wicked all moisture from her cheeks, a cleansing renewal.

Fidgeting in the passenger seat, Tripp slapped the dashboard like a conga drum. "My turn, little brother."

Parker obliged, downshifting and stopping in the middle of the road. Parker had only had a few beers, but Tripp was saturated and flying high. At any other time, a flat "No, thank you, leave me here by the side of the road" from Lisa would have been appropriate. But a black sky pierced with pinpricks of light engulfed them. There were no streetlights and no headlights ahead or behind. They were alone in an open space where even a child would be safe behind the wheel.

Parker leaned into the back seat. "Helen."

Helen squinted at Parker, one eye closed. "Is it rally time?"

He laughed, and the sound pierced Lisa's heart like Cupid's arrow, pinning her to the car. "Exactly. Rally time. Mind if I..." He gestured toward Lisa.

"Okay!" Helen shouted as if to invoke sobriety.

After Helen took the passenger seat, and Parker hopped into the back, Tripp peeled out, sending a shudder through the Scout. Parker put his arm around Lisa, sparking a different kind of shudder that nearly made Lisa forget where she was.

"Let's take this baby off road."

Tripp's words made it to Lisa's ears, but they were overshadowed by the sound of blood swooshing and a heart beating. Tripp took off into the black desert just as Parker pulled Lisa in for a kiss.

When Lisa first opened her eyes in the hospital, antiseptic cleaner and a faint odor of blood muffled a fuzzy recollection of the smell of burning rubber mixed with gasoline. The IV stand next to her pinned her between a privacy screen and a bare white wall.

"Welcome back." Charlie stood beside a chair near the window, her face inscrutable but her voice filled with relief.

Lisa vaguely remembered pain and red and—"Where am I?"

A woman in blue scrubs placed her hand on Lisa's arm, quieting her. Her feathery voice defied the gravity pulling the walls in on Lisa. "Focus on yourself right now, sweet thing. You're getting some medication to help you get back to sleep and manage the pain. Push that button if you need anything." She wrote something on a chart and exited the room.

Lisa's eyes connected with Charlie's, and Lisa stammered as she tried to choose between apologies and questions.

A low voice interrupted her. "May I have a moment with your friend?" A police officer stood near the doorway. He held a cowboy hat in his hand.

Charlie hesitated, eyed the officer warily, and left.

The officer placed his hat on a stool. "Jett Phillips, county police. We haven't been able to get any information from the others. Parker Harrison used the CB to radio for help, but he was unconscious by the time we arrived. The other two, whether from the alcohol or the concussions, don't remember anything past leaving the Ranch Hand. Can you tell me what happened out there?"

She reflexively attempted to sit up and winced at the pain shooting through her shoulder. "Out—what? Is everyone okay? I need to know."

The officer peered out the doorway then back at Lisa. "The girl and Tripp are just banged up. Parker..." He peered out the doorway again, and all feeling in Lisa's limbs disappeared. "Parker isn't going to make it. He never regained consciousness, and he just lost too much blood. The doctors said—"

Tripp's father barged into the room, his broad shoulders menacing in proportion to the meek privacy screen. "Jett, what's happening?" His voice, heavier than the hospital air, filled the room. "The nurse told me this one's awake." He looked at the officer with suspicion.

"Sir, I was asking this young lady what happened. Doing my job. Don't you think you should be with your fam—"

"Your *new* job, and based on the slow response to the ranch tonight, it might be your former job." Mr. Harrison's eyes narrowed, and he glared at Lisa. "Go on."

Lisa retraced the night, trying to find where the end to it had started, her head spinning over the news about Parker. She'd just been with him, and he couldn't be gone. They'd returned from the bar, and Annesley had stormed into the house. Helen had rallied, and Parker had kissed Lisa. Those soft lips. Then Tripp had suggested they head out.

"We went out to patrol the ranch," she said.

The officer shot a dubious look at Mr. Harrison, who stared more fully at Lisa in response, his eyes reddening with emotion.

It sounded ridiculous now. Lisa touched the IV needle in her arm and pushed it until it stung. "Tripp wanted to take the Scout. Oh—"

The full scope of events flooded her mind in a jumble. A sky full of stars, warm wind in her hair, Parker's arm around her in the back seat, a scream, a tree in the headlights, the smell of gasoline. Lisa jerked her arm at the realization buzzing through her brain, and pain shot from her shoulder to her wrist. She lost focus on the two men in the room.

The officer stepped closer to the bed. "Can you tell me who was driving? You were the only one still in the car when we arrived on the scene. Smart to wear a seatbelt."

Mr. Harrison stared down at her. The glint in his eyes caused the hairs to stand up on Lisa's neck.

"Tripp. Tripp was driving."

Mr. Harrison's face seemed to grow even larger, and its angry flush heated the room. Lisa's heart pounded, and she could see the heart-rate monitor responding, red lights blinking. She wondered how fast her heart would have to beat for the monitor to explode.

Mr. Harrison pushed around the officer. "Are you sure about that?" he sputtered. "It wasn't your little friend? She had a blood alcohol content of point eighteen." He looked agitated, out of place. The gregarious man who had raised a toast to "pretty girls" at dinner was not the man standing in front of her. The two men stood between her bed and the door like sentries.

"Yes, I'm sure. I mean, Helen couldn't drive a stick. None of us could. Charlie was the only one. Tripp said he'd show us the ranch.

I-I guess he'd been drinking too much, and we crashed." More memories flashed. "There was a tree." Her eyes filled with tears. "Where is Helen? Can I see her?"

Mr. Harrison's face went from red to purple. "This is bullshit, Jett. A bunch of drunk kids. Let's wait and talk with her when she's sobered up. Someone needs to pay for this."

"Her toxicology report was clean, Mr. Harrison. The only one." The officer slid to his left, partially blocking Mr. Harrison, and locked his eyes with Lisa's. "Anything else he'd been doing? Tripp, that is?"

Lisa remembered the baggie of coke in Tripp's pocket. Mr. Harrison cleared his throat. Someone in royal blue ran past the open doorway. Then Mrs. Harrison rushed by, accompanied by Annesley, who glanced in at Lisa, her eyes red.

The officer's radio crackled, and a garbled voice mentioned a code something or other. The officer lowered his voice. "Mr. Harrison, can I accompany you to the ICU?"

A flicker of pain passed over Mr. Harrison's face. With a glance at Lisa, he recovered, nostrils flaring and chest heaving. He didn't leave the room without a final look at Lisa. The look was not a reassuring, paternalistic one. "For now, you remember nothing."

She didn't want to remember anything. If she could forget, maybe it wouldn't have happened. All she'd wanted at that point was to close her eyes and wake up in Los Angeles.

# Chapter Forty-Four
# 2019
# Lisa

As Lisa told the story in the restaurant's dark corner, no one else spoke. She had yet to look at their faces. "The meds must have knocked me out again. When I woke up, Mr. Harrison was there with his lawyer and a non-disclosure agreement." Never had she said those words. And those words must have been the only thing inside her, because now that she'd set them free, she was a hollow shell.

She would have imagined that pouring out her story would be cathartic, a cool shower on a hot day. But it was a dust storm filled with guilt and a growing awareness of what she'd done. "Oh my God." Her hand flew to her mouth. But it was too late to put the words back. She didn't want to look at what she knew would be four sets of judging, hateful eyes. But she did.

Instead of reprobation, she saw confusion and concern. They looked more in shock than they had in the Escalade after the storm-chaser incident. Helen's face slackened in the shadows.

"Oh, Lisa. I wish you'd talked to us," Mary Blake said, as if it would have been easy.

Mary Blake had been safe in her room at the ranch, nursing her argument with Annesley. Now Annesley was the one lying. Lisa would have laughed if she had anything other than emptiness inside her.

"No one came to see me at the hospital. Not after Charlie left the room. I was in there with the lawyer and Mr. Harrison all by myself." She heard the self-pity mixed with accusation in her voice.

"The night was a blur," Annesley explained. "I think they said you were sleeping and we needed to leave you alone. And then... Parker..."

"I can't believe... I mean, they said Parker was driving." Charlie's face was flat, but her words sounded confused rather than judgmental. Still, Lisa knew where she was going. She didn't understand why Lisa would have let Parker take the fall, why she would have thrown a dead boy under the bus.

Lisa hastened to explain. "I couldn't have predicted when I signed the NDA that they would blame Parker." Suppressed anger mixed in with her words, and her stomach twisted at the thought of Mr. Harrison grieving while forcing her to sign the NDA. Her voice weakened, and the first tear fell. "After... after I found out, I told myself they'd already lost a son, and they didn't want to lose the other." It had made sense in a perverted, privileged way.

"Or they were just heartless bastards," Charlie said.

"Oh, Lisa. You've been carrying this for twenty years?" Mary Blake looked like she was going to cry on Lisa's behalf.

Lisa had little else to lose with this group, and her words spilled. "You know what's pathetic? They only paid me thirty-five thousand dollars to sign the NDA." A sound filled with mirth and disgust escaped her. "That probably makes me look like a fool. But it was a fortune to me. It was nothing to them to protect the family. And now I have a reporter calling me. A fucking reporter. Tripp—soon to be senate-candidate Harrison—has a history, and people are investigating." She buried her face in her hands. "I don't know what I'm going to tell Zander. I shouldn't have told you."

"Of course you should have." Mary Blake's soothing tone tugged at Lisa's heart, but the barbs of the NDA held tight.

"No. If reporters or political opponents find anything, it's going to pull us all in. Pick your female witness to a politician's past acts and look how that turned out. I am so sorry. So, so sorry." Numbness crept beneath her skin, a weightlessness reminiscent of isolation and exile.

Mary Blake placed her hands on the table. "It'll all be fine. I promise. We're all in this together. Delta Rhoadies. We'll figure this out—"

"Mary Blake," Charlie said, "Delta Rhoadies was a two-week thing two decades ago. And before that, we attended parties together for a few years. We were placeholders. You can't fix everyone's problems with a sprinkle of fairy dust."

Helen, who had been silent through Lisa's story, stared hard at Charlie. "Is that all we were to you? Placeholders?" Her voice caught on the last word.

Charlie's silence lasted a beat too long for Helen, who fled the bar.

"That's not... I didn't mean... fuck." Charlie threw down a twenty and went after Helen.

"Should we go too?" Mary Blake asked.

Annesley, whose own secret still burrowed through Lisa's conscience, stilled Mary Blake with her hand. "Yes, but let's give them a minute."

Lisa shrank into her seat, relieved that attention had been pulled away from her but unable to measure the distance between herself and the others. She hadn't thought about how bringing this up might affect Helen, the only other one of them who'd been in the car.

# Chapter Forty-Five
# 1999
# Helen

After the crash, in the syncopated flicker of fluorescent hospital lighting, Helen had lain splinted, bandaged, and hooked up to an IV when Charlie entered the room.

"You okay?" Charlie gestured toward the bandage on Helen's head. Charlie's hair hung loose, and her T-shirt and shorts looked like she'd pulled them from the bottom of a duffel bag.

"Thirteen stitches. Did you hear about Parker?" Helen blinked hard. Her brain wasn't working properly yet. She knew what the cops told her they'd found at the scene, but when she tried to recall anything from the crash, her memory played tricks and snuck in dim patches from a different night, one she'd pushed into the deep dark.

Charlie nodded. "I haven't heard much, but I heard that."

"I don't—" Confusion still clouded Helen's head. "I remember being at the house when we got back from the bar, but not much after that. Were you with us?"

"No, Helen. Jesus, I didn't go out with you. I came here with Tripp's parents."

"Charlie, I am so sorry about your car."

"What do you mean? Brent's car?"

"No one told you?"

"No. Told me what?"

"It's totaled." The words were a whisper, and the only way Helen knew she had made a sound at all was that Charlie's eyes flooded.

"I don't understand." Charlie shook her head like she was trying to erase the world. "I left the Scout in the carport. How would you have gotten the keys?" The realization unfolded across Charlie's face as quickly as remorse prickled Helen's gut.

Helen had retrieved the keys from the front seat where she had put them after Charlie told her she planned to leave Texas without her.

Charlie fought tears with a halting breath. "What the *fuck*, Helen?" The words blew into the room like shattered glass. Charlie's reddening face and manic eyes made her look like she could explode.

Helen's disorientation swirled. "You're worried about a car? We're in a hospital."

"Exactly. And Parker is dead because he bled out when *you guys* crashed my car."

The tornado in Helen's chest paused, as if to harness power from the emotion released by Charlie. When the paralysis released, it didn't transform into pain or apology. It turned into anger, a thick, pernicious heat that emerged from somewhere deep, somewhere Helen usually avoided. "Your car. Your trip. You. You. You. This trip has been all about you!" Tears welled in her eyes, but the tension in her face wouldn't let them fall.

"Me? All about me? Are you kidding?" Charlie stepped closer to the bed, and the thrust of her words hit with brute force. Helen's head pounded with each syllable.

Helen squeezed her eyes closed and pushed words out like punches of her own. "Your route. Your disappearing act. Your snide comments. Your tirades. Your broken fucking car!" She opened her eyes and dared Charlie to look away. "Brent is gone. And yes, it's sad, horrible, tragic, devastating. He's gone. But you need to focus on who's still here." She inhaled, and the whirlwind stopped.

"He was all I had."

The ensuing standoff lasted mere seconds, but it felt as heavy as a lifetime, a lifetime of Helen being nothing to Charlie, of Charlie considering herself and herself alone.

"Can't you think about someone else for one moment, Charlie?"

"You need to look at yourself before lashing out, Helen. You've seen this whole trip as a way to avoid being an adult. I can't be your babysitter anymore. And getting blackout drunk clearly isn't working for you."

Hatred was the only word that could describe the taste in Helen's mouth, a bitter, salty, iron-filled taint. Charlie stood posed in frozen animation, her mouth half-open, eyes wide.

"I don't know what you're looking for, Charlie. But it's not here." Helen turned her head away.

Charlie left the ranch before Helen signed out of the hospital.

# Chapter Forty-Six
# Helen
# 2019

Helen stood at the canyon's edge. In the dark, it was as if the chasm didn't exist. One step, though, and it would swallow you.

She'd thought this trip would take her back to a time when she'd put That Night out of her mind and allow her to find the fork in the path she'd missed on the last trip. Helen knew Charlie's words at the bar came from anguish and not vitriol. Lisa's story had caused Charlie to lose a piece of her brother all over again. But still, those words had pierced the flimsy membrane that remained of Helen's bubble.

That they had been friends for only four years was true. But Charlie was wrong. They hadn't been placeholders. At what point did a friendship count? They could have been together for four decades, four months, or four days. A friendship counted when it caused a ripple, when it nudged a person forward. Placeholders were ephemeral and disposable.

The Delta Rhos had been milestones, markers of a journey, of a place they'd been and of places they were going. Solid columns of granite.

Charlie's lean form eased up next to Helen, and a light breeze whispered across Helen's bare arms. Helen and Charlie had always been best when quiet, when words weren't what was needed. Words opened wounds. Words hurt. Helen touched the diagonal scar on her temple.

Charlie had not been a placeholder, and she knew it. She'd been bedrock. Helen had leaned on that foundation in college. When Charlie had decided in Texas to go off on her own, Helen had lost her footing.

And that led to a joyride, a decision with consequences that had wrapped razor wire around Helen's heart and pulled until all that remained in her chest was bloody pulp.

After the ranch, she'd dropped New York and clung to her childhood home, then Derek and, more than occasionally, a bottle of wine. Always someone or something that made her feel like she wasn't going to fall off the planet.

Mary Blake, Lisa, and Annesley approached, concern etched on their moonlit faces. With the five of them standing inches from each other and the edge of a natural wonder, that past and that separation felt as close as it felt distant.

Helen wrapped her arms around her chest. "Charlie, what happened? To us."

"I was an asshole," Charlie said.

"Well, that was easy." Helen laughed and held back tears. "Seriously, though. It didn't need to end like that."

"I failed you."

Helen's arms fell to her sides. "No, you didn't. I never should have taken the keys. You had every right to be angry."

"Not like that. I was angry. But I wasn't angry at you." Charlie kept her eyes focused on the darkness in front of them, as if the answers lay within. "I think the only thing I knew how to do was to blow things up so there was nothing left behind."

The breeze picked up, drawing goose bumps across Helen's arms. "I told myself I deserved what you said. If I hadn't gone out that night, if I hadn't downed all those shots, if I hadn't handed over the keys..." *If I hadn't drunk so many beers at the beach party. If I had gotten in the car with Lisa to go back to the condo. If I'd fought harder, screamed "no" louder. If I'd been sober enough to remember if I'd fought or screamed at all.* So many little things, simple things. "The Scout would still be here. We would have finished the trip. Parker wouldn't have—"

"Stop." Charlie's voice was insistent.

Helen hadn't forgotten the other three were there. Their collective warmth grounded her.

"I hated you," Helen said. A tear rolled down her cheek, and the salt tightened her skin.

"You deserved to. I said horrible things."

"I didn't hate you for saying what you said. I hated you... I hated you because you left." The tears flowed. "And now I'm a mess."

Charlie laughed softly. "You're not a mess, Helen. Your singing, maybe. Has Derek heard that audible catastrophe? If not, I recommend keeping it that way."

Helen pictured Derek brushing sawdust off his pants and beaming as he showed off the results of their renovations. Always building something, making it better. Derek's words whispered through the darkness. "You have to let me in."

An elderly man walked by and nodded at the women. He wore white orthotic shoes and shuffled with a slight stoop. Helen longed for Charlie to ask what his story was, to free her from the crevice she'd fallen into. She already had the answer, and it involved Corgis and Facebook and rediscovering lost love.

As Charlie opened her mouth to speak, Helen prepared her response.

Charlie asked, "What's Helen's story?" and all the air rushed from Helen's lungs.

If she turned to see the others, she would fall. And yet, their presence behind her was what kept her standing.

Helen stared off into the blackness and tried to picture her first-year college self in the distance. The story game had been a trick to mold the unknown into something approachable. Teachers raised in zoos, ferret aficionados, Clint Eastwood movies, transplanted Manhattanites.

Charlie, her body angled toward Helen protectively, was not seeking a deflection.

The other three moved to Helen's right, forming a line, but she didn't turn her head. The floral notes of Mary Blake's perfume lifted her heart, helped take her back.

Helen stared ahead, grateful for the blackness. "She's a girl who grew up playing Sudoku and listening to country music. She went to college, met some great friends, and sometimes even sang. Catastrophically, or so I hear." She nudged Charlie with her elbow, and the others allowed themselves a soft chuckle.

Their freedom to laugh unlatched something inside of her. "One night, she insisted on staying at a party when her friend left. She kept drinking, and when she woke up, she realized she'd been..." She'd never said it, never used the word. Why, she didn't know. Whatever force had kept things in the deep dark released, though, and the sounds combined on her tongue for the first time. "Raped."

Helen heard the gasps beside her and felt the shift in gravity as the five drew closer together. But the others said nothing, intuiting, perhaps, that she didn't want to hear platitudes.

What surprised her was that her own words continued to form, as if the jumbled strands in her mind were transforming into a map she could only follow by reading it out loud and trusting it would lead her to her destination. "She didn't know who. She didn't report it. But she told her best friend, and her best friend was there for her, and so were the others, even if they didn't know."

Not talking about it back then had tricked her into thinking she'd moved on. Brent's death had provided a new focus, followed by dreams of a shared apartment in Manhattan then planning a road trip.

Helen set her hand on Charlie's. Charlie squeezed and didn't let go. The warmth of five bodies filled the space. She imagined being them, the ones who were hearing this for the first time. Why had she thought people would judge her? She wouldn't have judged.

Annesley regarded her with the concern of a mother, the concern Helen would show if Josh were injured. And Mary Blake bit her lip as if it was all she could do to keep herself from flinging her tiny body toward Helen and squeezing her. The thought of a Mary Blake embrace both steeled her and brought warm tears to her eyes.

"I don't know when I started unraveling. I stayed in Richmond after the trip. It was easier than New York. I had my family. Then Derek and I got together, and I thought I left everything behind." After the crash, she'd suppressed it all.

But the shame had been wearing away at her from within, finding fissures and seeping out with a path of destruction that led to her outburst at her dad's party and after Josh's accident and in countless regrettable moments with Derek and lost moments with herself. "I thought this trip would help me reset."

"You haven't told Derek?" Charlie asked.

Helen shook her head. If she'd told him, he'd have seen the hollowness, the naiveté, the mistakes. And she'd lashed out at him in a mock show of strength. Only now did she realize, with these women standing next to her, caring and not judging, loving and not shaming, that opening up might have been the strongest thing she could do.

Helen inched closer to the canyon's edge and inhaled in the ancient air until she couldn't take in any more.

"Helen." Charlie's voice was soft with emotion and edged with determination. "I should have insisted on reporting it or encouraging you to find help."

"No. It was my fault, my decision."

"Your decision to keep information private, yes. But here's the deal. What happened at the beach was not your fault." Charlie looked into Helen's eyes. "You will never, ever be alone."

Helen bit her lip. She believed that. From Derek to Josh to the rest of her family in Richmond to this family standing with her in Arizona, she knew it was true. The air filled her lungs. When she couldn't hold it in any longer, she opened her mouth and screamed. The blackness engulfed the sound with only the barest of an echo reaching the rim. She screamed again, pushing her voice into the rocky crevices she couldn't see.

Helen squeezed Charlie's hand. She looked to her left and right to see all of them, hand in hand, from Charlie to Helen to Lisa to Annesley to Mary Blake. They all opened their mouths, and their screams wove into one.

# Chapter Forty-Seven
# 2019
# Lisa

They lingered at the canyon's edge, and no one seemed to want to let go. But the truth was they were tired.

Lisa trailed as the five made the short walk back to the hotel. After twenty years, revelations were inevitable, but the night had contained one after the other, from Mary Blake's relative breakdown to Helen's breakthrough to Lisa's broken mess. Annesley, her own secret undisturbed, limped but hid it well.

"We'll be right up," Annesley called to the others as they ascended the steps to the El Tovar entrance.

Lisa braced herself for a dressing down. For the lying, for her role in the night at the ranch, for ruining this trip by revealing her disgrace. Helen had granted a momentary reprieve, but Lisa had to face her own truth now that the others had digested what she'd revealed.

A dry thread of resignation wound down her spine, and the air prickled her nose with the smell of ancient dirt. She deserved whatever Annesley wanted to dole out.

"Out there," Annesley said, her words unraveling slowly, "You didn't even flinch when Helen talked about... when she said what happened."

No, she hadn't. She'd collapsed inside, though, for Helen, for the part of herself that had wondered for years if she'd misremembered or misinterpreted Helen and Charlie's conversation, and for the other part of her that had hoped she'd misinterpreted, since she'd done nothing about it. Lisa tried to swallow, but her mouth was too dry.

"You knew. And you didn't tell anyone. We could have helped, been there for her." She didn't sound like she was accusing Lisa of conspiracy. She was just stating that an opportunity had been lost, a hidden path left unexplored.

Lisa rubbed her neck. "It was complicated."

Annesley whispered, "Yeah." She winced and shifted her weight from her right leg to her left.

"You need to get an X-ray," Lisa said with the firmness she used when telling her kids to get off their screens. "Your bones are more susceptible—"

"We were rear-ended today. We're all sore. It's good to have normal aches and pains to focus on." Her eyes, exhausted and pained, said otherwise.

"Please go get some rest. It's been a rough day."

Annesley paused Lisa with a hand on her shoulder. She closed her eyes briefly as if to summon words. "When I was growing up, my mother punished women she thought weren't staying in their place. She would 'forget' to put them on a guest list, or she'd drop a scathing word into a conversation, and it would destroy them. She never expressed regret." Her forehead creased. "I used to believe I should never regret anything."

The light above them flickered, casting Annesley's face in and out of shadow.

"I know better now, but I don't know everything I've done or said that I should regret. I let my brother disappear for years before finally reconnecting. Other things, I can only guess at and hope I didn't leave any lasting damage, hope that I had a far smaller impact on people than I thought I did. What I most regret is not supporting my friends." Her eyes shone. "I'm sorry. I'm sorry about the probation. I'm ashamed of my secrecy and for brushing past what you went through."

Those things were so small that Lisa felt embarrassed at the apology. She opened her mouth to tell Annesley it was okay, but Annesley stopped her.

"No. It's important to me to get this out. I was, still am, too focused on myself. I'm sorry for every comment I ever made that made you feel bad. And I'm sure there were a lot. But I'm most sorry that I didn't support you and the others the way you deserved to be supported. You weren't supposed to be there to make me look good, but that's the way I saw the world."

The weight of Annesley's sincerity weakened Lisa's knees. She leaned against a railing, while Annesley continued to stand in her dancer's conditioned posture.

"And regarding my diagnosis. Thank you for not telling anyone. I'll take care of it soon. I just need a little more time."

Lisa shook her head. "Of course."

"And I'm sorry about making that comment yesterday about your things flying off the roof in Mississippi." Annesley's jaw clenched.

All Lisa could picture was a faded floral sheet flying above a highway like a trailer park ghost, and she smirked. Annesley cocked her head.

"It was humiliating, but it was funny," Lisa admitted.

A young couple walked past, arguing about how to pronounce the hotel's name. El TOE-var—him. El Toe-VAR—her. The woman was right, but the man was insistent.

"About the Tripp situation—" Annesley stopped and pressed her lips together.

Lisa didn't know what to say. She wanted to apologize. Again. Lisa had looked up to Annesley throughout college. Even in the years since, Annesley's stature, her command of moment, had been aspirational. Annesley stood before her in a new light.

Still, Lisa needed guidance. "What should I do about the reporter?"

Instead of forthright direction served with a side of condescension like her college self would have delivered, Annesley exhaled and gave a weak smile. "I'm still processing what you told us. Tripp driving that night... I mean, I guess it doesn't change the outcome. And the NDA, the reporter, the lawyer. Honestly, I don't know." She winced and rubbed her hip.

Lisa felt a pang of guilt for burdening a cancer patient with her legal fears. "I'll handle it. And apology, apologies, accepted. Now, will you go get some rest? We have a long drive tomorrow."

Lisa lingered alone in the lobby, unable to pull away from the hotel's shadowed corners. She pictured the bear-faced Mr. Harrison who had seen through her twenty years ago. Smoldering anxiety tightened her chest.

Her phone buzzed in her pocket, and she startled. She pulled it out with her eyes closed, but she had to see who'd texted. Zander. She checked the time: eleven thirty. She'd forgotten to check in.

*Zander:* Missed you tonight.

*Lisa:* Sorry! Lost track of time.

*Zander:* Talk to you tomorrow, love. Sleep well. Can't wait to see you.

*Lisa:* Love you too.

She was lying by omission again. An ongoing, chronic erosion. She couldn't be like this.

She thought of the others getting ready for bed after more sharing and emoting than they'd ever had together. And tomorrow, they would be in the Great White Whale together for the last leg, after which... apart? Or maybe not.

Even during college, there had been an ebb and flow. They all left for school breaks and came back together upon return. Boyfriends, course loads, a need to be alone—each pulled one or more of them away in any given semester. But they'd always flowed back to the five of them.

They were together again, and she was ebbing. *Damn that reporter. Damn the Harrisons and their money and their power. Damn herself for making stupid decisions and pulling her friends in on the consequences.*

She thought back to her college self and how she'd always felt like an "other," even when they'd been together. The five of them posing for photos at a frat party, the five of them packing for a tailgate, the five of them eating wraps under one of the ancient oaks on campus. They hadn't excluded her. She hadn't been on the outside. She'd never been on the outside.

The other girls had launched a two-thousand-mile trek across the country to help get her where she was going. She felt that sense of belonging, of joining hands and merging voices. They hadn't kicked her out or thrown her over the canyon's edge. They'd embraced her.

The time now called for her voice alone. And her voice, her words, held danger.

She had to handle the Tripp situation. The Harrisons didn't know she'd told anyone, and she trusted her friends. But that wasn't where the risks lay.

The possibilities flashed before her like she was flipping cable news channels: A phone call from a reporter telling her they'd connected her to the car that crashed. A news team interviewing an embittered Texas cop who'd kept his old notes, "just in case." Phone calls to her home and the medical office from opposition researchers and the news outlets desperate for a scandal to drive ratings. Her kids mocked at school. Her husband hurt by her lack of trust in him.

Even if she kept her mouth shut, the existence of a woman, a physician no less, who had a connection to the death of a rising politician's brother and who was paid to keep her mouth shut would be shark bait. Lisa had no chance of emerging professionally or personally intact.

If she went on the record, there would be a lawsuit. They would have to sell the house, sell the cars, stop sending money home to Mom and Dad, and declare bankruptcy. Added to that was the prospect of being the face on the television in front of a microphone if she did speak out against the Harrisons and expose their lies. She would be tarred as the shrew, the whore, the liar, the thief. They would make of her what they wanted. She'd seen it done before to any number of women. No politician or powerful man, and certainly not Harrison, would let a woman challenge his climb to the top without crushing her publicly until there was nothing left to salvage.

And if the reporters or the opposition couldn't get to her, or if she wasn't enough for them, it was a tiny step to link her presence on the ranch to each of the women upstairs in their hotel rooms.

She had so much and hadn't acknowledged it. She would never say she'd risen. That was pretentious. But she'd built a life, a family, a career, and a passion for living. She had things to love and to lose.

She activated her phone, opened the web browser, and started typing, "Tripp Harrison campaign manager."

# Chapter Forty-Eight
# 2019
# Charlie

Charlie woke up parched and restless from too much talk, too much emotion, and too much everything the night before. The clock read 4:20 a.m. She slipped into a pair of shorts and a T-shirt, put on her running shoes, and pulled the door closed behind her. Bypassing the hotel staff and the orange half-moons of light reflected by fixtures on the walls in the lobby, she snuck out into the still-dim morning.

Why she'd thought she could avoid emotional bombs on this trip, she wasn't sure. Those emotional concussions could crush plans and goals, like they had last time when she'd let emotions overrun everything. But last night, the bombs hadn't been destructive. If anything, they'd been more like blasts necessary for launch. She pictured Helen on that canyon edge, her face shifting from apprehension and fear to discovery.

The blackness of the canyon that had greeted them the night before took on more of a shape now, as though searching for the sun. She stretched her quads and listened for echoes of last night, for memories reemerging from the crevices in the shadowed canyon. She heard only the crunch of pebbles under her feet.

She'd always thought of herself as strong. Strong enough to resist getting emotional. Strong enough to avoid peer pressure. Strong enough to stand up to the general.

But last night had shown that Helen was the strong one, and Charlie had only made things harder for her by acquiescing to silence and, in the end, pummeling her with words.

Charlie's own life—a sparsely furnished condo, a dog who spent more time with the dog walker than her, employees who stayed out of her way so she could reel in the next big deal—felt as empty as the canyon.

She found the walkway along the edge and decided to run west and let the sun chase her. Her watch told her it was a brisk fifty-one degrees, and the slight chill invigorated her.

It had all started with going west, and here she was again.

Easing in with a measured jog, Charlie took stock of the tightness in her calves and the tension that pulled her shoulders together. Last night's wine seeped out in sweat that evaporated in the desert air almost as soon as it emerged. Perhaps the dryness was what had pulled so much from the women last night.

She still hadn't made sense of Lisa's story. Charlie had always maintained it wasn't the car's fault. But learning Tripp was the driver had upended her. She shook her head. It didn't matter who was driving. Lisa's situation with the NDA, however, *did* matter, and Charlie had a lawyer on staff. She decided to contact the attorney when she got back to the hotel. There were ways around contracts.

She accelerated until her toes felt light on the asphalt and she found a comfortable stride. Pedestrian traffic was light. She nodded at a pair of lean backpackers wearing headlamps, their features barely visible in the moonlight.

With the canyon still shrouded in shadows, Charlie focused on every movement of her body, every sensation. *Breathe in. Breathe out. In. Out.* The power in her shoulders propelled her with each pump of her arms, releasing the tension that had settled in overnight.

She'd been angry with the general for years, though that anger had dulled to an imperceptible din, like the refrigerator you didn't notice was humming until the electricity went out.

The sense she had now, with him lying in the ICU, was a deafening roar of emotion. What emotion, she wasn't sure. Anger, maybe. Or hurt. Both were warranted. Compassion or empathy? She searched and felt blankness in those areas, but she wouldn't have denied those feelings if they arose. Compassion and empathy made sense when one's father lay dying. What she refused to accept was guilt. Not about the general.

The general had engineered a distance between them, and it wasn't Charlie's job to close it. It wasn't her fault he'd been off on some officer junket when her mother died. It wasn't her fault her brother had been shipped off to fight instead of getting a stateside assignment or, better yet, not going into the military altogether in some attempt to emulate his father. The general was the one who should feel guilty.

Needles pierced her shins, and she lengthened her stride. Each inhale pulled in more dry air. Each exhale pushed out... she didn't know what. Some of it had come out as she screamed into the darkness with the others. Whatever it was, she wanted it gone.

The fresh rawness of her throat pushed her even harder. Each desiccated breath reminded her of her body's effort. But the breaths were pulling other thoughts with them: the general on a respirator; the *whoosh, thump, thump* she'd heard in the background of Lillian's phone call last night before Charlie went down to the restaurant; Brent dying in an undisclosed location while Charlie was with the Delta Rhos at some party. She wondered if someone had been with him when he took his last breath.

The two weren't the same, the general and her brother. But the invisible boulder pushing against her chest as she thought about them felt the same.

Her watch clicked—daily exercise goal achieved. She dodged three hikers occupying the path's full width and nearly stumbled toward the canyon side. She considered what that would be like, to fall and to fly. The sense of soaring free and ungrounded sent a jolt of electricity through her chest.

The dry air reminded her of the ranch, the billowing dust of a truck on a back road, and the vacant, absent, parchedness of loss. She accelerated until she could hardly keep up with her feet, and the lightening of the horizon ahead of her showed that the sun would not be outrun that morning.

Then she puked.

Charlie walked the last half mile back, head down, without a glance at the exposed canyon. Near the hotel, she forced herself to stand at the edge where they'd stood the night before. The sun, still at a low angle, bathed the gash in a golden glow, the depths still in darkness. A battle rumbled in her core, like wrestlers angling for a takedown in a space with no room to pivot.

Maybe the blame shouldn't all fall on the general. Maybe he reminded her of her brother, and she resented him for that. Her heart raced like it wanted to run again, down into the canyon this time. But she attended instead to the ghost of that little girl who'd taped the photo of the general to her bed and to the college girl who'd clutched Brent's letters. She would have given anything to have had one last moment with her brother. Perhaps she shouldn't be throwing away the same chance with her father.

An awkward grunt pulled her out of her daze. Annesley stood behind her, wilted at the waist like she had a stomach cramp.

"You all right?" Charlie asked.

Annesley straightened then held up a rock. "Stepped on a rock. There seem to be a lot of them out here."

"Rocks at the Grand Canyon. Huh. Who could have imagined that?" Charlie smiled. Somehow, light banter with Annesley softened the world's edges. "Any of that whiplash Lisa warned us about?"

"I'll be fine. How about you? A morning run must mean you're feeling well."

"I tend to run more when I'm not feeling well." The needles in her shins felt more like daggers now. "But it is getting harder to roll with the punches."

"Damn punches."

They shifted to avoid the backpacks of a group of teens trailing a barking chaperone who already looked tapped.

Charlie peered over the rail-less edge, contemplating the drop as she watched pebbles tumble to a lower ledge. "Can you imagine what it must have been like to come across this for the first time without ever having seen pictures?"

"I don't think photos could possibly do it justice."

Charlie pulled out her phone and checked the screen. No messages from Lillian. She considered taking a photo but slid the phone back in her pocket.

"Expecting a call?" Annesley asked.

Charlie's reflex was to shake her head, but words tumbled out instead. "Yeah. The general. He had a heart attack. I'm still waiting for news. He and I..." She couldn't think of how to explain the chasm between them.

"I remember." Annesley set her hand on Charlie's shoulder. "I'm sorry."

They stood in silence, their own inaction stopping nothing. The sun continued to rise. The air continued to warm.

The moment's ease made Charlie recall their time on Annesley's lake house dock, where water had lapped at the shore, birds had landed and taken flight, and two young women had forged a connection over brothers and skipping rocks.

# THE LAST ROAD TRIP

Charlie ached as if the canyon's power was compressing her into another pebble on the ledge. "This makes me feel like a blip. Here now, gone tomorrow." And seeing this place—the last stop on Brent's list—marked him gone forever. She took in a sharp breath.

Annesley shook her head. "No. Not a blip. This is proof we're forever." She swept the toe of her shoe in an arc across the ground. "Every drop of rain and every piece of dirt whipped by the wind left its mark here. We're not looking at rocks. We're looking at what millions of years of wind and water left behind." She gazed opposite the rising sun, where the shadows still hugged the cliffs.

"What happened with your brother? Last we spoke about him, he was off being the anti-bougie kid."

Annesley laughed. "We reconnected when I—" A troubled look contorted her face then vanished. "He's been a part of the family. My family. My mom still hasn't fully reconnected, but that's her way. She's always been one to hold a grudge. It was important for me to renew the connection. Family's important." She stretched out her arm, positioning the rock she held against the backdrop of the canyon. The sun caught the stone, its brownness unremarkable against the rainbow strata beyond yet unmistakably a part of the whole.

Charlie's phone buzzed and broke the spell. It seemed a violation of the quiet morning, with the sun exposing the history before her. She checked the screen and shared it with Annesley.

*Lillian*: Extubation successful. He's awake.

Annesley grabbed Charlie's hand, pushing the rock into her palm, then walked away without a word.

Charlie stepped back from the ledge. Her heart pounded in slow motion, thick thumps that vibrated in her throat. The colors before her blurred as if in their own time warp. He was awake. He was alive. She blinked to clear the colors before her, and her heart returned to baseline. Her thumb hovered over the call button. She pressed it.

"Charlie, dear. I'm glad you called." Lillian's up-tilted voice defied the early hour.

"How is he?"

"He'd like to talk to you."

"Yes, of course."

In an instant, the canyon seemed small, out of focus, and wavering. Charlie turned and walked toward a spot away from the tourists and their oversized backpacks.

"Charlotte?" The general's voice was rough, older than she remembered. But he still emphasized the second syllable of Charlotte, always pushing her, even when stating her name.

"Hi. How're you feeling?"

"Like I did when I went to Ranger School." He coughed weakly and excused himself to get a sip of water. When he resumed, his voice rumbled like a tank on gravel. "I feel older."

He said it with such contempt that Charlie laughed and felt her chest expand. She turned back toward the canyon. Her distance, even the dozen yards, and the sun's slow but persistent rise provided a new perspective. The colors of the rocks had already changed. Oranges had divided into more oranges, and pinks shone through, dazzling.

He coughed again, lightly. "Lillian tells me you're at the Grand Canyon."

"Yes."

"Your brother always wanted to camp there. Did you camp?"

The fact that he remembered that about her brother brought tears to her eyes, and she laughed. "He did. No, we didn't camp. Maybe I'll come back and do the camping version when I'm not on someone else's schedule."

He laughed. Sadly, she thought. Or maybe it was fatigue from trying to fight off death. She didn't know what sadness sounded like in her father. At Brent's funeral, he'd stood mute in his Class-A uniform, buttons shined until they looked like pure gold. When Charlie had returned for her mother's wake, he'd greeted her with only a nod. She was sure they must have shared some words, but none rose in her memory.

"You and your brother, exactly alike," he mumbled.

She glowed at the comparison despite the tone. "What do you mean?"

"Stubborn, smart, adventurous, independent. But mostly stubborn." He took another sip of water. "When you didn't go to law school, that was like when your brother wouldn't let me line up a prime commission for him. Damned kid was determined to head off to where he could get combat experience."

Charlie pivoted from the pinks and oranges of the rocks. "What? What did you just say?"

It took a couple of beats before he responded. "I said you're stubborn."

"No. After that. About... Brent."

He coughed then took another sip of water. "The commission. He wouldn't let me help him with getting a commission. Something prestigious, safe. Instead of something that would land him in a hot spot. But he had to do his own thing. Like I said, you two are exactly alike. You always were. That time you set up that tent? Goddammit if I expected that."

Charlie's brain spun. She gazed over the forever, her view interrupted by tourists stopping to take selfies. The sun's rays enveloped her, and every pore expanded to take in the liquid warmth. The rock from Annesley pulsated in her hand. She squeezed it tighter.

"Are you there, Charlotte?"

"When I set up that tent, why didn't you take me hunting with you and Brent?"

"You remember that little white dog of yours?" he said.

Her dog. The tennis ball. The screeching brakes. The general had dug the dog's grave while Charlie stood by crying.

"Yes, I remember." It had been mere months before the camping trip. Of course he hadn't wanted her to be exposed to violent death so soon after her grief.

"Why didn't you include me on all the camping trips?"

"I didn't know what to do with you, Charlotte." His voice was scratchy and fatigued. "I wasn't around enough, I know. Maybe I should have made more of an effort. But one thing I always knew is that you'd be able to take care of yourself."

Charlie wound her way back to the canyon's edge. She squeezed Annesley's rock in her fist, thick in the middle and broken at the end. She pushed its angles into her flesh. Its morning coolness had given way to the warmth of her palm, of Annesley's palm before that. "He wanted to see this. The canyon."

"I know. When you made that trip after graduation, you kept him alive for your mom and me through those postcards you sent home. I still have them."

Charlie pictured him paging through the postcards, searching for glimpses of Brent. In her mind, he was smiling. She'd never given him the benefit of a new perspective. She'd always painted him army green and never allowed for him to shine a different color.

"It's beautiful, Dad. I'd FaceTime you so you could see it, but there's no way you'd be able to appreciate it on a screen."

"Don't need to see it. I can hear it in your voice."

Charlie's heart pounded like she'd pushed past her top speed. She felt the swell of blood expanding the muscle beyond its limit. The fact of him hearing something in her voice—hearing her—almost broke her. "I'm not sure how far I am from Phoenix, but we can probably reroute, or maybe I can find a shuttle from here. They must have a shuttle from here. I could be there tonight even."

"Absolutely not." His voice, abrupt, took on a familiar tone, and her heart froze. He started coughing again.

"It's not a problem." She hesitated. Had she misread him? Was she setting herself up for disappointment? "I'll... I'll talk to the concierge."

"Can't you do one thing I ask you to do? For once?" His voice softened. "Finish it for your brother. For me."

There was a blank space in his words, and she wondered if he wanted her to do it for her, as well. "Okay. Our last leg is today. I'll come straight to you when I get back. You'll be there?"

"I better not be *here*. But I'll be here."

"Dad?"

"Yes, Charlotte?"

She had no more words. She did. "I love you."

There was no hesitation at the other end of the line. "I love you too. You were always my little general."

And just like that, she was a child, a teenager, a college student, her life compressed by time like a rock in the canyon.

# Chapter Forty-Nine
# 2019
# Lisa

The drive's last leg took them through the jagged features of western Arizona and into California. They all sat in the forward seats but not to gossip and sing along with the radio, though there had been a bit of that when cell phone service faded out. They sat closer because the revelations had somehow drawn them closer instead of pushing them apart, and they only had one day left together.

"You emailed who about Tripp?" Charlie's eyes bulged with incredulity.

"Whom," Helen said, earning an eye roll from Charlie.

"Tripp's campaign manager." Lisa had tracked down someone she thought might have a plan of action but who wouldn't broadcast the information. "I thought I could threaten to talk, and the campaign could come up with some way to make sure the reporter decided to move on from the story. Redirect, distract, offer something else, whatever it is campaigns do to make sure stories don't see daylight." But last night's blast of pride in her sleuthing succumbed to a bubbling anxiety that if Charlie showed hesitation, Lisa was in over her head. "They do that, right? Bury stories? Was that... Did I totally eff this up?" Heat burned her ears.

"I guess you're going all in." There was pride in Charlie's voice, but it did little to stifle Lisa's anxiety.

Typing the email after screaming on a cliff had come easier than she would have expected. But as the van lumbered into the lower altitudes and higher temperatures along the Mojave, Lisa prayed for overflowing inboxes or, better yet, a mailer-daemon notification winding its way through the ether to notify her the message had been undeliverable.

"Ah, we have service again," Charlie said when her phone buzzed. "Okay, Lisa. I got an email from Amissa, my attorney. I told her about the NDA situation this morning."

Lisa's heart rate didn't budge. A day ago, she would have freaked out about another person knowing about the confidentiality agreement.

"Just the need-to-know stuff. Don't worry." Charlie looked at the screen. "She says you can probably have the NDA voided. You've got duress, material misrepresentation, maybe even false imprisonment—"

"Imprisonment?" Lisa asked.

Charlie grinned. "I might have hyperbolized the part about you being kept in your hospital room away from your friends. Bastards. Amissa knows her shit. I didn't bring her on as chief legal counsel for nothing. The Harrisons have deep pockets and big lawyers, so you want to come to the table with stores of ammunition."

"I don't want to be at a table." She wanted freedom. She wanted to decide for herself what to say and to who—whom—to say it. She leaned her head against the window.

Clouds dotted the sky in puffs of cotton. She counted them like sheep. If they kept driving and never stopped, the bad things stayed at bay: reporters, lawyers, risk.

Charlie elbowed Lisa and squinted out the windshield. "What's going on up there?"

Lisa looked at the cars lining the shoulder. "I don't know."

Helen craned her neck. "Not another dust storm, I hope." She'd told them that she'd already reached out to Derek about counseling. There was a fragile peace about her now, and she seemed ready to take on another dust storm.

Mary Blake turned on the blinker. "I'm going to pull in somewhere, and we can go see. It's time for a wellness break, anyway. But you may need to pee in the ditch in front of all these people."

After Mary Blake wedged the van between an SUV and a Mini Cooper, Lisa climbed out and followed the others past the lineup of cars. The license plates were from all over: California, Arizona, New Mexico, Nevada.

Next to a Jeep Cherokee, a stocky woman in a wide-brimmed hat held a professional-looking camera with a wide-angle lens. She pointed to the right. "There's a super bloom from the recent rains. Incredibly rare, and it could disappear tomorrow."

Purple flowers extended like a shag carpet across the desert floor as far as the eye could see. Lisa had never seen anything more beautiful.

A car ahead, Helen posed for Charlie while Mary Blake and Annesley took a selfie.

Mary Blake hopped back over to Lisa, her ponytail swinging. "Isn't this gorgeous? And I'm wearing the perfect outfit." She posed coyly in her trim white sailor shorts and lavender boatneck T-shirt, which allowed her to stand out against the landscape without contrasting with the stunning violet blooms. "We're going to go up front for a group photo."

Lisa's phone buzzed and she checked the caller ID. "It's Texas. Probably the attorneys calling to tell me to cease and desist." The evenness of her voice cloaked the supernova in her chest.

"Whatever you decide to do," Annesley said, "we've got your back."

Helen and Charlie sidled next to Annesley, and four Delta Rhoadies stood in a line in front of Lisa, like a phalanx ready for battle. She answered her phone and braced herself for the smooth voice of Glenn Whiteford, Esquire.

"If it isn't Lisa Davis." The cocky drawl didn't belong to the lawyer or the female campaign manager she'd emailed.

"Tripp?" Lisa's voice cracked.

"I'm going to cut to the chase, Lisa." The arrogant, easy tone made Lisa's heart beat a hollow, echoing thump that pushed the air out of her lungs. "You signed an NDA. So this email you sent to my campaign manager, and I quote: 'I no longer consider myself bound by the contract. If pushed by the press, I will respond.'" He paused as if she needed to let what she wrote sink in. "Darlin', you have, by virtue of referencing the contract and declaring a breach, violated the NDA. Is that really what you want to be doing?"

The words she'd typed had been pixels on a computer. The idea of living those words hadn't felt real until now. Lisa looked at the other women. She owned this and wouldn't let Tripp take the lead. "Yes, Tripp."

"You won't do that." She could picture his entitled face taking on a condescending cast, eyebrows flat above cold eyes. "If this is an attempt at extortion, you're dealing with the wrong people. Don't make my family destroy you."

"I don't want your money." She would have given back what she'd already taken if she could. Erased everything. But she couldn't erase everything. Someone had died, and the person at fault was on the line. "And you can't destroy me if I have the truth." She tensed every muscle in her body and stood straighter in hopes of generating more powerful words. She started to move her hands to her hips, Wonder Woman-style, but almost dropped the phone from her shoulder. So she settled on a wide stance.

"The truth, darlin', is what's in the official police report. That's all that matters."

The image of Mr. Harrison bulldozing into her hospital room when she told the police officer it had been Tripp driving flashed through her mind.

Tripp bulldozed her memory with a soundbite. "Parker was driving, and the Scout had been jury-rigged with junkyard parts and crashed. It was tragic." He blamed his own brother with such ease.

"You know that's not the truth. I saw the police officer transcribe what I said. Your daddy having the money to destroy those records doesn't change that. Anyway, I don't care. I'll go public. The mere fact that I have an NDA will be damning enough for a family who probably has a thick history of rigging juries."

"Darlin', you can't afford it. You will get ripped to shreds if you get pulled into the spotlight. I know your situation: mortgaged to the hilt, a husband whose job is more of a hobby. And you still send money to support your parents, right? Do you think your marriage can survive bankruptcy? And think of the professional damage a medical professional would suffer for covering up something like this. You may think you're being a big girl right now, but have you actually changed from all those years ago? When you followed Annesley and the others around like some lovesick puppy, desperate for anything they might toss out to make you feel like more than an unmemorable charity case?"

"I don't care." Her voice quavered, though. He was right. She *had* craved that acknowledgement.

And she'd felt that thrill of inclusion when Mary Blake had called to invite her on this trip. But even if Tripp was right about her need for acceptance, he wouldn't be able to comprehend what she saw before her in her phalanx of women. They embraced her.

She looked out over the super bloom, one they wouldn't have seen had they taken a different route or driven a different day. The violet carpet contrasted with the black void in the canyon the night before.

Helen's screams echoed in her mind. As did Lisa's own inaction. She could have stopped everything that night at the ranch.

Her stance faltered, and she flexed her quads to lock in. "When they find out you were driving... Wait. Which is worse? That you were driving full of liquor and cocaine or that your family covered it up?"

"Darlin'—"

"Stop. Fucking. Calling. Me. Darlin'."

Shocked amusement took over the faces of the other women. Charlie's mouth hung open, and Mary Blake clenched her fist in you-go-girl encouragement. She'd surprised herself as well. The scene filled her with fire, and her feet pushed into the ground like she was a vector for every force contained beneath the earth's crust.

"I wasn't finished, Tripp." Lisa spat his name. "Anything else out there you might be just a tiny bit worried about surfacing? Who else might come out of the shadows if I do? If I show just one gruesome thing your family has covered up for you for years? I know your daddy has the police and God knows who else on the payroll, but the reporters will keep poking around until something shakes loose. They're already digging into old hospital records. I'm sure it wasn't the first time your daddy covered for you or paid someone off. You even said we wouldn't believe some of the shit you've gotten away with. 'It's the Harrison way,' right?"

"It was a long time ago. Memories fade. Your mind plays tricks. You'll sound like a pathetic middle-aged woman desperate for attention."

She refused to let his words slice her open. "Do you remember the attending physician's name? I do. The day nurse's? I do. The police officer's? All of that will check out. It will be hard to trip me up. I can be super helpful with reporters or opposition researchers. I have relived that twenty-four hours on an infinite loop."

"I can't be responsible for something my father did or didn't do. And I can say whatever I want about that night. Hell, it could have been you driving that car." Tripp's voice sounded more defensive than condescending.

"I was sitting the back seat and wearing a seatbelt."

"It could have been Helen."

"She couldn't drive a stick. For God's sake, now you're the one who sounds desperate. Here's the deal, Tripp. You can have all my money if you want to go after me for breach of contract. But as you apparently already know, there's not much for you to take. Call off your attorney. I'm ready to answer questions if it comes to it. Texas loves political scandals, and this should do wonders for the Harrison family name and your web of family business arrangements, like that fracking contract in front of the regulatory agency right now."

"I see you've been doing your research. But you have no idea what you're up against."

"Oh, but I do." She grasped Mary Blake's outstretched hand. "And I have people who will have my back. How about you? I can picture the headline: Senate Wannabe Killed Brother and Lied So Brother Took the Blame for Crash. How's that for a news channel scroll? How about everything your daddy has done? Who will continue to take your calls? Who will let you see your children more than every other weekend after your wife decides your scandal is getting her shunned by the Junior League and leaves you?"

She closed her eyes and took a leap with her feet planted more securely on the ground than she could ever remember. "I will be referring future press calls to your attorney. Or… maybe I'll answer their questions. I don't know yet. Most importantly, I will make my own decision on this. You and your family no longer have any control."

"You wouldn't risk it." He didn't sound as confident as he had at the beginning of the call.

"Try me... darlin.'" She clicked off her phone. She was trembling with anger and excitement. The power coursing through her needed an outlet.

The other girls looked at her expectantly. Annesley stretched out a hand. They were waiting, holding a spot for her because they had always been stronger together.

# Chapter Fifty
# 2019
# Annesley

Three hours after Lisa out-bloomed the flowers in the desert, Annesley alone seemed weighted into her seat, her bones feeling chalky beneath her skin as they navigated I-10 through LA.

Annesley knew Lisa had idolized her in college. Bestowing confidence by mere proximity had given Annesley purpose. She hadn't expected Lisa's admiration to last into adulthood. But back in the lobby of Rancho Verde, which seemed a million miles and as many years ago, Lisa's visible calculation of Annesley's clothing and hair had telegraphed the doctor's reconsideration of every choice she'd made when she packed for the trip. And that had caused Annesley to revert to the comfort of her younger self. She'd taken advantage of Lisa to ease her own sense of powerlessness. There was a fine line between sharing a confidence as a sign of trust and telling a secret as a mode of control, and Annesley had grasped control by telling her secret to a compliant Lisa.

Mary Blake, her hands at ten and two on the giant steering wheel, had regained her spark. She turned up the radio and sang along, bobbing her head like she was recording a TikTok. She'd pulled off this trip, all five of them in California and Frank in the rearview mirror. In a sense, Annesley's job was done. But they still had one last night, and Annesley needed to tell her, all of them really, before she flew home for her port surgery. And then chemo. But how? Cancer with sunset? Lies with breakfast? Guilt at withholding the truth ate at her insides like rust dissolving metal.

Lisa's raspy alto joined in with Mary Blake's lilted soprano, and Annesley took a picture of them singing into their invisible microphones.

Annesley formulated her plan between Monterey Park and Culver City, while Lisa showed off photos of her kids and Charlie changed flight plans and figured out how to set up an out-of-office message so she could visit her father.

Everyone knew Annesley had been limping. Only Lisa knew the doctors had seen the tell-tale shadows in the images that proved cancer had infiltrated her bones.

Under any other circumstance when there had been a car crash and she had this pain, it would be perfectly reasonable to get an X-ray. While Mary Blake gossiped about her Hollywood encounters, Annesley googled and found an urgent care center in Malibu. She would see the doctor, get the X-ray results, and tell everyone the doctor had discovered the cancer had returned. They would then know the truth but not that she'd hidden it from them, balance restored. Annesley shifted in her seat and grimaced. No position comforted her.

"Thirty-five more minutes," Helen said.

Thirty-five minutes to absorb the plan and neutralize the guilt. Thirty-five minutes to think about what brought them here, what brought her to a passenger van on an LA freeway with women from a distant past who had somehow given her hope.

At the end of the last trip, Annesley had spent months, years even, processing what had happened and where that left her. The last road trip—the good and the bad—had exposed more about herself than she could have ever seen in a mirror, as if fate had granted her the gift of seeing through the eyes of Charlie and Luke and Lisa.

She'd left the Harrison ranch midday, after Tripp was released from the hospital, and she felt only a hollow blandness in the place of what she'd thought was love. A southwestern wind blew so strong that the flags in front of the house cracked as they whipped. The other girls had already left, and the last person Annesley saw was Tripp's mother.

Mrs. Harrison stood in the open doorway, wearing a cotton dress, its pure white a bold stand against the elements and the dark circles under her eyes. The dress fluttered in the hot wind and molded to her stooped frame. Her grief obliterated Annesley's heart. This woman who had greeted her with an icy hand was an empty vessel. Annesley sympathized with her for the loss of her son and for the loss of joy Annesley assumed had happened years or decades before.

Then it struck her. Mrs. Harrison was Annesley's mother. She was any number of women who had enjoyed a cocktail at her mother's garden parties. Those women would leverage any opportunity to control others in an attempt to fill emptiness.

On the trip, outside her mother's framework, Annesley'd had the potential to be full color. Messy, lovely, mean, exuberant, wrong. She'd been free to feel the hurt and the love, and most of all, she had the possibility of being content in life. It only now occurred to her that her mother may have never lived in full color, and that permission to live and to love was Annesley's gift to her own daughters, her own legacy.

The road curved, and the sun blinded her. She pushed down the visor and blinked away the afterimages.

The carbon monoxide soup of the interstate gave way to the breathtaking views of the Pacific Coast Highway. Soon, they were on the winding roads that led to Mary Blake's new home.

Mary Blake flipped up her visor to make it easier to play tour guide. The sun hid behind the houses and peeked out intermittently over landscaped side yards. "This one is owned by an oil magnate who only uses it one week a year. And that one over there with the gate sold for four and a half million dollars last month, even though the prior owner had mirrors installed on every ceiling in the house."

To homeowners peeking out their curtained windows, the group in the Great White Whale must have looked like tourists on a celebrity homes tour.

Around a bend, Mary Blake turned on her blinker. "This is it! You're my first real guests other than the dogsitter."

A modest bungalow sat at the end of a steep driveway. Annesley knew enough of Malibu and Mary Blake's tastes to imagine a welcoming interior and a view that went on forever.

Two King Charles spaniels ran to greet them, jumping and yipping with Mary Blake-like ebullience. After shushing the dogs with treats, Mary Blake settled Charlie and Helen into a guest bedroom, while Annesley pulled Lisa into the living room.

Pale-blue grass cloth wallpaper covered the walls, and a white oversized couch sat centered under a capiz-shell chandelier. A wall of glass overlooked a view of the ocean.

Lisa returned to doctor mode. "Are you feeling okay? Do you need to contact your physician about getting stronger painkillers?" No judgment marked her face, only concern.

Annesley opened her mouth to ask Lisa to come with her to get an X-ray, but the image of Mr. Harrison appeared in her mind. Her heart dropped like a steel sphere to the bottom of her stomach. Both she and the bear-man had asked Lisa to lie. And she didn't want to do that again. She clamped her mouth shut. That man had controlled and crushed Lisa for twenty years. What was Annesley trying to control with her own lie? Lisa? Mary Blake? The cancer? The hollowness expanded, engulfing her intestines, her stomach, her liver, her metastasizing lungs. She was deluding herself by imagining she had control over anything.

Mary Blake popped back into the room and fluffed a blue chenille pillow on a side chair. "I'm going to order delivery, and we can sit out on the deck and watch the sunset." She herded Annesley and Lisa toward the sliding doors.

"Mary Blake, your home is stunning," Annesley said, recognizing a lamp and some knickknacks from Mary Blake and Frank's home. She pointed at a painting. "That's new." Hanging above a white hall table, the blues and reds of the abstract piece popped in the fading light.

Mary Blake turned. Her hands went to her hips. "Y'all have got to be kidding me." She lifted an envelope from the credenza and opened it. "The painting is a thank you from Frank. And I quote, 'For finding Monica and me our new castle. Let's get together to catch up, just you and me.'" Mary Blake slid the note back into the envelope. "My dog sitter must have let him in. This painting was at an open house. You know, the one I was cohosting when you texted and we planned this trip."

"Oh, hell no," Annesley said, yanking the paper from Mary Blake's hand.

Mary Blake stepped back to consider the piece, unperturbed by Annesley's indignation. "It looks fabulous there."

Annesley readied herself to lecture Mary Blake on self-respect and paths that led nowhere. She stopped herself. Mary Blake didn't need Annesley telling her what to do.

Helen and Charlie bounced into the room and stopped short on seeing the other three staring at the painting.

"Frank sent this," Mary Blake said.

Charlie rolled her eyes. "Oh, boy."

"It's just a painting." The glint in Mary Blake's eye faded when she noticed Annesley's frown. "I'll send it back, okay?"

Annesley needed to tell her. Now. Mary Blake was her best friend. But telling her in front of the others seemed cruel. She recalled her own anger when she learned Mary Blake's secret at the pharmacy in Texas. Her fury at learning the others knew before she had. She looked at the four sets of eyes that were now on her, questioning. Then she remembered the five of them together in the restaurant, on the canyon edge, and on the side of the road at the superbloom. She would need their combined strength. So would Mary Blake.

She caught Lisa's eye. Lisa nodded her support.

Annesley turned away from the painting. "Can we move to the couch?"

Mary Blake sat next to her, and Annesley took her hand. Annesley thought back to that first day on campus, when Mary Blake had swooped in and pulled Annesley from her mother's grip. She remembered when Mary Blake had helped her feel normal during her first bout with breast cancer.

"A couple of you don't know this"—Annesley looked from Charlie to Helen—"but I had breast cancer in my thirties."

Concern filled their faces. Lisa grabbed Annesley's other hand. Charlie and Helen reached out to where Lisa held her hand, forming an intertwined mound that pulsed with warmth.

Emotion pressed against the back of Annesley's throat. "The cancer is back."

"What? No." Mary Blake's fingers froze in Annesley's grip. The blacks of her pupils overtook the blue irises as she shook her head.

Charlie sucked in her cheeks. Helen grabbed Mary Blake's free hand.

"I've known this whole trip, and I should have told you." Annesley squeezed Mary Blake's hand and almost melted when Mary Blake reciprocated.

Mary Blake's face tightened, the tiny crows' feet deepening and making her eyes look like blue stars.

Annesley swallowed the lump of emotion in her throat. "I'm so sorry. I needed to have control over something one last time, and that wasn't fair to you, not after all you've done."

"All I've done?" A tear fell across Mary Blake's cheek.

Annesley wiped it away. "Please don't cry. I don't want to cry. I'll mess up my mascara." Annesley's attempt at a joke drew only a sad chuckle from Charlie. "You do so much and sacrificed so much to helped me."

Mary Blake put her face in her hands. "I'm a horrible person."

Annesley hesitated. She'd expected anger or disappointment at her deception. She hadn't expected self-deprecation. "What are you talking about? You are the kindest, most generous person I've ever known. You give, give, give, and ask for nothing. Having you on my team has been one of my life's greatest blessings."

"No, I'm not. Last time, when you were sick, it was awful and scary. But—" Mary Blake looked out toward the sun, which had begun to disappear into the water. "I was useful and busy. And I got to be with you and your girls. It was one of the fullest times of my life. I miss my time with them. And you." Distress twisted her face. She looked like she was in physical pain, and that wrenched Annesley's gut in a way sickness couldn't. "I've been so lonely, and thinking of that time is so selfish. Who does that? Who can find joy at the same time her friend has cancer?"

Annesley wrapped her arms around Mary Blake. "That's part of your magic. It was an awful and scary time, but having you there gave us hope and joy. It means the world to me that you found some too." She released her grasp and locked eyes with Mary Blake. "You'll do it again, right? My girls need you to make sure they turn out okay. *I* need you." She turned to the group. "All of you."

Silently, they watched the sun sink lower, melting across the water and infusing the sky with color even as it disappeared.

# Chapter Fifty-One
# 2019
# Lisa

The next morning, everyone rose early, not willing to squander a moment. Lisa helped Mary Blake set a breakfast buffet on the deck: halved grapefruits, bowls of granola and yogurt, smoked salmon with capers, and champagne for mimosas, all interspersed with sprigs of rosemary. Thanks to Instacart, a small container garden, and Mary Blake's flair, they didn't need to be at a posh hotel for five-star treatment.

"Did everyone sleep okay?" Lisa tried to keep the physician out of her voice.

"Yes, doc." Charlie saluted.

"So, Mary Blake," Lisa said, "what are you going to do about the painting?"

"I haven't decided yet." Mary Blake's eyebrows pulled together. "I might keep it. It reminds me of you guys."

Lisa examined the red circles floating against the blue backdrop and wondered which was her. It didn't look like she was the only one thinking that, and no one objected to the possibility of the painting staying, as long as it didn't involve keeping Frank in the picture.

Charlie teetered her chair back on two legs. "MB, you've got a great place here. I could learn to love California."

Lisa followed Charlie's gaze. Grasses below them rustled in the soft breeze. The water lapped the beach. A man threw a stick into the water, and a golden retriever splashed in after it.

"Open a Malibu office!" Mary Blake exclaimed with a clap of her hands. "I'll design it."

"Don't tempt me."

"Maybe we'll get all of you out to California." Lisa caught herself and looked sheepishly at Annesley.

"Connecticut's pretty nice. Y'all can come visit me."

"That's a given," Helen said between spoonfuls of yogurt. "It's a quick trip from Richmond. Is your flight on time, by the way?"

"Yes. In fact"—Annesley glanced at Charlie's luggage—"I need to finish packing. Be back in a bit."

After Annesley was out of sight, Helen set her spoon on the table. "I don't think I'd be able to hold it together."

Lisa felt the same, but she'd seen plenty of patients go through diagnosis and treatment. "Everyone's experience is unique. But the most important thing is that she has a support system. She's got a tough road ahead."

"She has us."

The four of them didn't speak while clearing the plates. Mary Blake and Charlie rearranged the chairs, Helen went to get her travel bag, and Lisa moved to the railing where the salty breeze was strongest. Last night, the deep watercolors of sunset and the tears of shared grief over Annesley's news had given way to an ink-black sky. This morning's sky was white blue, a clean slate.

Lisa's life wasn't a clean slate, not with Tripp's candidacy blemishing the canvas, but she'd made peace with the situation. She turned to see Charlie at Helen's shoulder.

Helen hovered over her notebook, writing road trip updates in her precise hand on a half-filled page.

"There are an awful lot of empty pages in there," Lisa said.

"That doesn't mean we have to do this again, does it?" Charlie asked with an exaggerated loll of her head.

"We're Deltas forever," Mary Blake sang.

Charlie rolled her eyes but didn't hide her smile.

Mary Blake flipped on the TV. "Frank's Monica is supposed to be on some cable news show about pregnant TV personalities. I know you're dying to see her."

Charlie checked her watch. "Better come on quick. My Uber will be here soon. Where's Annesley?"

Annesley's voice rang from inside the house. "Don't leave without saying goodbye to me!" She appeared in the window, arms wide.

Lisa's jaw dropped. "No way."

Juvenile squeals pulled Annesley onto the deck, where she did a somewhat limping catwalk strut. She paused, her crab-emblazoned TOOLOULOU T-shirt front and center. She pivoted, lost her composure, and settled onto the couch in joyful laughter.

Lisa knew for a fact no one had bought a T-shirt at that dive bar in Louisiana. And the only way to get that particular T-shirt was to work there. Or win amateur night. "Carpe Diem List?" Lisa asked.

Annesley stuck her chest out to show off the crab. "Yes. I went back." She gave a seated curtsy.

"Wait," Charlie said. "Did you…?"

Lisa recalled the waitress's comment "No one wins if they don't take it off."

Annesley held up a hand. "I always do what it takes."

"Oh my God." Mary Blake picked up the TV remote and turned up the volume. "It's about Tripp."

On the TV, a news ticker ran under an empty podium: "Texas Senate watch… Harrison announcement…"

The lap of ocean waves clashed against the pulse echoing in Lisa's head. While the other women crowded closer to the TV, Lisa inched back until the railing pressed against her spine.

Panic buzzed her brain with a new thought. She hadn't considered that Tripp might not wait for the reporters or the opposition, that he might go on the offensive against her to preempt and control the narrative, in which event she was in no position to react. She had no publicist, no lawyer, no machine. She looked around, and her gaze fell on Helen.

In that Texas hospital, with Helen's scream echoing in her ears and Mr. Harrison and his attorney looming over her bed, Lisa had wished she'd matched Helen beer for beer that night, enough to black out everything that had happened.

For twenty years, Lisa had suffered regret for not putting an end to things early that night.

# Chapter Fifty-Two
# Lisa
# 1999

The dry Texas heat had dissipated soon after the sun disappeared, but Lisa was warm in the back seat with Parker, his soap and hay scent filling the space around them while Tripp tested the Scout's off-road chops. After spinning donuts and bouncing over uneven off-road trails, Tripp pulled the Scout to a stop with a quick brake that sent the wheels skidding on rocky dirt. "You're up, Hellcat."

Helen laughed at her new nickname. She was blitzed, and Lisa was clear-headed enough to know it. But from the moment Parker had climbed into the back seat with her, nothing other than the six feet of leather seating they shared mattered.

Tripp, his voice full of whiskey and hot Texas air, had moved on from Annesley's dismissal. Or maybe he'd leaned into it. "You know you want to try." Helen hadn't passed up a drink or a challenge from him all night. "Charlie will never know."

Helen slid to her left while Tripp jumped over the door on his side and stumbled around to the other to take shotgun. Helen stalled the car on her first attempt, and Lisa joined in the laughter and jokingly put on her seatbelt in an elaborate show of humor. Tripp guided Helen through the steps of starting and shifting as Helen jerked the car forward, tossing Parker practically into Lisa's lap.

"Maybe this isn't such a great idea," Lisa said.

"It's wide-open spaces out here," Parker assured her. "No one around for miles."

The vastness of the plains felt expansive, all the better to accommodate the fullness of being the center of his attention. Nothing existed other than the four of them and the Scout. She leaned against Parker and prepared for more harmless fun.

Helen struggled with the steering wheel, laughing through slurred words. "There's no power steering."

Tripp bellowed. "Maybe it needs a little lube."

"Don't be disgusting," Helen said in Annesley's accent.

Lisa laughed along with the mocking of the friend who hadn't been able to take a joke.

Helen changed gears and accelerated, finally getting the hang of it. The wind whipped her hair across her face. The Scout's headlights formed an indistinct portal in the blackness of the Texas flatlands.

Helen cranked the music, and Tripp stood with his arms raised. Helen swerved, and he fell back into his seat, sending Helen into peals of laughter. Tripp leaned toward the driver's seat.

"Stop it!" Helen's bark sliced through the music.

Tripp's hand slid up and inside her shirt.

She slapped it down. "I said, stop."

"Oh, come on. You know you like it. I've heard you're a wild one."

"What's that supposed to mean?" Helen asked.

"I heard about you at the beach."

Helen turned toward Tripp. Moonlight washed out her slackened jaw and highlighted the fear in her eyes. The only other place Lisa had seen that look had been from the hallway at the beach condo, when Lisa had overheard Helen and Charlie. And Lisa had done nothing then. Lisa leaned forward, and the seatbelt tightened across her hips, holding her back.

# THE LAST ROAD TRIP

Tripp reached over and put his hand between Helen's legs. He leaned toward the driver's seat, blocking Lisa's view. Helen screamed, and the Scout lurched as her foot bore down on the accelerator. As the car accelerated like a drunk moon rover over the rocks and brush, Helen released the wheel and backhanded Tripp. A low, wide tree appeared in the overlapping cones of light cast by the headlights. Tripp reached for the steering wheel, but he couldn't get purchase in time.

Afterward, in the hospital room, when the cop told her everyone else had blacked out and asked who had been driving, Lisa blurted Tripp's name out of pure protectiveness.

# Chapter Fifty-Three
# Lisa
# 2019

Thanks to some kind of gift of fate by way of a severe concussion multiplied by inebriation, Tripp hadn't remembered what happened that night in the desert. Only Lisa did. Lisa trailing at the back of the pack, Lisa the smart one, Lisa in the back seat.

And what Tripp didn't know couldn't hurt them.

Helen's voice pulled Lisa back to the deck. "He's about to start."

The camera zoomed in on Tripp Harrison, dressed in a navy suit and red tie. Lisa searched his face, and he stared back at her, eyes piercing the ether. The left side of his mouth rose and pulled into the self-satisfied grin that hadn't aged.

Tripp placed his hands on the podium as if he had built it himself from wood he'd planed by hand. When he clenched his jaw and his eyes flickered, Lisa knew he was looking right at her. He didn't see her standing with Charlie, Annesley, Mary Blake, and Lisa, but maybe he was picturing them. He resembled his father, from the pompous posture to the piercing eyes. But she realized that the piercing look from Mr. Harrison—the same look she saw on screen now—hadn't been anger or superiority. It had been fear.

She had been the one with the power that morning in the hospital, and Mr. Harrison had known it.

Mary Blake placed her hand on Lisa's arm. "You okay? You look like you went somewhere else."

Annesley and Helen, on either side of her, squeezed Lisa's hands. They'd ended up in a chain again, as if channeling their powers.

"I'm exactly where I'm supposed to be," Lisa said.

# EPILOGUE

*Delta Roadies Notebook*
December 1, 2019

Travel (Mary Blake coordinated airport pickup):
   Mary Blake arr: Nov. 30th (stayed with Annesley last night)
   Charlie arr: 12:30 p.m. (Delta Flt 7865)
   Lisa arr: 3:00 p.m. (American Flt 683)
   Helen arr: 11:00 a.m. (Southwest Flt 9203)
   Lodging: Crisfield Manor Bed & Breakfast, Bradington Road (203-555 9840)
   4:30 p.m.: Travel to Annesley's house (2.5 mi.). Stop & Shop/liquor store: frozen limeade, Sprite, beer & tequila

> THIS IS CHARLIE. I have commandeered Helen's notebook, which reads like a ~~fucking~~ manifest. We're here to see Annesley, who kicked the shit out of chemo and is getting ready to take down radiation. It's worth noting that Helen looks like a million bucks. Maybe I need to take up kickboxing too. P.S. The margs were good.
>
> THIS IS LISA. Charlie said it was okay for me to write in here. (I hope you're okay with it, Helen!) I'm so glad we could be together to see Annesley. We'll be back to see her next year, maybe after radiation. Her medical team is incredible, the best in the country. I went to med school

with her oncologist. Thinking positive thoughts. Oh, for posterity and all, I thought it was worth documenting that the new Texas Senator is Maria Fuentes. After Tripp Harrison decided "for family business reasons" (yeah right) not to run for senate, the field opened up. Sorry, I'm digressing. Love you guys!

THIS IS MARY BLAKE!!!! I'm so happy to see everyone!! I wish we were here for a different reason. :( But Annesley is worth every minute and every mile. Chemo was soooooo hard, but she is strong and beautiful, and her girls are too. <3 <3 We've got this, ladies! Delta Rhoadies forever!! <3 <3 <3

ANNESLEY HERE: I found this on the table when the girls took you out to see the chicken coops. I hope you'll indulge me.

*My dear Delta Rhoadies,*

*Never in my dreams did I think we would get back together to finish our trip. It was only a road trip, right? Five girls—we really were just girls—who had no idea who we were or what the future held for us. But even if we were young and stupid (present company included), we were pretty incredible.*

*YOU are pretty incredible.*

*I can only credit divine intervention (or Mary Blake, which I suppose is the same thing) for the truly unlikely reunion we had. I gained so much on that second trip, and I'm not just talking about the weight from all the food. You—we—are a force. You embody everything I want my girls to be.*

*Lisa, you standing up to Tripp inspired me. And the jade silk scarf you sent me when my hair fell out kept me laughing about roadside yard sales and parties in Alabama.*

*Charlie, I'm so happy you and your dad—sorry, The General—are spending time together. If he's anything like my mom, he'll still annoy the crap out of you, but he'll defend you to the death.*

*Helen, people are always telling me I'm strong. I tell them to STFU because they haven't met you.*

*Mary Blake, my dear Mary Blake, I can't live without you. And without you, I wouldn't have these other women to lift and support me. I hope my girls grow up to be surrounded by people who love and support them no matter what.*

*I didn't want to get sappy here (sorry, already did!), but let's be honest, my prognosis isn't good. Maybe I'll be in that 5% the doctors mentioned, and you'll still have to be dealing with me in five years. Hell, maybe we can do another road trip. But either way, I am blessed. Maybe I don't deserve to be blessed, but I'll take it. I'll take you. Thanks for being here. Next time, margaritas are on me.*

*~A*

# Acknowledgements

*The Last Road Trip* was inspired by my husband and his friends, who drove cross-country during college. Their trip is legendary (in their own minds) and has been the topic of video compilations, anniversary celebrations, and countless (loud) late night conversations over the years. But since their excursion didn't include a tragic death in Texas or toxic secrets that led to decades of estrangement, it simply wouldn't have been as fun a story to write as what ended up becoming *The Last Road Trip*. So, while the guys inspired the book, I can confirm that I changed every single thing, including the gender of the cast.

Thank you, Bryan, Phil K., Eric, Matt, Phil M., Ti, and Chuck. Your friendship is one for the ages, and I cherish being in the circle with you and your families.

The Fellas may have inspired the story, but my Gamma Phi Beta sorority sisters were on my mind (a road trip across Texas to New Mexico in particular) while I wrote. I miss you all!

While writing this book (and giving up on it multiple times), I was fortunate to have the help of many in my reader/writer/expert network. Thank you to Negeen Papehn, who told me someone had to die and was right; Tiffany Yates Martin for your editorial insights and your patience each time I quit; my mom, the enthusiastic beta reader every author needs; Amy Feranec and Heather Frimmer for your medical consulting (all errors are my own); my dad for instilling in me an appreciation for badass cars; Daryl Williams, Elizabeth Harris, Julie Kyle, Erin Baldecchi, and Joey Gaines for your feedback on early drafts; my neighbor Dave Lauer for owning a drop-dead gorgeous emerald green International Harvester Scout II that screamed out to me to be put into a book; Kim Grant and Elizabeth Emerson for your Texas-sized encouragement; my Sherwood neighbors, who have been persistent cheerleaders; the Women's Fiction Writers Association and the Ink Tank for camaraderie and support; Red Adept and Lynn McNamee for believing in this book; Alyssa Hall for your editing work; Leftie Aube, Audra McElyea, and Barbara Conrey for early critique reads; and Sarahlyn Bruck and Janet Rundquist for being synopsis sounding boards.

Most importantly, my love to the Fab Four. Will and Audrey, your wit and creativity bring light to my every day. And Bryan, with whom I would drive anywhere, thank you for making sure I can write books and start companies and not worry about the world around me falling apart.

# About the Author

*USA Today* bestselling author Jennifer Klepper was born and raised in Iowa and Nebraska, respectively. After attending Southern Methodist University and University of Virginia School of Law, she worked in Texas and Massachusetts before settling in Maryland. She's worked for Big Law, small law, start-ups, and Google, and most recently, she cofounded the tech company Early Works.

Jennifer is an ardent consumer of podcasts and books that challenge her with compelling and unfamiliar topics. When she's not writing, she's crossing things off a never-ending to-do list and hoping to catch that next sunset. She lives in a forest by a river in Maryland.

Read more at https://www.jenniferklepper.com/.

## About the Publisher

Dear Reader,

We hope you enjoyed this book. Please consider leaving a review on your favorite book site.

Visit https://RedAdeptPublishing.com to see our entire catalogue.

Check out our app for short stories, articles, and interviews. You'll also be notified of future releases and special sales.

Made in the USA
Monee, IL
03 February 2025